Rosie stood before Josephine smiling [...] embarrassment at her nudity but in am [...] until Josephine sprang from her chair, turned her back on Rosie and barked, "Put something on, will you?"

—*La Belle Rose*, Julia Watts

I pulled Bashful by the shoulders away from Sleepy, and I took her place, between Sleepy's legs.

—*A Butch in Fairy Tale Land*, Therese Szymanski

Mina leaned down and kissed Charlotte's neck. "And I love the feel of you in my arms." She dropped the book and ran her hands along Charlotte's arms and then across her bosom. Charlotte couldn't help but arch into her touch, and then she twisted so they were face to face. She closed her eyes, yielding to Mina's mouth and tongue and fingers. As Mina pulled her in closer still, she could feel their hearts beat in unison. Her breath caught in her throat as Mina caressed her through her clothes, her hands gliding over breast and belly and hips to thighs.

—*Charlotte of Hessen*, Barbara Johnson

There were lesbians all around them, maddeningly ready to share a night of passion. They were all beautiful, appealing, sexual – and utterly forbidden. Their pheromones spilled into the air like blood in water, unmistakable. Ariel found it increasingly difficult to ignore the pulsing between her legs. She drew herself up proudly, not wanting Laveena to see how badly she needed more than song.

—*A Fish Out of Water*, Karin Kallmaker

WHAT CRITICS HAVE SAID ABOUT THE AUTHORS...

"Johnson's *Stonehurst* will fan the flames of your summer heat right into the coolness of fall . . ."

—*National Gay and Lesbian Reader*

"This best-selling author doesn't follow any formulaic plotline and Karin Kallmaker delivers an entertaining story with a whole cast of quirky and highly likable characters *à la* Rita Mae Brown."

—*Lesbian Review of Books*

"Szymanski is a master at pacing . . . The sex scenes are very hot and believable . . . She knows how to hook her readers from almost the first page."

—*Lambda Book Report*

"Watts expands her repertoire of characters, creating an extraordinary world that is fascinating, fun, and very moving."

—*Bay Area Reporter*

Once Upon a Dyke

New Exploits of Fairy Tale Lesbians

Fairy Tales with an erotic twist by

Barbara Johnson
Karin Kallmaker
Therese Szymanski
Julia Watts

Bella
BOOKS

2004

Bella Books, Inc.
P.O. Box 10543
Tallahassee, FL 32302

Printed in the United States of America on acid-free paper
First Edition

Editors: Karin Kallmaker and Julia Watts
Cover designer: Sandy Knowles

ISBN 1-931513-71-6

CONTENTS

FOREWORD

Why Fairy Tales?

Fairy tales are about sex. Plenty of serious books have been written on the psychosexual aspects of fairy tales. These books enlighten readers about the sexual symbolism of forbidden forests, candy houses, and tempting poisoned apples.

This is not one of those books.

We're here to have fun. We don't want to pin down the butterfly that is the fairy tale so we can dissect it and study it. We do want to play with it, though, and see if it will fly off in a different direction once we set it free.

For contemporary women, and especially for contemporary lesbians, the old fairy tales can be appallingly rigid. Young is beautiful, old is evil, and a woman's worst enemy is another woman. We all grew up with these tales, whether they were the original, grisly stories or Walt Disney's "sanitized for your protection" Cult of the Princess versions. And for those of us who were not destined to grow up to be the heterosexual princess type, these stories raised some serious questions: Why were the heroines always pretty, pure, passive little things who needed rescuing? And even if a girl did need rescuing (as we all do from time to time), why did she have to be rescued by a handsome prince? Why not a handsome princess, or a comely peasant girl, for that matter? What was so charming about Prince Charming anyway?

The short answer to all of these questions is that fairy tales were a product of their time and culture. But the tales in *Once Upon a Dyke* are a product of *our* time and culture. Some of the tales will take you back to traditional fairy tale land, but with decidedly non-traditional twists. Others use a fairy tale as inspiration for a story set in a different time and place. There is more than one road to Happily Ever After.

But no matter what approach the authors in this volume take, these are our tales, tailored to adult lesbian tastes, with heroines that are nobody's gender stereotypes and love scenes that don't fade to black after the first kiss.

Fairy tales are about sex, and we're not shy.

Julia Watts & Karin Kallmaker
January 2004

La Belle Rose

by Julia Watts

"Beauty could not help fretting for the sorrow she knew her absence would give her poor Beast . . . Among all the grand and clever people she saw, she found nobody who was half so sensible, so affectionate, so thoughtful, or so kind."

—*from "Beauty and the Beast" by Mme. Leprince de Beaumont*

Chapter 1

Not as long ago as you might think, a couple of years after your great-great grandmother threw out her corset and hemmed her dress to show her ankles, but a few years before she bobbed her hair and started drinking bathtub gin, there lived a girl named Rose Bell, although everybody just called her Rosie. Where Rosie lived is neither interesting nor important except that it was a small town in the mountains—the kind of town where many people come from, but where only the least adventurous souls want to stay.

Rosie was an adventurous soul.

But where our story begins, when Rosie was twenty-two years old, she didn't know that she was adventurous yet. She had always lived in the little mountain town in the same house where she'd been born, and her only adventures came from the books she checked out of the tiny public library to read and re-read. In those pages, Rosie had traveled to hundreds of places and kissed dozens of lovers, and when the pages came to an end she always felt a twinge of sadness as she returned to her duties of baking the biscuits or washing the dishes or sweeping the floor. For while Rosie's mind soared off to exotic lands, her body was relegated to the most mundane tasks.

Of the three Bell siblings, Rosie was the youngest and the most attractive, with thick, waist-length auburn hair and big hazel eyes. A light sprinkling of freckles dusted her nose which, while highly unfashionable at the time, would have been regarded as quite adorable by anyone wise enough to turn up her nose (freckled or otherwise) at the flighty fickleness of fashion.

Rosie's older sister, Violet, was married and lived up north. Their brother, Claude, was married to a dull but good-hearted woman named Helen and lived just a couple of miles up the road. In Violet's letters to her sister and during Claude and Helen's weekly visits, the same question always came up: "So, Rosie, when are you going to get married?"

"I don't know when I'll marry," Rosie would always reply, whether on paper or in person. "Somebody's got to take care of Daddy."

Rosie's mother had died of pneumonia four years before, and part of Rosie's father had seemed to die with her, leaving him thin, sad-eyed, and frail beyond his years. Like many men of that day, Mr. Bell was utterly helpless without a wife to look after him. It was through no fault of his own, as boys of his generation were never taught the workings of a household. But his total ignorance of simple domestic subjects never failed to amaze Rosie.

How clothes went from dirty to clean, to him, was a miracle on par with turning water into wine. The process of transforming flour, shortening, and buttermilk into biscuits seemed as impossible to his gender as giving birth to a baby. He didn't know how to crack an egg, let alone scramble one.

Because Rosie was the unmarried daughter and because she both loved and pitied her heartbroken father, she chose not to leave home after her high school graduation, but to stay with Mr. Bell and keep the house and take care of him. Early each morning before he went to work at the lumber mill, Mr. Bell would sit down to a full breakfast Rosie had cooked for him: eggs, bacon, biscuits, and in the summertime, sliced homegrown tomatoes. Rosie would make sure he never left the house without two sandwiches wrapped in waxed paper for his lunch, and when he came home in the evening, a hot supper would be waiting for him.

Now a less kind man than Rosie's father would have accepted Rosie's cooking and cleaning as no more than her womanly duty. But Mr. Bell appreciated his daughter's efforts and often felt downright unworthy of them. Many evenings, after he had sopped up the last drops of bean soup with his cornbread and sat at the kitchen table drinking his coffee, he'd say, "Rosie, don't you stay around this place on my account. A pretty girl like you shouldn't be wasting her time looking after an old man like me. I could always hire a woman to come in a couple of times a week and take care of the housework."

Rosie would always say, "Why pay a stranger to take care of you when somebody who loves you can do it?" And she'd pour him more coffee and kiss the top of his balding head.

It was on an evening such as this, after the beans and cornbread and during the second cup of coffee, that we leave behind all the exposition and start getting to the juicy parts of the story.

After Rosie washed up the supper dishes, she went into her bedroom, changed into her light blue sailor dress, and pinned back her hair. Her gentleman friend John was coming to take her to the carnival. This was the carnival's last night, and Rosie didn't want to miss it. Ever since she was a little girl, Rosie had loved the carnival that rode in every summer. The many-colored lights, the smell of popcorn and candy apples, the fast-talking pitches of the carnival folk brought some much-needed excitement into the dull little town.

It is appropriate that until this point, the narrator has neglected to tell you about John, Rosie's gentleman friend. John was somewhat of an afterthought for Rosie, too. She thought of him far less often than did her father and siblings, all of whom were hopeful that Rosie would stop short of spinsterhood and marry him.

After all, John was a nice young man. He was two years older than Rosie and very thin, with parted-in-the-middle hair (which despite our current disdain for it, was very fashionable among men in those days) and a pair of thick spectacles perched on his rather beak-like nose. Clearly he was no matinee idol—no one would ever mistake him for Douglas Fairbanks or Francis X. Bushman—but he wasn't a bad-looking sort. And he was indeed nice, although painfully shy. More comfortable with numbers than with people, he toiled daily as the bookkeeper at the lumber company where Rosie's father worked.

Until the day our story begins, John's shyness had worked in Rosie's favor. Because he was so timid, he either did not mind or did not have the nerve to say he minded the glacial pace at which Rosie insisted they conduct their courtship. In the two and a half years that Rosie and John had been seeing each other, most couples would have been engaged or even married. But Rosie, unlike many girls who pressured their suitors to hurry up with a ring, was content to let their relationship creep along at the pace of an arthritic turtle.

After two and a half years, the most intimate way Rosie would refer to John was as "my gentleman friend." She could not bring herself to call him her sweetheart. Growing up in the country had given Rosie a complete understanding of the birds and the bees—or the cows and the pigs, as was the case in her neighbor's back yard. John, both out of fear of Rosie's father and brother and out of the sexual timidity of the time, had never tried to do more than hold Rosie's hand. For Rosie, even this physical contact sometimes seemed a bit much. When Rosie did dream of lovers, they were from the pages of books. Her dreams were populated by strong, dark lovers whose brooding exteriors hid warm and kind hearts. These lovers she could imagine holding hands with . . . and more.

This particular night, the night that would change Rosie's life forever, after she put on her sailor dress and pinned back her hair, she heard John's tentative knock at the door. As was the custom of the day (a custom designed to strike fear into the hearts of young men everywhere), when a male suitor knocked on the door, it was the girl's father who answered.

"I could barely hear you," Mr. Bell said, letting John in. "You don't knock. You scratch at the door like a cat." His words were teasing, but his tone was kind.

"I'm sorry, sir." John held his hat in his hands. "I just didn't want to disturb you."

"You couldn't disturb me if you tried," Mr. Bell said. "We're always glad to have you." At this point, Rosie emerged from her bedroom, and Mr. Bell boomed, "There's your girl! Just look at her, John! That blue dress is mighty becoming, ain't it?"

John's face turned azalea pink.

"Don't be silly," Rosie said. "You've both seen me in this dress a hundred times. Ready, John?"

John held out a slightly shaky arm, and to please him and her father, Rosie took it.

The carnival was spread out in a field on the outskirts of town. Even before you could see it, you could hear it and smell it: the brass band playing, the frying onions, the hot popcorn. Rosie and John walked down Main Street in the direction of the sounds and smells, past the dry goods store, the drug store, and the barber shop with its candy-striped pole. The closer they drew, the faster Rosie walked, until she was practically dragging John by the arm.

"Look at you," John laughed, "you're just like a child!"

"There's nothing wrong with that," Rosie answered peevishly. "Adults could learn a lot from children when it comes to having fun."

The carnival was full of games designed to take advantage of the male ego. The game operators called out to young men with their sweethearts, "Look at them muscles on you, boy! Come and test your strength and win that pretty lady a prize!"

Burly youths who did heavy work out at the lumber mill would pick up the mallet and swing it over their shoulders, expecting to bring it down hard enough to ring the bell and win their sweethearts a blue-eyed chalk dog or a piece of colorful, opalescent glassware. More often than not, though, they came up short, and the few young women who carried around chalk dogs or glass sugar bowls did so with a look of Darwinian pride that their mates were the fittest of the pack.

Even scrawny, bespectacled John wasn't immune to the carnies' pleas for him to prove his masculinity. He knew he didn't have a chance at the "test your strength" game, but he did plunk down a nickel at the booth where a greasy-haired man in a checked suit ordered him to "knock down just three pins and win that pretty lady a prize!"

Each ball John threw made contact with a wooden pin but failed to knock it down. So he plunked down another nickel to try again. And then another.

"Really, John, I wish you wouldn't waste your money this way," Rosie chided just as John was about to plunk down yet another coin. "My life won't be any poorer for not having a chalk dog."

"I just wanted to get you a little souvenir, that's all." John glared at the wooden pins as if they were issuing him a personal challenge.

"Well, if you really want to get me something, I think that nickel would be better spent on a candy apple."

At the concession stand, bright rows of candy apples gleamed like red patent leather. "Aren't you having one?" Rosie asked John as he handed the lady at the stand a single nickel.

"No," John said, "too messy to eat in public."

This was one of the reasons John and Rosie would never be compatible. John would never dream of looking anything other than neat and respectable in public, whereas Rosie would never let the fear of messiness or the opinions of others keep her away from something delicious.

After Rosie had gobbled her apple and John had dabbed at her sticky face with his handkerchief, they decided to go on the carnival's only ride (for rides were fairly rare in carnivals in those days), the carousel. Ever since she was a little girl, Rosie had loved the carousel, with its merry calliope music and lights and mirrors and painted ponies. She was about to climb on a white pony with red roses in its golden mane when John said, "Let's sit on the bench instead. Going up and down on the horses upsets my stomach."

John had paid for the ride, so Rosie felt it would be rude to argue. She sat down on the gold-painted bench and watched with amusement how seriously children took the decision of which pony to ride. The calliope music swelled, the carousel began to turn, and Rose leaned back, enjoying the breeze in her hair.

"You . . . you look pretty like that," John said.

Rosie, who had momentarily forgotten John was there, said "Thank you."

"Rosie," he began, taking her small white hand, "there's something I've been wanting to ask you for some time now."

Rosie felt a churning in her stomach which was not entirely due to the fact that she was spinning around rapidly with a belly full of candy apple.

"Rosie," he continued, "would you . . . would you be my wife?"

For the past two years, Rosie had known that this moment was inevitable, that all those sodas at the drug store, all those Sunday afternoon picnics, all those long walks in the woods, were designed to lead up to this question. Rosie knew, too, that John had planned his proposal carefully. I'll take her to the carnival, he had thought, and propose to her there. Wouldn't that be a story to tell the grandchildren? How, Rosie wondered, had she failed to see this disaster coming?

The spinning sensation that had filled Rosie with pleasure now filled her with panic. She was spinning so fast with the tinny calliope music filling her ears, and yet she was going nowhere. She was trapped on the carousel, trapped and spinning, just like she would be trapped with John, spinning daily through the duties of wifehood and (inevitably) motherhood, but never going anywhere.

One thought throbbed in her head: I have to get off. She jerked her hand from John's, jumped off the bench, and leapt off the spinning carousel. She fell to the ground, but got up just as quickly as she fell, and ignoring the ride operator asking, "Lady, are you all right?" she ran as if she were being chased by an enraged maniac instead of an enamored suitor.

She did not look back when she heard John yelling for the operator to stop the carousel; she was too busy running, past the games, past the concession stand, past children with their balloons and popcorn. She ran and ran and ran and ran until she hit something that nearly knocked the wind out of her.

"Lady, watch where you're going!" a voice from the ground called.

Rosie looked down to see a tiny man wearing an immaculate dark suit, bowtie, and derby hat. She realized, with some horror, that she had just run right over the top of him. "Oh, I'm so sorry." She reached out her hand. "Let me help you up."

"Don't need no help." The little man's voice was surprisingly deep. "Been standing on my own since I was one. You here to see the show?"

"Show?" Rosie asked. Had she not been distracted by both running away from her would-be fiancé and running over a man almost half her size, she would have noticed she was standing in front of a large green tent festooned with a painted banner reading **HUMAN CURIOSITIES . . . FREAKS OF NATURE . . . GUARANTEED REAL AND ALIVE!**

Other banners with crudely painted portraits on them hung from the sides of the tent. The portrait labeled "Tennessee Tom . . . the Smoky Mountain Giant" showed a huge, smiling man in a ten-gallon hat standing astride two mountains. The one reading "Wilma Waddles—500 pounds and still gaining" showed a rotund woman dressed in a girlish pink dress surrounded by piles of roast chickens, bread loaves, and fruit. "Alligator Al" was shown rising from swampy water, the skin of his arms and chest covered in green scales. And

"Colonel Peanut—World's Tiniest Man" was pictured as a little doll in a dress military uniform of indeterminate nationality.

It was Colonel Peanut with whom Rosie was now speaking, although he probably wasn't really the tiniest man in the world, he definitely wasn't a colonel, and his real name was Stanley Simpson. "Yeah, the show," he said. "It started five minutes ago, but I can still let you in if you're willing to pay full price."

Rosie had been looking over her shoulder to make sure John was nowhere in sight. When she turned around, it was not one of the big, bright banners that caught her eye, but a small sign on the ticket stand, roughly printed in pencil on tablet paper:

HELP WANTED

GIRL

"Actually," she nodded toward the sign. "I'm here about the job."

"Oh, then you'll want to go to the office, the little tent around back," he said.

"Thank you." She glanced over her shoulder one last time and hurried around the side of the tent.

"No need to look over your shoulder like that," Stanley Simpson called behind her. "Whoever it is you're worried about will never think to look for you here."

Chapter 2

When Rosie came to the small tent, she wasn't sure how to make her presence known to its occupant. After all, you can't really knock on the door of a tent. Finally, she decided on pulling the flap back slightly and calling, "Hello?"

"Yes?" a mellifluous tenor answered.

"I'm here about the job?" As is often the case with people in situations in which they are unsure of themselves, Rosie found it impossible to speak in any form except that of a question.

"Come in."

Rosie ducked into the tent, happy to be out of sight, since John was no doubt still pursuing her.

The "office tent" obviously doubled as someone's living quarters. In the left corner was a cot covered by a handmade quilt stitched as finely as if Rosie's own grandmother had made it. In the right corner was a large metal bathtub, with a bucket beside it. Between the bed and the tub was one of the most beautiful objects Rosie had ever seen—an Oriental folding screen, decorated with delicate paintings of gray and white cranes and pink cherry blossoms. Rosie was so transfixed by the screen that she didn't even notice her potential employer until she heard the words, "You're here about the job?"

"Oh, yes. The job." For the first time she noticed the person sitting at the rickety table in front of her, a slight, small-boned man with dark, intense eyes and a full beard which reached his chest. In a time when most men had shaved their beards or at least trimmed them short, he looked strangely old-fashioned, as if no one had told him about the turn of the century.

"Forgive my rudeness," the man said, rising, and Rosie saw that his suit hung loosely on his frame, as if he might have suffered a long illness and lost a great deal of weight. He gestured to the chair on the opposite side of the rickety table. "Please sit."

Rosie sat. "What kind of job is it?"

"We need somebody out front to sell tickets. Stanley's usually our talker, trying to lure folks in to see the show, but right now he's having to talk and sell tickets, which is hard for him. Especially because since he's so short he tends to disappear behind the ticket box."

"When do you leave for the next town?"

"We'll break down the show tonight and be on the train at seven tomorrow morning."

"Immediately" would have been a better answer as far as Rosie was concerned, but this was still satisfactory. "I'll take the job if you'll have me."

"My, aren't we eager?" the man smiled. "Are you an experienced worker?"

"Not really."

"Are you an honest person?"

"If I wasn't, do you think I'd tell you?"

He smiled again. "A good point. But I will warn you, if you aren't honest you'll find yourself out of a job very quickly. A lot of shows are crooked. They shortchange the rubes as a matter of course. But not here. I can't speak for the other vendors in this carnival, but in my show, we're strictly a Sunday School operation."

"I understand."

"Well, then, it sounds like you've got yourself a job." He offered his hand which Rosie was surprised to find no larger than her own.

A sudden thought came to Rosie. "Why did the sign say help wanted—girl? Couldn't a man sell tickets just as easily?"

"I suppose so," the man replied. "But it never hurts to have a pretty girl up front. Also, there is another part to the job if you're willing to do it."

"What's that?"

"Well, occasionally we need a girl to help out on stage. Alligator Al, our alligator-skinned man, has a knife-throwing act. The girl who sold tickets before would put on this shiny costume and stand propped up against a target while Al threw knives at her. But of course, she's not with us anymore."

Rosie pictured the poor girl pinned to the wall, a human pincushion stuck with daggers. "Is she . . . dead?"

"Oh, no," he laughed. "I did phrase that badly, didn't I? She's not with us anymore because she quit. She ran off with the fellow who used to be the weight guesser. You see, when we hire normal-looking folks to work in the show, they don't usually last long. Unlike our human oddities, the normal have other options. And sooner or later, they take them. I expect it will be the same with you. In the meantime, though, you'll be most welcome."

He rose from the table. "If you'll excuse me for just a moment, I need to get ready for the show." He stepped behind the screen.

"Should . . . should I leave?" Rosie couldn't imagine being in the same room with a man she had just met while he undressed, even if he was hidden from sight.

"No need. Just stay where you are," he called from behind the screen. "You haven't even asked me anything about money," he said.

"Well, anything you pay me is more than I'm making now."

"How does a dollar a day plus room and board sound?"

Rosie was astonished. A dollar a day may seem like next to nothing to us now, but to Rosie's ears this sum sounded astronomical. "It sounds like more money than I'd know what to do with."

"Oh, I'm sure you'll figure out something to do with it. You know, it just dawned on me that I haven't even asked what your name is."

"Rose. Rose Bell. But everybody just calls me Rosie."

"Rose Bell. You couldn't hope for a more beautiful name than that, could you?" To Rosie's amazement, her new employer stepped from behind the screen, dressed in an emerald green satin gown cut tight across what was by any standard a magnificent bosom, a narrow corseted waist, and rounded hips. The beard was decorated with a mother-of-pearl and silver filigree barrette.

Rosie gasped.

The figure before her spoke. "I am Josephine."

"Oh . . . oh, my!" was all Rosie could manage at first, then she managed to blurt out. "I'm sorry. It's just that . . . that—"

"You thought I was a man?"

"Y-yes."

The corners of Josephine's lips, which Rosie could now see were much too full to belong to a man, turned up in amusement. "It was a logical assumption. When I have business to do in town, as I did today, I often put on a man's suit so as not to be bothered. I used to go out in a dress with a veil over my face until an unfortunate incident with a woman in a store in West Virginia, who kept raving about gypsies robbing her blind."

Rosie couldn't take her eyes off Josephine. Again and again, her gaze roved over the bosom, the hips, the hands, the beard. In the past few seconds, Rosie had experienced two separate shocks: first, her shock that Josephine was a woman, and now her shock that she had been blind to the obvious signs of Josephine's gender. It should have been perfectly obvious, even when she was dressed in a man's suit: her long-lashed eyes; her thin, small nose; her full lips; her small hands; her thick, black, waist-length hair.

Rosie felt like a fool, and her face turned as red as her floral namesake.

And yet anyone might have made the same mistake, even those of us with more modern sensibilities. Any woman who has ever worn a pair of jeans or waxed her upper lip knows that a pair of trousers and some facial hair do not a man make. And yet, how many of us, when confronted with a woman such as Josephine, would have made the same assumption that Rosie did?

"I don't mean to stare," Rosie said finally.

"Stare all you like," Josephine said. "If people like you didn't stare at people like me, I'd be out of a job." Josephine smiled, a mustachioed Mona Lisa. "You're going to have lots to stare at in this job, Rosie. You're not in the normal world anymore. You're in Madame Josephine's enchanted kingdom, where the freakish is normal and the normal is freakish. If you're not ready to live in a world like this, then you should probably stay here in . . . in whatever the name of this town is."

"I am ready," Rosie said. "The last thing I want is to stay here."

"Well, then," Josephine said, "in that case, you'd better come see the show."

Josephine extended her arm, and, without hesitating, Rosie took it.

When she stepped up on the stage, Josephine wore an emerald veil which hid the lower half of her face. Rosie watched her from the audience, or as Josephine had called it, "the tip," as her new employer sat down next to an enormous woman who had to be Wilma Waddles.

Wilma didn't quite live up to the "500 pounds and still gaining" claim on the banner that advertised her, but still, she was nobody's idea of svelte. Her huge, doughy limbs spilled out from beneath a short, frilly, pink frock of the kind that a little girl might wear on Easter Sunday. Her feet, which looked impossibly tiny compared to the rest of her, were encased in black patent leather Mary Janes. A large pink bow sat atop her blonde curls. Wilma smiled demurely at the crowd and fanned herself with a ladies' magazine.

In the center of the stage, Colonel Peanut, who stood just a little more than three feet tall, was clowning around with seven-foot, one-inch Tennessee Tom, who lifted the colonel in his arms as the crowd laughed with delight. "And now," the colonel announced from his piggyback perch on Tennessee Tom's shoulders, "the most exotic of all ladies . . . Madame Josephine!" He yanked off Tennessee Tom's hat and dropped it so it completely covered his own head, milking one more laugh from the crowd.

Josephine rose from her stool, walked to the center of the stage, reached up, and slowly removed her veil. The crowd gasped.

"In the past," Josephine said, "some people have accused me of wearing a false beard. So I always like to select one member of the audience to help me prove that this is, in fact, real." She cast her dark eyes over the audience, then let them rest on one member. "You, young man. In the second row."

A little boy, no older than nine, pointed to his chest and mouthed, "Me?"

Josephine smiled. "Yes, you. With the freckles. Come up on the stage. Don't be afraid. I hardly ever eat little boys—they're all tough and stringy."

The freckle-faced boy climbed on stage, and Josephine said, "I bet you've never pulled a lady's beard before, have you?"

The boy grinned a gap-toothed grin. "No, ma'am."

"Well, I'd like you to do it now." She leaned over so he could reach her face. "Give it a good tug. You won't hurt me."

The boy shyly pulled her beard, and when he met resistance, cried out, "It's real!"

"That's what I wanted to hear. Thank you, young man. You may take your seat," Josephine said, and then spoke louder to the audience, "I come from the backwoods of Kentucky. When my mother was expecting me, she was frightened by a wild boar that came charging out of the woods at her. When I was born, my face was covered in coarse dark hair just like a boar. As I was growing up, other children and even people in my own family called me a beast, a monster." She held out her arms outstretched, letting the audience get a long look at her.

"But I ask you, ladies and gentlemen, do I stand before you as a savage beast? I have taken great pains to educate myself, reading the great books and learning the feminine arts such as music and needlework. I made the dress I am wearing." She reached behind her stool and retrieved an instrument which Rosie had always called a fiddle. When Josephine played it, though, it was a violin. She didn't saw out a jaunty tune like "Turkey in the Straw," but instead stroked the bow over the strings, producing notes of such sweet sadness that tears filled Rosie's eyes.

Rosie didn't know the name of the song, yet it was song that had been playing in her heart all her life—a song of longing for something different than what the girls around her wanted, a song of being different and the beauty and pain it brings. Rosie cried like she hadn't since her mother's funeral, and a few of her fellow audience members looked at her more strangely than they looked at the human oddities on the stage.

After Josephine finished playing, it was Alligator Al's turn to perform. Wearing only a pair of short black trunks, Al was a normal-looking middle-aged man from the neck up, but from the neck down, his skin was the texture of an alligator-skin purse. He rolled out a wooden target, and with great speed and accuracy, pitched a dozen daggers at it. His accuracy was a great relief to Rosie.

After Alligator Al received a round of applause, Colonel Peanut reappeared and said, "We're through on the main stage, folks, but that's not the end of the show. For just five cents more—one nickel, ladies and gentlemen—you can see the greatest attraction of them all. If you will direct your attention to the back of the tent, behind the red curtain is the most amazing attraction on the face of the globe—Harry/Harriet—a real, live half man/half-woman! Is he a she? Is she a he? Harry/Harriet is both . . . and is guaranteed to be one hundred percent real and alive! Only five cents to see this added attraction . . . but adults only please, because of the shocking nature of this exhibit."

"So what did you think of the show?" Josephine asked Rosie as the crowd filtered out.

"That song you played . . ." Rosie said. "It was lovely."

Josephine smiled. "Thank you. The first thing people comment on after seeing the show is not usually my musical ability."

"It was my favorite part," Rosie said. "Listen, I need to go get my things. I'll be back in a couple of hours. Promise you won't leave without me."

"Don't worry. We'll wait for you."

When Rosie got home, her father was already asleep. She tiptoed around in the dark, grabbing her hairbrush, her toothbrush, and her three good dresses. Deciding not to wake her father, she scribbled a note and left it on his bedside table:

Dear Daddy,

For the past three years, you've been telling me I need to stop devoting all my time to you and to start living my own life. Well, I have finally taken your advice. A lady who tours the country as a musician has asked me to travel with her as her personal secretary. I figure that this may be my only opportunity to get to see some of the world. Please tell John not to come looking for me. Daddy, I love you and will write and send money every week.

Your daughter,

Rosie

Chapter 3

Rosie lay in the bathtub in Josephine's tent, letting the hot water soak the tension from her muscles. (And given that several hours of her working day were spent having knives thrown at her, her muscles were quite tense indeed.) Josephine had let Rosie know on the first day of her employment that she was welcome to use the bathtub any time, as long as she fetched and heated the water herself and scrubbed out the tub afterward.

"The men in the show," Josephine had said, "are content to rinse themselves off with cold water straight from the pump. They make fun of me hauling this bathtub everywhere I go. But there's something about a woman that makes her want a hot bath. I'd let Wilma use the tub, too, but I don't think she could fit more than her right leg in it."

So now, after three days on the road, Rosie lay in the tub in a tent which was currently pitched in a little town in North Carolina.

Josephine was on the other side of the Oriental screen, letting Rosie have her privacy and reading one of the fat Victorian novels she favored.

"Do you mind if we talk?" Rosie called through the screen.

Josephine set down her book. "Of course not. I'm glad for the company."

"I was just wondering . . . that story about your mother being frightened by a boar, causing you to be born with hair on your face . . . that's hogwash, isn't it?"

"Some of it is," Josephine laughed. "A lot of the stories showfolks tell about themselves are pure hogwash. Colonel Peanut isn't a colonel. Al wasn't raised by alligators in the Everglades any more than you were. And as you well know from taking your meals with her, Wilma doesn't eat six whole chickens a day. People like a good story to explain what they see and make it interesting, so we try to give them one."

"Well, your story is good," Rosie said. "Even if it isn't true."

"My story is truer than some. I was born in the backwoods of Kentucky, and my mother and father did believe that I looked the way I did because Mother had been frightened by a boar when she was carrying me. But of course, the very idea is . . . as you said, hogwash. But it's not hogwash that this idea was very real to my parents, and that my mother was so frightened of her hairy little baby that she refused to put me to her breast. My father pitied me enough to feed me cow's milk so I wouldn't starve. But he acted out of pity, not love."

Rosie, who had been adored by both her mother and father since the day she was born, could not conceive what it would be like to grow up without the security of parental love. "How sad," was all she could say.

"Yes, it was sad," Josephine said. "Mother and Father insisted on keeping me away from my sisters and brother, all of whom were normal, as if I had a disease they could catch. I was hardly ever allowed in the house. I slept in the barn loft, and Mother would leave me biscuits or cornbread from the night before when she came to milk the cows in the morning. She always made her feelings for me quite clear: I was a mistake of nature, a beast instead of a human, that I had been cursed by God, and that no one would ever love me."

A tear slid down Rosie's cheek. "How could a mother talk that way to her own child?"

Josephine sighed. "In her mind, I was not her child. She was kind to the other children. They never wanted for anything. Unfortunately, there are limitations to many people's ability to love, and my mother was one of those people. When I was thirteen, my beard grew thicker, and the problems with my mother grew worse. Once, she tried to shave me, but the stubborn hair started growing back within just a few hours. Finally, one day my parents came to me in the barn carrying a washtub, a cake of soap, and a new dress. They told me to wash and dress—they were taking me to town."

"Were they taking you to a doctor?"

"No," Josephine said, with a humorless smile. "They did not have your kind heart, Rosie. And of course, I was afraid because they had never taken me anywhere, and I knew they hadn't just got the sudden urge to treat me to an ice cream soda at the drug store. As it turned out, they were taking me to the carnival. They introduced me to a pudgy, good-natured man named Samuel Perkins, then they said, 'You want her for your show? If you pay us'—and they quoted an amount—'you can have her.'"

Rosie could not believe what she had just heard. "They sold you?"

"Just like a cow at the market, yes. But as it turned out, being under Samuel Perkins' care was not a bad thing. He was kind-hearted and took a liking to me. Soon I was calling him Pop, and he had legally adopted me. He was an educated man. He spent three hours every day tutoring me, teaching me to read and write and do figures. You see, up until that point, I'd never had any education at all. But I was a quick learner, and soon I left behind the McGuffey's Reader and moved on to Charles Dickens. Pop gave me a good education. Better than most girls get."

"Which is why you don't talk like you're from the backwoods of

Kentucky." Rosie was amazed that Josephine, who had never been to school, had achieved such a remarkable level of sophistication.

"Pop taught me how to speak properly, how to play the violin. Taught me all about the carnival business, too. When he died, I was twenty-five years old. He left the whole show to me. As far as I know, I'm the only woman in the country who's running her own show."

"So your story has a happy ending."

"Does it?" Josephine said. "Is it happy that I had to lose the one person in my life who ever gave me anything like love, just so I could make a little money? I would give up every penny I make if it would bring Pop back."

Rosie felt like ducking her head underwater and disappearing. "I'm sorry. I didn't mean that the way it sounded—"

"No, I'm sorry," Josephine said. "I didn't mean to snap at you. Sometimes, though, I get in the grip of this melancholy and can't wrest myself from its control. Cheer me up, Rosie. Tell me about your life."

Rosie told all the funny stories she could think of: how her brother had once tried to help her pull a loose tooth by tying one end of a string to the tooth and the other to the doorknob and when he slammed the door, the doorknob came off, but the tooth didn't. She told the story of her grandmother going out in the dark and falling over a cow, which then ran through the pasture with her still lying over its back. She didn't tell Josephine about her mother's drawn-out death or about the years she had spent caring for her lonely father. She wanted to hear Josephine laugh, to bring some light into a life that had known so much darkness.

After Rosie finished talking, Josephine took out her violin and played a lovely, light melody she said was by Mozart. When the tune was through, Josephine said, "Rosie?"

"Yes?"

"Isn't your bathwater getting cold?"

Rosie looked down and saw goosebumps on her milky skin. She laughed. "It's freezing! But I was enjoying your company so much I didn't notice."

◦⟶◦

After Rosie had put on her dressing gown and was about to excuse herself to go to her own little tent, a melodious but genderless voice from outside called, "Guess who-o?"

"Come in, Billy," Josephine said. Billy was the real name of the sideshow's top-grossing act, "Harry/Harriet," the half-man/half-woman.

When not wearing the costume that made him/her look female on one side and male on the other, Billy dressed in a plain white button-down shirt and trousers. Billy would have looked like a smooth-skinned young man, were it not for the fact that one side of his/her hair was clipped short, while the other side was long and curled. "It's not just me," Billy said. "It's the whole crew." Wilma, Stanley, and Tennessee Tom, who had to duck to get in the doorway, followed behind him. "Guess what? We found out where the bootlegger in this burg lives," Billy said. "We sent Al in to deal with him."

As if on cue, Al appeared, wielding a bottle of whiskey. Rosie had already discovered that when the folks from the show wanted something from the "normal" world, be it a bottle of aspirin or a flask of whiskey, they would send "Alligator Al" to get it. In a long-sleeved shirt and trousers, Al's reptilian skin was completely hidden, so he wouldn't attract the same stares and harassment as his colleagues.

"Well, aren't you clever?" Josephine laughed. "I know I've got some glasses around here somewhere." She rummaged under her cot and produced an apple crate filled with glasses, cups, and dishes cushioned by newspaper.

"I swear, it's untelling what all she keeps under that bed," Billy said. "She's got a whole library's worth of books under there."

Josephine handed them each a glass, and Al made the rounds filling them. When he got to Rosie, she protested, "I'd better not."

"You'd better, too," Al said, filling her glass anyway. "It'll steady your nerves after all those knives I threw at you today."

Rosie had never taken a drink of alcohol before—both of her parents had been Temperance—but she felt in this situation, it would be rude not to. The whiskey tasted strong and bitter like medicine, and it burned going down, but it left a nice, warm glow in her belly.

"Your eyes are watering, honey," Wilma laughed.

"Oh, it's just a little stronger than I'm used to," Rosie said.

"I know what you mean, hon," Wilma said. "I'm not much of a drinker either. You'd think as big as I am, that I could put it away and not even feel it. But one little drink, and I get silly, then sleepy. Tom's not much of a drinker either, but little Stanley over there can put it away like both of his legs are hollow."

Rosie found that the more she sipped, the less she minded the taste. Soon she was feeling cozy, comfortable, and curious about the unusual people around her. "I'd love to know," she said finally, "how you all ended up in this show."

"Put a drink in a normal one, and that's always what they ask," Billy said. "It's like they all write for the same newspaper or something."

"I'm in the show," Al said, draining his glass, "because it beats working for a living."

"Hear, hear," several of the others said, laughing.

"A few years back, though," Al said, "this do-gooder came around and had me convinced my skin was the way it was because I was sick. 'These carnival people are just taking advantage of you,' she said. 'Come to this hospital and get cured of your disease, then you can have a normal life.' So I went to the hospital and laid in bed for weeks, only to have them tell me there wasn't no cure for what I had. But they still wanted me to stay there on accounta being 'sick.' Finally I said, 'I ain't sick; I feel just fine,' and I walked right out of that hospital and went back on the road."

"There's no place for us to go except the show if we want to earn a living," Tom said. "My back gives me so much trouble from being so tall I can't do regular labor. And I've got a wife and two kids to support."

"With me, it was different," Wilma said. "I just got sick of my husband. He told me I was so fat I ought to join a carnival, so I left him and took his advice." She laughed uproariously, so Rosie did, too.

"I've worked regular jobs before," Billy said. "But it's always the same. It doesn't matter if I'm washing dishes in a restaurant or picking apples in an orchard, sooner or later the other fellows will start going on about how soft my voice is or the way my hips sway when I walk. Women's work might be better, but I can't quite pass for a regular female. So here I am. The people I work with leave me alone, and if other people are going to stare and make fun, they at least have to pay me for it." He leaned in close to Rosie. "You know, a lot of the performers you see claiming to be he/shes are grifts. But I'm the genuine article. I was born with a little something extra." Billy poured another glass of whiskey. The bottle was almost empty now. "And if I drink enough of this stuff, I just may show it to you."

Rosie blushed furiously, and Josephine interceded, "No more vulgarity, Billy. You're in mixed company."

Billy grinned. "Even when I'm alone, I'm in mixed company."

"What it seems like to me," Al said, "is that it's obvious why all of us are here except for you, Rosie."

"That's true," Wilma said. "The normal people who have joined up with us in the past have mostly been on the run . . . from the law or a bad situation at home. But here you are, a pretty girl with good manners from a nice family, choosing to spend your time with the likes of us."

Rosie knew that there was an implied "why?" at the end of Wilma's speech, and she was expected to answer it just as much as if it had been said out loud.

But what could she say? True, she was "on the run" in a sense—on the run from a man she didn't want to marry. But there was more to it than that, wasn't there? As meek as John was, she could have just politely declined his proposal, and while he would have been hurt, he would have been nothing but polite right back to her. Was her decision to join the show really about running away from John, or was it about running toward something else?

All she knew was that even though she grew up surrounded by people who loved her, whom she loved back, she had always felt different. Not the kind of different that everybody notices immediately, like Josephine's beard, but an on-the-inside difference that only she noticed. Inside her there had always been a longing, a longing made no less intense by the fact that she didn't know exactly what she was longing for. She just knew that the obvious path—husband, home, and children—that seemed to satisfy all the other girls would not be enough for her.

But what would be enough? Rosie still didn't know, but she did know that in the past few days, living on the road, being a part of the show, and becoming fast friends with Josephine, she felt closer to happiness than she had ever been before.

Chapter 4

The bathtub conversations continued, and Rosie found that she looked forward to them more and more. After a long, hot day of selling tickets, getting knives thrown at her, and joining the other showfolk in making fun of the marks or rubes, as they called the audience members (Rosie quickly discovered that whatever nasty comments the audience members made about the so-called "freaks," it was nothing compared to what the freaks had to say about them), Rosie looked forward to slipping into a warm tub and a long conversation with Josephine.

Rosie didn't quite know what it was that made her and Josephine's conversations so special. Maybe it was because Josephine treated her as an equal, as someone whose thoughts and opinions were of value. And Rosie valued Josephine's opinions, too. John had commented on Rosie's good looks a thousand times, but his flowery compliments never touched her as deeply as a simple "you look nice" from Josephine.

Rosie's bathtime conversations with Josephine were her favorite part of the day. Until one night after several weeks of these talks, when things took a strange turn.

Rosie had finished her long soak and had washed her hair with the sweet floral shampoo Josephine always kept around. Rosie had gotten out of the tub and was toweling off when she lost her balance and upset the Oriental screen that separated her from Josephine. For a few seconds, Rosie stood naked before Josephine, the droplets from her wet, fragrant hair sparkling on her white shoulders and breasts.

Now Rosie's time was before our current "salad days" in which girls think they should only nibble the occasional lettuce leaf so they can show off the skeletons beneath their skin. Girls in Rosie's day ate three square meals a day and wore their curves with pride (and Rosie's curves were definitely something to be proud of).

Rosie stood before Josephine smiling, then laughing, not out of embarrassment at her nudity but in amusement at her clumsiness, until Josephine sprang from her chair, turned her back on Rosie and barked, "Put something on, will you?"

Rosie was shocked and puzzled. "I . . . I was going to." She reached for her dressing gown. "I'm sorry. I didn't mean to embarrass you. Of course, it seems like if anybody should be embarrassed it should be me." She tied her dressing gown. "You can turn around now."

Josephine turned around but didn't look Rosie in the eye. "Rosie, perhaps it would be better if, from now on, I left the tent while you bathed."

Rosie's heart deflated. It was not just the pleasure of the baths she came for, but the pleasure of Josephine's company. "But why? There's no shame in women seeing each other with no clothes on. Especially as close as we are. Why, in the past couple of months, you've become like a sister to me."

"A sister?" Josephine laughed, but somehow there was no humor in it. "Rosie, I'm tired. I think I'll go to bed early. Good night." She turned her back and waited for Rosie to leave.

Over the next two days Rosie stayed away from Josephine's quarters. They saw each other in the show, but they didn't speak except about business matters. At night, Rosie washed off the sweat and sawdust with icy water from a bucket, the coldness stinging her skin like Josephine's coldness had stung her heart.

On the third day, she couldn't take it anymore. She had to find out what had upset Josephine so much.

That night she called "Josephine!" once outside the tent door and entered before Josephine could try to send her away. Josephine looked up from her knitting, her expression shuttered.

"I have to know," Rosie said. "I have to know what I did to make you turn away from me."

"You did nothing," Josephine said. "It's because of me that our friendship cannot continue."

"But that makes no sense! Everything was fine until I knocked down the screen."

"Yes," Josephine said. "You knocked down the screen, through no fault of your own, and let me see what I want so desperately but cannot have."

Confused, Rosie thought that Josephine was saying that Rosie's smooth, feminine form had made Josephine wish that she herself could look like a normal woman. "But you shouldn't feel that way at all!" Rosie said. "You should never wish to look like other women. Why, girls like me are a dime a dozen, but you . . . you're extraordinary. And . . . lovely. I thought so the second I saw you in that green silk dress."

Josephine smiled sadly. "You're very kind, but you misunderstand me." She sighed and nervously twisted the pearl ring she wore on her left hand. "Rosie, I'm going to tell you something that may very well make you run screaming from this tent. But even if you do, at least you won't spend the rest of your life wondering why I sent you away." She paused, searching for words. "My beard isn't the only thing that makes me different from other women."

Rosie knew this was true. Josephine was different from any other woman she'd ever met—more independent and more intelligent. But she sensed it was Josephine's turn to talk and said nothing.

"Do you remember when I told you about my parents selling me to Samuel Perkins when I was thirteen?"

"Of course."

"Well, there was an incident leading up to that event which I neglected to tell you about. A few days before, my mother had caught me in the woods with a girl who lived on the neighboring farm. When Mother saw us, we were . . . kissing."

Rosie didn't understand. "Kissing like sisters?"

"No. Kissing like sweethearts."

Rosie couldn't decide what surprised her more—the fact that two girls could kiss like sweethearts, or the fact that this possibility had never crossed her mind before. She would never have thought it could happen, and yet why couldn't it? Girls had lips, didn't they? Lips that were softer than boys'. Rosie felt a little leap in her stomach like she felt the first time she saw the bright lights of a carnival. "Oh," she said.

"My mother took what she saw as a sign of how cursed I was. The beard, the unnatural feelings toward girls, even the fact that the cow had stopped giving milk—these were all signs of my cursedness. So she decided to get rid of me." Josephine shrugged.

"Oh, Josephine," Rosie sighed. "Such cruelty."

"Of course, as it turned out, selling me to Pop was good for me in that respect, too. Pop preferred the company of men—well, of one man in particular. He and Mario, the carnival's strong man, had been together for ten years before I even joined the show. So the fact that I cared only for girls was fine with Pop. He wished me the same kind of happiness that he and Mario enjoyed. The only problem was that few girls cared for me. There are few enough girls in the world who prefer female companionship, and those who do want women of their own smooth-skinned kind, not women who look like me. So in a way, my mother saying that I was cursed such that I would never know real love has come true."

Josephine paused and looked at Rosie. "But in another way it hasn't. I know you, and I love you, even though I know you can never love me." A tear formed in Josephine's eye, then slid down her cheek and disappeared into her beard. "When I saw you the other night, standing before me like Aphrodite rising from the foam, it was more than I could bear. I had to turn away. Now you know why."

Rosie didn't run away, as Josephine had thought she would. Indeed, her feet seemed glued to the spot. "You . . . you love me?"

"Yes."

"Like a sweetheart?"

"Yes."

Rosie didn't know exactly why she started crying. Was it her reaction to Josephine's bravery in confessing her feelings? Was it because she was touched or just because she was so overwhelmed she didn't know what else to do? "I . . . I don't know what to say."

"You don't have to say anything. I'm just happy you haven't run away yet."

"I don't want to run away. I want to . . . understand. Explain it to me."

Josephine wiped away a tear. "Words can't explain it." Then, perhaps figuring that the worst that could happen was Rosie slapping her face and running away, she took a step closer, reached up, and passed her fingers over Rosie's thick auburn hair. When Rosie didn't jerk away, Josephine leaned in close and pressed her lips to Rosie's.

Rosie closed her eyes and let herself be kissed. Josephine's lips were full and relaxed, very different from John's thin, tight ones, and Josephine's beard was not at all wiry and scratchy (as Rosie could remember her grandfather's beard being), but as silky and soft as the hair on Josephine's head. Through her lips, Rosie felt the power of Josephine's love—not the safe, comfortable love that men and women settled for when they followed their parents' and society's wishes and took their vows before church and state.

No, this love was something else entirely—a love that had nothing to do with the wishes of anyone but the lover, a love so powerful that it trampled over the rules of mothers and fathers and polite society in order to make itself known, a love that bloomed in a world different from the world where Rosie had always lived. The sheer force of this love nearly made Rosie swoon, even though she wasn't the swooning type.

When Josephine broke away, Rosie was as dizzy as a child who has ridden the carousel one too many times. Her senses were overwhelmed. "I . . . I have to go" was all she could say.

"Of course you do," Josephine said with a knowing sadness, sitting back down to her knitting.

All the showfolks looked forward to playing the bigger towns. In the little burgs where they most often performed, they slept in tents, washed as best they could, and lived on sandwiches and pots of beans they cooked over the campfire. But in the bigger towns like Richmond and Raleigh and Louisville, there was usually a hotel or boarding house that welcomed show people. The proprietors of these places didn't care if their customers had three legs or two heads or scales instead of skin, as long as they paid in cash. With their pockets nicely lined, they were happy to provide any assortment of people with a hot meal and a real bed and bath.

The night after Rosie and Josephine's kiss was the group's first night in Raleigh and Rosie's first night in a real hotel. When she went up the narrow stairs to the room she was assigned, she was surprised to see Josephine already there.

"After you left last night, I figured I would be having this room to myself," Josephine said.

"You thought I was leaving?"

"You said you had to go."

"I didn't go far. I just went to my tent."

Josephine let herself smile a little. "Well, I want to make clear to you that you have nothing to fear by sharing a room with me tonight. It's a matter of economy, really. It's too expensive for everybody to get a room alone. Billy does because a person of both sexes demands some privacy, but everybody else always bunks down together. Al and Tom share a room, and Stanley and Wilma."

"Stanley and Wilma share a room?"

"Yes. The two of them have been together for over a year now. I always register them in hotels as husband and wife. They would be husband and wife, too, if the husband Wilma left would go ahead and give her a divorce. He's just holding out on her to be mean. I've got half a mind to offer to pay him to divorce her, so she and Stanley can tie the knot, and I can bill them as World's Strangest Married Couple. Married acts really bring in the crowds."

"I had no idea about the two of them," Rosie said. "Does everybody else know?"

"Yes. In normal circles, it would cause quite a scandal that Wilma is still married. But we don't judge each other." Josephine looked away for a second, then said, "The reason I told you this has nothing to do with Wilma and Stanley. I just wanted you to know that you're rooming with me because it was the only choice, not because I was trying to be alone with you."

"I understand."

"Good. And I understand what it meant when you walked out of my tent last night. I'm just glad my little display didn't drive you from the show entirely."

"What did it mean?"

"I beg your pardon?"

"You said you understood what it meant when I walked out of your tent last night," Rosie said. "I was hoping you could explain to me what it meant because I'm not so sure I understand myself."

"Well . . . my understanding was that it meant you did not return my feelings."

"Hm," Rosie considered for a moment. "Maybe it meant that at that moment I was having too many feelings—more than I could possibly make sense of."

Now it was Josephine's turn to say "Hm."

Rosie sat down on the floor near Josephine's feet and looked up at her. "Josephine, you're not anything like who I ever imagined myself loving, but all my imaginary loves were heroes in books. All I know is that I spend my days looking forward to being alone with you. I don't know if it's love or friendship or sisterhood I feel for you, but I do know I feel more for you than I ever did for John."

"John?"

"The man who proposed to me the night I joined the carnival."

Josephine laughed. "That's one way to turn down a proposal." But then her smile faded. "Rosie, I want you to understand the seriousness of what you would be doing if you chose to . . . to become closer to me. By being with me, by staying here in the carnival, you would be leaving behind all that the world says is normal and natural. We would create our own life together, but it would be a life that would make no sense to anyone except us and our family of showfolk." Before Rosie could say a word, Josephine rushed on, as though if she didn't say everything in her heart right then she wouldn't have another chance.

"That's what I want, Rosie, a whole life with you. I know that many before me have been drawn to your great beauty, and heaven knows, I am, too. But even more than that, I find myself drawn to your inner light . . . a light that brightens the darkness that has surrounded me my whole life. Mine is not an easy path, Rosie, as you will see if you join me on it. And a woman with your beauty can always choose an easy life. But to choose me you have to take more than a vacation from the life in which you grew up. You have to leave it forever. It is a lot to ask—perhaps too much—and if you can't give it, don't toy with me. It would be better for you to go back to whatever little town I found you in and say 'yes' to your would-be fiancé."

Rosie thought of her life back home and all those evenings spent with John when she would rather have been at home with a good book. How was it, she wondered, that she had found so much more happiness in one month with Josephine than she had in two years with John? But when her thoughts turned to her father, she felt a twinge. Leaving John behind was easy—she had already done it. Thinking of her father sitting down to a lonely cold supper every night, though, caused her real pain. Still, hadn't he always told her to get on with her life, to find happiness?

Finally, Rosie gathered her thoughts enough to speak, wondering if she could even hear herself over the pounding of her heart. "Josephine, the world I've found here with you is the only place where I've ever felt like I belong. And the days that we didn't speak to each other were the saddest days I've spent since my mother died. So, if I can still visit my family occasionally, I am prepared to say no to the rest of the world if it means saying yes to you."

Josephine gathered Rosie in her arms, kissing her hair and whispering her name, her voice choked with tears. Soon their lips touched. A few short kisses melted into a long one with parted lips and slippery tongues. When they pulled apart, Rosie panted, "I don't remember the last time I was so out of breath."

Josephine smiled. "Did kissing what's-his-name do that to you?"

Rosie laughed. "The only time John made me out of breath was when I ran away from him after he proposed to me."

"Come to think of it, you did look a little winded the first time I saw you." Josephine reached up and stroked Rosie's cheek.

Rosie started to speak, but the dewy look in Josephine's eyes said that the conversation was over. Rosie's excitement was sharpened by a flutter of fear. "Josephine," she whispered, casting a nervous glance at the iron-framed double bed, "I need to tell you that I've never . . ." How could she say it? "I mean, not with a man or a woman either . . . I know a little about it with men from books, of course, but with you . . . I don't know what to do."

"Well," said Josephine, her arms encircling Rosie's waist, "I will be more than happy to teach you." She kissed Rosie's cheek, then left a trail of kisses down her neck. "I think you'll be a very good student."

Rosie felt a tremble of anticipation as Josephine took her hand and led her to the bed. The fact that she wasn't even sure what she was anticipating made it even more exciting. Standing by the bed,

Josephine unbuttoned Rosie's dress and let it fall to the floor, so Rosie stood before her in her white lace chemise and bloomers. Josephine motioned for Rosie to sit on the edge of the bed, then knelt on the floor at her feet, where she slipped off Rosie's shoes and rolled her stockings down each leg, kissing her from knee to toe.

"So beautiful," Josephine whispered as she pushed Rosie back on the bed and moved down to kiss the hollow of her throat and the plane of her collarbone. She loosened Rosie's chemise and kissed her white, freckle-dusted shoulders.

Rosie lay back, savoring each kiss, but was suddenly struck by self-consciousness. Freckles were far from the fashion of the day, and Rosie's sister had always offered Rosie salves and advice in hopes of getting rid of them. "Sorry about the freckles," Rosie muttered.

"They're beautiful," Josephine breathed. "Like little stars."

Soon Rosie's chemise was on the floor with her dress, and Josephine was kissing down from her collarbone to her full, white breasts. How strange and yet how lovely it was for Rosie to feel Josephine's hands stroking places that Rosie had only touched per-functorily while bathing—to feel Josephine's lips where no one's lips had been before. It was as if these places on Rosie's body had been incapable of sensation before Josephine's lips touched them, and now each kiss woke them up to pleasure. Rosie gasped and sighed, amazed by both Josephine's kisses and her body's response to them, and reached down to stroke Josephine's lustrous black hair.

When Josephine's fingertips touched the waistband of Rosie's underwear, she asked, "May I?"

"Yes," Rosie whispered, not wholly sure of what she was saying yes to, but still confident that "yes" was the right answer.

Josephine slipped off Rosie's underwear and slowly stroked Rosie's thighs and belly until Rosie moaned in a mixture of delight and frustration. When Josephine finally stopped to stroke the soft auburn hair between Rosie's legs, she said, "You see, all ladies have beards; they just don't display them most of the time."

Rosie didn't laugh for long because she was too distracted by the blissful sensation of Josephine stroking her softly with her fingertips and then bending down between her thighs and planting soft kisses there. "Can . . . can we do this?" Rosie gasped, for such an act had never occurred to her.

"We," Josephine said, pausing to plant a light kiss on each of Rosie's inner thighs, "can do anything we like."

Josephine's wandering mouth soon found a spot that most girls today are thankfully familiar with but which until that moment, Rosie hadn't even known existed. She cried out as Josephine's tongue touched it and felt herself melting into the bed as Josephine continued to caress it rhythmically, each stroke liquid fire, making Rosie soften and burn white-hot like metal in a blacksmith's forge. To Rosie, the world had shrunk to the size of her and Josephine and the bed and the pleasurable flames she was sure were surrounding them. And then that tiny world exploded, and Rosie shook and cried out, "Josephine!" It was amazing that she could say Josephine's name at that moment since she could scarcely remember her own.

When Josephine slid up the sheets to lie beside her, she murmured, "You can let go of the headboard now."

Until Josephine mentioned it, Rosie hadn't noticed that she had been holding onto the headboard so hard that her knuckles had turned white. Still too short of breath to talk, she released her grip and snuggled into Josephine's soft beard and bosom. When she could finally speak, she said, "How . . . how did you know . . . how to do that?"

Josephine kissed her forehead. "I don't know. I suppose I've always known what I wanted."

Rosie smiled and snuggled closer. "Funny, isn't it, how you've always known what you wanted, and I didn't learn what I wanted until just now."

Chapter 5

They had to eat breakfast in the hotel's kitchen so they wouldn't scare the other guests. But since the cook filled their plates with just-fried eggs and biscuits straight out of the oven, it was hard to complain. Rosie sat next to Josephine but mostly kept her eyes on her plate. When she looked at Josephine, she couldn't help smiling, and she was afraid the smile might turn into a giggle.

"You two have an awfully good appetite this morning," Billy said to Rosie and Josephine. "You must have *slept* really well last night."

The way he said "slept" made it clear that he wasn't talking about sleeping at all, and Rosie felt her face heat up.

"I know Stan and I always get a lot more *sleeping* done in a nice double bed," Wilma said, digging into her second plate of bacon and eggs as Stanley beamed at her.

And just like that, Rosie and Josephine were accepted as a couple. Rosie moved her few possessions into Josephine's tent and scooted her cot alongside Josephine's to form a rickety double bed that often collapsed during their energetic lovemaking.

Rosie knew she was living a life that would shock anyone in her family or hometown. But it didn't matter because it made perfect sense to her and seemed to make sense to the people around her.

One night when she was changing out of her red and pink satin costume backstage after the show, Billy came up to her. "Hey, can I borrow some of that cold cream?"

"Sure."

"You know, doll," Billy said, smearing the cold cream over his face, "I've been meaning to talk to you."

For some reason Rosie couldn't name, a knot of dread clenched in her stomach. "Really?"

"Yeah. You know, sometimes girls . . . pretty ones like you, who can walk down the street and have people think only good things about them . . . Sometimes a pretty girl will decide to have an adventure—maybe to sample an exotic dish before she goes back to her regular diet of meat and potatoes."

"I don't know what you mean."

Billy pursed his lips in frustration for a moment, then said, "All right. What I mean is that Josephine really loves you."

"I know that."

"And I'd hate to think that she was just a little adventure for you until you found a nice, normal man to settle down with."

"What makes you even say that?"

Billy's blue eyes stared at her from the white cold cream mask. "Because I've seen it before. Girls like you have more choices than our kind do. Sooner or later, most of them choose a nice, comfy home and a husband over a life of tents and sawdust."

Rosie's voice was cold. "I love Josephine."

Billy patted her shoulder. "I believe you mean that, now. But I've never met a girl like you that didn't get tired of the traveling life after a year or so."

Rosie was furious that Billy would assume that her soul matched her normal-looking exterior. "You never have met a girl like me."

Billy smiled. "I hope that's true. Because I've seen Josephine's heart broken before, and I don't want to see it again." He patted her hand. "I know you're mad at me now, and I'm sorry. I like you, doll, I really do. But I owe my life to Josephine, and so I feel like I have to look out for her."

"You owe her your life?"

Billy nodded. "When Josephine first saw me, I was lying in the street, covered in blood, surrounded by a pack of drunk sailors who had been entertaining themselves for the past hour by beating me to a pulp . . . and doing worse. Josephine happened to be walking down the street, dressed in her men's clothes, and when she saw what the sailors were doing to me, she took out her little pearl-handled pistol, fired it into the air, and said, 'I'm not going to waste my second bullet.'

"They scattered, Josephine helped me up, cleaned me up, and asked me to join the show."

Rosie's heart swelled in admiration for her lover. "That's quite a story."

"Josephine's quite a woman. You be careful with that heart of hers."

"Billy and I had an interesting conversation tonight," Rosie told Josephine, who was lying on her cot reading *Madame Bovary* (Josephine, Rosie had noticed, in addition to her appetite for fat Victorian novels, was also partial to French literature).

Josephine set down her book abruptly. "Really? What about?"

"About you and me," Rosie said, taking the pins out of her hair. "About how I'd better not break your heart. Apparently regular girls like me are not supposed to be trusted around girls like you. It stopped just short of being a warning, really."

"Well, I wouldn't worry about it," Josephine said with a hint of a smile. "Billy is a little overprotective of me because of something that happened a long time ago."

"He told me," Rosie said, sitting down next to Josephine on the cot. "There was something else Billy said, too. Something about someone else breaking your heart."

Josephine reached out to take Rosie's hand. "Before I met you, I used to think I was born with a broken heart. But yes . . . there was someone Billy was talking about. Her name was Mildred. She had the same job you have . . . this was a little over three years ago. And in case you're wondering, no, she wasn't anywhere near as pretty as you."

Rosie couldn't muster a smile. The story was making her too uneasy and not because she was concerned about how the other girl's looks compared to hers.

"What Mildred and I had together was very different from you and me. With her, it was more of a flirtation. She shared private jokes with me and winked at me on stage during the knife-throwing act. She'd hint, too, for little presents from the local stores—new stockings, a bottle of perfume—and I would buy them for her. There were a few kisses between us . . . some handholding. I would have liked more, of course, but Mildred always stopped things before they went too far. She didn't feel well, or she was afraid we'd get caught, or she had to be up early the next morning. The depth of my feelings for her were as shallow as a mud puddle compared to what I feel for you. But at the time, if someone had asked me if I loved her, I would have said yes."

"So what happened?" Rosie asked, only slightly comforted by Josephine's reassurances.

"The same thing that always happens to normal girls who join the show. She met a man—a big, strapping Bible salesman who stopped by the carnival one night to tell us how sinful we were. She left with him two days after she met him, but not before she told me that she never really cared for me. She said the only reason she had made nice with me because I had money and could buy her things. To tell the truth, she said, just looking at me made her sick . . . I was an ugly monster on the outside because of the unnatural way I looked and an ugly monster on the inside because of the unnatural way I felt."

Rosie was sure that if Mildred were standing before her, she could happily practice a more lethal version of Alligator Al's knife-throwing act on her. "Why that little—"

"Don't say harsh words about Mildred," Josephine said. "True, for a full year after she left I was so sick at heart I hardly slept or ate. But now I'm grateful to her."

"Grateful? Why?"

"Because she gave me quite an education. She taught me that smiles and kisses can be just as dangerous as scoldings and whippings. She taught me that what seems like kindness can be something else altogether. She taught me not to be so trusting."

Rosie stroked her lover's shiny black hair. "Poor Josephine. What a terrible lesson to learn."

"Terrible but valuable."

"Maybe so, if you don't lose all trust entirely. You trust me, don't you?"

When Josephine looked at Rosie, her dark eyes glittered with tears. "Most of the time. But sometimes . . ." She looked away. "Never mind."

"What?"

"Sometimes I wonder how someone like you could ever love someone like me."

Rosie wrapped her arms tight around Josephine and rested her head on Josephine's shoulder. "How could I not?"

Usually when Rosie and Josephine made love, it was Josephine who leaned in for the first kiss, who pushed Rosie back on the makeshift double bed. But this night it was Rosie who pushed Josephine back, who unbuttoned her butter-yellow dress, who unlaced the old-fashioned corset that Josephine always wore during the show to accentuate her feminine curves. Josephine lay back, tears still in her eyes, as Rosie stroked her skin lightly with her fingertips.

Rosie always touched Josephine with the utmost gentleness, as though her kind fingers could undo some of the cruelty Josephine had endured in her life. Rosie knew that Josephine would never believe how beautiful she found her, that Josephine was blind to her own beauty.

But Rosie loved Josephine's smooth golden skin, the strength of her arms and the softness of her breasts and belly. She loved the smell of the vanilla extract Josephine dabbed behind her ears and the slightly spicy smell, like cinnamon, that emanated from Josephine's skin. She loved Josephine's thick, lustrous, flower-scented hair, her soft beard with its mother-of-pearl barrette, and the silky hair between Josephine's thighs. When Rosie stroked her there, softly in the place Josephine loved best, Josephine smiled and sighed. Rosie felt Josephine relax under her touch, then stiffen as her pleasure grew more intense. When Josephine cried out, Rosie was sure that she could be heard outside the tent and possibly in the next county.

When Josephine opened her eyes, she reached out for Rosie's hand and squeezed it hard. "Promise you'll never leave me," she breathed.

Rosie rested her head on Josephine's bosom. "I promise."

Two weeks later they had set up in one of the tiny mountain towns where the carnival was always a great source of excitement. It was the first show of the first night, and the sideshow tent was so packed with rubes that there was no fresh air to breathe.

Rosie walked on stage in the pink and crimson satin costume she always wore for the knife-throwing act. She smiled at the crowd, then pressed her back against the large sheet of plywood where Al's knives always landed.

Al picked up the first knife and aimed it, and Rosie, as she always did, turned to look in the crowd with mock terror, as though she were starring in *The Perils of Pauline*. But the face she saw when she looked in the crowd made her stomach leap in real fear.

It's difficult to say what happened first: Al's knife sailing through the air, or the man in the crowd jumping up and yelling, "Stop! That's my sister!"

Rosie flinched, and as she did, the knife's blade grazed her left shoulder. She looked down to see a thin ribbon of blood unfurling down her arm. But there was no time to think about it because Claude was already beside her, grabbing her other arm and dragging her off the stage.

Outside the tent, he dabbed her injury with a clean hanky. Rosie was having a hard time taking in the events of the last three minutes. "How . . . how did you find me?" she asked.

"Well, it wasn't because I spent a lot of time looking for you." Claude's brow was furrowed in irritation, and Rosie couldn't help noticing that his hairline was already creeping back like their father's. "I happened to be here on business and saw a poster for the carnival at a diner downtown. The picture of the girl in the knife-throwing act looked just like you."

"Stanley drew it . . . Colonel Peanut. He's a good artist, I think."

Claude did not comment on Stanley's artistic ability. "Of course, I didn't really believe it was you until I actually saw you. You've always been such a sensible girl, Rosie. I'm shocked that you'd run off and do something like this."

Rosie inspected her cut, which, luckily, was shallow and clean. "Maybe I was tired of being a sensible girl." She looked up at her brother. "Has Daddy gotten the money I've been sending?"

"He has. And he's so proud, thinking you're working for a famous singer or some hogwash like that. I suppose it's a good thing you didn't tell him what you're really doing. Performing in a traveling carnival, wearing hardly any clothes . . . something like this could ruin a girl's reputation."

"Claude, I don't care about my reputation. I'm having the time of my life."

"A girl like you shouldn't be having that kind of time. It's way past time you settled down." The rubes were pouring out of the tent. The show was over. "But we'll have time to talk about this later. You're coming home with me."

Rosie stamped her pink-slippered foot in indignation. "I most certainly am *not* going home with you! You've made your life back home. I've made my life right here—"

"Turn off that redhead's temper for just a minute," Claude said. Now his tone was kind. "I'm not asking you to come back for me. I'm asking you to come back for Dad. There was a logging accident—"

"Is he—"

"He's hurt. Both legs broken, plus one arm. He's been in the hospital for two full weeks now. The doctor says it will be some time before he can walk again. With someone Dad's age, you can never be certain. What is certain, though, is that when he comes home, he's going to need somebody to take care of him. And our sister can't come home and do it because she's busy with her new baby."

Rosie wanted to believe this was all a lie to get her to come back home, but when she looked into Claude's eyes, which were the same color and shape as hers, she knew it was true.

How, she wondered, could she go back to a life of cleaning house and cooking soup beans when everything she loved was right here? Well, not everything she loved. She loved her father, too, and when she thought of him alone and hurting and wondering where she was, she knew she had no choice. "I'll go," she said. "I just need to get my things and talk to Josephine."

"Who's Josephine?"

There was no way to answer the question in a way Claude would understand. "My . . . my friend."

Outside the tent she and Josephine shared she said, "Why don't you wait outside for a minute while we talk?"

"Nonsense," Claude blustered. "I can have all your things packed in the time it takes for you to talk to her. Besides, I'm your brother. There's nothing you girls can say that you can't say in front of me."

And so, much to Rosie's irritation, Claude followed her into the tent.

"There you are," Josephine cried when she saw Rosie. "I've been looking for you. I keep a first aid kit here. Sit down. I'll bandage your arm for you."

Rosie sat down, and Josephine dabbed gently at her wound with an alcohol-soaked piece of gauze. The cut hurt Rosie a little, but not as much as the knowledge of what she was about to say. She looked over at Claude and saw he was looking at Josephine the way all the other rubes did, with a mixture of amazement and disgust. His thoughts—*Is that really a woman?* and *Is that beard real?*—were so obvious they might as well have been printed on his forehead. "This is Claude," Rosie said, to explain his presence.

"I'm her brother," Claude added.

"Yes, I gathered that from what you shouted during the show," Josephine said, securing the bandage to Rosie's arm. "If you had been able to withhold that piece of information until the show was over, your sister wouldn't need this bandage."

"Now look here," Claude said, "there's no need to be rude."

"Not rude," Josephine said, "just matter-of-fact. Common sense should tell anyone over the age of six not to yell at the top of his voice when a man's about to throw a knife in the direction of his sister."

"I . . . I just didn't want her to get hurt." Claude was clearly annoyed at being dressed down by a woman whom he'd just met, let alone a woman with a beard.

"Well, you didn't do a very good job of preventing it, did you?" Josephine said.

"Actually, I think I am doing a good job of preventing it—at least in the long run." He looked at the four dresses hanging on a line stretched across the back corner of the tent. "Rosie, are these yours?"

"Yes." Rosie's answer was almost a whisper.

"Why does he care about the whereabouts of your dresses, Rosie?" Josephine's voice seethed with suspicion. "Could it possibly be that he's helping you pack your things?"

Rosie hadn't expected to be put on the defensive like this. It made what she had to say even harder. "Josephine, it's not what you think. There's been an accident. My father is hurt. I need to go see him, and I may need to stay with him a while . . . a month, maybe two. But I'll catch up with the show after that. I'll be back."

"Every person—every normal person—who has left the show has said that." There was a catch in Josephine's voice. "But they never came back."

"Well, she won't be back if I have anything to do with it," Claude announced as he snapped Rosie's traveling trunk shut.

"Well, you don't have anything to do with it!" Rosie shot back at him.

"Oh, I imagine he does," Josephine said. "Him . . . your father . . . your sister . . . Why choose to live in a family of freaks when you can have the luxury of walking down the street without people screaming or fainting? Sooner or later, normal people choose to be with their kind and live normal lives. It's natural—like calls to like. And when you have the luxury of choosing, a normal life is certainly an easier life. I might choose it myself . . . if I had the luxury."

"Josephine, it's not like that!" Rosie's chest felt so tight she feared her heart might explode. "I'm not like all the others . . . I'm not normal. I don't want what normal people want; I just need to take care of my father."

"I understand that," Josephine said. "You're a loyal daughter, and you're right to do your duty. But I also understand that once you've been out there for a while, it gets harder and harder to come back here."

"You're all packed," Claude said. "Let's go."

Rosie wondered how he could be so blind to the emotional scene he was witnessing. "Well," Rosie said, her voice choked, "I will see you again, Josephine."

Josephine rested her hand on Rosie's cheek. "So beautiful. Inside and out. I wish you a beautiful life."

Rosie couldn't find any more words. She leaned in and kissed

Josephine's cheek, and when she did, she tasted the salt of her sweetheart's tears.

"What a strange woman," Claude said, as he carried her trunk across the carnival grounds.

"I suppose she is," Rosie said.

"Does she always make speeches like that?"

"Not always." Only when someone has broken her heart, Rosie thought.

They passed Wilma and Stanley beside the candy apple stand. "Are you all right, Rosie?" Wilma asked. "When I saw that knife graze your arm, I thought I was going to faint dead away."

"I'm all right," Rosie said. "I'm leaving for a month or two, though. My father's had an accident."

Wilma said, "I hope he gets well soon," and Stanley said, "Take care of yourself, kid," but what Rosie heard them say as she walked away was, "Poor Josephine."

At the edge of the carnival, they ran into absolutely the last person Rosie wanted to see. Billy was in a dressing gown to cover the "half male/half female" bare chest he displayed in his show, but other peculiarities—the half made-up face, the long wavy locks on one side and the short mannish hair on the other—still made Claude stare slack-jawed.

Billy took in Claude, the trunk, and Rosie. "Leaving so soon?" Billy purred.

"Well—" Rosie began.

"This would be your boyfriend, I presume," Billy interrupted.

"No, my brother," Rosie said coldly. "My father has been in an accident. I need to go see him—"

"Yes, well, home and hearth always call your kind back one way or another," Billy sighed. "I expect I'd better go see to Josephine."

Claude made chit-chat all the way to the train station. Rosie knew he was probably talking about Helen and the baby and their home and his job. But she didn't hear a word he said.

Chapter 6

The hospital in Rosie's hometown was a twelve-bed infirmary, with six beds in one room for female patients and six in another for males. When Rosie stepped into the men's ward to see her father, he lay on his narrow bed, casts on both legs and one arm. He was the only patient in the room. Rosie thought she had never seen anyone so alone and helpless.

When he saw her, he smiled. "Rosie, you came!"

Rosie leaned over and kissed his cheek. "Of course I did. I just wish I had known sooner."

A middle-aged nurse bustled into the room, pretty and efficient-looking in her white uniform.

"Well," Mr. Bell said. "Judith here's been taking good care of me, haven't you, Judith?"

The nurse smiled as she fluffed Mr. Bell's pillows. "I've been doing my best. He's the only patient in the men's ward right now, but you'd be surprised how busy he keeps me. You must be Rosie."

"Yes, ma'am."

Judith smiled. "Your father talks about you all the time. He says no man ever had such a smart, beautiful, honest daughter."

The "honest" stung Rosie since she had been lying to her father about her job, but she forced herself to smile back at Judith anyway. Now was not the time to clear up misunderstandings.

Rosie sat with her father every day, reading him the newspaper in the morning and the cowboy novels he loved in the afternoon. Claude stopped by to visit but not often; clearly he thought that the responsibility of caring for a sickly parent should fall to a daughter, not a son.

But Rosie was not the only person caring for Mr. Bell. Judith was quite attentive, too. And Rosie was beginning to wonder if Judith's attentiveness went beyond the bounds of mere professional responsibility.

Once Mr. Bell had joked that the first thing he was going to do when he got his casts off was chase Judith around the room. Judith, with her salt-and-pepper hair and finely lined face, had giggled like a teenager.

Another time, when Rosie had gone outside for some fresh air, she had returned to find Judith holding Mr. Bell's good hand. She dropped it as soon as she saw Rosie.

One afternoon while Mr. Bell was napping and Judith was gathering the linens from the women's ward for laundering, Rosie asked, "Judith, could I speak with you for a moment?"

Judith smiled, but Rosie thought she saw some apprehension in her eyes. "Of course."

Rosie wasn't sure how to say what she wanted to say, but she decided to go ahead and blunder her way through it. "I couldn't help noticing that my father really seems to like you."

Judith became unusually absorbed in stripping the sheets from a bed. "Your father is a very dear man," she said without looking up.

"I know he is. And you're a very nice lady." Rosie touched Judith's shoulder. "Judith, what I'm trying to say is . . . if there's something between you and Daddy . . . something more than a nurse-patient relationship . . . nothing would make me happier."

Judith looked back at her, beaming. "Really?"

"Really. Dad's been so lonely since Mama died. I worry about him so much."

Judith sat down on the hospital bed and patted the spot beside her. "Rosie, I'm so happy . . . and surprised . . . to hear you say that. Your father didn't want me to tell you because he was afraid you'd think he was being unfaithful to your mother."

"He can't live the rest of his life being faithful to a memory."

"It's true," Judith said. "And I've been so lonely, too, these years since my husband passed. Your father and I are both staring at old age, Rosie, and that's not a part of life you want to face alone."

"Well," Rosie squeezed Judith's strong hand. "I'm glad neither of you have to."

At the house that evening Rosie sipped tea and thought about the unexpected happiness that two broken legs had brought her father. For the first time since she had come home, she dared to think of her own chance at happiness. With Judith there to care for Mr. Bell once he came home, Rosie would be free to go back to the carnival and back to Josephine. But her heart hurt when she thought of Josephine's parting words to her. She would go back to Josephine, but only if Josephine would have her, if she could make Josephine believe that she would never leave her again.

Rosie's brooding was interrupted by a knock on the door. She opened it to find John, standing in the doorway, beaky-nosed and bespectacled. Had he always looked so much like a ferret, Rosie wondered, or had she just never noticed before?

"Hel . . . hello, Rosie," he stammered.

"Hello, John," Rosie said, resisting the urge to slam the door and lock it.

"May I come in?"

"If you like."

John waited for Rosie to sit, and she chose the chair rather than the couch so he couldn't sit down beside her.

"How's your father?" he asked.

"Much better. The casts come off next week, and the doctor says he shouldn't suffer any long-term damage."

"That's excellent news."

"Yes, it is," Rosie said, but what she really wanted to say was, what in the name of heaven are you doing here?

"Rosie . . ." John fiddled with the hat he held on his lap.

"Yes?" Rosie knew her voice sounded impatient, but she didn't especially care.

"I just wanted you to know that I think it's wonderful how you came back here to care for your father. It shows how sensible and mature you've become—"

"I love my father. Of course I came back to look after him."

"See? Sensible and mature, just like I said. And I . . . I want you to know that I forgive you for what happened that night at the carnival."

Rosie's spine stiffened. She didn't like where this was going. "Thank you, John. It's very kind of you to forgive me."

"And—" He looked down and fiddled with his hat some more. "Now that you've obviously changed . . . matured, as I said, I'd like to make you the same offer I made that night."

Rosie sprang from her seat in shock. "John, are you asking me to marry you *again?*"

"Yes. As I said, I forgive you, and I'm prepared—"

Rosie's arms were folded tight across her chest, and her eyes flashed with anger and exasperation. "Honestly, John, how many times does a girl have to say no to you?"

"I just figured you'd had time to do some thinking."

"I have. And running away from you that night was the best decision I've ever made."

He stood and slapped his hat onto his head. "Well, if that's the way you feel, I might as well leave. I was just trying to do you a favor, you know. To save you from spinsterhood." He stood in the doorway, then turned around. "Think about it, Rosie. Your last chance is about to walk out the door."

"My last chance? For what?"

John looked at her as though he was regarding a none-too-bright three-year-old. "For happiness."

Rosie laughed. "What makes you think you hold the key to my happiness? There are other ways for a girl to be happy than having a husband and a houseful of kids."

"Well, there may be," John said. "But they're not normal ways . . . not respectable."

"Well, maybe having a husband and children isn't normal for me," Rosie snapped. "And maybe I can find ways of being happy such that I can still respect myself."

Standing in the doorway, John shook his head as though Rosie had just said the most ridiculous thing he had ever heard. "Well, whatever those ways are, I hope you find them."

Rosie thought of her days with Josephine, of their nights on the shoved-together cots. "I already have."

Judith became the second Mrs. Bell in a quiet ceremony the day after Mr. Bell returned home from the hospital. Rosie cried at the ceremony—both for their happiness and for her uncertain future. She knew she was free to go back to Josephine, but she couldn't help replaying Josephine's words in her mind—"Why choose to live in a family of freaks when you have the luxury of walking down the street without people screaming or fainting? Normal people choose to live normal lives because they can."

Josephine had been so hurt and betrayed so many times by the normal world that Rosie feared she would never be able to fully trust a girl such as herself . . . a girl who could always choose to run away and find acceptance in the larger society.

Then it came to Rosie what she must do.

Chapter 7

It took Rosie nearly three months to complete the task she had set for herself. Like any heroic task, it was long and painful, but even in her most difficult moments, she bore the pain by closing her eyes and picturing Josephine. And then she had an even harder task ahead of her.

With today's technology it is alarmingly easy to find someone you're looking for. In Rosie's day, this was not the case. She traveled through small towns in Virginia, North Carolina, and Tennessee, sometimes stopping to do a day's work apple picking or dishwashing to earn more train fare, always asking when the carnival had last been to town. If a carnival had been there in recent memory, she always asked a second question: Had there been a bearded lady? All too often, the answer was no.

In Georgia, though, she felt she might be getting the scent of a trail. An old man picking peaches beside her said that a carnival had been to town two weeks before. "There was a bearded lady, too," he said. "Woulda been right pretty if it wasn't for the whiskers. Called herself Madame something. Started with a J, I think."

"Josephine?" Rosie asked, squeezing a peach so hard that juice dribbled down her wrist.

"That sounds right. My brother lives in Versailles, the next town north of here. Said the carnival was there last week."

So they were moving north. At the rate the carnival moved—one town per week—they should be in the next town up from Versailles, Rosie thought. She thanked the old man and announced that she was through picking peaches.

Rosie made it to the carnival in time for the last show of the night. Wearing a long black dress and long black gloves despite the heat, she bought a ticket from a seemingly normal man she didn't recognize and crowded in with the rubes inside the tent.

When Josephine took the stage, Rosie was shocked by her appearance. The once snug-fitting emerald green gown she favored for performing now hung loosely from her narrow waist and hips. Had heartbreak made her so thin? Tears pooled in Rosie's eyes.

"I come from the backwoods of Kentucky," Josephine was saying automatically. "When my mother was still expecting me she was frightened by a wild boar that came charging out of the woods—" Suddenly Josephine was silent, and her eyes met Rosie's.

After a full minute of silence, Wilma nudged Josephine, who said, "I'm sorry. I'm sorry, everyone. I was just thinking about . . . the past. But you don't care about my story anyway, do you? You just wanted to see me. And you have. And now you must excuse me."

She stepped off the stage and walked through the audience toward Rosie. The rubes parted, as if afraid that brushing against Josephine might make them freakish, too.

"Rosie?" Josephine said, as the rubes stared at them.

"Yes." Try as she might, Rosie couldn't read the look on Josephine's face.

"How is your father?"

"Recovered . . . and remarried."

"Rosie," Josephine said again.

"We can't talk here," Rosie said, feeling the dozens of pairs of eyes on them. "Take me to your tent. I have something to show you."

In her tent, Josephine hugged Rosie so tight she could scarcely breathe. "I never thought I would see you again."

"I told you I'd come back."

"And I wanted to believe you. But I couldn't because they . . . they never do." Josephine let Rosie go. "And even though you have come back, how do I know you'll stay? If you left again, Rosie, I couldn't endure it. The normal ones always choose to leave because they can. They—"

"I'm not a 'they,' Josephine." Rosie took Josephine's hands in hers. "I am me. And I'm not like all the other rubes. I am one of you."

Josephine released her. "I . . . I don't understand."

"Remember how I said I had something to show you?" Rosie pulled off her long black gloves and unbuttoned her dress until she stood before Josephine in just her chemise.

Josephine, who was used to causing shock in others but not to being shocked herself, gasped. Rosie's fair skin—her shoulders, arms and hands, her legs and feet, were now decorated with trailing green vines, thorns, and leaves which led to fully blooming red roses. On her left forearm a butterfly lit on a rose. On her right thigh, a hummingbird fluttered over another rose to sip its nectar. A honeybee hovered above a blossom on her shoulder.

"You see," Rosie said. "I'm not Rosie Bell anymore. I am La Belle Rose, the Tattooed Lady. And my life isn't out there with the ordinary people. It's here with you."

Josephine moved closer and trailed a finger down a snaking vine on her arm. "So beautiful. But so much pain . . . for me?"

"It was nothing compared to the pain of being away from you."

When Josephine's and Rosie's lips met, the two worlds they knew—the normal world and the carnival world—faded to black, and there was nothing but the two of them.

Josephine led Rosie to the narrow cot, pushed her back, unbuttoned her chemise and gasped again to find another surprise—

Rosie's lovely breasts were white and devoid of ink except for a heart-shaped vine tattooed on the left over Rosie's own heart, with the name "Josephine" in script inside it.

With tears in her eyes, Josephine leaned to Rosie's ear and whispered, "Your name is written on my heart, too."

Josephine kissed each picture on Rosie's body: licking the rose petals, biting the bumblebee, tracing her tongue and fingers up the vines that trailed from Rosie's ankles to Rosie's calves to Rosie's thighs to the part of Rosie that was free of illustration and exactly the way Josephine remembered it. There Josephine lingered, her face dipping down like a nectar-thirsty hummingbird over a rose.

And to Rosie it felt like the speed of a hummingbird's wings with which Josephine's tongue flickered against that most sensitive spot. This sensation, she knew, was what she had always wanted even before she knew she wanted it. Rosie was soaring with joy, carnival lights shimmering in her head, her breath coming in great gasps, her hands tangled in Josephine's long black hair. When the carnival lights burst into fireworks, she cried out, "Oh, Josephine! My sweetheart!" Her thighs quaked, and her hips bucked so hard that the flimsy cot collapsed beneath them.

Rosie laughed as she sprawled naked in the sawdust, but Josephine still asked, "Are you all right?"

"Never better," Rosie said.

Josephine held out her hand to help Rosie up. "We'd better get dressed. It's time for the second show. And as delighted as many audience members would be to see you in your current state, I think it would be wise for La Belle Rose to make her debut with at least a few stitches on."

Rosie smiled. "Will my old costume from the knife-throwing act do?"

"It will until I sew you a new one. You'll need a new costume now that you're here permanently." Josephine kissed Rosie's shoulder blade as she zipped up her costume.

"Yes, permanently," Rosie said.

The love she and Josephine carried in their hearts was as permanent as the ink on her skin. It would be with them all of their days.

A Butch in Fairy Tale Land

by Therese Szymanski

Chapter 1

I knew something was up with Sal and Sheila. I mean, it really didn't take a brain surgeon to figure it out—a few months ago, they started arguing a lot. They tried to hide it from me, but I knew. Every time I walked into a room, they'd suddenly shut up and go into a tense silence. What other explanation could there be but that they were fighting?

But then one day, Sheila came over to return some books. She was sporting a nasty black eye.

"I ran into a door," she said.

"Yeah, right." I couldn't believe she'd hide the truth from me, of all people. "What's going on, Sheila?"

"It's nothing to worry about. Everything's all right, really Cody."

"That doesn't look like all right to me. And I know you didn't run into any door."

"Okay, fine, you're right. I didn't run into a door. But you don't have to worry about it."

"It was Sal, wasn't it? I mean, I've seen how you two have been acting lately."

"Fine, it was Sal—but you don't have to worry about it. Everything's fine."

"You keep saying that, but—"

"Cody, I know how much you love saving damsels in distress—but I'm not one. There's a perfectly reasonable explanation for this. I just can't tell you what it is right now."

Sheila was making concern for a friend sound like a psychological disorder. " 'Damsels in distress?' I don't have a thing for damsels in distress! I just worry about my friends is all."

"Cody," Sheila said, running her soft hand lightly over my cheek. I felt a flush start to rush up my neck. "Face facts. You like helping femmes."

"And that's a bad thing?"

"It is when they don't need saving. I mean, Linda's cat, for example."

"It was up a tree for chrissakes."

"The same tree it always got into—and out of—all by itself. If you had bothered to ask her, you could've avoided another trip to the emergency room."

"I still don't know why it bit me when I was just trying to help." Why did they have to keep bringing up that cat? It was an honest mistake—and I paid for it with the stitches and two days in the hospital!

"Word to the wise—most people would have dropped the cat after the first dozen bites."

"I'm tenacious if anything."

"What about the time Diane was worried about her ex stalking her, so you decided to keep track of her?"

"I was just trying to help, I—"

"Cody, Diane's paranoid. If you had remembered that, Sal and I wouldn't have had to bail you out." She took my hand in her warm one and led me to the couch. We sat down facing each other. "You jump to conclusions and take your own actions. That time Diane just thought you were her stalker. But then there was Patrice, whom you really were stalking."

"Oh, c'mon, that girl was so lost she made Hansel and Gretel look like they knew the way home. She was always losing her keys, tripping her circuit breakers, driving over nails and misplacing her car."

I shuffled nervously. Sheila had her pegged. "Plus she was cute."

"Cute? Uh-uh. She was drop-dead gorgeous! But she did need help!"

"And you wanted to be the one to always give it to her. Cody, you spooked her so bad, she moved to another state."

"Have you heard from her lately?"

Sheila rolled her eyes as she stood up. "Cody, we've known each other since high school. We roomed together in college—I know you." She leaned over to ruffle my short brown hair, just like she'd been doing for more than a decade. "I love you, but you're an incurable romantic."

I shrugged. "I just want to help."

"You read way too many romances, too many fairy tales in college. The real world's never as easy as all that."

I can't remember how many times she'd harassed me about that damned fairy-tale class I took as an English major. I was devoutly grateful I had never told her I'd toyed with the idea of doing graduate studies in fairy tales. A butch could only take so much teasing.

"Listen, just know that everything's all right with Sal and me—never better, in fact. So don't worry." She turned back for one last parting warning. "And don't be going all stalker-butch on us either."

I knew there was something going on. After all, Sheila had displayed all the classic signs. In fact, they both had, for several months. I was an idiot not to have seen it sooner.

Fortunately, for me and Sheila, all reason indicated that it would be some time before Sal got really out of control—after all, didn't the anger and fighting escalate before an abusive spouse finally went too far?

I couldn't believe this was surfacing now. They had been together for more than a decade, but I had known Sheila for longer than that. I remember when they first met, how Sheila went on and on about this hot new butch she was seeing, and how gallant and sexy and smart she was and everything. Then she'd finish by saying, "But she's just after my money, like every hottie I meet."

Made me wonder when they filed their wills.

Thank goodness it was Spring Break and the swim team at Paul K. Cousino High School didn't need me. I decided to follow them. But if there's one thing I've learned through all my many misadventures, it's how to properly follow someone so they won't know I'm there.

During the week I didn't see anything overtly threatening, though it did look as if they had a few heated conversations—apparently about some paperwork, which I figured was their wills, because they kept pulling out bound manuscripts of some sort. Sheila had money, and some property, stocks and such, so her will would be very long and complicated, especially if she was giving stuff to more than one person. If she wasn't planning to leave everything to Sal that could explain the fighting.

When the weekend rolled around though, it looked like I'd hit the jackpot. They were obviously preparing to go away for a few days, or maybe longer, considering how much they were packing.

I quickly went back to my own place to pack my car, and then carefully tailed them out of Royal Oak to I-94, then out past Port Huron, and even the village of Lexington, to a cottage secluded in a forest. It was at least an hour off the main road, so that even I was worried about them seeing me. As soon as I saw the cozy little place that was their apparent destination, I immediately backed down the road, out of sight. I waited plenty long enough for them to unload their copious baggage.

And then I waited a bit longer. Well, okay, I kinda snuck through the woods to peer through the trees so I could keep an eye on them to make sure they were actually gonna stay at this cottage out in the middle of nowhere. Once I was sure they were there to stay, and they were out of sight inside, I slunk over to it, carefully hiding behind whatever objects were available. As I approached, I heard Sal's and Sheila's raised voices. Well, hell, they weren't raised voices, they were yelling. Screaming. At each other.

I peered through the window, not wanting to make any abrupt moves. If it was just shouting, that was one thing. Hitting was another.

Given Sheila's lecture of earlier in the week, I didn't want to go barging in until something actually was going wrong. I couldn't jump the gun, not this time. I had to wait.

But I didn't have to wait long. Sal's arm went flying, and then so did Sheila—all the way onto the couch. Had Sal been working out?

I was through the door in less time than it takes for The Scottish Play to go bad. After all, given my life, I had practice breaking down doors. Of course it helps when they're ajar so I go flying into the room like a total idiot.

"Cut!" I heard someone yell. Then that someone turned to me, looking very irritated. "Who the hell are you?"

"Cody!" Sheila yelled, jumping up from the couch. "What the hell are you doing here?"

"Ummm . . . helping?"

"Goddamned dyke," Sal said, turning from me in disgust. "I told you to stay away from her," she said to Sheila.

"She's been my friend for longer than I've known you. I couldn't just tell her to get lost, not without a reason."

I looked around at the camera and lighting equipment that hadn't been visible through the barely open blind. Out the back window of the cottage I spotted a large van and two more cars. "What's going on here?"

"We were shooting a movie, until you came charging in," the snotty butch who had first spoken said. I was sure I could take her and Sal at once. But there were several other women in the room as well, all in the shadows. I had an impression of a pair of fine black eyes from behind the camera, watching every move I made.

"Cody, I told you not to worry—and I believe I specifically mentioned that you should not follow us," Sheila said. She looked up at me from the couch, completely uninjured.

"But the black eye—"

"Darcy here—whom you might remember from college?—is making a movie. It's very low budget, so she asked Sal and me to star in it."

"But . . ." I suddenly remembered Sheila had been a theatre major. "But why couldn't you tell me?"

"In case it sucked totally and we didn't want anyone to know about it. Sal and I were rehearsing this fight scene, by ourselves, when she got too close and clobbered me. I told you everything was all right—so why the fuck didn't you believe me?"

"Now we've got to take it from the top," Darcy said, throwing her hands up.

"Why couldn't you for once listen to someone?" Sal asked.

"I . . . I'm sorry—"

"Just get the fuck out."

I looked around at all of the accusing stares aimed at me and gave them a slight smile. I felt like an asshole.

"I specifically told you not to follow us, Cody," Sheila said.

I did the only thing I could think of—they wouldn't let me apologize, so I turned and ran. I didn't pay any attention to where I was going, I simply ran into the woods. I didn't even think to try to find my car. I just needed to be elsewhere.

Chapter 2

I ran and I ran and I ran. Okay, so maybe I just ran and ran. Gotta give up that pack-a-day habit. Anyway, it was quite enough running for me to get totally turned around in the dense forest. I had no idea where I was, nor where I had come from.

Maybe in more ways than one.

I tripped over something and went flying into a tree. Fortunately, I was still together enough to put my arms up to protect my head. But it still knocked the wind right out of me and gave me a mouthful of dirt. I spit the dirt out the best I could.

I lay on my stomach for a moment, still catching my breath while I listened for sounds of pursuit. Then I put my head down in my arms and cried for a while. I couldn't believe the disappointed look in Sheila's eyes when she said she'd told me not to follow them. I couldn't believe they were just making a bloody movie!

Really, I was the injured party here. C'mon, I was just trying to help out a friend. I've read all about battered partners and all that, and of course I look out for Sheila—we've been friends since grade school! No one could ever be good enough for her. Not even Sal.

Now, okay, fine. Maybe sometimes in the past I was a bit over eager and all, but I knew this time I had been fully within my best-friend rights. I pushed myself to my feet, wiped my face on my sleeve, and sat down on a rock to catch my breath and try to figure things out. And light up a smoke.

I already knew I felt like an asshole, and should've listened to my best friend when she told me it was all right. But still, I would have expected Sheila to come after me, to look for me. I couldn't have come so far that I'd be beyond her yelling my name.

But I didn't hear anything.

I couldn't even see the underbrush I must have trampled before barreling into that tree. Then I saw a flash of red through the dense branches, which really didn't make a lot of sense unless it was someone looking for me.

"Hey!" I called out, and the red stopped briefly, then rushed along even faster than before. I got to my feet to follow. It wasn't hunting season, and besides, didn't those guys usually wear shades of obnoxious and toxic orange?

Besides, whoever it was—and as I chased after the red, I knew it was a person—was either a dwarf or a child wearing a long, red hooded cloak.

It took a bit, but eventually I got a peek at what was under the hood. She was young, a teenager at the most, with blonde hair that curled around her face. Red glanced behind her once or twice, as if to see if I were following—but never acknowledged me.

She looked vaguely familiar. She carried a picnic basket in one hand and moved quickly, yet surely, through the woods, as if she were afraid a big, bad wolf was out to get her.

I followed little Ms. Red Cloak, hoping she'd lead me back to my car, or to someone who would know where I might've parked. After all, this forest couldn't be so big anyone who lived here wouldn't know where the cottage was.

So I followed her over the river and through the wood, feeling safe lagging far behind her because her red cloak would make her visible all the way through the Hundred-Acre Wood.

This forest was a lot bigger than I thought it was. And a lot hillier than anything in Michigan had a right to be.

Finally, after what seemed like hours, she arrived at a neat and tidy little log cabin that looked like an oversized version of Lincoln Logs. Red walked up the stone pathway that led to the front door (from the middle of the woods?) and boldly knocked.

"Grandmother?" she cried. "Oh grandmother! I have come to bring you a basket full of treats from my mother!"

Speaking of treats, my stomach growled. I inched closer until I could smell the fried chicken. Now that was a treat that could get me to do my Snoopy dance.

"Grandma? Where are you?" Red pounded on the door again. "Please answer, darkness comes swiftly and I am afraid of the wolves in this forest."

Oh, ya gotta be kidding me.

"Dear," a gravelly voice croaked from inside the cottage, "I am very sick and can't get out of bed."

"But then whoever will let me in?"

"The door is unlocked. Come in and tend to your poor, ill grandma."

Now, I know lots of women and lots of men. Lots of TGs, TSs, TVs and every other possible combination and degree in between— and one thing I could tell you was that wasn't a woman with that voice. I wasn't quite sure what it was, but it wasn't a woman, of that I was certain.

While I was trying to decide what to do, the girl in her red cloak opened the door and went in.

Red cloak, with a hood. Little girl in the woods. Isolated cabin.

Okay, now all of that could either belong in a horror or porn flick. But add in the sick *grandmother*, who was unquestionably not a woman, with a gravelly voice, and it all added up to one thing. One thing that was, without a doubt, not possible. Nonetheless, one couldn't be too safe, so I quickly found the obligatory axe by the woodpile.

It was heavier than it looked. Grandmother must've had someone doing the chopping for her—someone like the local woodcutter perhaps. That is, unless she was The Little Old Lady from Pasadena, mixed in with the woman who wears a purple hat, and Miss Universe.

The cutting edge looked dull, so I found a slice of rough, thick leather, and did my best to sharpen the blade. Unfortunately, I cut the leather into two pieces. Oh, god, why couldn't I have taken some sort of knife class in college? Maybe even a good culinary course? Well, okay, those would've had me sharpening blades with something metal.

Oh well. I'd done the best I could. I brought the heavy axe up to rest on my shoulder and went to the cabin. I didn't have all day to waste, after all.

Having learned my lesson not too long ago, I tried the door before charging through it. It was unlocked, so I silently entered.

"Grandmother, what big eyes you have!"

"The better to see you with, my dear."

Okay, so when I was dashing through the forest, I ran into a tree, hit my head, and was now out cold, lying on the damp forest floor, probably with a concussion, and lots of little animals nibbling at me.

"Grandmother, what big ears you have!"

"The better to hear you with, my dear."

Oh, well. As long as I was here, I might as well do something. Especially since I knew how this story went.

"But Grandmother, what big teeth you have!"

I didn't bother trying the bedroom door first. Instead I opened it with a swift kick. Thank god for kickboxing!

What greeted me was so much like a scene from a Disney movie that I almost laughed out loud. A wolf lay on the bed, wearing a little old lady's cap and nightgown, and speaking English.

"The better to eat you with, my dear!" the big, bad wolf shouted, leaping from the bed and grabbing Little Red Riding Hood.

"This is so overdone," I said, bringing up the axe with both hands and swinging it from my shoulder to lop his head off. Or at least, that was the game plan. What actually happened was the swing threw the wolf back onto the bed with a deep red gash across his throat.

I thought I heard his neck crack on the second swing, but I still wasn't sure, so I tried again. It took four swings total for me to be sure the big, bad wolf was dead. And the head was still kinda attached. Okay, so I was no woodcutter.

I turned to the stunned girl, really not wanting to look at the really dead, bloodied, neck-skewed wolf's corpse any longer. "For chrissakes, when was your grandmother ever quite so furry? And are you gonna even try to tell me her nose was anywhere near so prominent?"

"That, that wasn't my grandmother!"

"Duh. Now run and get me a nice sharp knife." She stood still, looking at the blood pooling on the floor. "Yo, Red, can we hurry it up a bit? Your grandma's being digested even as we speak."

Red ran to out of the room and quickly returned with an evilly sharp knife. I took it, hoping to god I was right about this, because I was sure Red would be really sad if granny was dead. If memory served, grandma could still be retrieved from the wolf's over-extended belly. (Really, did Red think grandma was pregnant or what?)

I took the knife, looked away, and aimed toward the beast's gut— only stopping my own hand at the last moment. I couldn't exactly do a random stab-in-the-gut now, could I? Grandma was in there!

I thought about lighting a smoke, but Red was staring at me expectantly, and I really did think the old woman was being digested. And I remembered why I decided against becoming a surgeon—I mean, I even had trouble dissecting Marsha, my dead frog in ninth grade bio!

I looked at the girl, then turned and sliced the beast open, gutting him like a fish. Wow. A sharp knife really does make a difference.

And there was grandma, gasping for breath. The wolf had swallowed her whole.

Just then, the front door burst open, and the woodsman came charging in, his own axe in hand.

"You're a little late," I said, kicking away my axe.

I washed my hands and the knife on the way out, slipping the handy blade into the back of my jeans. Maybe I wasn't in a movie, but I knew the time for a quick exit. But that still didn't stop me from grabbing a piece of that mouth-watering chicken from Red's basket.

Back into the dark woods I went, munching happily on a second piece of chicken. It was gonna play hell with my cholesterol, but it was all a dream. A really silly dream. And I was gonna wake up now.

How long did this forest go on for anyway?

Yup, right now, I was gonna come to on the forest floor and get some grub and go to the hospital for the concussion I was sure to have. My stomach rumbled its compliance with the decision to get food before going to the hospital. All I had to do was wake up and find my car.

Right now. As in, this instant.

But the scenery didn't change. I was still walking alone through the woods, and when I looked back, I couldn't see Grandma's cottage, nor any hint of smoke from the chimney.

I hadn't walked that far. It was as if the structure had simply disappeared. That wasn't possible.

But I had just slit open a wolf—*ick!*—and had a woman jump from its tummy, unharmed. I had just met Little Red Riding Hood, for fuck's sake. Nothing was possible because it was all a bad dream. A nightmare.

Thank god I wasn't on Elm Street. Then these dreams would

have some guy with knives attached to his fingers, wanting to kill me, instead of damsels in distress, wanting me to save them. Oh no, what if this dream was being prompted by my thoughts? Freddie Krueger could be around any boulder or pine!

A white rabbit leapt across my path, scaring the shit out of me. I half expected to see a blonde girl in a blue dress to be following the rabbit. Poor innocent little bunny. I ate rabbit once. It was rather tough. Not the least bit like chicken. But of course, that might have just been my mother's non-existent cooking skills.

Somehow, regardless of the chicken wings, I was still hungry, and even remembering that godawful rabbit dinner made me realize this simple forest was teeming with potential food. Birds warbled in the trees overhead, a deer leapt into a thicket, and small furry critters burrowed happily in the dirt. It was chock full of good things for my grumbling tummy. But that would require hunting, killing, skinning and cooking—none of which I was good at. I wasn't even sure if I could start a fire without matches or a lighter.

But, of course I had a lighter. That pack-a-day habit comes in handy! Speaking of, I suddenly realized why I was so tense. I hadn't smoked in a while. Took a bit for me to forget to smoke.

I pulled the pack from my jacket pocket, extracted one, and lit it. The smoke filled my lungs as the nicotine filled me with a sense of calm and relief. God, I needed that.

I knew I couldn't actually hunt, kill and eat innocent woodland creatures, even though I had just killed a wolf. But that was a dream. Having to really premeditate, beyond sharpening an axe, would be so . . . premeditated.

As the nicotine filled my system, relaxing me and giving me a mild buzz, I looked around and realized that Disney wasn't that wrong. Trees and underbrush and animals could look quite menacing and monsterific in the dark. They towered over me, like they were leaning toward me, stalking me, reaching for me.

No. Bad thoughts. Couldn't have those thoughts now. Perhaps I should wonder if all the animals were as close as they sounded. It was as if they had never seen people—they weren't scared of me, not running away or anything. Peculiar, really.

Except that maybe these weren't all cuddly bunny-type animals that wouldn't attack me. Maybe these were more wolf types ready to devour my lean, tender flesh, and enjoy its succulence.

Okay, no more bad thoughts. Don't think about Freddie, I warned myself. Of course, then all I could think about was Freddie. For a distraction I wondered what really was around me. I flicked my lighter (everything's afraid of fire, right?) and I realized I was looking at a patch of wild strawberries. Now, they weren't as large as regular ones, but I knew they wouldn't kill me. So I knelt and began a major scarf-fest. I could forget about the dirt and whatever had recently crawled over them, since this was a dream. Wasn't it? After all?

They were food, and that was all that mattered. I could hunt and ingest these all right. They were probably organic and therefore extra good for me.

But they didn't last long. I ate my way through them and was still hungry. I looked around for more berries, or something else that I knew I could safely eat, and that's when I saw . . .

A trail of bread crumbs.

Chapter 3

They were big bread crumbs, more like bread chunks, and I was hungry. I began scavenging for them, eating them as soon as I found them. They were dirty and disgusting and tasted like chalk, but they were food, nonetheless.

Damn, I was hungry!

"See, the crumbs will again lead us home," I heard a very young, high-pitched voice say. There was a squeak of alarm. "Who are you, and what have you done with my crumbs?"

I looked up and saw a blonde-haired, blue-eyed boy looking down at me. He stood next to his equally blonde-haired, blue-eyed younger sister.

They were adorable.

I stood up and held out a hand. "Um, yeah, sorry about eating your bread crumbs. I was just really hungry."

"We were too. Yet we left the trail so we could find our way home."

"After your parents left you in the woods, right?"

"They didn't leave us, they simply—"

"Forgot you. Misplaced you?" I stood up to my full height. "Listen, we're all hungry here, and I think we'll find food just ahead. We just need to wander around a bit, and we'll find it."

"How do you know this? We're—"

"In the midst of famine. I know. There's no food to be found anywhere. And that's why your mother and father brought you to the middle of the woods. They told you they were gathering food, but really, they left you so they would have fewer mouths to feed."

"Don't say that! Our parents love us!"

Hold on, these children should be speaking German. I don't know German. I shouldn't understand them, yet I did. It was a dream. Nothing I did really mattered, because it was a dream.

The little girl was beating against me with her fists. "Our pawents wuv us!" she screamed.

"Oh, for chrissake's kid, learn to pronounce your 'Rs.' It isn't cute, it's annoying. Next up, your folks left you in the woods, all alone. Deal with it."

"They said they were going to come back for us," the little boy said.

"Okay, Hansel, right? You heard your parents saying they were going to get rid of you—I mean, this isn't the first time they did this, is it?"

"Nooo. But the Lord has watched over us."

"Yeah, well, unless I'm an angel, he's just checked out, 'cause if memory serves, you're wicked hungry with no way to find your way home."

"Had you not eaten our trail of bread crumbs, we would already be home."

I laughed at this. "Get a clue, I mean, bread crumbs? In a forest? If I hadn't eaten them, the birds or fuzzy critters woulda made short work of them. They'd already eaten most of the trail anyway."

"Are you weally an angel?" Gretel asked.

I ignored her, and instead studied the sky. If memory served, Hansel and Gretel found a white bird they followed to the witch's house. Of course, that was only after three days and nearly starving to death.

I didn't really relish that thought . . . relish. On a hot dog. With onions and chili. Ah, a Coney Island chili dog sounded like a wonderful idea. Okay, focus now; focus would be good here.

The bread crumbs had been in a fairly straight line, and I was pretty sure that if we followed along their path, we'd find the kids' cottage. Or come close enough so they'd recognize the area and be able to find their way home.

But that wouldn't really solve the problem now, would it? Their parents would just try to lose them again when I wasn't around to help. We had to first find the witch's house, eat a tasty meal, kill her before she steeped us in marinade, and rip her off. Then I could take them home.

"Okay, move out."

"Where are we going, sir?" Hansel asked.

I looked at him, then down at my clothes, and decided against correcting him. "We're off to find the Wicked Witch of the West. Come on." I'd use the sun and stars to navigate our course. 'Course, I'd still mark some trees to ensure we could find our way back. I'd already had enough embarrassing mistakes today to last a lifetime. For most people. For me, enough to last, say, a day if I was lucky?

"Did the angel just say we're gonna meet a witch?" Gretel asked.

"Are . . . are you sure you know what you're doing?" Hansel asked me.

I'd had enough of people questioning my help. "Listen, kid, I don't see you coming up with any hot ideas of your own. But if you do, feel free." I waved a hand back toward the forest.

"What are we gonna do?" Gretel whispered to Hansel.

He shrugged. "Follow our angel."

I kept scanning the sky, hoping to see the white bird that would eventually lead the kids to the witch's house. According to the tale, it took three days for them to see the bird. I was hoping it had taken them three days to notice the creature.

We kept trudging forward, and it seemed like hours, but it *was* probably hours. I tried pinching myself to wake up, but it didn't work. I musta really clocked myself.

But, looking on the bright side, at least Gretel hadn't been saying anything too much. Darn good thing I was a dyke, 'cause I just really couldn't deal with kids unless I could make them drop and give me fifty.

When I looked back at them though, they were having trouble keeping up. I couldn't help but notice how pale and shaky they looked. Though they could probably last a few days, or maybe a week, they really needed to eat soon. I'd heard starvation was not a pleasant death. I think it ranked right up there with being slowly eaten by dung beetles. I grinned. Now, being slowly eaten by a woman would be something entirely different.

Oh, god. My mind was wandering and I was starting to get weak. I had to eat if I was going to be any match for the witch.

Now, logically I knew these kids would get by all right on their own, but it wouldn't be a pleasant experience. And, as a good dyke, I knew what these kids were going to have to go through would mar them for life. They'd need years of therapy to get over it!

I looked around for something we could eat. I might seriously have to consider killing something. Too bad there wasn't a stream, 'cause maybe I could handle fishing. That wouldn't be too bad, killing a fish, would it?

Then I heard gasps and I looked into the darkening gloom. At the edge of the glade there was a house made of food. The roof was cake, the walls were bread, and the windows were sugar.

"Let's eat!" I yelled, charging forward and grabbing a handful of wall. I noticed Hansel and Gretel went straight for the roof and windows. Just what I needed, munchkins on sugar highs.

"Nibble, nibble, nibble," came a high, croaky, aged voice from inside the house. "Who's nibbling on my house?"

Before I could stop him, Hansel responded, "The sun and the wind!"

This response would've made much more sense had the sun not just set. I glanced around, looking for something I could use as a weapon. According to the tale, the kids would get out of this, but only after a week of torture. Hansel would be held captive and fattened, while Gretel would have to eat shells.

Not on my watch they wouldn't. The witch was supposed to get shoved into the oven when she tried to show Gretel how to check its heat, so she really wasn't that powerful. I walked around the house, looking at the surroundings.

If she had an oven, it was probably heated by wood, given this area and age. Thus, she must have a woodpile somewhere, and as I'd already proven once today, where's there's a woodpile, there's an axe.

Bingo! I hefted the axe in my hands. Major déjà vu. Before today, I wasn't sure if I had ever *hefted* anything before in my life. Ah well. I checked the blade with my finger. It really wasn't that sharp. It was rather dull, actually.

I tried to imagine aiming it at the witch's neck, swinging it toward her and . . .

But . . . Okay. So from the tales, this witch isn't really too powerful, she just has some odd eating habits. But what if the tale is wrong? What if she is really a real witch, with like masso-destructive powers? C'mon, I watched Buffy the Vampire Slayer. I knew what a powerful witch could do.

Besides, I didn't like the idea of lopping someone's head off in the first place, but to have to swing and hit repeatedly? Giving her a chance to fight back? No way José. This wasn't some old wolf playing grandmother, this was a witch.

Then, well, I was a good dyke and I'd been to Michigan. The festival, not the state. Well, I'd been to the state too, I lived there and I was pretty sure this forest was still in Michigan, but that's beside the point. I'd done the festival in the hot muggy summer rain, chanting with Holly and Molly and Muffy. I'd done Muffy, too, but . . . focus, Cody.

The point I was struggling with was, well, what if this was a misunderstood good witch, a victim of patriarchal mistrust of feminine nature and oppression of old womyn and their unusual abodes? What if I chopped up a good Crone? How would I ever go topless and share tofu again? Well, now that I thought about it . . . maybe the key was to just get it over with quickly. Trust the fairy tale. Next time I was passing the talking stick around the bonfire, I just wouldn't mention this little episode.

I looked around for something to sharpen the blade with. I wanted it nice and sharp. And of course, the only thing was another of those bleedin' leather straps. Oh, well, if this kept up, I'd be an expert with them.

I went back to join the kids just as the witch came out and tried to seduce them with pretty words. I tried to see her as a worthy Crone, but when she seemed to be measuring Hansel to see if he'd fit in a particular cook pot she had in mind, I decided politically correct hesitation might be fatal.

Not that I didn't hesitate some more. Let's think about this. I was just worrying about having to kill cute, fuzzy animals, and here I was about to lop the head off a person. But, again, I had just dissected a wolf, so, I guess I could put it all into perspective.

It was all a dream. I swung the axe and her head went flying while her body collapsed. Both spewing blood. Lots of blood. Some of it flying back onto my favorite Timberlands. *Ick*!

I dropped the axe and looked at the dumbstruck kids. "She was a witch. A really evil, wicked witch who wanted to eat you. She likes eating children. Likes the nice, tender meat."

"Oh, then it's all right," Hansel said, shrugging and continuing with his speed eating. The kid could really pack it away, too.

I knew we had more to accomplish here, plus this bread, cake and sugar meal just wasn't hitting the spot with me. The witch was a carnivore, after all, and even if she did like young children, she must eat something else as well. I went in, careful not to pull apart the somewhat sticky and flimsy door. I wondered if this climate was cool enough so that she never had to worry about it melting. Or had she rebuilt after every heat wave?

I looked around and called out, "Hansel, Gretel, dinner's served!"

After our tasty meal of . . . well, I didn't want to think what the meat was, but given the size, it was probably venison (oh, god, my ex Anne would never forgive me for eating Bambi!), but at least she had already prepared and cooked it. All we had to do was find the mustard.

We couldn't go anywhere safely until daylight because the forest was probably haunted and had trolls and such. Besides being bewitched. But as long as the predators thought the witch was still alive, we'd be fine in her house.

So I went and dug a makeshift grave into which I buried her body. I went back inside and searched the house with the help of the kids. We found the pearls and other jewels I knew were there, and I piled them up.

"In the morning, I'll take you two home. We'll take as many of these as we can carry, because these are what'll keep your parents from trying to lose you again."

"But what do we do tonight?" Hansel asked.

I looked around. "We crash here. You two share the bed. I'll sleep on the floor. No one will bother us. After all, they think the witch is still here."

Gretel jumped off the bed and hugged me. "We'll be safe with our angel."

Kids could grow on you. I left them with the blankets, but I took the witch's pillow and crawled up on the floor, pulling a shawl over me.

The floor was hard, I didn't have my air purifier, and I was cold. The damned kids had just better not snore, or I'd have to *lop* off their heads, too.

I wasn't gonna sleep a wink.

Chapter 4

I rolled over and got scratched by a branch. Hold on, I was just asleep on a floor. When had a tree grown in the room?

Actually, I had just burst into the room and stopped Sal from beating Sheila again. I took Sal out with a single roundhouse, and Sheila collapsed in my arms, "Thank you, brave Cody. What would I do without you?"

But that had just been a dream. Just like falling asleep in the witch's cabin with Hansel and Gretel had been. And now I was finally coming to.

I knew I had hit my head in the mad race through the forest. I should be careful. I probably had a concussion. Maybe something worse. Like bugs crawling all over me.

I jolted upright, brushing away all of the non-existent bugs I knew were all over me.

I opened my eyes to make sure I was bug free and immediately covered them with my arm. It was sunrise, and I had awakened on the forest floor. I must've been out all night. Why hadn't anyone come looking for me? Didn't they care? Was I that shitty of a friend? That horrible to be around? Come on, I was the one who would help with flat tires, with emergency moves when couples broke up, the one who could fix pipes and put together furniture—I was always helpful and friendly. People liked me. I had friends.

But apparently not friends who really cared about me.

I hoped Hansel and Gretel had listened to me and found their way home, with all their riches, safely. So they could live happily ever after.

That was just a dream. This was reality. I knew that was a dream because I remembered lopping off the witch's head, and getting her blood on me, and now I was clean. I checked the Timberlands carefully—nope, no blood, and, thankfully, no bugs either. Damn, the wicked sharp blade I had taken from the cottage was gone, too.

I slowly stood. Everything seemed to be in working order. I looked around. I was in a deep, dark forest. I still couldn't believe such a thing existed in the thumb of Michigan, but apparently, I was wrong.

It just seemed big. If I kept walking, I'd get to a road. I'd be able to find my car, then, and get home.

Using the sun as a guide, I started walking east. I was surprised I wasn't hungry. I hadn't eaten in—I glanced at my watch—at least twenty-four hours. I should be starving, but my stomach was acting as if I really *had* eaten a huge dinner the night before.

I glanced up at the sun to check my course, and saw the tower. It was massive. Huge. Made of stone. It was tall and thin, as towers go. It looked like something I'd find in England, or somewhere like that. Not here. Not Michigan. Except maybe on a college campus, but then it'd be surrounded by students, other buildings, a coterie of protestors and falafel carts, a city, for fuck's sake.

I walked around the building, studying it. There were no doors, no ladders. There was just a single window, high above the ground.

Why the hell would anyone ever build something like this with no means of entry? This was strange. But hold on, what if it was the Michigan Militia? There'd be a hidden access tunnel somewhere near. Could I be onto another of their paranoid plans?

I glanced around the forest, looking for some access to underground tunnels, and then I heard the most beautiful song that had ever graced my ears.

Her voice was music itself. And the words . . . the song immediately took me to a place of serenity and love. I looked around, trying to find the source of this pleasure, and realized it came from above.

It came from the single window. I looked up at it, and a beautiful woman leaned out, singing to the new day. She had the face and voice of a goddess. She sang to the world with yearning. With hope. With dreams and prayers. It was as if she had been locked away from everything forever, and she dreamed of something more.

Oh, shit, it was corny, but the look on her face was wistful. I don't think I'd ever used that word before in my life, but it was the only word that fit.

Her face and her voice were wistful.

I knew how that felt. I knew how it felt to want more than the nine-to-five and a basic existence with just enough pleasures to keep you going—a DVD player, a CD burner, a car you didn't have to use gum on to keep running. I was living the good life, by all accounts and measures, but there was a reason I realized she was wistful. We both wanted real and true love.

And I didn't realize that until the moment I saw her.

Chapter 5

I shook my head to pull myself back to reality. I had to remember who and where I was. And then I looked back up at the slender structure. A tower with no means of access. A single window and a beautiful damsel with a voice that could make you forget your own name.

A gorgeous femme trapped in a tower, drawing me to her with her beauty and voice.

I couldn't remember my name, I think it began with a C, or some hard sound like that, but I knew her hair was a long, golden mane. A mane long enough to reach the impossible length between her window and the ground below.

And although I can't quite remember my own name, as distracted by her voice as I am, I know her name.

And I know what I must say, I know it in my heart. "Rapunzel, Rapunzel, let down your hair that I may climb the golden stair!"

My throat was dry, and my words came out a harsh croak. She ceased her song and in moments I was taking hold of the golden braid. I pulled myself up and into her room, then rested on the sill, just looking at her.

"Who . . . who are you?" she asked. Her hair was still draped over the sill.

"I'm a friend, Rapunzel." She was breathtaking. Long blonde locks (talk about a femme making a butch's dream come true and never cutting her hair!), full red lips, a petite body, soft voice, breasts just big enough to fill your palms, and big, innocent green eyes.

Her gown was a simple robe of shimmering rose, settling around her feet like a fine mist. She was a dream come true. Totally.

She was young. I should keep my distance. Just here to save her, after all.

And leave her for some prince. Who would repeatedly leave her for other women. Princes were all alike, I was sure of that.

"A friend? I have never had one before." Her brow was furrowed in thought.

"You need to leave this tower."

"But this is all I know."

I swept my fingers through the silken locks that still draped the window sill. Again, what a butch's dream, well, at least the first six or seven feet of it! "You're a captive here."

"But there are no doors. How shall we escape?"

I held her gossamer hair in my hand, and looked around the room. I wasn't sure there was anything else that could hold our weight for a climb down. "We cut your hair."

"But then how shall grandmother come to visit me?"

"You won't be here any longer. You'll be out in the world. Living."

A smile touched her lips then. "Out there?"

"Yes, out there," I assured her as I pulled my switchblade. It was not as sharp as Red's grannie's knife, but it would cut hair.

She gasped at the sight of my blade. "I am but a helpless maiden.

What are you to do with me? Do you plan on ravishing me like some roguish pirate?"

Did I detect a hint of anticipation? I reached forward to caress her soft cheek. "I'm rescuing you, like the handsome prince of your fantasies." I swiftly sliced through her hair, leaving her with locks that fell halfway down her back (the perfect length!). Stray wisps were like the caress of silk on my hand. I used a ribbon to tie off the loose ends of the braid, then attached it to the hooks sunk securely into the windowsill.

Laughing, Rapunzel shook her hair loose. "My head is so light now. I could fly!"

She danced around the room, her lithe, nubile body enjoying its new-found freedom, freed from the weight of her hair.

She was so young, virginal, untouched and unlearned. She was probably all of maybe about eighteen, at the oldest. Plus she was waiting for some prince to come and rescue her. One that would be so stupid he wouldn't pull her out of her lonesome tower when they first met—not until after they did the wild thing and the old witch found out. Which was what happened in the fairy tale—her prince just kept visiting her till they were found out, the moron.

Then the witch would pluck out his eyes and put him in a desert, or some such nonsense. Maybe the witch had the right idea, keeping all this beauty safe from unappreciative princes.

So, over all, by pulling her out of here early, I'd be saving the prince from a horrible fate, and this beautiful princess from a godawful future, perhaps short-circuiting her right to her happily ever after.

Anyway, for fuck's sake, I was still conked out cold, and sleeping away my unconscious time in Fairy-Tale Land, so why shouldn't I have some fun? None of this mattered, really, so why should I care? Why should I even think about how old she was? How inexperienced she was? It was all a dream, anyway, right?

She was still dancing around the room, by herself. Her hair glistened in the sunlight. I wondered if I could teach her how to flip her long locks over her shoulder.

The very thought made me hot. As did watching her pirouette around the tower's circular room as she sang of her release.

God, she was beautiful. And now flipping her hair over her shoulder. I wondered again if my own thoughts were creating this reality. The potential of unleashing my nightmares had been terrifying, but right now I hoped my good dreams were all about to come true.

I couldn't take it any longer. I glided into her orbit, into her aura, and then she was running into me. She was in my arms, and we danced together. Her laughter was light and contagious. She wrapped her arms around me, pulling me closer as we swung around the room, dancing, around and around.

Her innocent green eyes looked up into mine. "You have set me free, my prince. I feel so strange, as if there is more . . . more you could teach me, show me."

This really was a Very Good Dream.

We spun around, getting closer and closer until finally, I pushed her against the wall, pressing into her. My thigh was between her legs, pressed into her heat.

Time seemed to stop. We caught our breaths at the unexpected electricity of our union, until finally she gasped, and her bosom pressed against me. We were looking right into each other's eyes. I could feel her breath on my lips.

She was so soft in all the right places. I ate last night, now I hungered for something else.

My leg was between hers. My hands were on her hips. Her arms were around my neck.

"I've read about things," she whispered. Her breath was like a feather against my cheek. "Are you my prince? My knight in"—she paused, glancing over my leather jacket and jeans—"leather?" I was the metal to her magnet. I couldn't resist. I brought a hand up through my hair in the back, expecting to wipe away sweat.

I leaned closer. Moving toward her lips. I gave her a chance to move away, but she didn't. So I brushed my lips against hers. They were just as soft as I thought they'd be.

She kissed me back. She didn't resist when my tongue entered her mouth. She followed my lead. She was my damsel, whom I was rescuing.

I could get used to this entire damselling bit.

She gasped when I ran my hands over her curves, enjoying my touch. Her body seemed to swell against me.

She was mine. She was giving herself to me, to her prince.

If I could be an angel, why couldn't I also be a dashing prince? We could both be in our very own fairy tales. And I'd rescue her, and she wouldn't have to deal with all the sadistic elements of a Grimm Brothers tale. We could escape, and if it was meant to be, she'd still meet with her true prince.

She pulled me in closer, obviously enjoying the fit of her body against mine, the feel of my tongue in her mouth. And I was in her mouth, deep and firm, sharing kisses that sent sparks up my spine. She was following my moves like Ginger Rogers, just not backward and in high heels. Though I couldn't say for sure, 'cause I hadn't seen her shoes yet.

I'd let her know what my tongue could really do. Give her a feel for options other than doing her duty for God and Country.

I went for her neck, kissing, nibbling, and biting.

"Oh, my prince . . ." she moaned. "Your kisses make me feel things I've never felt before."

The material of her robe was thin, but the ties that held it shut were incredibly complicated. I needed her naked, now! I needed to fuck her. I needed to make her squirm, feel true pleasure, and scream my name.

But I don't think I had told her my name.

I took both of her hands in one of mine and held them above her head. She struggled against me, humping my thigh. I knew there was a reason I worked out. "You're gonna be screaming my name soon, my beautiful treasure. So know that it's Cody."

"Cody, Cody, Cody," she started repeating, panting, like a magic chant. "Prince Cody, show me the tender mysteries I can see in your eyes."

Her breath was hot on me, her body was squirming against me, pushing herself into me as much as she could—fitting into me—wanting me. I had to do this without hurting her. I had to be careful and gentle. I hoped I could do this right, make this nice for her. I loosened my grip on her hands.

I pulled back and looked into her eyes. "Rapunzel," I whispered to her, moving in on her neck. "Rapunzel," I murmured again.

Her neck was so soft, and her moans as musical as her singing had been. "Let down your clothes for me." Carefully watching the tip of my blade, I cut the laces on her gown. They were in my way.

She gasped as the shimmering cloth rippled off her shoulders, falling into a puddle at her feet to expose her luscious body. She tried to pull away to cover herself. "What are you doing?" she whispered.

Our gazes locked as I tried to reassure any fears she might have. "If something doesn't feel good, I'll stop." I ran my hands over her naked arms and hips, still looking into her eyes. I wouldn't have been so abrupt about stripping her if I'd remembered they didn't wear real underwear back then.

She moaned and pushed against the wall, stretching her neck to entice my lips to return to it.

I wasn't one to allow a damsel to continue in her distress. I cupped her face in my hands, running my fingers lightly over her cheeks, and finally allowed my thumbs to trace her lips. She slipped her tongue out to flick over them. I went in for another delightful kiss. We nibbled lightly on each other's lips, then I slipped my tongue again into her mouth, exploring her. I kept reminding myself that she was a young virgin, so I needed to go slow and be careful.

She wrapped her arms around my neck, finally, pulling me again closer. When her hands wound into my hair, securing me to her, I ran my tongue over her neck, tenderly nipping lightly at her pulse point, enticing her to further moans. I kept my hands on her arms at first, then allowed myself to feel her sides and her outer thighs until she began to press her warm heat down on my thigh still between her legs.

"My prince, my Cody. Do with me what you will. Set me free of my past, my sweet prince."

Still looking into her eyes, I cupped her breast in my hand, enjoying the feel of her hardening nipple against my palm. I dropped my gaze down to her breast. I was the first person to ever touch her. She knew nothing of sex, nor of what her body was capable. I had a sudden vision of Rapunzel as a mature woman, self-aware and sexy as hell. She'd cut a swath through the butches of my world, leaving us panting like puppy dogs. And if I thought about that much more I'd get performance anxiety.

I lowered my head to run my tongue over her nipple. She grasped my head to her. I kept my thigh against her crotch, pushing into her.

"What is it I'm feeling?" she gasped.

I ran my hands down over her naked hips, pulling her into me. I began to lick and tease her other nipple, flicking my tongue over it. I wanted to bite it, but I didn't know her, or her body, yet. And she had never experienced anything like this before. I needed to make this good for her. Very good.

"Oh, sweet Cody."

I tightened my lips around her nipple, sucking it into my mouth as she began to move more urgently against me. She was arching up into me, searching blindly for greater satisfaction. Her fingers were tightly wound in my hair, and she urged me from one breast to the other, forcing her erect, swollen nubs into my mouth.

I wrapped my lips around her luscious flesh, pulling it into my mouth as I lightly tugged and teased the rigid, reddened tip.

"Oh, yes, yes, please . . . What is this I am feeling?"

"You're feeling pleasure, darling Rapunzel. Enjoy it." I looked up at her with a feral grin on my face. Yup, I was a predator. I was going to eat her. I was going to taste her and feel her and make her mine. Damn it, this was my dream, and I was going to enjoy it! And she was going to, too. I hoped. I needed her to.

I sucked a hardened point back into my mouth and whipped it with my tongue.

"Oh, sweet prince!" she screamed.

I could feel her wetness through my jeans. She was wicked turned on. I nibbled on the other breast, reminding myself that I had to go slowly. But her urgent bucking against me made me momentarily lose control.

I bit her nipple.

She screamed and thrust against me, yanking me into her, spreading her legs for me.

I knew she wanted me to do that, so I did it again, and pulled her smooth hips into me. Deep in her primal senses, she knew what I was doing to her, and she wanted it.

And good lord, I was being so dykey and over-analyzing everything to death. I had a hot and willing woman in my arms, spreading her thighs for me, needing me to make her day.

I bit the other nipple, causing her to thrust against me again.

I'd do my duty. To God and Country and Rapunzel and my own strange subconscious. I was gonna enjoy this, dammit!

Willingly.

I dropped my hand between her legs and felt her. Lubricated my finger with her sweet juices.

"My prince," she gasped.

I lightly plunged a finger into her. Into her wet, inside of her. Feeling her. She was tight.

She went beyond words. Now she only made sounds.

Goddamn, it was so fucking hot.

I bit one nipple while twisting the other. I slipped that same finger back into her, curling it up so as not to hurt her, and she collapsed against me. What could I do but carry her to the bed?

"What . . . what are you doing . . . to me . . . making me feel . . ."

"Ssh." I whispered into her ear, kissing it lightly. "Just enjoy." I touched her perfect body all over, feeling her everywhere, including inside of her.

She was *very* wet.

"Have you ever touched yourself?" I asked.

"I wash my hands. I wash . . . myself."

"Have you made yourself come?"

"What?" Her confusion was obvious.

"How much pleasure have you experienced?"

She moaned as I curled that singular finger inside of her. "I have . . . I have . . . I enjoy poetry . . ."

A true virgin. In mind, body and soul. A butch's dream come true, maybe. But not mine. Her inexperience was scary. But she was here and sweaty. I was horny. And she was willing. And it was all just a dream anyway.

I treasured her breasts and nipples with my lips and mouth, while I caressed her clit with my fingers. Every time I withdrew that finger from her warmth, she arched, trying to recapture it. But when I pressed more deeply, she squeaked. Loudly. It was too much for her.

I looked into her eyes. "Do you like my touch?"

"Please, don't stop!"

I slid that finger back into her tightness and she moaned, arching up into me, wanting more. She had no idea what was going on. She was wet, and I made her feel good. I'd make her come. She would remember me for the rest of her life and, I hoped, require the same depth of pleasure from her princelings, male and female. Everything about her said she was not meant for an ivory tower, though a princess she would always be.

She was naked beneath me. She moved against me, her body knowing what she wanted even if she didn't.

I withdrew and fondled her clit. She arched against me, asking for me inside of her again. My finger slowly slid back into her shuddering cunt.

She grabbed my hair and forced me to look into her eyes. "My prince . . . Cody . . . please . . . I am yours . . ."

She had her own fairy tale in mind. And yet I loved her in that moment. I loved her naiveté, her youth, her beauty.

I couldn't really fuck her, not without hurting her. And I didn't want to hurt her.

"Do you trust me?" I asked.

"I am yours, my love." She tried to sit up, but I pushed her back with a kiss.

I slowly licked my way down her perfect body, gently nibbling along the way. I worshipped her breasts for a few moments, while spreading her legs under my body, and pushing into her, causing her to arch against me.

And I continued my descent down her pale flesh, bringing it to life and causing her to squirm. As soon as she felt my hot breath on the tender flesh between her legs she almost threw me from the bed.

I held her down. And then I put my head between her legs, draping her thighs over my shoulders while I reached up to fondle her full breasts. I took a deep lungful of her musky scent, and slowly, softly, ran my tongue up her.

"Oh . . . oh . . . oh . . . dear Lord!" she screamed.

I used my hands to hold her down and keep her against me. I carefully brought my lips against her heat, trying to gradually ease her into what she was beginning to feel. I used my breath and lips on her for a while, first causing her to squirm, then to calm down and moan deeply. Her wetness was dripping out of her.

I needed to taste her, and make her scream again.

Unable to resist further, I brought my tongue back into play. I slowly licked up where she was dripping, enjoying the sweet taste of her. She was hot and pulsing right in front of my face, and I knew she needed me.

That was a rare feeling for me. Having such a delicious femme want me so badly.

I drew my tongue up her, enjoying the taste and feel of her. I wanted to bury my tongue inside of her, but knew I had to go slowly. So I continued softly licking her, listening to her breathing and groans—listening to her body.

I lowered my hands to her stomach, and felt the quivering within her. I became more forceful with my tongue, working up to stroking her clit with long, hard motions. Then I pushed my tongue up into her, causing her to shove her cunt into my face.

I continued tongue fucking her, while again running my hands over her smooth, firm, young flesh, until she began seriously bucking against me, begging for release.

"Please, please, oh my prince . . ." Her head thrashed deliriously from side to side.

I swirled my tongue into her depths and then returned to licking her, but this time I was more forceful, and I slipped that same finger back up into her, curling it to touch her G-spot.

"Cody!" she screamed, bucking against my mouth, pushing my arms out of the way so she could pull me to her crotch harder, deeper.

She was delicious, and I ate her. I took her. My finger inside of her, my tongue attacking her beautiful clit.

She tightened around my finger, and her legs crushed my shoulders.

I went after her and kept going after her. I wasn't here long, so I had to make this last—for the rest of her life, and maybe even mine.

"Cody!" she screamed again, and her body was all at once rigid and melting.

God, she was beautiful. No longer an untouched innocent, nor beautifully coiffed . . . she was sweaty and trembling, flushed and covered in sex juices . . . and positively edible, but for different reasons.

And increasingly beautiful still when she gazed at me with her luminous eyes and said the one word I ached to hear. "More." Her soft girl's voice had found the assured timbre of a woman's confidence.

For the first time in my life, I truly felt like a prince.

I had to make her come a few more times before I'd let her sleep. And I was gonna make her keep on coming, enough for a lifetime maybe.

And I just knew she'd let me go on for a Toblerone plus. With just my tongue and a single finger.

After all, this was for a lifetime.

Chapter 6

Apparently, I had done all I needed to do with Rapunzel, 'cause it seemed that I was like that time-tripped dude in that TV show: I would move on when everything was done and right.

You remember the show, right? (The first star got killed on set, and the replacement is now on some Star Trek spin-off. As if that doesn't describe a lot of actors.)

Anyway, this time I woke up in a gutter, just as a Mercedes pulled up and splashed me.

"Huh?" I asked, quite succinctly while trying to wipe the water from my eyes. My eyes were level with an exquisite pair of ankles, which suddenly pulled away from me.

"How did this . . . creature . . . get here? Please remove the rabble!" a uniformed man said, waving his arms maniacally. It was almost as if I had X-ray eyes, 'cause I could almost see the stick shoved up his ass.

I looked up at a beautiful woman with short blonde hair. She regarded my filthy figure with caring and understanding. I glanced at the Mercedes, complete with a driver holding the back door open for his passengers.

This wasn't some forested glade. The last I knew I had been in a tower with Rapunzel, giving her more than her dreams. Now I was a gutter-snipe at the well-heeled toes of an elegant lady who was . . .

Familiar.

"Don't get in that car," I said, standing. God, I was wet. I really had been lying in a gutter. I knew I smelled foul. But I didn't know how long I had here, so I looked her in the eye.

"Is there something I might help you with?" she asked with a regal British accent. Maybe she had once been a mere kindergarten teacher, but I had just stepped into a modern-day fairy tale whose unhappy ending I could change. Not a fairy-tale princess, a real one, a tragic one unless I could save her.

"Don't get into that car. Your driver has been drinking."

"Go get yourself a cuppa or whatever else you might need," her escort said, trying to give me money. I pushed his hand away. I only appeared at turning points. This had to be the night.

"Please don't get into that Mercedes."

"Do you require help?" she asked.

Just then two men in uniform charged me. I tried to duck their blows, but then I was hit. My head hit the curb and everything went . . .

. . . black.

Chapter 7

I awoke lying flat on my face and breathing dirt, which I quickly determined, due to my acute senses and keen mind, was because I was lying on a dirt road. There were corn fields to my right and left, stretching into the distance in the wan moonlight. I pulled myself to my feet and looked down the road. Nothing.

Thank god. I was worried that I was about to be surrounded by maniacal children intent on killing all adults in a bloody harvest ritual. I stood, grateful that again, apparently, I had awakened clean. I'd hate to smell like that sewer, and failure. I had to take my mind off it. My failure. And my nose liked being away from the gutter.

The moon was full, but shadows fell beneath the tall trees over the road in that direction. The leaves rattled maliciously in the darkness, whispering secrets to the ghosts and demons that surely lived nearby.

I decided that really wasn't a good direction to go in.

I turned around to see if the other option was any more inviting, and was nearly bowled over by a really big, dumb-looking guy.

What the fuck was this? Where were the damsels in distress? I needed some damselling to get that black Mercedes out of my mind!

I looked around his formidable form and there was nothing. Just more of the same dirt road. Not even a good, old-fashioned haunted forest. "Yo, dude, watch where you're going," I said, looking up at this farmer's son. "Would you happen to know where I can find the damsel, or damsels, I'm supposed to help?"

All I could figure right now was that the damsels must be in the woods. So when he didn't immediately reply, I turned toward the thick trees and started walking, with behemoth, the walking lunkhead, following behind me.

Once among the foreboding groves, which I had thought were a mere hundred or so feet long, I realized it was a full-fledged spooky, miles-deep forest.

"I do not understand what you speak about," the doofus said, again coming up behind me. "But I can tell you that when I was young, my mother used to tell my brother and me the story of Brier Rose, a beautiful, modest, sweet damsel. That is the only damsel of which I know."

"Okay, so tell." He began walking again, and I had to all but run to keep up with him.

"Tell what?"

"Brier Rose. What's the sitch?"

He stopped and looked at me. "You speak queerly. I do not quite understand most of which you say."

"Tell me about Brier Rose."

"I only know that which my mother told me."

"And what was that?" I was being patient, trying to pull his story out, word by word. And if he hadn't been built like a stone wall, I'd have already jumped him and beaten the crap out of him, just to make him talk to me.

"Turn right at the next town, and you'll find it."

"What's it?"

"A huge brier hedge, full of thorns and prickles. One large enough to cover a castle." He turned to me, earnest. "It is all but a legend. But the damsel within all that is the only one of which I've ever heard, before I met you."

His mother told him a fairy tale, and he believed it.

"I have always been tempted to try to help that maiden myself, but I was afraid of the briers and dragons and other things between myself and her."

I contemplated following him. After all, maybe he needed my help as well. But when I considered the seriously hot damsel who needed me even more, he left my thoughts entirely.

After all, what was a poor, simple butch to do?

Chapter 8

At least this time I didn't have to wake up in a sewer, or with a mouthful of dirt. All I had to do was walk. And walk. And walk even more.

Left turn at the town, my ass. Yeah, that was the right direction, but he didn't tell me how far it'd be. Or if there were any other turns or such along the way. All I knew is that my stroll in the woods had turned into a vision quest. I walked even more.

Fine, I'll admit that I occasionally wandered off the path when I saw a likely looking bunch of thorns. I kept hoping to find the brier patch. And also hoping that Peter Rabbit wouldn't hop out of any of them.

I wanted to rescue another hot chick, not some flopsy or mopsy creature. It was wicked weird that my dream left me so far out. Okay, so maybe there was something I was supposed to learn here. It would be nice if the powers that be were a little more clear on what they wanted! I started to get that resentful feeling that useful information was being withheld from me. You know, like when your soon-to-be-ex says something like, "If I have to tell you what's wrong, there's no point."

I needed something to drink. I even found myself licking dew off grass. I was parched. Thankfully, most of the distance had been flat, but this new hill was killing me.

I was thirsty and hungry and my legs were killing me. Now, I was in reasonably good shape, but . . . this . . . was this what folks in olden times went through? Was this what you had to do back then to survive? To be a hero? To rescue others?

Frankly, this was pretty boring. And tiring. And trying. And really hard on my knees!

I got to the top of the hill and dropped to a squat, breathing harshly through my parched throat. My kingdom for water.

I was on my knees, gasping, when I realized I was looking at a big bloody rose bush, thorns and all. Big enough to cover, say, a castle.

I was an English major in college. In spite of the teasing I'd gotten, I'd read all the fairy tale versions I could. Considering the dream I was having, I would get the last laugh on that decision.

I'd learned things that are utterly useless in the day-to-day world. But this was no ordinary place. I looked at this overgrown, under-tended rose garden gone wild and was able, once I got over the whole "Let's stay away from that unless my entire body was Armour Guarded" idea, to remember how idiot boy, whose parents were obviously at least first cousins, referred to Brier Rose, et cetera.

Brier Rose had another name, a Disney name, brought forth out of the three-page Grimm fairy tale. And, since I really, really need to invest my next paycheck in a brain, I didn't remember this until I saw this huge thorn patch.

Brier Rose was Princess Aurora, a.k.a. Sleeping Beauty.

I knew what I had to do. I stared at the Cody-maul patch, and realized that I was wicked glad I had never seen the Disney version of the story. Lord only knows what this would be if I had.

I really didn't dig facing dragons, beasties, or other evil shit without a good weapon. Or several. Well, actually, without an arsenal. A nice rocket launcher or a fast-acting herbicide would have been handy as well.

Alas, I didn't have anything but, well, me, right now. Me and my clothes.

Ah well, damsel and all . . . Butch in scuffed leather . . .

I started down the hill. Slowly, 'cause I knew going down a hill too quickly could be hell on the knees. God I was getting old. And I didn't want to pull a Jack and Jill.

I walked, keeping my pace, down the steep hill, toward the brier-covered castle, thankful that I had on my leather. It could afford some protection.

As I neared I kept my eyes open, and that was the only reason I saw . . .

Him.

Shining armor and all. Silver, or some nice shiny stuff like that. White horse.

I hated him on sight.

But I couldn't out-race a horse. Nonetheless, I started moving faster, knees be damned.

I ran down the hill, right up to the thorns, and as I reached out with my hand, I swore I saw a shimmering—as if something was happening.

And I remembered . . .

The prince in shining armor does not save Sleeping Beauty. She just happens to be awakening from her hundred year sleep when he shows up. He's just *lucky*.

So, okay, choice time. I can let the "gallant" prince "save" her, or go for her myself. I can let her first kiss be with me. I smirked. Rapunzel had been pleased I'd gotten there first. So Sleeping Beauty might be equally pleased to know her first kiss from me, so much so she falls madly in love with me. Or I can let him do it, the lucky bastard.

He leisurely trotted up to the thorns. We looked at each other over the yards of brambles between us. He took off his helmet and studied me. He'd only try to keep me from the girl. This was a challenge I was supposed to win. Wasn't I?

Granted, he had the horse, so could move faster. He had a sword to clip through all the thorns and bushes in his way better than I.

Then I realized that if I rescued the princess and won her love, it wouldn't matter, because I would be off to another tale, another rescue, and she would be left with her love for me, but I wouldn't be there.

I really hated losing this one, especially to the other team. I mean, it's one thing to lose a woman to another woman, but to a man?

Yet he lived here and had come for her. We both had. Now, he had probably come farther (on horseback, so he could not be anywhere near as thirsty as I!) but . . .

We looked at each other. And I gave him The Butch Nod.

They'd live happily ever after, and right then I needed to believe in it.

Sometimes you have to realize the others' forever after, and get out of its way. Even if you'd like to know how well you'd face thorns and prickles, dragons and demons, and sleeping beauties. Even if you wish you could know how good you and a particular princess would be. Damnable thought—maybe not all princesses want to be rescued either.

Oh, hell. Fairy tales really aren't that interesting. Few pages each, and gruesome. Stephen King can't compare. At some point, I hesitantly admitted to myself, I had to live in a real world and accept that every problem wasn't mine to fix.

The prince plunged into the thorns without even putting his helmet back on.

That had to hurt!

I reached out, quite tentatively, to see what I was missing . . .

And faded to black.

Chapter 9

At least this time I woke to the now-familiar, simple and understood surroundings of another forest, complete with trees and birds chirping. I was face down in grass. My clothes seemed clean, yet again, and leather intact, as if I had taken another shower between adventures and been dry cleaned.

It was like I had woken having to pee really bad. You know how sometimes that just wakes you up? That pressure in your bladder? You don't know why you're awake, but then you realize you had better hightail it to the bathroom?

So that was how this felt. Being awoken by bladder pressure. But when I thought about it, I didn't have to pee. So what woke me?

And that was when I heard the voices in the distance. The voices were what actually woke me.

"Heigh ho, heigh ho, it's off to—"

"Get our nails done!" one voice cried above the others.

"Wench! That's not our song, and you know it!"

"I really don't care anymore, Lust. My nails are a wreck from all of this low-paid grunge work. Don't you just wish for a real manicurist?"

"That's not how we do things around here." This time it was a butch voice. Deep and guttural. I hated it immediately. In the rule book of Cody's Fairy-Tale Land, it's one butch per dream.

"So, okay, like we spend all our days digging around in dark, dirty—"

"Buggy—"

"Buggy places, looking for valuable stuff, like gold and silver and—"

"Diamonds!" came a swooning voice.

"But how do we eat? What keeps food in our mouths and a roof over our heads?"

"Don't ever ask such questions!"

"Diamonds! Don't you just love how glittery and pretty they are?" It was the swooning voice again, but this time not so much on the swooning. "I just don't understand what you keep bitching about, Wench. At least we're after something worthwhile."

"We're in dank and disgusting places all day long, Lust. Getting our nails and 'dos all messy and icky. Where is the bright side here?"

"Money. And bright, sparkly objects that are pretty," Lust replied.

I did a slow push-up, trying to raise myself from the forest floor.

And that was when I saw it. Big and hairy and all glossy-eyed.

I swear it was the biggest spider I had ever seen. Really, you had to have seen this monster. Especially up close, when you first wake up. Right in your face. Big, black hairy. It was awful. Truly scary. Terribly icky.

Confronted with such a horrid beast, I did the only thing natural: I screamed. I don't care who says I shrieked, it was a scream, or maybe a bellow, but regardless, it wasn't a screech. It was a deep, butchly yell.

But anyway, a voice I hadn't heard before said, "What was that?"

"What was what, Sleepy?"

"Someone shrieked," Sleepy replied, yawning.

"I didn't hear anything," Lust answered.

"Nor did I," Wench added.

"Girls, girls, let's not get into some sort of a cat-fight," Butch said, just before muttering under her breath, "It's just like any other day. Why do we always have to go through the same old shit?"

"I heard that, Doc," someone else said. Then, resigned, "Why is every day just like every other day?"

"Okay, Lace, Doc, we all know we do the same thing over and over again. Wench complains about our work and we all end up arguing. Can we just try to do something different for a change?"

"Um, Lust . . . ? I . . . I . . ."

Oh, for fuck's sake, where's a score card already? How many of these chicks were there? I carefully crawled through the brush trying to see them, but this time I was careful of noises. And big, hairy spiders. Even cockroaches. Or Killer Slugs From Hell.

"Bashful! Could you get it out already?"

Great, just what I need, yet another name. I needed to place the names with the faces or I'd never keep them straight. I had a procedure for remembering these things, and I needed to stick to it or . . . ACK! Was that a slug?

"I . . . I think Sleepy was kinda breaking our entire routine by hearing that strange noise." Bashful again.

It *was* a slug!

I brushed it off with my hand. It got stuck. To my hand. "EeeeYack!" I screamed, in a good, deep, butch voice, shaking it off me as I plummeted through the brush and shrubs and trees to land directly at the feet of . . .

Six incredibly beautiful women, femmes all. And one butch who didn't seem to be too happy with me. Okay, fine, the butch was . . . well, she wasn't that tall, or that rugged.

But when I say six incredibly beautiful femmes, I mean these babes were All That topped with a lemon and salt around the rim. Long legs, exposed by modest, knee-length dresses, with slits up to their hips. Their bodices revealed bountiful cleavages, suckable collar bones, and tanned, shapely bodies. It was like being on the set of Xanadu, times six.

I didn't care if I was dead. I could be dead, for all I knew. I mean, I had gone down on a forest floor. I had bitten the dust in the forest, and I kept having forest-based dreams. Except for those that weren't.

But did any of that really matter? Here I was, lying at the feet of these gorgeous women, and almost no matter what my taste, I would find something for my appetite here. Busty, lusty, curvaceous, slender, blonde, brunette, redhead. Oh, it was a veritable buffet for a butch. Pick and choose, pick and choose . . .

"Who are you?" It was the butch, Doc. Her arms were crossed in front of her, and she stared down at me. She didn't look real happy. And why should she be? Another butch had just invaded her turf.

Served her right, keeping such goodies all to herself.

"Oh, you're a cute one now, aren't you?" said one of the femmes, in a voice I didn't recognize, as she reached down toward me, offering me a hand up.

"Sleepy, I guess you were right," Doc said. I realized she had thick arms, broad shoulders, narrow hips, thick quads, short black hair, and deep blue eyes. I could see why she could keep this many femmes happy.

But still, she really wasn't all that rugged. She wasn't all that. Not really.

I took the offered hand, which helped bring me to my feet, under Doc's watchful eye. Or eyes, really, since she had two of them. Both of which were fixed on me.

The important thing was that she wore really heavy boots. One of which quickly hit the side of my head. I did what anyone else would: I blacked out.

⁌⁍

Those were heavy boots, I thought, as I tried to swim back up toward consciousness.

My head was pillowed on something soft and warm. Delicate hands stroked my forehead. It occurred to me that Doc was probably thinking she had put down a potential rival, but she had miscalculated.

It had taken me years to learn what Doc had yet to realize: femmes wear the real pants in the family—they control what goes on. If Doc kicked me off a cliff, her harem was likely to kick her off right after me.

These luscious women were surrounding me when I came to, butting between me and Doc, all but swooning over me. Making me lightheaded with views of their ample cleavage and long legs in their slitted skirts.

"Be careful," Doc warned them. I didn't blame her. I'd want to keep this bunch for myself, if I could.

"Oh, she's coming to!"

"How many fingers am I holding up?"

"What's your name?"

"Are you okay?"

"H . . . H . . . How are you d . . ."

"Hot damn, you're cute."

"Cody, and I think I'm okay," I said, focusing on Cleavage's . . . well . . . cleavage. God, I wanted to feel those breasts in my hands. Funny how I was able to identify voices with names now.

Cleavage pulled my head against her breasts, while Lust checked my head, more stroking my hair than checking, really. All of the other girls had at least one hand on me. As if they wanted me, or I was a curiosity.

They'd apparently had just one butch for quite a while, so I was different. But I glanced up at Doc's watchful eyes, paying especial attention to her powerful arms, and realized I wasn't so much a diamond in a forest of coal, as, perhaps, maybe . . . Well, fuck, I couldn't think of the analogy. Doc and I were equals and (okay, maybe she was a bit more of a prize than I), but still, they were interested in me.

She was much more the butch than I, but I was different.

I gave it up and lay there, quite comfortable despite the monster headache (fuck, I'm a butch, I was enjoying the view), when I realized all of the women surrounding me were wearing bodices and laces right out of some Renaissance Pleasure Faire. At least that's what I thought they reminded me of.

Why'd I have to keep falling into fairy tales? Why not a good porno flick for a change of pace?

I had to think past the boot-induced concussion I was still recovering from. A bunch of really horny girls and one butch. Girls names, let's see. Bashful, Sleepy, Cleavage, Wench, Lace, and Lust. Oh, and of course, Doc.

Doc . . . Doc . . . that wasn't in Grimm or Hans Christian Andersen . . . that was pure Disney.

Considering the day I had, I knew where I had to go. I looked up and beyond Lust's bust and said, "Take me to Snow White."

"How—"

"What—"

"Who—"

"Snow . . . Beautiful . . . White as . . . Black as . . . . Shames us all. Doc . . ." All the words melded into one. I couldn't tell one word, one woman's voice, from any other.

"Enough!" Doc yelled. Always the butch top. I could see the veins pop on her forearms.

I rose with the gentle assistance of about ten soft, womanly hands, walked around the cleavage that separated us, and looked Doc in the eye. "She's in trouble, and I can help."

The femme babble erupted again. "Trouble? . . . We knew that . . . What's going on? . . . Who is this woman? . . . God, she's handsome . . . It must be that woman . . . We can protect her . . . What does this woman know?"

"You know her, and where she's at," I said.

Doc harrumphed and grumped quite realistically, looking around at her little harem and gaining their consent first, and then she looked at me. "Snow White is at our cottage. She is quite safe there."

"Except from the evil queen, her stepmother."

"I knew she had to be a princess . . . Royalty! . . . She's special! . . . We knew that! . . . Snow White? . . . She likes to lead . . . Why does she keep grabbing Doc's attention? . . . Anything for a new . . . Please tell me she ain't a butch who likes other butches . . . I . . . I . . . I think . . ."

Then, as one, they all said, "What is it, Bashful?"

"I think we should trust her," Bashful said all in a rush before blushing and looking down.

"No way in hell!" Doc crossed her thick arms in front of her and put her foot down. Hard. So it stomped. I liked her boots.

Goddamn, I wanted to show Doc who was boss. I wanted to pound her down into the ground and beat her till she bled.

Alas, I knew who would win if we fought, and it wasn't me.

"You just want to keep Snow all for yourself," Wench said to Doc.

"Do not!"

"The rest of us could use a bit more attention, you know," Cleavage said, giving me a slow once over before wrapping her arms around me and pushing the ample reason for her name against me.

Needless to say, although I'm no Albert Einstein, I didn't argue. Of course, maybe he might have. I, on the other hand, had a real brain. So I smiled stupidly down into Cleavage's uh, er, cleavage. I could get lost in there and never be seen again.

Sounded like a great way to spend the rest of my life. Where's a snorkel—cause I'd dive right in!

"Oh, no Cleavage, down girl—you try to grab everyone just for yourself!" Lust said, coming up on my other side.

"Like you're not trying the exact same thing!" Lace now.

"Not before me!" Lust.

{Yawn} "You're cute."

"I . . . I . . . I like her, too."

They were surrounding me, all trying to touch me, to seduce me, to take me. Oh, this was nice—Butch's choice of a bevy of beautiful babes? After Rapunzel's innocence, a no-need-to-explain-just-fuck-me-baby-till-I-cry orgy sounded *really* good. Works for me.

"Girls, girls, girls! There's plenty of me to go around!" Then I looked over at Doc and saw she was way not happy, which reminded me that my purpose here wasn't to have a lot of fun, although I wouldn't shirk my duty to these lovely lasses who were so obviously in need. I was really here to help Snow White.

Which could wait, couldn't it?

I looked over at Doc. "Quite a handful you've got here," I said, wrapping an arm around the two nearest femmes, and pulling them in for a kiss one at a time. One tasted like strawberries, the other like mint. Cleavage was already undoing her bodice, and Lace and Lust were undoing each other, squirming to get out of their clothes as quickly as possible.

Doc was fully glowering at me by now, wholly unheeded by the lusty wenches surrounding me, including Lust and Wench. I sure wasn't winning any friends in the Doc camp, which could be really detrimental to my mission here, so the best way to begin was by offering an olive branch.

This was a perfect opportunity.

I met Doc's eyes, taking a brief moment from the more-than-handful of Cleavage's bosom, but leaving my hands on Bashful's and Lust's asses, both of which were quite nice and shapely. "I think we have our work cut out for us," I told Doc, with a grin and a wink.

"Oh, please, please, I need you now," Lace said, pushing up against me.

Doc looked shocked. "Us?"

"Six horny hotties? I think they can keep the *both* of us busy all night long!"

Doc grinned. "Everybody naked, *now!*" she ordered, then looked at me. "Except for you, of course."

I watched the group striptease, and really wished I had some lube on me. Well, at least I had my ChapStick to ensure my lips and mouth were ready. I kept my Zippo and ChapStick in my right pocket, tissues in the left. I automatically reached for the familiar tube, and then felt the little packs of lube I didn't remember putting there.

Oh, what the hell. I had chicks, and it was really handy that I now had lube. It was a dream after all and it was getting incredibly good.

I grinned back. "Of course." And then I pulled Cleavage into my arms, running my hands down over her bare form, grabbing her by her shapely ass so that she rode my hard thigh, which was between her legs, even harder.

"Oh, god, yes," she cried. "That's how I like it!"

I pulled her up off the ground, so she rested solely on her wet cunt. I could feel her through the denim of my jeans. I was molesting her mouth with mine when I felt someone trying to ride my other thigh. I turned around so my back was against a tree, for leverage, and let both Cleavage and Wench ride, my hands on their asses, taking turns kissing them.

I glanced over and saw Doc working on Lace and Lust. Bashful and Sleepy had definitely decided to work on each other, and it was incredibly hot—bosoms, hair, wet cunts, fingers. Wow.

I had my hands wrapped around Cleavage's and Wench's thighs so that my fingers were teasing their tender wet places, lubricating my fingers with their juices. I kept dipping inside of them, so they pressed themselves even harder against me. Between the Bashful/Sleepy bold and wide-awake performance and the two greedy darlings in my arms, I was so far past heaven I knew I hadn't even dreamed of having this dream.

Sleepy grabbed Bashful, kissing her deeply, but pulling back enough so I could see their tongues dancing with each other in the cool evening air. Sleepy cupped Bashful's breasts, tweaking the nipples, hard. Bashful snaked her hand down Sleepy's toned tummy and into the nest of red curls between her legs. She pulled away from the kiss long enough to look over at me and smile, then she spread Sleepy's lips, showing off the other woman for me.

I all but drooled at this display.

Doc caught me at it, and said, "I love watching them make each other's day." I had to agree. Women who knew what they wanted and how had always rocked my world.

I swapped places with Wench and Cleavage, shoving them both against the wide oak, hard. I kissed and sucked Cleavage's neck while fondling their breasts, pinched their nipples, then squeezed and twisted them till both women cried out. I turned my attention to Wench's neck and the other breasts.

"Oh, yeah, baby, I like being teased," Wench groaned.

The area was now a field of blooming "Yesses!" and "Do mes!" called into the twilight.

I took one of Wench's nipples between my teeth, and ran my teeth over it while my hands played down over their bellies—feeling, touching, teasing. I licked the nipple, sucking it into my mouth, then bit it, softly at first, then harder.

She tangled her fingers in my hair and pulled me as hard as she could toward her, pressing me against her wonderful softness. "Yes, like that," she moaned.

I trailed my hands down, then up, their inner thighs. First one, then the other.

I nibbled and sucked Cleavage's ample nipples, teasing them both, on and off, while my fingers continued playing with them— running up and down their thighs, around but never in their wetness. I wanted them to beg.

"Oh, god, please, do me—there!" Wench said, trying to force my hand between her legs. I let her lay my hand where she wanted it, but I just let it lie there, feeling her heat, her pulse.

Still on my knees I looked up at my two girls. They opened their eyes and looked down at me. "Please," they both mouthed.

I brought my hands down between their legs. I continued to look at them while I ran my index fingers over their clits, soaking my fingers in their juices, then up into them.

They both gasped.

I brought all the fingers on both hands to play, fully fingering them and opening them to the cool night air. I knelt as if worshipping them, which was what I *was* doing.

I glanced behind me to see Sleepy's head buried between Bashful's thighs, Bashful pulling Sleepy into her by her hair, urging her on.

Doc was giving Lace a nice fingering while she went down on Lust.

Two pairs of hands forced my attention back to the treasures in front of me. I kissed Wench's and Cleavage's inner thighs, pulling them so they stood, braced back against the ancient oak, thigh to thigh. I inserted another finger into each, then another, and then I pulled out.

I ran the backs of my hands through their wetness, thoroughly lubricating my hands and wrists. I stood, kissed one girl, then the other, then I dropped back down to my knees and entered them both, at the same time.

One finger. Fuck 'em with that. Rapunzel had taught me the power of using just one digit.

But these girls weren't blushing virgins, so I added a second finger, bringing them out then in again. The palms of my hands fondled the sensitive tissue between their legs.

Three fingers. In, out, in . . . My thumbs playing with their clits.

"Oh, stud, give it all to me," Cleavage ordered.

Both women were panting hard and trying to hump my hands.

I'd give them what they came here for.

I squeezed in the fourth finger, just down to the knuckle, into both of them. I felt around inside of them, slowly assessing what I could do. I looked up at them. They both had their eyes closed and were focused solely on what was happening to them.

They were both grinding against my hands—wanting, needing, more. I removed my hands for a moment, pulling out the lube and slathering my hands with it.

"Yes," Wench said fiercely.

"Whatever that is, if it makes it easier to fill me, use it. Fill us both," Cleavage added.

I shoved my fists up into them, impaling them both on my hands.

"God!" they screamed in one voice. I pulled them together with my fists, so their hot cunts were inches from my head on either side.

"Squeeze each other's nipples," I ordered. I waited until they were doing so before burying my face between Wench's legs, licking up her sweet juices. "Harder," I said, running my tongue up and down the sweet folds of her pussy, exploring her.

I twisted and turned my fists inside of both of them, making their legs shake, making them moan and groan. I focused on Wench's clit, still moving my fists, while I beat her with my tongue.

Wench began to moan even more loudly, bucking against my face, riding my tongue and fist. She was coming close, so I pulled away and turned to Cleavage, leaving Wench groaning with desire.

"Faster." "Harder," they each ordered in turn.

I began to fuck them with my fists, pulling them out, then shoving them in again while I ate Cleavage out, exploring her, whipping her pussy with my tongue, just like I had with Wench.

But I didn't stop. She pulled me into her, with Wench squeezing her nipples tightly. I beat her clit with my tongue hard, right across the nub, hard and fast, back and forth, my fists in and out of them, fucking them both. At the same time.

"Yes! Yes! Yes!" Cleavage screamed, falling onto the ground so I had to pull out of Wench to continue fucking her. Fucking and riding her hard, while Wench feasted on those incredible tits of hers.

"Oh, god, oh, god, again!" Cleavage yelled, coming again, squeezing my fist hard. I fucked her and ate her and made her come again. And when she lay panting and exhausted, with a pleased gleam in her eyes mingling with tears, I withdrew my hand and pulled Wench off her chest and threw her back onto the ground, burying my fist again inside of her while I bit her nipples. Hard.

"Oh, god, eat me!"

I went down on her. Eating her out. Enjoying her taste, and the feel of her legs tight around my head, squeezing, with her hands in my hair, trying to pull me even closer.

I shoved my whole hand back inside of her, causing her to cry out, while my tongue worked her clit. I twisted and moved my fist, feeling all around inside of her, getting to know her better than her gynecologist, while my tongue beat her pussy.

I fucked her hard, made her ride my fist like a pony, while I hit her with my tongue, back and forth, causing her to ride higher and higher, pressing down onto my fist, pushing for it, riding it . . .

"Yes. Yes! Yes!" she screamed.

And I continued. My tongue and my fist. I let my spare hand run over her breasts, squeezing her hard nipples till she cried out. I wanted her to feel ravaged.

"Oh, god!"

I slipped the little finger of my left hand into her asshole, and it threw her over the edge one more time.

When I withdrew, she lay immobile next to Cleavage. Then, with matching sighs, they curled up into each other.

I ran my hands over their sweet curves. I thought about going back for more on these two, but then I remembered Bashful and Sleepy.

I turned around to see Bashful between Sleepy's thighs.

I looked back at Wench and Cleavage. They were out for now. Satisfied, with three apiece.

I was needed elsewhere.

I stood and approached the two. Sleepy was crying out, but only slightly, as I came to them.

I knelt on one knee behind Bashful, caressing her ass. She pulled up slightly, away from Sleepy, so I whispered, "That's so fucking hot."

With my right hand, I entered Bashful as she ate out Sleepy. My hand was well-lubed now, so I was able to add digits easily, till she was gasping.

Sleepy looked up at me and said, "Whatever you are doing, do it more. She's loving it!" She arched her pussy up into Bashful's face harder.

Bashful screamed in pleasure when I shoved my fist into her tight cunt. Then I inserted two of the well-lubed fingers of my left hand into her asshole. She writhed and squirmed and yelled into Sleepy's cunt. Sleepy looked about to burst as she watched Bashful writhe between us.

"Eat her out. Good." I all but felt fingertips through the thin membrane inside of her. I explored and felt her. I was all the way inside of her and fucked her good, up the ass and cunt.

She was on her knees to eat Sleepy, now she separated her knees further, opened herself wide for me, inviting me into her most private places.

As one, I pulled both my hands out, then pushed in again. She ate Sleepy, who moaned lightly, while I rode Bashful hard. I fucked her.

Then I heard Sleepy cry out more loudly, so I looked up from the delicious ass and pussy I was fucking and met Doc's eyes. Lace and Lust were now curled together like Wench and Cleavage.

Doc winked at me. She was worshipping Sleepy's nice, firm breasts. Teasing her nipples into even more of a frenzy.

Then something caught her eye. "Do you have your fist entire hand inside of her?" She pulled away from her treat to stand and walk up next to me. "Oh, god. Now that is fuckin' hot," she breathed, looking at what I was doing.

"You've never fisted these girls before?"

"Well, no, nor have I touched them back there . . ." Doc actually blushed. She might be beginning to trust me. And want to play as a team together.

I pulled out of Bashful, even as she pushed back, still wanting me. I caressed her ass and kissed it, assuring her she'd soon get good and properly fucked.

I took Doc's right hand in my own, and thoroughly lubed it with another pack of lube. I'd have to dream up a couple of gallons of the stuff to leave behind. After this, Doc was going to need it regularly.

"Kneel here, now." She did as instructed. "Put a finger into her.

Now another." Apparently she now thought of me as a friend because she did so. "A third. Feel how easy you slide up into her?"

While Bashful was groaning out words that just made me want to do it all again, harder.

"Oh, godunfuckingbelievable," Doc groaned, sounding close to orgasm herself. On her own she pushed in a fourth digit, and then, slowly moving it around, feeling her way, she fisted Bashful.

"Oh, god, yes!" Bashful screamed, shoving herself back to further impale herself on Doc's fist.

Doc ran the index finger of her other hand over her right fist, when she was outside of Bashful, and then slipped it up into Bashful's ass.

Bashful again squealed. "I don't care who does it, but take me again!" she screamed.

I watched Doc fuck Bashful for a few moments, enjoying watching the sight of someone inches from me attacking a woman's private parts. I liked seeing those parts opened up for us. Spread for us.

Invaded by us.

I pulled Bashful by the shoulders away from Sleepy, and I took her place, between Sleepy's legs.

I fisted, fucked, ate her. I made her come repeatedly while she said things so hot I was on fire to fuck her over and over. She damn near dislocated my shoulder when she squeezed her legs so tightly around me on the last climax.

Doc and I started to hug, then remembered ourselves and pulled back, glancing around at the sound-asleep women scattered like leaves.

Doc grinned, pleased with herself. "I think I've got this under control," she said, watching the six femmes. "But you wanted to meet Snow White, yes?"

"Yes. Something is going to happen to her, and I need to help her." I suddenly forgot the smells wafting around the forest, the smells lingering on my hands, and all that I had just done.

Doc pointed to an opening from the clearing. "Take that path. Turn left at the stone in the stream, and you'll find her. She's in our cottage."

"So you'll take care of whatever arises here?" I asked with a wicked grin.

She looked me dead on. "These are my girls. I think my interest in Snow is only through them. I need to remember I have enough here." She smiled as she glanced over the peacefully resting femmes. "I need to wake them each, one at a time, for some personal time. That's all they need, and what I need, too." She looked back to me. "Thank you for making me realize that."

I went off into the forest, hoping that now she really liked me and wasn't merely sending me to meet some evil dragon, sorcerer, or really big bear.

I was trying for the cool, distinguished butch, but when I slipped off a rock and fell into the river, I lost all that. I stood up, sputtering, and realized I was a distance from Doc and all the femmes. I didn't have to keep up any charade at the moment. I had no reason to be embarrassed.

And then I realized I was about to meet the heroine of the tale, and so I ought to wash myself. Especially considering where my hands had just been.

The water was cool and clear. It felt refreshing.

Although I kept waking up clean, washing the sweat and scent of other women off my skin felt cleansing to body and mind.

I'd been through a lot over the past few days. Or however long I'd been knocked out. And it had given me time to think about, and experience, some things. I liked helping women, still liked that, even though I had done a lot of that of late. But that there had been so much rescuing made me realize that it wasn't enough.

Sex helped, but even with that, it wasn't enough.

I thought about the wistful look Rapunzel had when I first saw her. That was when I knew there was something missing in my life. That I, too, was wistful. But I didn't really know what it was that I wanted.

I undressed, wringing out my clothes and putting them on the shore to dry while I continued washing.

I'd had a few girlfriends, and some one-nighters, as well, but none of them had really lasted very long. It was as if, maybe, my humdrum everyday life couldn't hold my interest. Like I just wanted someone to help, and once I'd helped them, and done all I could, there was nothing left.

Of course, there were a few girls whom I couldn't help, and those I just gave up on.

But, you know, I always seemed to go after the same type of woman. Maybe I needed to find a new type? I mean, I knew I had to do something to make my hopes of finding my own perfect mate happen. I just didn't know specifically what I needed to do.

Oh, well. I pulled myself out of the river and got dressed, hoping my clothes would dry by nightfall. At least my short hair should dry quickly, and it wouldn't look too bad wet, either. I might as well carry on helping the damsels in distress, even though my heart really wasn't so much in it anymore.

I hoped, after I cleaned myself, that I was on the right path. And I also hoped that was a good omen.

I was going to meet the much lauded Snow. I tried to get excited about it. I knew I could help her. Save her. But I just wasn't as into rescuing as I had been.

I almost went wrong at the rock in the river, but I found my way, and it seemed again as if I walked forever. More than forever. But then on the path I saw an aged old hag and a beautiful young woman with skin as white as snow and hair as black as coal. Oh, fuck, she was hot, and I knew it was Snow White. So I had to save her.

I stepped forth, knowing the truth about the apple the old woman held. Well, okay—knowing what it could do to her. That piece of fruit was nothing but trouble, as was the evil queen in disguise who offered it.

I ran forward. "Wait, Snow, no!"

But still she took the apple. And then she threw it into the woods.

She turned to the hag. "C'mon, do you really think I'm going to keep falling for your tricks, stepmother?"

I stopped dead in my tracks. I could almost see smoke pouring out of the crone's ears, but then she stomped off into the wood.

Snow looked me up and down with fine black eyes. "Now who are you, and did you really think I was going to take yet another evil object from yet another old hag?"

"It's okay," I said, "Doc sent me. I am here to, well, save you from your Evil Stepmother." Her hair was as black as night, her skin white as snow, her lips red and full and begging to be kissed. Just as advertised!

"Oh, like I needed saving. How stupid do you think I am—that I'd just keep falling for her machinations?" She turned her back on me, walking swiftly toward a cottage in the distance.

I had to almost run to keep up with her long legs. "I'm sorry. It's just, I thought—"

She wheeled around to face me. "What? That I'm some sort of damsel in distress you need to save?" She stalked off again. "You're just like Doc and all the others, thinking I'm not too bright and can't be trusted to do anything by myself."

The cartoons couldn't have been more wrong. I had never liked Snow White, but now that I saw her in the flesh, I was in love. I raced forward, grabbing her arm and turning her back toward me.

"What? You want to carry me back to the cottage because you don't want me to get my dainty little feet all dirty?"

This girl had ovaries! I backed off, holding up my hands in peace. "Hey, I can see that you can take care of yourself." I looked down at the ground, toeing it with my boot. "It's just that I have no idea where I am." I kept my head down, but looked up at her, giving her my best puppy-dog eyes. She was beautiful and sexy, and could use *machinations* in a sentence, and I really didn't want her to send me packing this quickly just because she could take care of herself and was tired of people trying to help her.

"My name is Cody, by the way."

"Whatever. Why are the others not here? What did you do to them?"

I didn't know what to say. I didn't want to make her jealous. "Um, well, Doc and I kinda delayed them. They're still coming home from the mines."

Her black eyes snapped with intelligence and fire. She was everything I had ever wanted, hoped for, dreamed of in a woman. She lifted one of my hands and sniffed it. "I was hoping perhaps a second butch had helped calm those girls down." She continued fondling my hand.

"You were hoping I'd done the girls?"

"Something about you makes me think they're happy right now." She sighed and I couldn't help but watch her magnificent chest rise and fall. "They've had Doc all along and I've had little to call my own." Her dark, luminous gaze left me breathless. "Maybe I could call you my own, just for a night."

My mind spun. I let her play with my hands.

She laid one of my hands against her breast. "If it's Lust, I know I can get your mind off her." Her heart beat beneath my palm. I cupped her breast and looked at her full, ripe lips.

Anything I'd say would sound stupid, so I put my other hand to the back of her head and brought her lips to mine.

"Doc is always so afraid of making the others jealous," she whispered, pushing my head down to her bosom. "It's nice to have someone who is just mine. If only for now."

Our tongues tangled, danced, and did the waltz together. "God, Snow, the others can't compare with you." I had thought about taking her back to the cottage, but here and now would work just fine. I pushed her down into the grass, lying on top of her and pressing my body into hers.

She arched up into me, and my hands traced her body through her clothes.

"Oh, please," she said. "Help me with this dress."

Laughing, I explored the laces, ruffles, and underthings. She let me roll down her stockings and seemed to appreciate little kisses on her knees.

"Yes," she said, guiding my hands over her curves.

"You are so beautiful, Snow," I said, pushing her again to her back. The carpet of grass cushioned us, and I had one arm beneath her head, holding her to me. I draped one leg over hers, opening her up, as I traced a fingertip over her collarbone and down between her breasts.

The smile that graced her lips was one of the most beautiful things in this world. She closed her eyes, so her long, black eyelashes lay on her pale cheeks. Mona Lisa had nothing on this girl.

I trailed my fingers over her stomach, and then brushed against it with my hand, studying her beauty, enjoying the softness of her skin. So smooth and firm, her body filled me with a sense of awe and wonder I had never felt before.

Our eyes met, and I was entranced. She was liking that I could spend this time worshipping her. She was enjoying my attentions. So I knew I had to go slow, and take my time. And I *love* taking my time. I knew she wasn't a virgin, not with Doc and the rest of them, so it wasn't like Rapunzel. It wasn't like anyone else, either.

I leaned down to kiss her, gently at first, allowing our lips to become reacquainted again, then she opened her mouth to me.

I wanted her to feel entirely loved. I started by lightly caressing her arms, stomach, legs and collarbone. Then my hands became more and more adventuresome, and I lightly touched her breasts. She began to wriggle slightly.

"Nobody ever takes the time for kissing," she whispered. "More, please."

I was more than happy to oblige. Kissing could be a destination unto itself, though I had no intention of stopping there.

Her barely audible moans were music to my ears.

I pressed my thigh into her, between her legs, and began sucking her neck, nibbling on the tender flesh there. I found her pulse point and nipped it gently. I moved firmly on top of her, taking both her breasts into my hands and finding her nipples, which I rolled gently between my fingers and thumbs.

She was arching up into me, searching for greater contact.

I pushed down harder against her, giving it to her, while I again found her mouth. Her groans filled my mouth as I continued to fondle and caress her body. She brought her hands under my clothes and dug her nails into my back, making me moan in turn at the delightful torture.

I lightly ran my tongue over each of her ears in turn, then worked my way back down her neck, suckling it. I bit at her collarbone as my hands trailed down from her breasts and over her waist.

"Oh, dear heaven, please," she moaned, trying to push my head down, but her legs were wrapped around my body, pulling me into her as much as possible.

I continued downward, licking a nipple, then running my tongue around it as I gently sucked it. I brought one hand up to give butterfly caresses to the other, while my other hand caressed her leg, telling her my intentions of knowing her fully and intimately.

I moved to the other breast and switched sides with my hands. Working her slowly up, causing her to mumble and groan, even as I started to tenderly tug at the already extended flesh, bringing it into my mouth to bite up and down its extended length.

When I had worked up to a good, hard bite, causing her to cry out and writhe against me, I went back to the first nipple to give that the same loving, thorough treatment.

And then I worked my way down, running my tongue over her abdomen, gently nipping at times, while my hands returned upward to toy with her breasts.

"Please, dear heaven, please, Cody," she mumbled, her head moving from side to side. She put her hands on my shoulders and pushed them down toward her heat.

I licked and teased each inner thigh, the heady scent of her arousal filling my brain.

"Please, I need you!"

I bit one thigh and then moved my head directly between her legs. I looked up at her. Her eyes were closed. She put her hands in my hair and pulled me toward her, trying to force me to do what she needed.

I gleefully acquiesced. I put my mouth between her legs and ran my tongue over her dripping slit. This was a taste I could continue feasting on for the rest of my life. I let my mouth hang open as I buried my face between her thighs, tasting her, up and down, again and again.

I ran my hands up and down her body while I feasted, loving the feel of her trembling flesh beneath my hands, even as I used them to keep her in position, to hold her down. I put my tongue up into her, causing her to squirm into my face, and then I focused on her clit, beating it side to side. Every few strokes I would let my tongue glide up and down the length of her, enjoying the taste of her and making it all last that much longer. I wanted her to enjoy this as much as I was.

I slowly slid two fingers into her, lubricating them on the way, making her come.

"Oh, dear heaven, yes! Yes!" She screamed and I felt her squeeze my fingers as she writhed around me.

I wanted more than one orgasm from her. She needed it. I kept eating, even as she briefly tried pushing me from her.

She gave that up after a few moments.

I pulled the rest of the lube packets from my pocket and ripped them open, covering both hands, and went back to where she was pressing me.

It only took a few more moments with my tongue for her to come a second time, flooding my face. Did she climax easily, or could it be me? I didn't care one way or the other, but I was going to spend a really long time finding out. I wanted to take her places she'd never been before—I wanted to be as special to her as she was to me.

I put my right hand back to her pussy, entering her once again, starting with two fingers.

"Yes, again, I can again . . . please . . ." Snow threw her head back, her chest heaving.

I worked her like that, then added a third digit, then a fourth. Doc had said she'd never done these girls with either her fist or anally, so I could hope I might make a real impression here. I didn't want her to remember me for the rest of her life, I wanted her to need me for it, and want me there to please her.

"Don't stop, please don't stop," she mewled when I tried to put my entire hand into her. She lifted her hips toward me, one hand in my hair in a death-hold, keeping me to her. I pushed the rest of the way in, causing her to scream out loud, squirming and tightening around my fist. I thought she was gonna break it, but there was no way in hell I'd pull it out.

Once she calmed, I began moving my fist around inside of her, twisting it and turning it, causing her to mumble incoherently and squirm further. I continued lapping up her sweet juices, knowing I needed to get her going again before I could do much more.

I listened to her body, and when she began squirming and moaning again, moving under my mouth, I brought my other hand up to her ass, working my way between her cheeks and to her tight, virgin hole. I snuck the tip of one well-lubricated finger into her.

She gasped. "Dear heaven, how can that feel so good?"

"Let it happen," I said soothingly. "Let it feel good." I worked my way into her with that finger and felt her pussy contract around my fist.

"It's good, don't stop, no, no, don't stop . . ."

I moved my finger around inside of her, enjoying how I could feel my fist inside her, and feel that one finger with my fist, even as she pushed herself into my mouth.

I fucked her with both hands while eating her, tonguing her back and forth while she tightened her legs around my head, all but ripping my hair out.

I lost count. All I knew was that I was wet to my elbows and she had soaked the front of my shirt. My back was wet with exertion and I never, ever wanted to stop.

"Oh, heaven above," she said breathlessly. "I really can't take any more."

Her body had relaxed around me, and her legs were limp, as were her hands.

I withdrew as gently as I could, wiping my hands on the soft clover and drying them with tissues.

Then I cuddled her into my arms and gently kissed her face and lips. She curled around me and held me. I could not remember a time when I had felt so calm and at peace. She brought out things in me I wanted to remember.

I had . . . patience and insight.

I felt . . . better . . . with her.

A while later, she sat up to look at me. "That was incredible." She leaned over me for a deep kiss and I was pleased to notice her arms were trembling.

I went along with it when she pushed me away. Her eyes were still somewhat glazed. "Just give me a few more moments, and I'll return the favor," she whispered, pulling my head down to rest on her breast.

"No need," I said, though I was horny as hell. I didn't want to be some sort of rollover butch, after all.

She shoved me down with surprising strength. "Cody. I want to. Please?" She leaned over me, gently nibbling on my lips, then kissing me fully. She trailed her hand down my body, feeling my breasts and abs. Then her hand found my belt buckle, and I put my hand on hers.

"You're not the only one who likes the taste of a woman. Please?" she asked, looking down at me with lust-fogged eyes. I drew back my hand, and she undid my belt and unzipped my pants.

She sat back, then said, "Sit up." I did so, and allowed her to pull my T-shirt and sports bra off. When I tried to cover myself with my arms, she pushed them away and pressed her naked body against mine. She kissed my neck and down, until she began suckling on my breasts.

I groaned when she stopped. She moved to my feet to remove my boots and jeans and boxers till, for the first time in this dream, I was naked. I would've complained, not allowed it, but she climbed on top of me, pressing her warm, supple, naked flesh against mine.

Against my will, I found myself pushing my crotch up into her naked thigh. It felt good. Really good.

She was biting one nipple and twisting the other, making me groan as sensations raced through my body. She spread my thighs so she lay between them and I let her move down.

I stopped her, my hand on her head, just before she hit where I really needed her.

She looked up at me. "Please, I want this. I need this. Let me do this. I want to."

I was speechless. I surrendered to sensation as her tongue dove into me, as it caressed me and made me shudder. I was so turned on, after doing her, after all I'd been through, and she was good, realizing I needed release.

"Snow . . . Like that, yes, oh god, like that!" My insides were churning as my legs clenched around her, securing her to me as I bucked against her lithe form . . . I saw stars behind my eyes and might've blacked out for a moment . . .

We fell asleep on the forest floor, our naked bodies entwined. I wasn't sure if I could move. So I murmured, "I love you."

Snow burrowed further into my arms. "I love you, too."

Chapter 10

"Cody? Cody! Wake up!"

I shook my head, struggling to sit up while trying to tell Sheila to stop slapping me. Finally, I trapped her hand in one of mine.

"We were so worried about you!" Sheila said, running her hand through my hair. I think she was looking for an injury. "You ran out, but we found your car, and you weren't in it. You must've knocked yourself out on a branch or hit your head on a rock or something."

I stared at her. A jumble of memories pounded through my head, and I tried to understand the why's. I knew I had left here, and gone elsewhere, but I couldn't tell anyone about that, or prove it.

"I'm fine. Really," I said, sitting up shakily. I was leaning heavily on Sheila, with Sal looking at us disapprovingly.

Someone moved on my other side and I found myself staring at a woman with hair as black as coal, skin as white as snow, and lips as red as passion. Her fine black eyes snapped with intelligence and wit. I was a goner, all over again.

"Cody? Cody?" Sheila said, trying to get my attention again.

"I'm Selina White," Snow said to me, kneeling at my side.

"Selina's part of the crew on the film—the camerawoman," Sheila explained.

I took Selina's hand and just stared.

"Do we know each other?" she asked, with a mixture of humor and disbelief.

"Yes," I said firmly.

Her eyes sparkled and I could smell clover and the scent of her hair.

We seemed to have forgotten about everyone else.

I went to her.

I didn't have a choice.

After all.

Charlotte
of
Hessen

by Barbara Johnson

Chapter 1

*L*ong, long ago in a land far, far away there lived a young woman as beautiful as she was intelligent, and as kind as she was spirited. Left to run wild after her mother's untimely death, Charlotte von Hessen was as comfortable in her father's forests as she was in his sitting room. Life does not always stay the same, however, a lesson good for all to heed, and one that Charlotte was about to learn.

On a misty morning that seemed like any other, Charlotte crept into the forest just as the household was beginning to stir. Baron Heinrich von Hessen, her father, would be shocked to know that his only daughter, clad in the garb of a common peasant, ventured into the forest before dawn each day to search for animals caught in hunters' traps and snares. Like her mother before her, she could not bear to see creatures in pain.

On this day, those not too badly injured she set free, but a red fox had suffered a crushed foot. She scooped him into an old flour sack and carried him off to her secret place.

"You poor, little thing," she crooned to calm the frightened animal while she bound up its injured paw. "You'll be safe here now."

In this hidden part of the forest, she'd found the ruins of an ancient church. She guessed it was centuries old, but its crumbling façade provided just enough shelter for her collection of wooden cages. She'd found the place when she was nine, and in the five years since, no one had ever disturbed her. Deep in the forest as it was, surrounded by brambles and thorns and inhabited by all manner of creatures, including snakes, she figured most people found it intimidating and scary to venture so far into the woods. Most of her father's tenants were a simple people, given to superstition and fear.

She placed the fox gently in a wooden cage and covered it with a dark cloth. She'd powdered some valerian root and given it to him in water. The mild sedative would calm the creature and keep him quiet through the day.

"And how are you doing this fine morning?" she asked as she uncovered a red-tailed hawk. "Your broken wing seems to be healing nicely." The bird of prey stayed calm as she carefully stretched out the wing and ran her fingers along the delicate bones. "I think in a day or two I'll be able to set you free." She fed him some mice she'd caught in the barn.

One by one, she checked each animal; she had ten to care for this week. All were doing well, until she got to the last cage. "Oh, I'm so sorry," she said as she lifted out the lifeless body of a spotted fawn. Caught in a leg-hold trap, its injuries had been too severe. She stroked the soft fur as tears welled up in her eyes. "When Papa comes home, I will ask that he ban the use of these traps on his lands."

Finished with taking care of the animals, Charlotte settled on a boulder to eat a breakfast of bread slathered with butter and quince jelly. She took a sip of honeyed tea, since grown cold. She sighed, deeply content.

She looked around her hideaway. The weathered grey stones of the church were covered with moss and lichen. On all sides of the overgrown clearing, pine trees grew dense and tall. Little light filtered through their branches, but in the afternoons the boulder upon which she sat would be bathed in sunshine. She inhaled deeply. There was nothing she liked better than the scent of a pine forest and rich, verdant soil. She rested back against the boulder, using her rucksack as a pillow. She could hear the distant gurgle of a stream. It made her thirsty, but she didn't want to sit up to take a drink. She closed her eyes. The animals around her, both caged and free, skittered through pine needles and underbrush. A languidness overcame her as the forest sounds faded.

"Well, what have we here?"

Charlotte woke with a start. In the shadowy sunlight, a form stood before her, hands on hips. She felt the pounding of her heart, and struggled to control her panic. She sat up and squinted at the intruder. She unconsciously grabbed her knife. "Move to where I can see you," she demanded, hoping she didn't sound as scared as she felt.

The figure moved out of the shadows, allowing the pale sunlight to illuminate his face. Dressed in the leather pants and tunic of a huntsman, he appeared rather young, possibly only two or three years older than Charlotte. "Don't worry, I won't hurt you." The voice was surprisingly feminine.

Charlotte leapt from her rock and stood at her tallest. Still clutching her knife, she appraised the young man before her. His garb and demeanour both identified him as male, yet his voice and face were those of a woman, and an educated one at that. Confused, she could only say, "You are trespassing."

The youth laughed. "Ah, this old church belongs to you? And who might you be?"

Haughty now, Charlotte raised her chin. "I am Charlotte,

daughter of the Baron Heinrich von Hessen. This forest is on his land. And you are?"

With a low bow, he replied, "I am Willi, son of my father and my mother."

Despite herself, Charlotte couldn't help but smile at his clever reply. An identification, and yet not. And she noted that he did not remove his hat. Very discourteous indeed. "From whence do you come?"

He indicated the boulder. "Do you mind if I sit down? I've had a long walk this morning." He sat without waiting for an answer. "Where I come from does not matter. Suffice it to say it is a great distance."

Charlotte sat next to him. "In all the years I have come here, no one has ever discovered my secret place."

"You are a rescuer of animals I see."

"I do not like the slow death from trapping. I prefer a quick and fair hunt."

"I find that admirable."

Charlotte felt herself blushing under his intense gaze. She was suddenly self-consciously aware of her drab brown skirt and less-than-white peasant blouse, garments that she'd talked Elke into acquiring for her. She wore leather sandals, and she noticed her feet were filthy. She tucked them under her ragged hem while she tried to smooth her tangled hair into some semblance of order.

"Is Willi really your name?"

"Of course. Why do you think I would lie?"

Was it her imagination, or did his voice get noticeably lower? It was her turn to gaze intently upon him, noticing the smooth, delicate hands and the distinctly feminine mouth. What would she find if she snatched away his hat? He seemed uncomfortable at her perusal.

Charlotte stood up. "I do not think you a boy at all."

"Of course I am!"

"Then prove it. Remove your hat."

"I . . . I cannot. I have a . . . a disfiguration."

Charlotte waved her hand around. "I have seen horrible disfiguration in the animals I rescue. I am not some weak female given to vapours. If you have nothing to hide, you'll remove your hat."

He took a deep breath. "Very well then." With a flourish, he removed his hat to reveal a mass of unruly reddish-brown curls that fell below his ears. The colour reminded Charlotte of a newborn fawn. His brown eyes crinkled at the corners when he smiled, and that amazingly feminine mouth curved to reveal bright, white teeth. "You expected something different?" he asked to Charlotte's silence.

"I feel so foolish. I was sure you were a girl."

"And you are not so sure now?" His smile got wider.

"I . . . You are confusing me!" She turned away, feeling her cheeks redden. "I think I must get back to the house. My servants will be wondering where I am."

Willi took hold of her arm. "Please don't go. I want to see all of your animals."

His touch on her arm was like a bolt of lightning. She stared at his fingers, long and unadorned, with short, buffed nails. Despite his garb, this was no peasant hunter. As he continued to hold her, she felt the stirrings of unknown feelings in the pit of her stomach. Elke had told her that one day she would meet a boy who would cause such feelings. She had scoffed at the idea. She'd been around boys her whole life, from her father's stable boys to the sons of visiting merchants. She'd found them all sorely lacking, nothing more than uncouth boors. And now here was a boy she'd barely met, and he made her feel all giddy inside.

She turned from his grasp and approached the first cage. With shaking fingers she removed the cover. "This is a red-tailed hawk. I found him caught in a snare intended for rabbits. His wing was broken."

Willi stood close to her. She felt the heat from his body and smelled the animal scent of warm leather. She wanted to touch his smooth cheek.

"What a magnificent bird." He turned and smiled at her. "And lucky that you found him."

She uncovered the next cage. "These rabbits were orphaned. I don't know what got their mother. I hid them in my room in the beginning. They needed food round-the-clock."

"How did you keep them from being discovered by your servants or parents?"

She laughed somewhat bitterly. "My father is never home. I hardly see him when he is. He blames me for my mother's death."

"I am so sorry."

She felt a rush of shame. "No, I am sorry. I know my father loves me, as I love him. I think I remind him of my mother, and the pain is just too great."

"You look like her, then? She must have been very lovely."

His words pleased her. "We have a painting of her in our formal dining hall. I see the resemblance, but she was much more delicate. Her hair was like moonlight."

Willi touched Charlotte's hair. "And yours . . . Yours is like an early morning sunrise. All red and gold."

Charlotte could feel the flush spread across her face. She knew she should move away, yet could not. This young man . . . The words he spoke . . . They were much too intimate.

As if sensing her discomfort, Willi dropped his hand. "How old were you when your mother died? Do you remember her?"

She felt the prickling of tears. It had been a long time since she'd cried for her mother. "I was seven. She was killed by a coach and horses." She had never wanted to relive that day, but something about Willi made her want to explain so he would know about the pain she carried from all too unwittingly being the cause of her mother's death. "She pushed me out of the way and was struck herself."

Willi gasped. "That must have been horrible."

"That day is a blur to me still. But for her I would have been trampled too. My memories of her also have faded. It makes me sad, but I know she is with me. It was she who taught me to love all God's creatures."

She continued down the row of cages, showing off the forest animals and birds that she cared for. She was proud of her skill as a healer, and it showed in her voice. At the last cage, she faced Willi. "You will probably think I am crazy to rescue this creature," she said as she pulled aside the cloth to reveal a prickly porcupine. Willi backed away. "I'm not sure what attacked him, but he was clawed pretty badly." She moved the cage slightly so the animal was in the sunlight. "You can see the scars on his face. At first I thought he'd been blinded. I know I need to let him go, but I've grown quite attached to him." She could feel the sting of tears. "It's the hardest part of what I do here."

Willi seemed to sense her pain. "Why don't we release him together?"

Charlotte couldn't answer. The tears threatened again as her throat tightened up. Why was she so reluctant to release this animal? Then she felt Willi's hand on her arm. "Come," he said.

Charlotte turned toward him. She had to look up, though he was not too much taller. The sunlight touched on his hair, making it glow like burning embers. His brown eyes were gentle and understanding. She looked away. She felt an urge to kiss him, and she shook her head to rid herself of it. What was wrong with her? She'd never wanted to kiss a boy before. It seemed so . . . so unhealthy.

She smiled. "All right."

She went to lift the cage. "Let me do that," Willi said.

He picked up the cage, holding it away from him as the porcupine's quills began to stand up. Charlotte motioned for him to follow her and led him to a stream a short distance away. They knelt together beside the running water. Willi carefully untied the twine holding the cage door shut. Charlotte took a deep breath, willing herself not to cry. It was so childish. Willi took her hand as the porcupine hesitantly crept out of the cage and sniffed the air. It then walked away from them, pausing briefly to turn and look back before it disappeared into the underbrush.

They stood up together. Willi raised her chin so she looked into his eyes again. He smiled and gently wiped the tears from her cheeks, and then brushed his lips softly against hers. She felt as if her head could explode, the rush of blood was so intense. "Do you like me, sweet Charlotte?" he murmured, his breath warm on her neck.

She backed away. "I hardly know you. I *don't* know you. How can I like or dislike you?"

"But you feel something between us?"

Willi cupped her face with much tenderness. She shivered. She'd had her monthly cycle for about a year now, but it was only recently that she'd begun to feel strange sensations in her body, sensations that Elke had assured her were normal. There were even times when she pleasured herself, but here and now the mere touch of Willi's hand on her skin was unlike anything she'd felt before.

"I . . . I don't understand. What is happening to me?"

"I feel it too."

They stared into each other's eyes. Charlotte felt that something more could happen, but she wasn't sure what. He moved toward her, then paused. Charlotte thought she saw uncertainty in his eyes. He moved toward her again and then kissed her full on the mouth. Dizzy with an unnamed desire, Charlotte wrapped her hands around his neck. His tongue teased her. Her hands seemed to take on a life of their own as she brought them down over his shoulders and across his chest. She gasped and pulled away. She'd felt the unmistakable swell of breasts.

"You *are* a girl!"

Willi caught her. "Does that bother you?"

"But . . . but how can that be? You call yourself Willi. You wear men's clothes."

"Only so I can travel unmolested. My parents would send me off to a convent if they knew."

"Your hair—"

Willi, or whatever her name was, smiled ruefully. "I was almost disowned for that." She ran her hands through the curls. "It was much shorter than this, but I promised *mein Vater* I would let it grow out again."

For a few moments Charlotte could say nothing. So many thoughts raced through her mind. She'd never encountered a girl like this. "So, what is your real name?"

"Wilhelmina."

"I like that much better than Willi, but I will call you Mina."

Mina took Charlotte into her arms again. This time Charlotte did not resist. She was inexplicably drawn to this unusual girl. "I would like to see you again."

"I would like that too." And in that instant, she knew it was true. She did want to see this strange girl/boy again. She rested her cheek against Mina's chest. The leather tunic was soft and warm. Despite the fact that Mina was female, it felt so right to be in her arms. Charlotte pulled away reluctantly. "But now I must get back. I'm sure my maid is wondering where I am, and she'll give me quite the scolding as it is."

Wilhelmina kissed her hand. "I'll come back here every day until I see you again."

Chapter 2

"**W**here have you been all day?" Elke scolded when Charlotte returned. "And look at you, dressed like a common peasant. I should never have given you those clothes."

Safely in her spacious bedchamber, Charlotte stripped off the skirt and blouse so she was wearing only her linen chemise. "Better that I wear these in the forest than my finery. What would Papa say if he had to keep replacing those expensive dresses?"

Elke poured hot water into a tub. "I don't understand why you like to go there. Those woods are all full of spiders and snakes and such." She shuddered. "And bears."

Not even Elke knew of Charlotte's menagerie in the woods. "I find it peaceful." She stepped into the tub and sighed with contentment as she slid into rose-scented water. As much as she enjoyed her forays into the wild, she did like coming home and getting clean again.

Elke shook her head. "It's no place for a girl like you. You should be studying, learning how to be lady of the manor. You're getting to the age when you can marry."

Charlotte wrinkled her nose in distaste. "I will never marry." An unexpected image of Wilhelmina flashed through her mind. She felt momentarily confused. It wasn't as if she'd never thought of marriage before. After all, what other course was there for a girl like her? But suddenly now the thought of marriage to some boorish man held no appeal.

Elke laughed. "You say that now, but one day soon a young man will come along who will sweep you off your feet. And I'm sure your papa will make sure he is very handsome and very rich."

"I don't think Papa will do anything of the sort. He is too busy with his business to care about me." Again, Charlotte visualized Mina. *She* was very handsome.

Elke combed Charlotte's hair, gently working out the snarls. "You poor dear, I know it hurts that your papa is away so much. You know that he loves you though." She stroked Charlotte's cheek. "It's just that you look so much like your mother. She was a lovely lady, so kind and sweet."

Charlotte yanked away, scowling fiercely as her hair pulled painfully from the comb. "It is not my fault that I look like her. He shouldn't punish me for it."

"There, there, dear," Elke soothed, "he does not punish you. I have never seen a man suffer as much as he did when your mother died. And the fact he has never remarried . . . Well, there aren't many men who would stay alone that way."

"Perhaps it would be best if he did. Remarry, I mean."

Elke continued combing Charlotte's hair. "At times I think so too, but would you like a new mother?"

"She would never be my mother."

"Of course not."

The maid finished with Charlotte's hair and helped her wash. The girl then stood and wrapped herself in a big, fluffy towel. "I suppose I should dress for dinner. It seems so ridiculous since it's just me. Why won't you let me eat with you in the kitchen?"

"When you were a child, that was acceptable. But you are a young lady now of fourteen. You need to act like one."

Charlotte threw her arms around Elke. "I love you so much. You're my best friend in the whole world, and I'd rather be with you. Please don't make me sit all alone in that big dining room."

The maid smiled. "All right. Just this once. Your papa will be home tomorrow, and you can be a lady then."

After dinner, Charlotte went early to her room. She needed to be alone with her thoughts—thoughts of a girl named Wilhelmina. Would she really come to Charlotte's secret place as promised? She found herself almost in tears, thinking that it might all have been a lie. She'd never felt this way about anyone, ever. As she drifted off into an uneasy sleep, she feverishly prayed that she would indeed see Mina again.

There was a great commotion in the courtyard the next morning. Charlotte had snuck out early as usual to care for her animals, but this day had returned soon afterward because she knew her papa was coming home. She had lingered for a little while, hoping Mina would show up, but then hurried back. She'd actually gone back to bed, and it was the clattering of horse's hooves against cobblestones that woke her. She rushed to the window and looked down. There was not one, but three coaches in the yard. Charlotte couldn't help but admire the magnificent horses—perfectly matched pairs on all three. She wondered where her father had found the money to pay for such an extravagance.

Just as she was about to leave her window view and rush downstairs in her nightgown, a footman opened one of the coach doors and helped a finely dressed woman step out. Awed by the sight, Charlotte could only stare in open-mouthed astonishment as not one, but three ladies alighted from two of the coaches. She could not see their faces, but the colourful bird plumage on their hats was exceptional indeed. The sun glinted off silver and gold threads in their travelling coats, and the brilliant flash of diamonds on one gloved wrist almost blinded her.

The door banged open behind her. "Lady Charlotte," Elke said, her face all flushed, "you've got to get dressed quick! Your papa has brought home a new wife and daughters."

"A wife and daughters? But that can't be true. He said nothing to me."

Elke was already taking off Charlotte's nightdress. "We were all caught off guard, but that is neither here nor there. We have to make you look beautiful for they are fine indeed."

"I don't want to see them. I want my Papa!"

"Hush, child. You want to make a good impression on your new *Mutter*."

It was with some trepidation that Charlotte descended the stairs a half hour later. Elke had done her best to make her presentable. Just as she reached the bottom stair, she saw her father follow someone into the receiving room. Trying to collect her thoughts, Charlotte paused to look at the portrait of her mother. There had been a time when her papa used to tell her she was her mother in miniature. She could only hope she was half as beautiful.

With a nervous flutter in her stomach, she entered the room. Still wearing travelling clothes, four people turned as one to look at her. She held her head high and smiled, but the three women who stood before her were frightening indeed. Tall and bony, they all had hair as black as coal and dark, beady eyes like crows. The younger of them had a pockmarked face, probably from some childhood disease, and they all had blood-red lips compressed into a thin line. Their ruddy complexions made them look as if they spent too much time outdoors. It was obvious indeed that they were related.

"My darling," her father said as he came over to give her a big hug. "I have brought you a ready-made family." He guided her to them. "This is your new mother, Gudrun, and her two daughters, Lisette and Truda."

Charlotte curtsied. "Pleased to meet you, madam."

With a disdainful raise of an eyebrow, the older of the three looked her over like she was examining a piece of meat for the family dinner. "Charlotte." Her voice was scratchy, as if she had something stuck in her throat. "Your father, my new husband, has told me much about you."

Charlotte's stomach flip-flopped. How could her father have done this? And with no warning! She struggled to control her dismay. She faced each sister in turn and bowed her head.

"She's not very pretty, is she?" the one called Lisette said.

Truda with the pockmarked face laughed. "So rough looking."

The baron laughed, too. "That's my Charlotte for you." He took Gudrun's hand and kissed it. "I trust, dear wife, that you will take my child under your tutelage as if she were your own. You can see that she has sorely missed a woman's guidance."

Mortified, Charlotte could feel herself blushing furiously. How could they talk about her this way, as if she wasn't even in the room? "Papa," she hissed under her breath.

He turned from them with a swirl of his great cloak. "I will leave you four to get acquainted while I attend to other matters. It is wonderful to be home."

Charlotte watched him leave, feeling as if she was going to be sick. Taking a deep breath, she indicated the ornate brocade and silk couch. "Please, sit down. I will ask the servants to bring tea."

Without a word, Gudrun pulled off her gloves and hat, placing them carefully on a settee. Her two daughters did the same. Then they took off their cloaks and all sat down, mirror images of each other as they carefully smoothed their stick-straight black hair before spreading their skirts around them. Only then did Gudrun look at Charlotte. "Well child, what are you waiting for? Where is that tea? We have had a long journey, and the roads were very dusty." Charlotte turned to go. "And would you mind terribly taking our travelling coats and hats to our rooms?"

"I . . . but of course, madam." She piled the items in her arms, taking care with the hats and their extravagant feathers. One of them tickled her nose, and it was all she could do to keep from sneezing. Elke met her outside the door.

"Lady Charlotte, what are you doing? Give me those."

Charlotte allowed the maid to take them from her. "My father's new wife asked me to take them to their rooms." She frowned. "Do they even have rooms? You'll have to get some aired out."

"The housekeeper has already ordered it done." Elke leaned close. "She's not very happy."

"I didn't think she would be. Thank you for taking those. I have to get to the kitchen. Her Majesty wants tea."

"Oooo, you'd better not let her hear you talking like that."

Charlotte hurried to the kitchen and ordered tea, as well as *brötchen* with butter and strawberry jam. Then she returned to the receiving room to discover that the three women were in exactly the same positions as when she had left. They looked up expectantly at her entrance.

"The tea will be here shortly," she said, observing Gudrun's frown. Sitting in an overstuffed chair, she continued, "This is all much a surprise to me."

"Well, the marriage was very unexpected. Your father asked me not two weeks after we'd met."

Charlotte couldn't help herself. "And where was that?"

Gudrun frowned again. "It will not do for you to talk to me in that manner. Your father told me you were an unruly child. You're worse than I imagined."

"I quite agree, Mama. She is so coarse. To think I have to call her Sister."

"Now, now, Lisette. You don't have to do any such thing. She is, after all, just a stepsister. Why, I expect you won't even have to share the same floor with her."

Furious that once again they spoke as if she wasn't there, Charlotte retorted, "All the sleeping chambers are on the same floor. Unless that is, of course, you'd rather bed below stairs."

"Mother!"

"Insolent girl! You apologise to Lisette immediately."

"I have nothing to apologise for."

"Your father will hear about this, and then we'll see. You may have had your own way all these years, but that will change. I am mistress here now, and you will do as I say."

Charlotte stood up. She could feel the blood rushing to her head and the sting of hot tears in her eyes. This nightmare could not be happening. She blinked once, then again, hoping this was a bad dream and they would all disappear. It was not to be.

Clutching her skirt so tightly that her nails stabbed her through the material, she turned away and ran from the room, almost knocking Elke over in her haste. She bounded up the stairs and flung herself into her bedroom, where she ripped off her expensive silk gown with its accompanying pannier and corset, replacing them with the drab peasant garb. Overcome with an anger at her father that she'd never felt before, she hurried down the stairs and snuck out through the kitchen, taking time only to grab a bottle of milk, a loaf of bread, some fresh-churned butter, and an apple to stuff into her rucksack.

Running most of the way, it wasn't long before she arrived at her hideaway. Its calm beauty and the animals she kept there couldn't cheer her up. She flung herself onto the boulder and wept, deep gulping sobs that tore through her whole body. She gave a small scream when someone touched her shoulder.

"Charlotte, what is wrong?"

It was Wilhelmina, looking exactly as she had yesterday.

"This is the most miserable day of my life since the day my mother died."

Mina sat next to her. She pulled a handkerchief from a pocket. "What happened?"

"My father came home with a new wife and two horrible daughters."

"Did you not know?"

Charlotte shook her head. "He said nothing before his trip. And not even one letter while he was away. I can't go back there. I just can't."

Wilhelmina stroked Charlotte's hair. "But you can't stay here. It's fine for woodland creatures, but not for one such as you."

Charlotte angrily pushed Mina's hands away. "I am no weak girl. I can take care of myself."

"I did not mean to imply otherwise." She gestured toward the small rucksack. "It does not seem to me that you have come prepared to spend many a night in these woods."

Charlotte felt her anger drain away. "You're right. I left without thinking. I just had to get away from their smug faces and cruel smiles." She was silent for a moment. "I'll sneak back to the manor and take extra food and then I'll run away."

"And what about your animals? Who will take care of them?"

Charlotte threw herself into Wilhelmina's arms. "Oh, Mina, what am I going to do?" She pulled back. "You can come to my father as Willi and ask to marry me."

Mina laughed. "But as you said yesterday, you don't even know me."

Charlotte sighed. "You have a good and kind heart, and that's all I need to know. I don't care if you're a farmer's daughter. You can come to my father as Willi and tell him we're getting married. Then we'll go away together. You can be Willi or Wilhelmina, whatever you'd like."

"You're a sweet girl," Mina said as she brushed the tears from Charlotte's eyes. "I wish it could be so easy."

Once again, her touch sent shivers of delight through Charlotte. Were these the feelings Elke meant when she said Charlotte would one day meet a boy who would change her life? But Wilhelmina wasn't a boy. As confused as she was, Charlotte's only thoughts right now were of her plight. She was, after all, only a girl of fourteen who'd been left to her own devices for these past seven years. And now, suddenly, she had a new stepmother and two new stepsisters who obviously disliked her. Her father was as oblivious to Charlotte and her needs as he had been ever since her mother was killed that awful day.

She pushed all thoughts of stepmothers and stepsisters away and let herself relax in Mina's arms. It felt so safe. "Where do you come from?" she asked. "I know you're not really a huntsman or even a farmer."

"I guess I'm like you. I want to get away from my everyday life. I will only tell you that my father is a very important man, and because of that I live under so many expectations. Sometimes I just want to be an ordinary person."

"It's not very ordinary for a girl to dress and act like a boy."

Wilhelmina laughed. "If you think about it, sweet Charlotte, you may be wearing a dress, but you are no ordinary girl either. That's something that could make me go mad, trying to live up to the expectations of our parents."

"I never really thought about it. I was always allowed to do whatever I wanted. I can ride and hunt as well as I can embroider and dance."

"You're lucky then. And your father must love you to have taught you."

"No, his gamekeeper. I don't even think my father knows."

"I'm sure he does."

Charlotte sighed deeply. "I have a feeling my new stepmother will not be so understanding. My maid, Elke, and the other servants know but let me do as I please. I think that will all change."

Mina lifted Charlotte's chin and looked into her eyes. "Whenever you can get away, I will be waiting for you here. And if on some days you cannot, I will take care of your creatures. I too have some healing capabilities."

Charlotte wrapped her arms around Mina's neck and kissed her. It seemed like the natural thing to do. "Thank you," she said, but Mina silenced her with another kiss. Her hands played across Charlotte's shoulders and back. And then her fingers were fumbling with the laces of Charlotte's blouse. As the laces loosened, she kissed Charlotte's neck and then her lips pressed against the mounds of Charlotte's breasts spilling from the low-cut chemise. Charlotte moaned, her heart pounding from these unexpected and unfamiliar sensations.

"So sweet," Mina murmured. She kissed Charlotte again, softly, then more urgently, then soft again. It was almost as if she fought with herself. With a groan, she pushed Charlotte away.

"You need to go." Her breathing was ragged, her cheeks flushed. Her eyes glittered with an unnamed desire. Or was that shimmer simply tears?

Charlotte's breathing was not much better. Her bosom heaved, her skin burning where Mina's lips had touched. "I don't want to go."

"You must."

"But why?"

Mina turned away. "I can't explain. Please, just trust me. It's better this way."

"I'll only go on one condition."

Mina looked at her again. The sadness in her eyes tore at Charlotte's heart. "What is it?"

"You have to promise you'll come back here tomorrow. I'll come early in the morning and wait for you all day if I have to."

"Charlotte, we shouldn't see each other again."

"Please. Promise me."

Charlotte watched the play of emotions across Wilhelmina's face. There was joy and unhappiness both. She held her breath. Joy won out.

"Very well. I promise."

Charlotte felt as if a great weight lifted from her. For a few moments, she'd been truly afraid she'd never see Wilhelmina again. She laid her hand upon Mina's soft cheek. Mina grabbed her hand and kissed it fervently and then bounded off into the woods like a young stag. Charlotte placed her lips against her hand, feeling the warmth from Mina's lips still lingering there. With a deep sigh, she left her secret sanctuary, not realising it would be weeks before she returned.

Chapter 3

"Where have you been, you unruly girl?"

Charlotte winced in pain at the pinch from her new stepmother. "I just went for a walk."

"Liar! You've been missing for hours. And look at you! You're a disgrace to your father, dressed as you are like a common peasant."

Charlotte backed away from her. She couldn't remember the last time someone had raised a voice to her. In fact, she didn't believe anyone ever had. Out of the corner of her eye she saw Elke cowering in a corner. She looked again. Was that a bruise she saw on Elke's cheek?

Gudrun grabbed her arm and spun her about. "Look at me when I speak to you, girl."

"My name is Charlotte."

Gudrun slapped her. Hard. The sting of that hand against her cheek brought tears to her eyes and a gasp to her lips.

"You'll not be impudent with me. You may have been left to do as you will all of these years, but I am mistress of the house now and you will obey me."

Charlotte struggled to control her temper. Was this nightmare really happening? Where was her father, and would he allow this harridan to treat her thus? How could he have married her? She took a deep breath. "I am sorry, stepmother. I would never presume to take your place."

Gudrun seemed somewhat mollified. "Go to your room and change for dinner. It will be our first as a family. I want your father to be pleased."

Charlotte hurried away, beckoning Elke to follow. All the way up the stairs, they said not a word. Once inside the privacy of her room, she threw herself sobbing into Elke's arms. The maid smoothed Charlotte's hair. "There, there," she soothed. "It will be all right."

"No, nothing will ever be all right again."

"Your papa will not let anything happen to you. It's just an adjustment period for everyone."

Charlotte looked up. "Is that why you have a bruise on your cheek?"

Elke touched the discolouration. "I spoke out of line."

"It is never right to strike a person. I hate her. I don't understand my father."

"He is a man who has had no wife for all these seven years. It is only natural he would want his daughter to have a mother. And two sisters! How lucky for you."

Charlotte flung herself away in disgust. "It's not lucky and you know it. It is a living hell." She stripped off her clothes, angrily tossing them into a pile on the floor. "If I were a boy, I would run away." She paused, thinking of Mina. Perhaps they *could* run away together. Mina had passed easily as Willi.

Elke helped her dress into something more suitable for dinner. "Then we have to be thankful you are not a boy."

The meal was an interminable affair. Watching her besotted

father, Charlotte knew her worst nightmare had come true. She loved him still, but did not know if she could forgive him for what he'd done, especially because he'd not talked with her first. Charlotte did not know that night just how much of a nightmare her life would become.

For the next few weeks, Charlotte was unable to leave the manor for her forays into the forest. Her only consolation about her menagerie of animals was that Mina had promised to take care of them. It did not even occur to Charlotte that Mina would not come; she trusted her new friend implicitly. And late at night when she tossed and turned in her bed after another long and tedious day, her thoughts of Mina would turn to a more intimate nature. She remembered the softness of Mina's lips and the feel of her hand on her face. She would moan aloud while she pleasured herself, imagining all the while that it was Mina's fingers stroking her. During those exhausting weeks, Mina became much more than a friend to Charlotte's lonely heart.

Every morning she would be determined to somehow escape from the house, but she never could. She would sit for hours with Truda and Lisette, learning all manner of subjects from a boring tutor. It wouldn't have been so wretched if Charlotte had not already known most of what she was being taught. Worse, however, were lessons in the deportment of young women from a wrinkled hag who enforced her strictures with a far-reaching, knife-edged cane.

As the time passed, the lessons got shorter and shorter, so Charlotte was able to sneak away more and more, especially when her father would be away for weeks at a time. Mina became so much a part of her life that when Charlotte's fifteenth birthday came and went without the acknowledgement of her family, it was only Mina who could console her.

❧

And on yet another fateful day the winter when Charlotte was fifteen, the three girls left the classroom to discover the entire household in a sombre mood. As she descended the stairs, Charlotte felt an ominous foreboding. The servants all looked at her with obvious sympathy. Several struggled to control their tears. The three young women were led into the formal receiving room, where Gudrun awaited them. She turned, a fleeting smile on her face before she too turned sombre. "Sit down, my children. I'm afraid I have bad news."

Charlotte felt the blood drain from her face. "Something has happened to my father."

"I'm sorry to say that is true."

Charlotte gasped. Feeling lightheaded, she sank into a chair. "What happened?"

"It seems that on this last trip to Köln, he was flung from his horse when it slipped on wet cobblestones. He struck his head and died instantly."

Charlotte felt as if someone had hit her in the stomach. "No! No, it can't be true!" A swirling blackness seemed to surround her. She shook her head and lifted tear-filled eyes to Gudrun, searching her face in the hope it was all a lie.

Gudrun's eyes were cold. "They are bringing his body home. I'm sorry."

The next few days passed in a blur. Her father was brought home and buried in the family vault next to Charlotte's mother. Overcome with grief, Charlotte did not venture from her room for weeks. Emotionally numb, she could only lie abed and stare at the ceiling. She ate barely enough to keep a very young child alive, and hardly noticed the changes in the household. One servant after another was dismissed and replaced with someone new. Only Elke remained, though she had been reduced from lady's maid to mere kitchen help.

The painting of Charlotte's mother disappeared, as did all the beautiful or valuable objects her mother had brought to the house. The baron's belongings were destroyed or given away, until all traces of his existence were gone. And then early one spring day, Gudrun came to Charlotte's room. She unceremoniously yanked open the heavy draperies covering the window. Charlotte blinked as the bright sunlight stung her tear-filled eyes.

"I have coddled you long enough. It is time to come out of this room. In fact, I believe I have found a room more suitable for you now." She glanced around as if assessing what changes she would make.

Charlotte barely had the strength to raise up on one elbow. "You're moving me out of my bedchamber?"

"You need to earn your keep, girl. You've had enough time to grieve for your father, self-indulgent fool that you are." She stood with hands on hips. "Well, what are you waiting for? Get up out of that bed and go to the kitchen. You can help our new cook."

Too numb to even argue, Charlotte got out of bed and splashed cold water from the basin onto her face. Gudrun watched impassively as she struggled into her clothes, not even bothering to offer assistance. As Charlotte headed for the door, Gudrun called out.

"Wait!"

Charlotte turned. "Yes, stepmother?"

"Those clothes you used to wear? The peasant garb. Where are they?"

"Elke would keep them for me."

"You'll need them. What you're wearing now is much too fancy for the work you'll be doing."

And so it came to pass that Charlotte, daughter of the late Baron Heinrich von Hessen, became nothing more than a common servant in her own home. The weeks turned into months, which turned into a year. While her stepmother and stepsisters spent the inheritance that was rightfully hers, she waited on them hand and foot. The servants were let go one by one as the money ran out, until there were only the bare minimum to tend to the needs of the perpetually unhappy mistress of the house and her ungrateful daughters.

Charlotte continued to escape to her hidden sanctuary whenever possible, happy on those occasions when Wilhelmina would be there as well. Stolen moments with Mina became the only joy in her life.

Charlotte lived for the times they could be together. They would care for her wounded animals, Mina's gentle hands growing more sure every day. Afterward, they would enjoy breakfast or lunch together. And if time allowed, she would sit nestled in Mina's arms while Mina read to her.

"I love the sound of your voice," Charlotte said.

Mina leaned down and kissed Charlotte's neck. "And I love the feel of you in my arms." She dropped the book and ran her hands along Charlotte's arms and then across her bosom. Charlotte couldn't help but arch into her touch, and then she twisted so they were face to face. She closed her eyes, yielding to Mina's mouth and tongue and fingers. As Mina pulled her in closer still, she could feel their hearts beat in unison. Her breath caught in her throat as Mina caressed her through her clothes, her hands gliding over breast and belly and hips to thighs.

She had to admit she enjoyed their kisses and fondlings, although she sometimes wondered, and wished, if such pleasures could become more, though she knew not what. She knew there were physical intimacies that men and women enjoyed together. After all, her own dear mother had been married and with child by the time she was eighteen, only two years older than Charlotte now was. But Charlotte wasn't interested in finding out what intimacies men and women shared; she only wanted to be with Wilhelmina.

"You are a good friend, Mina," Charlotte said one day after they'd set free a dove. "I don't know what I would have done without you all these long months."

"I only wish I could help you more. It is unfair what those witches have put you through. If I were a man—"

"I know. You would marry me and take me away to a far-off land and shower me with jewels and silks." Charlotte laughed playfully. She did not laugh often these days.

"Yes, I would. You would never be unhappy again." She grabbed Charlotte's hand and kissed it.

The touch of Mina's lips always made Charlotte warm and tingly inside. Feeling unexpectedly bashful, she smiled and pulled away.

"Are you all right?" Mina asked with a slight frown.

"Yes. Just a little tired maybe."

Mina spread her cloak over a sunny patch of pine needles. "Come, lie down."

Charlotte did as she was bid. She closed her eyes and felt her whole body relax. The sun felt good. A shadow fell across her face, and she opened her eyes to find Wilhelmina staring down at her. Charlotte's lips parted, and Mina leaned down as if to kiss her but then pulled back. Charlotte could not read the expression in her eyes, but with an inexplicable longing she reached up and pulled Mina toward her. The sensation of Mina's tongue in her mouth drew a deep moan from Charlotte. Their kiss deepened, leaving Charlotte dizzy. And then Mina's hands were roaming all over Charlotte's body, making her feel on fire. Charlotte did not, could not, resist when Wilhelmina undid the laces of her corset and blouse and yanked her chemise down enough to take a hardened nipple into her mouth.

Charlotte gasped at the unfamiliar, yet powerful, sensation. "Mina—"

"Shhh, sweet Charlotte. Let me love you. I cannot wait any longer."

The forest sounds and smells faded deep into the background of her senses as Mina stripped off the rest of Charlotte's clothes and continued to play with her body as with a fine-tuned instrument. The sun caressed her naked form. Embarrassed at being so exposed, she tried to cover herself, but Wilhelmina gently pushed her hands away and kissed her sensitive skin. She couldn't help but moan. She'd never experienced sensations like these before. Mina's fingers gently explored the contours of Charlotte's curves, while her mouth kissed her eyelids, her lips, her throat, her shoulders. Charlotte arched in response and moaned again when Mina's warm mouth found a nipple and sucked.

Mina's hands explored further, travelling over Charlotte's body. The soft, tender caresses, in places only she herself had ever touched, warmed her, sending tingles coursing through her veins. As Mina continued to nibble at her hardened nipple while gently squeezing the other one between her fingertips, the tingling became like a lightning bolt, jolting through her.

Then Wilhelmina's fingers found their way between Charlotte's legs. Charlotte gasped and arched up, her hands tangling in Mina's hair, instinctively urging her on and pressing Mina's mouth to her bosom. She was panting and sweating while she squirmed under Mina's gentle ministrations.

Wilhelmina stroked Charlotte's nipples and breasts as she continued her exploration. Charlotte cried out when Mina's fingers eased into the wetness between her legs, caressing her slick folds. In all her sixteen years, Charlotte had never felt anything so incredible.

She was quivering now as her breathing became more ragged. Mina's mouth on her breasts and her fingers sliding through the curls between her legs created a flood of sensations. Had she been standing, she was sure her knees would have buckled by now—all her energy was focused between her legs. She closed her eyes tight, seeing red against the eyelids. She gasped for air. Her hands grabbed Mina's hair.

Then all thought ceased; she was only what Wilhelmina made now. Her body lost all control as she cried out and arched and bucked against Mina, crushing their bodies together, holding Mina's hand in place with her own tightly pressed thighs.

Charlotte wasn't sure if she had fallen asleep or merely swooned, but her next conscious thought was the realisation that she was encircled in Mina's arms. A breeze played across her bare skin, making her shiver. Wilhelmina held more tightly.

"Are you cold, my love?" Mina asked as she kissed Charlotte's forehead.

"A little."

Wilhelmina reached over and quickly pulled her cloak over them. "Better?"

"Mmmm, much." She took a deep breath. "I've never experienced anything like that in my whole life."

"I hope it was a good feeling."

Wilhelmina gazed at her so intently that Charlotte felt herself blushing. The things Mina had done to her body . . . Overwhelmed with feelings she couldn't understand, she reached up and touched Wilhelmina's cheek. "More than good. Incredible." She felt the prickle of tears. "I don't ever want to go back. Please take me with you."

Wilhelmina kissed Charlotte again. "You and I will be together soon. I promise you that. Now, let's get you dressed and home before darkness falls."

Feeling a little like something was missing, unfinished, Charlotte dressed quickly and made as if to set out for home. Once hidden behind the trees, she turned to watch Mina leave. Mina slowly picked up her cloak and held it to her face, appearing to take a deep breath. Her eyes were closed, and as she lowered the cloak, Charlotte could see that she smiled. Charlotte couldn't help but smile back. As Wilhelmina put on her cloak and hat and then strode away from the sanctuary, Charlotte felt a sense of loss.

"Mina," she whispered.

Nothing would ever be the same again. She had changed. She was a woman now, a woman who wanted to be with the one she loved. But that could never be. She was trapped, destined to live out her life as a servant in her own home, stealing brief moments of happiness. With a sigh, she started her journey back.

Chapter 4

$\mathcal{L}$ isette and Truda were all aflutter when Charlotte returned to the house. They did not even berate her for having been gone the whole afternoon. And Gudrun only gave her a cursory glance when she sidled into the kitchen to help prepare the evening's repast. Elke took Charlotte aside. "They have received an invitation from the palace."

"The palace? How do the stepdaughters of a mere baron warrant an invitation to the palace?"

Elke furiously peeled potatoes, as she was wont to do when excited. "The prince has returned home from abroad and is in need of a wife. The king and queen are holding a grand masquerade ball in one fortnight, and have invited the daughters of anyone titled." She gave a disdainful sniff. "Not that anyone would mistake those two bad-mannered females for nobility."

Charlotte giggled. It was true that her two stepsisters had turned out to be inelegant young women, lacking in even the most basic of social skills. Their months of lessons with the old woman had not given them brains. They could not hold an intelligent conversation, and though they dressed elegantly, their lack of grace became apparent when they moved. They could not sing or dance with any felicity, or even paint a decent watercolour. Gudrun had held a couple of cotillions to introduce them to eligible males, but their raucous laughter and coarse manners were enough to dismay even the most desperate of men. Try as she might, she could not believe any man would want to touch either of them with the love and tenderness she had experienced with Mina.

She paused in her washing of the turnips. "Then I too am invited to the ball."

Elke stared at her. "Oh mistress Charlotte, you could not go to such a ball, as much as you deserve it. They would never let you go, and what would you wear?"

"I have a dress of my mother's. Gudrun never found that one." Charlotte's eyes misted with tears. "You remember the dress, don't you Elke? All silver and white voile. The lace overskirt was covered with seed pearls. She wore it for my seventh birthday."

"Oh yes. Your mother looked so beautiful."

"I will wear the dress and go to the ball too."

Laughter startled them, and then Gudrun's raspy voice mocked them. "I can just see it now. You, a mere servant girl, introduced to the prince."

"I am not a servant, stepmother. I am my father's daughter, and I have as much right to be there as Lisette and Truda."

Gudrun looked at her. As usual, she made Charlotte feel like an insect under scrutiny. "Very well then," Gudrun said. "You may go if your chores are finished and you do indeed have such a dress. Of course, you'll need all the accessories too. Slippers. You can't dance in clogs." With that, she swept out of the room.

Charlotte looked at Elke in disbelief. That had been entirely too easy. Her stepmother was never that agreeable. It made Charlotte suspicious. "I don't trust her."

"Just as well that you don't." Elke gave her a big hug. "And don't you worry, we'll find what you need to go with your dress. You'll not disgrace your mother or your father. God rest their souls."

Soon the masquerade ball was only a few days away. Gudrun and the other two had kept her more busy than usual, but Charlotte had found the time to alter her mother's dress, and had managed to buy some silver ribbons for her hair. One of Elke's friends who worked for another family had borrowed a pair of shoes from the daughter of that household, unbeknownst to that daughter. They were not a perfect fit for Charlotte, but were still better than Truda's oversized shoes or Lisette's smaller ones.

"Oh, you are the vision of your poor, dead mother," Elke told Charlotte as she put the finishing touches on the voile dress.

Charlotte looked in the mirror. She smiled in delight, for she did indeed look very fine. It had been months since she'd worn anything other than the plain attire of a servant maid. She removed the ribbon from her hair, letting red-gold curls flow down beyond bare shoulders. "Do you think I can leave my hair loose for the ball?"

"'Tis not proper for a young woman to do so," Elke said. She lowered her voice. "Only strumpets do that."

"All right then, you can put it up. It's a good thing Gudrun did not let you go. I would not trust myself to her lady's maid, even if she would consent to it."

"Well, well, what have we here?"

Charlotte turned to find her two stepsisters watching from the doorway. It was the first time they had ever come to her room since she'd been banished to the servant's quarters. In the dim light they appeared even more like haunted wraiths, with their skeletal bodies, pale skin, and black hair. Lisette, the older one, grinned evilly.

"What do you want?" Charlotte asked.

The two sisters slowly flanked Charlotte at the mirror. Elke backed away. She'd felt their wrath more times than she cared to count. Charlotte felt nervous, but refused to let it show. Lisette began to stroke her hair.

"Don't you look pretty. Hmmm, I never knew how soft your hair was."

Trapped between them, Charlotte felt her skin prickle with unease. "What do you want?" she repeated.

"Why, we just wanted to help you. The ball is only a couple of days away. Do you have everything you need?"

"Thank you, yes. Please leave."

Charlotte turned to escape from between them, and as she moved away she felt a tug on her dress. Before she realised what was happening, Truda shoved her forward. As she fell, Charlotte heard an ominous ripping sound as the delicate voile of her skirt tore away from the waistline. Little seed pearls popped against the floor. Elke gasped.

"Oh my, I am so sorry," Truda said. "The heel of my shoe was caught in the hem of your dress."

"I'm afraid mine was too," Lisette said. "What a shame. It must be that the dress was so old. The material was just too fragile."

Kneeling beside a weeping Charlotte, Elke glared up at the two sisters. "What have you done?"

"It wasn't on purpose," Truda said, her voice dripping with feigned regret. "We only wanted to help."

"Please leave us," Elke said.

With a swish of their taffeta skirts, the sisters turned to leave. "Oh, look," Lisette said as she paused beside Charlotte's bed. "Why, these appear to be the shoes that Ursula misplaced. How fortunate that you found them." She smiled, and it was enough to make one's blood turn cold. "I'm going to be seeing her this evening. I'll return them for you."

"They are the most evil creatures I've ever known," Elke said after they'd left. She stroked Charlotte's hair. "There, there, mistress Charlotte. I am sure we can fix the dress."

Charlotte sat up and angrily pushed her away. "There's no time before the ball. I hate them so!"

"What are you going to do?"

Charlotte felt her anger drain away. "There's nothing I can do."

"It's not like you to give up like this."

"I'm not giving up, but I just can't fight it anymore. I'm resigned to my fate."

"'Tis not right. You're the daughter of a baron. You shouldn't be scrubbing kitchen floors and waiting on harpies."

Charlotte stood and replaced the tattered dress with her normal attire. "Can you take care of my chores this afternoon? I need to get away."

"Of course. Will you be back before nightfall?"

"I don't know, Elke. But I can't bear to see any of their smug faces."

Charlotte stopped by the kitchen to grab some bread, *wurst*, and cherry brandy before leaving the house. She did not notice the beauty of the day as she fled to the only safe place she knew. She was crying as she stumbled into the crumbling ruins and then into the arms of Wilhelmina.

"Charlotte, my love, what's the matter?"

Sobbing, Charlotte melted into Mina's strong arms. She smelled of leather and sweat. "My life is a nightmare."

Mina led Charlotte to their favourite rock. She took the brandy from the rucksack and opened it. She made Charlotte drink from the bottle. "Tell me what happened."

The fiery brandy made Charlotte cough. She felt its heat course through her veins. "You'll think I'm being silly."

"No I won't. Tell me."

"You might have heard the king and queen are having a ball."

Wilhelmina frowned. "Yes."

"They want to find a bride for the prince."

"So I've heard."

"Our household received an invitation. I really wanted to go."

She felt Mina tense up. "Oh, don't worry. I wasn't going because I was interested in becoming a princess." She smiled as she lightly stroked Mina's cheek. "I just wanted to dress up and dance."

Wilhelmina took Charlotte's hand and kissed it. "What does that have to do with Gudrun and her daughters?"

Charlotte sighed. "I had an old dress of my mother's that I altered to fit me. I was putting the final touches on it today when Truda and Lisette came to my room. They claim it was an accident, but they tore the skirt. It's unrepairable."

"Surely you have other dresses?"

"Not anymore. Not since my father died."

Mina took Charlotte into her arms and kissed her throat. "Mmmm, you are beautiful without all that finery."

Charlotte felt the familiar heat warm her blood. She tipped her head back, giving Mina easier access to her neck. She moaned deeply as Mina's hands travelled up her arms and across her breasts. She could feel her nipples strain against the fabric of her chemise. Almost frantically, she unlaced her blouse and pulled it over her head. There'd been many a night since that first time that she'd relived the moment, wishing and hoping Wilhelmina would make her feel that way again.

Mina took her hands and pulled her up so they stood in front of the rock. She reached around, undoing the fastenings to Charlotte's skirt so that it pooled around her feet, then pulled her chemise over her head. She quickly untied the ribbons on her stockings and pulled them off as well, leaving Charlotte completely exposed to the warming rays of the sun.

Mina spread a blanket over the pine needles. "Lie down," she said, easing her to the ground. Mina knelt above her, the passion smouldering in her eyes.

Charlotte felt the blood rush to her cheeks. She'd dreamt of being with Mina like this again, but now she felt a little scared and unsure. With a deep breath, she covered her breasts with her arms and crossed her ankles.

"No, none of that, my sweet," Mina said, fondling her collarbone before carefully taking Charlotte's wrist and pushing her arm away from her breast. "You're beautiful, and I love looking at you." She moved the other arm as she leaned over Charlotte, feathering kisses up her neck and to her lips.

The familiarity of Mina's soft kisses relaxed Charlotte. She closed her eyes, letting Mina's mouth soothe and warm her. When the kisses turned more fervent, she forgot her embarrassment and pulled Mina to her, holding her tight, tangling her fingers in Mina's hair and returning her kiss with an ardour stronger than she'd known before.

Mina's sure hands caressed Charlotte—down over her hips, across her stomach, up her inner thighs. She cupped Charlotte's breasts, tenderly teasing the hardened nipples, until Charlotte was again squirming, aching for more.

Charlotte gasped for breath, breaking the kiss. They stared into each others' eyes, and then Charlotte urged Mina down to her breasts. Mina obliged, tenderly suckling first the left, then the right. Charlotte arched up and automatically spread her legs. Mina moved quickly between them. Charlotte arched against Mina's hips, enjoying the pressure of Mina lying against her, pressing into her.

Mina began kissing her way down Charlotte's body, bringing up both hands to caress and tease Charlotte's breasts. She grasped the nipples between her fingers, squeezing them and sending pleasurable jolts through Charlotte's body, down between her legs. She moaned loudly and pushed up against Mina more urgently. She felt as if she was on fire, burning from the inside out.

"Please, please . . . Mina!"

Mina was nibbling her tender flesh now, licking and kissing and planting teasing bites as she moved down Charlotte's body. Then her chin was pressing gently but firmly against Charlotte's most intimate spot. Her tongue flicked.

Charlotte gasped and tried to sit up. "What . . . What are you doing?" Her primal self fought with her reason. Wilhelmina's mouth felt so good, but it couldn't be right. Not down there!

Mina looked at her and smiled reassuringly. "Just lie back, darling. Close your eyes. I won't hurt you."

"But—"

"Trust me."

Charlotte lay back, breathing deeply, trying to think about the way the sun shone above, the way the birds sang, the way the breeze tickled the leaves in the trees. Anything but the way Wilhelmina's mouth and tongue moved against her. Her body trembled. She clutched the blanket. She closed her eyes tight.

She felt a warm wetness against her most intimate and private spot, and it sent the heat of a royal fire through her. She cried out even as she opened her legs wider to Mina, involuntarily bending her knees and bringing them upward. Mina grasped her ankles and pulled them down, then held her legs firm against the blanket.

Mina was gently licking up and down, probing and examining with her tongue, her hands and fingers playing and fluttering across Charlotte's skin. Every nerve in her body seemed to be alive. "Mina!" she gasped. "Oh, Mother in Heaven—" Her hands alternately grasped the blanket and Mina's hair.

She was sure she couldn't withstand any more heat—it was going to burn her until she was a giant ball of fire, just like the sun. She squirmed, writhed, and arched under her lover's urgent ministrations, until Mina started to focus on one spot between her legs, licking and sucking until the world itself seemed to turn upside down. The sensations flowed through her body like a flood, rising and falling from her toes to her head and back again. She screamed again and again, gasping for air until she thought she would faint.

A flock of blackbirds flew from the trees as if shot from a cannon.

"I don't want to leave you," Charlotte said as she snuggled into Mina's arms. The sun was beginning to set, and she grew cold. Mina grabbed her cloak and pulled it over them.

"You can't stay here after dark. It's not safe."

"Take me home with you."

Mina's grip tightened, then relaxed. "I . . . I wish I could, but that is not possible. Not yet."

Charlotte looked up at her. "In all this time, you've never told me where you live. Or even your full name."

"That's not important."

"Do you have something to hide? Are the shire's reeves looking for you?" She briefly wondered if she should be wary, then shook her head. "I wouldn't care if they were."

Wilhelmina laughed. "No, I am not some rogue hiding from the sheriff. I told you when we first met that I too like to get away from my daily life. My parents would marry me off to some old landowner if they could, but fortunately my brother is enough of a worry that they forget about me most days."

Charlotte sat up. "You have a brother?"

"I don't want to talk about him, especially now." She kissed the tip of Charlotte's nose. "Let's not spoil a lovely afternoon."

Charlotte stood up and stretched. She smiled when she saw the expression on Mina's face in response to her nakedness. She felt wonderfully wicked and free. As Mina reached for her, she danced away.

"I guess I should get dressed and head back to the manor." She sobered. "How can I face them?"

"You'll not let them get the upper hand." Mina helped Charlotte into her clothes. "I want you to be back here in two days. Promise me."

"Yes, I promise."

"Good, now go home."

"Just one more kiss."

Mina laughed and took Charlotte into her arms. One kiss led to another, and suddenly the sun had moved behind the pines. Charlotte pulled away reluctantly. "I'd better go."

She turned away to hide her tears. Their parting was always bittersweet.

Chapter 5

True to her word, Charlotte returned to the church ruins in two days. She was disappointed that Wilhelmina was not yet there, but she took care of her animals while she waited. Her menagerie had decreased, and she now had only three creatures that could never be set free again. She fed one of them, a hoot owl, some ground-up raw meat. The raptor no longer had to be kept in a cage, and seemed content to reside in an old dead tree. It had been many weeks since he'd tried to fly with his useless wing. It never occurred to her what might happen to him should she ever leave her home. When she'd been a girl she had imagined she would become an old crone who lived in the woods alone and scared the village children. She wasn't a girl anymore, though. Her future was so uncertain.

She stretched out on the rock and let the sun warm her. As the light played across her face, she could feel the tension begin to ease from her body. The woodland sounds soothed her; if she listened closely she could hear the nearby brook. She was tempted to strip off her clothes and plunge into its cold water. She'd had a particularly bad morning; her stepsisters were more demanding than usual and Gudrun had actually slapped her. She touched her cheek, still feeling the sting of Gudrun's fingers.

"Why don't you let me do that?"

Startled, Charlotte opened her eyes to see Wilhelmina leaning against a tree and looking at her. She couldn't help the smile that lit her face. Mina looked wonderfully like Willi that day. Charlotte liked her in the tight leather huntsman breeches and scuffed brown boots, and with her unruly brown curls hidden under a cap she looked like a cocky young man. Sometimes Charlotte envied Mina her freedom.

Charlotte sat up and held out her arms. Mina shook her head slightly and stepped back. The crackling of leaves made Charlotte look behind Wilhelmina, and she was surprised to see an older woman leading a donkey.

"This is Anna," Mina said. "She was my governess many years ago, and now she helps me sometimes with my adventures."

"Hello, child," Anna said. "My Wilhelmina has told me much about you."

With a chiding glance at Mina, Charlotte slid off the rock and curtsied in deference to the woman's age. "Pleased to meet you."

"I can tell Wilhelmina has not told you about me. I am her little secret. She keeps her boy's attire in my cottage and passes herself off as my nephew."

"I have to say I did wonder how she was able to leave the house dressed as she does. I don't think her parents would approve."

"They wouldn't even notice," Mina said.

"I didn't raise you to be so bitter, Wilhelmina," Anna said.

"The only one my parents care about is my brother."

"Well, my dear, it's because he's the—"

"It doesn't matter now," Mina interrupted. "Show Charlotte what you've brought."

Anna opened the small trunk the donkey was carrying and shook out a velvet ball gown the colour of a blush rose. The luxuriance of it took Charlotte's breath away. She touched the material reverently. "This is the most exquisite dress I have ever seen."

"And it will look even more so on you," Anna said, smiling. She also showed Charlotte a stomacher elaborately embroidered with white and silver roses.

"This is all for me?"

"Yes, so you can attend the ball."

"I don't know what to say. Where did it come from?"

Anna looked over at Wilhelmina. "It belonged to Anna's daughter," Mina said quickly.

Charlotte raised an eyebrow. The gown and stomacher were much too rich for a governess' daughter, if she even had a daughter, which Charlotte doubted. There was obviously something the two women weren't telling her, but she decided to play along with their game. "Tell her I am grateful for the use of her gown."

"There is a hunter's cottage at the edge of the glen. Can you be there the night of the ball?"

"It will have to be after Gudrun and the others have left."

"Anna will be waiting for you there."

"What about you?"

"I'll see you at the ball."

"So, I was right."

"Right? About what?"

"I never did think you were just some village girl, for all that you tried to pretend."

Anna laughed. "She never has wanted to be who she is, not in all the twelve years that I've known her."

"Oh, Anna, I could not possibly have given you that impression when I was a mere girl of six."

"You were always wanting to wear your brother's clothes. No lace finery for you." Anna threw up her hands. "And always wanting to play with the village children and skip your lessons."

Charlotte was delighted to hear about Mina's childhood. She'd never told Charlotte anything about it. In fact, she'd been so secretive that Charlotte had seriously begun to think she was indeed a fugitive. Now it seemed she merely wanted to deny her noble birth. She looked at Anna. "Just who are Wilhelmina's parents? Perhaps my father was acquainted with them."

Anna looked incredulous. "She's never told you? Why, she's—"

"Not now, Anna. You may go. Thank you for coming with me."

"Very well." She turned to Charlotte. "I will see you in two days' time."

Charlotte watched in silence as Anna led the donkey away. She was even more curious now about Wilhelmina's true identity. She turned toward Mina, who took her into her arms and kissed her before Charlotte could say a word. As always, their kiss pushed all thoughts of anything else away. She melted into the sensations of Mina's lips on hers, of her hands gripping her arms, of her hips pushing against Charlotte, insistent. She could feel her heart beat faster.

She wrapped her arms around Mina's muscular form, pulling her as close as possible, though that still wasn't close enough. She wanted them to meld into one being. "Closer, I want to be closer—" Charlotte moaned, starting to pull off her own clothes as she guided Mina's hands onto her body.

They fell to the ground together, Mina helping Charlotte out of her clothes. As soon as she was naked, she started pulling at Mina's clothing, wanting. . . no needing. . . to feel Mina's skin warm against her own.

Mina stopped her. "No, Charlotte. Please, let me do this—for you."

At the look of love in Mina's eyes, Charlotte succumbed to her wishes. She lay back, giving herself to the woman she loved. "I just want to be with you, to be close to you," she said, placing Mina's hands on her bare breasts.

Mina began their lovemaking gently again, but Charlotte felt an urgent need, something she couldn't put a name to, but she needed . . .

wanted . . . it desperately. She kissed Mina passionately, putting all of her love and devotion into the meeting of their lips, urging Mina on in any way she could think of. Mina's lips kissed and caressed her, her teeth grazed and nibbled her skin. Charlotte took Mina's hand in her own, pushing it down over her body to the wetness between her legs. She moaned long and loud as Wilhelmina's fingers found their mark.

The passion and heat within Charlotte blazed hot, but now a need was there as well, filling her to near bursting, but leaving her empty still—still needing, wanting, craving. She hoped, with each touch, that she would be fulfilled.

Mina gently bit one of Charlotte's nipples, squeezing the other one—softly at first, then more harshly. Charlotte whimpered but didn't stop her. Instead, she arched into Mina's mouth, pushing her head against her. She didn't want to lose the delicious feelings Mina was giving her, but she needed so much, oh, so much more. Mina was fondling and teasing her sensitive places, driving her mad. She twined her hands in Mina's curls, urging her down, down toward where the wet flowed and gushed.

Mina obeyed, kissing and licking her way down Charlotte's body until her breath was tickling Charlotte there, tickling and teasing and making her even more wet and hot. Mina's lips and tongue performed their magic, making Charlotte squirm and moan. She again felt the tide rise and fall. Just as it seemed she couldn't take any more, she felt Mina's hand between her legs again, then felt Mina's fingers inside of her, not too far but enough make her gasp at the wonder of it.

"Oh Mina! Wilhelmina!" The feeling was intense, it bound them together. Wave after wave of pleasure surged over her, through her. Mina was inside her, making them one, making them whole. "Yes!"

The day of the ball dawned clear and bright. Charlotte woke excited, though she knew she'd have to temper that excitement so the others wouldn't suspect anything. As far as they were concerned, she was saddened over the fact she'd be unable to attend the ball. The bells were already ringing by the time she got to the kitchen.

"You're looking flushed this morning," Elke commented as Charlotte hurried to fix the breakfast trays. "Are you all right?"

"I'm fine. I just know it's going to be a hectic day. They'll keep me running." She dropped a china cup as the bells began ringing again.

"Let me help you with those," Elke said as she took a tray. They headed up the stairs together. "It isn't fair that Lisette and Truda ruined your gown. You have more right to be at that ball than they do."

"There's no sense in wishing for things that can't be." Charlotte felt a bit guilty that she'd not told Elke of Mina's gift, but there was no way to tell her for she knew nothing of Mina's existence. She silently vowed that if she ever was able to leave, she would take Elke with her.

"It's still not right." She pushed open the door to Lisette's room and disappeared inside.

Charlotte continued down the hall to Truda's room, which was still dark, though her stepsister was awake. Charlotte placed the two trays she was carrying on the table before pulling open the drapes. Sunlight spilled into the room, illuminating the disarray. Charlotte wrinkled her nose; the room did not smell pleasant.

"Good morning, Truda. I made your favourites."

Truda mumbled under her breath, but Charlotte had picked up the second tray and was already out the door. She hesitated before her stepmother's door. If anyone would be able to tell that she was happy about something, it would be Gudrun. And indeed, as she entered the room, Gudrun was sitting at her dressing table and looked sharply at Charlotte.

"Your cheeks are flushed today. Are you well?"

Charlotte placed the tray on the table and poured the first cup of tea. "I'm fine, stepmother."

Gudrun's eyes narrowed, but she spoke quite pleasantly. "I heard about what happened with your mother's dress. I am sorry my daughters are so clumsy."

"It's nothing," Charlotte lied.

"Well, it's been a while since you've been out in society. It probably would have been quite awkward for you."

"I expect you're right."

"Are you happy, child?"

Charlotte shifted nervously. What was Gudrun up to? "I really must get back to my chores."

"Please, we haven't talked in a while. Sit."

Charlotte sank down onto a settee and sat on the edge. She felt like an animal in a snare. The silence deepened as Gudrun ate her breakfast. She barely glanced at Charlotte, who felt her nerves begin to crack. "Really, stepmother, I must go."

Gudrun pushed her plate away and took another sip of tea. "Tell me. Where do you go when you disappear in the afternoons?"

Charlotte felt her stomach churn. "How—?"

"Oh, Elke tried to cover for you. It worked for a while. It is unseemly for a girl your age to go out unchaperoned."

"I'm sixteen!"

"Yes, and a good age to marry. I was thinking of Manfred, the coachman's son."

Charlotte stood up, feeling the blood rush to her face and her heart begin to pound. It was not the same sensation she felt when she was with Wilhelmina. It was fear. "You can't be serious!"

Gudrun gave her a hard stare. "Perfectly."

Desperate, Charlotte searched for an argument. "Truda and Lisette are both older than me. It would not do to marry off the younger daughter first."

"My dear, you are the stepchild. It is only natural that I would want to have you out of the house. I can't have a younger, prettier girl around to compete with my daughters. Well, I am hoping one of them will catch the prince's eye tonight." She gave a dismissive wave of her hand. "You may go. We will discuss this further later."

Charlotte took the breakfast tray and scurried to the kitchen as fast as she could. She didn't care what Wilhelmina said—it was time for her to leave this household. She would never see a penny of her rightful inheritance, and her stepmother would marry a baron's daughter off to a coachman's son. So upset was she that she stumbled into the kitchen, almost dropping her tray.

Elke caught her. "Lord, Miss Charlotte, what has happened? You are as white as a sheet."

The other two servants in the room hurried over as well.

"Gudrun would marry me off to Manfred, the coachman's son!"

The three servants looked at each other. "Here, sit down in front of the fire," said the cook. Even though she had replaced the previous cook, she knew it was not right how Gudrun treated Charlotte and had said as much to Elke.

"She also knows about my forays into the forest."

"Oh dear, I've tried to cover for you."

"I know, and I'm grateful. What am I going to do?"

Elke dried Charlotte's tears. "No need to worry today. All three of them will be thinking of tonight's ball and not of you."

Charlotte got to her feet. "Yes, you're right. I'll worry about Gudrun's marriage plans tomorrow." Somehow, she would get Wilhelmina to take her away. She could live as Willi, and no one would ever know. They could even marry. Why would Gudrun care whether Charlotte married a huntsman rather than a coachman's son?

Gudrun, Lisette, and Truda did indeed keep her busy all day. The two sisters could not decide on which gowns to wear. Charlotte was running up and down the stairs, carrying one gown after another to the wash room to be ironed. And there wasn't a single corset or stomacher to be found that could give either of them a decent décolletage. They were as thin and bony as they'd ever been.

At long last, it was time for them to leave for the ball. Seeing them sitting and waiting for the coach reminded Charlotte of the day they had arrived—a day that had changed her life forever. It really was astounding how much all three looked alike, despite the age differences. Their cold, black eyes stared at her as she held their fur-trimmed cloaks, waiting for word that the coach had pulled up. She tried not to fidget.

"I hope you have a good time at the ball," she said finally, hoping to break the uneasy silence.

"I'm sure we will." Truda giggled like a schoolgirl. The sound was not becoming to her. "And if the prince picks one of us to be his bride—"

"Let's not get our hopes up, dear," Gudrun said.

Charlotte was surprised that she would say such a thing. She was sure Gudrun felt either of her daughters would be a great catch.

"Mama!" Truda said.

Before Gudrun could reply, a footman came to tell them the coach was waiting. Charlotte helped each one into her cloak and watched as they climbed into the coach. In a way, she almost felt sorry for Lisette and Truda. If none of the local men had taken a fancy to them despite the extravagant parties thrown by their mother, how could they think the prince would even look at them twice? He was reputed to be very handsome indeed, but also very wild. She wondered if Wilhelmina's brother was a friend of the prince. Thinking of Wilhelmina made Charlotte smile. It would be interesting to see her dressed as a woman tonight. Charlotte wondered if she would even recognise her.

As soon as she was sure the coach was on its way, Charlotte hurried to the kitchen to grab her own cloak, her hidden rucksack with her only good underthings rolled inside, and a lantern. She'd rarely gone into the woods after dark, and she had to admit it made her a little apprehensive. She thought about asking Elke to accompany her.

"Where are you going?"

Charlotte let out a little shriek. "Elke! You scared me."

"It's not like you to go sneaking out this late."

"Can you keep a secret?"

Elke's eyes sparkled. "I love secrets. You know you can trust me."

"There's no time to explain now. Just grab your cloak, something to eat, and a lantern and come with me. Hurry!"

They left the manor house without being seen. Neither thought about explaining their absence to anyone. If the other servants acted according to human nature, they too would take advantage of all three mistresses being gone from the house at the same time.

As they hurried through the dark woods, their lanterns casting a pale light, Charlotte tried not to think of the wild creatures like bears that were always on Elke's mind. "Elke, you have to give me your word that you'll not breathe a word of this to anyone."

"I promise."

"Swear on my dear dead mother's memory."

"I swear, really I do."

"You know when I go into the forest? Well, I have a secret place there, and I met someone. Someone who is helping me so I can attend the ball tonight."

"I can't believe you've not told me of him. After all our years together."

Charlotte felt bad when she heard the hurt in Elke's voice. "It was better so. That way you wouldn't have to lie for me more than you already do."

"Well, tell me. What's his name?"

"Willi," Charlotte said without hesitation. It wasn't a lie, not really. Wilhelmina would indeed be Willi if she helped Charlotte escape her life of misery.

"How can he help you go to the ball? Is he a nobleman?"

"No, a huntsman. You ask too many questions, Elke."

"Can you at least tell me where we're going?"

"To the hunter's cottage at the edge of the woods. I am meeting a woman there. Now, hurry."

Charlotte was relieved to see a light in the window of the cottage. She'd worried that Anna would not come, that it had all been a dream. Although she knew Mina would not be there, her heart took a leap when she saw a well-dressed male figure standing beside the old governess. He turned, and she saw he wore the livery of a coachman. He bowed low and then smiled appreciatively when he saw

Elke. Charlotte felt her heart gladden when she saw the light in Elke's eyes, who lowered her lashes and blushed like a schoolgirl. Anna shooed the man outside.

"Miss Charlotte, there's not much time," Anna said as she began pulling off Charlotte's drab clothing.

"This is so beautiful!" Elke exclaimed as she picked up the pale pink velvet gown from the crude wooden bed.

Anna led Charlotte over to a metal tub filled with hot water. It was only then that Charlotte noticed the fire roaring in the fireplace. Charlotte sighed as she lowered herself into the fragrant water. It had been months since she'd had a real bath. Most days she had to make do with a quick splash of cold water or else an icy plunge into the brook near the ruins. Elke bustled about, falling easily into her old role of lady's maid. She laid out the new clothes, clucking approvingly as she unwrapped one piece of finery after another.

When Charlotte finished her bath, they wrapped her in clean, fluffy towels and rubbed her down in front of the fire. Next came the layers of underclothing, starting with stockings tied with pink satin ribbons. Then came her chemise, corset, pannier, two petticoats, and stomacher. The velvet gown fit her slender frame perfectly.

"Oh, Mistress Charlotte, you are a vision," Elke said as she worked Charlotte's hair into an elaborate coif. "It makes me cry to see you thus for it is as it should be. You do not belong in a kitchen working like a common scullery maid."

"I wish I could see myself. Do I really look pretty?"

"You look like a princess. Your mother and father would be so proud."

"These are a gift from Willi," Anna said as she brought over a pair of kid slippers covered with silver silk and decorated with diamond buckles.

Charlotte gasped. They were the most exquisite shoes she had ever seen. They fit her feet as if they'd been custom made for her.

"Only one more thing," Anna said as she handed Charlotte an elaborate feathered mask. "You have to leave at midnight to return here. The coachman needs to be back at the castle before the end of the ball so he can take his master and mistress home."

"I promise," Charlotte said as a footman handed her into the coach. She looked out the window and waved to the two women standing side by side, illuminated by the light in the doorway.

Chapter 6

When the coach arrived at the castle, Charlotte hesitated getting out, wondering if she should really go inside. It had been so long since she'd attended such an event. She hadn't even been allowed to go to her stepsisters' cotillions. And then suddenly Wilhelmina was there, dressed in a simple gown of white satin. In her brown curls rested a diamond tiara.

"You look breathtaking," she said as she helped Charlotte down the steps. If the footmen thought it odd, they showed no sign of it.

Charlotte smiled even as she felt herself blushing. It pleased her that Mina thought her beautiful. "Thank you. You look—"

"Don't say anything," Mina said, her eyes glittering dangerously. "I'm going to get out of this accursed gown as soon as I can. Willi is making an appearance tonight so he can dance with you."

Charlotte hid a smile. If the truth were told, she did prefer Wilhelmina in men's attire. As they entered the majestic foyer,

Charlotte could not help but stop in open-mouthed awe. The Italian marble, Grecian mosaics, and French crystal chandeliers were unlike anything she'd ever seen before. There were so many candles burning it was like daylight. Wilhelmina took her hand and led her past watchful footmen. Their shoes clicked softly across marbled floors and up the grand staircase to the enormous ballroom.

"Put on your mask," Wilhelmina whispered. "We don't want your stepmother and stepsisters to recognise you."

Charlotte complied, still unable to speak, so overwhelmed was she by the sights and sounds that greeted her. A footman started to announce her arrival, but Wilhelmina silenced him with a gesture. Again, if he was surprised, he did not show it.

"Let me introduce you to my parents and my brother."

She led Charlotte over to where the king and queen sat overlooking the festivities. Next to them sat a bored-looking young man. Charlotte felt about ready to faint. Wilhelmina's parents were the king and queen? Her brother was Prince Sigmund? It would explain to some extent the freedom she enjoyed. It also explained the restrictions and duties Wilhelmina found so vexing.

"Charlotte, daughter of the late Baron Heinrich von Hessen."

Charlotte curtsied deep. She wasn't sure it was proper to keep her mask on when introduced to the king and queen, but it was too late to remove it now.

"Their majesties, the king and queen, and Prince Sigmund, my brother."

"Your Highness," Charlotte said.

The prince stood and bowed, then took her hand and kissed it. She thought he must be quite tired if he had to kiss the hand of every maiden here. She examined him through her mask. He was indeed very handsome, just as people said, but there was a melancholy in his brown eyes that was disturbing. She would venture a guess that marriage was not something he wished to do.

"We hope that you enjoy the ball," said the queen. She turned to her son. "I think it's time for you to mingle with your guests. Surely there are a couple of young ladies who have caught your eye? What about the Lady Charlotte here?"

Charlotte flushed furiously.

"Would you care to dance?"

She curtsied low again. "I would be honoured."

As the prince led her onto the ballroom floor, there was a murmuring throughout the crowd. "Don't pay attention to them," Sigmund said kindly. "You are the first woman I have asked to dance tonight, and I must say my sister has wonderful taste in women."

"You are most kind," she replied, but she thought his choice of words odd.

"Willi will be joining us later this evening."

She looked at him in surprise, and he chuckled. "I know all about her exploits. I envy her the freedom to do so. As the princess, my parents do not expect much of her. At least, not yet." He sighed. "They want to marry me off first."

"Forgive me for being presumptuous, but it seems to me that you are not happy about it."

"You are perceptive. No, I have no wish to marry, but as the heir apparent I have no choice. Oh, what I would give to have been a younger brother."

"I am sure you have broken many a young girl's heart."

Again he sighed. "Not a young girl's—"

At that moment it came time to change partners. Prince Sigmund led away an awestruck girl who couldn't have been older than thirteen while Charlotte ended up with a vapid young man with sweaty palms. As she was twirled through the crowd, she looked for Wilhelmina. At one point she caught Lisette glaring at her, and she was glad for the masquerade mask. She then saw Gudrun and Truda huddled together, whispering behind their ivory fans. She felt their eyes boring into her back as she danced past, and it sent shivers up her spine. She changed partners yet again, all the while keeping an eye out for Wilhelmina. Where had she gone?

Then suddenly she was in Willi's arms. Despite the elaborate boar's mask, Charlotte knew immediately that it was her Wilhelmina. In tight, fawn-coloured breeches and a gold brocade frock coat, she cut quite the handsome figure.

"Did I tell you tonight how ravishing you look? I would like to take you upstairs to my boudoir and have my way with you."

Charlotte blushed for what seemed like the hundredth time that night. "Why didn't you tell me who you really are?"

"Would you have been as free with me if you'd known the truth?"

"How could I? You're a princess and I'm nothing but a common servant."

"Neither common nor a servant, my love."

Mina led her toward the balcony, where they slipped through the curtains unnoticed. The stars were bright in the clear, dark sky. Mina took off Charlotte's mask and then her own. Her kiss was soft. Charlotte felt the familiar weakness in her knees.

"I like this gown," Wilhelmina murmured as she kissed the tender skin of Charlotte's breast above the low-cut neckline.

Charlotte moaned and tilted her head back. Mina moved up to kiss the hollow of her throat and then upward again to her neck. She ran her hands down Charlotte's arms and across her back, pulling her close. Charlotte had felt pretty as soon as she put on the gown; now, with Mina's hands on her body, caressing her through the lush velvet of her dress, she felt truly beautiful.

The fine fabric of Mina's clothes felt slick and soft to Charlotte's fingers, long accustomed to only the coarse wool and rough leather of Mina's hunter disguise. She played with the buttons on her satin waistcoat, longing to see Wilhelmina naked, to make her experience the same sensations she made Charlotte feel. She wanted to touch Mina's bare skin, wanted their bodies pressing together. She pulled Mina close, kissing her lips, biting her neck. Mina moaned.

"Charlotte," she breathed. "Stop."

"I want you."

"No, no, my love. Someone could come out here any minute."

"But Wilhelmina, I want you so." She pulled Mina against her, boldly caressing the warm spot between Mina's legs.

"Oh, God, I want you too, but now is not the time."

Charlotte kissed her again. "Promise me. Next time—"

"Soon, my love. Soon."

Wilhelmina pushed her away. They were both breathing hard. Their eyes locked. Charlotte took a step toward her, but then they heard the sounds of footsteps and immediately put on their masks. Another young couple came into view, laughing and flirting as they too melted into the shadows.

"Come," Wilhelmina said as she took Charlotte's hand and brought her back into the ballroom. Almost immediately, the prince came over and led Charlotte onto the dance floor. She was aware of everyone looking at her, and as they passed her stepmother and step-sisters, she was again glad for the feathered mask. The look in their eyes was chilling. If they knew who she really was . . .

The prince danced her around the ballroom. She felt flushed from her interlude with his sister on the balcony and hoped he would think her colour came from dancing. Just as she was about to ask that they stop and get something to drink, he spoke first.

"Will you consent to marry me?"

Charlotte looked at him, disbelieving what he'd just asked. "What did you say?"

"I want you to marry me."

"Marry you? Your Highness, I'm flattered, but I . . . I cannot."

"You would turn down the opportunity to become queen one day?"

"But you don't even know me."

"I don't know any of the women here. My parents do not expect me to marry for love. They only expect me to pick someone here tonight, anyone. And I choose you."

Charlotte was beginning to feel uncomfortable. This was the prince, the heir to the throne. What was she thinking? How could she refuse him? In desperation she looked for Wilhelmina. She glanced up at the king and queen. They were smiling as they watched her with their only son. Could he have already told them his intentions?

"If it makes you feel any better, it would be a marriage in name only. I know you and my sister are lovers."

Charlotte could not help but gasp. "How—?"

"We tell each other everything. And I too have a lover."

"Then why don't you marry her?"

Sigmund laughed. "My lover is a he."

"Oh."

"Wilhelmina and I have it all figured out. I will marry you and she will marry Josef."

"She said nothing to me."

He twirled her around the floor. "Oh dear. She'll not forgive me for revealing our secret . But it will work out, you'll see." He led her to the side and bowed. "I'd best be nice to some of these other ladies. I don't want my parents to think I have succumbed too easily to their wishes."

"What a beautiful ball gown."

Charlotte recognised Gudrun's voice immediately. It sent chills up her spine. She turned and faced her stepmother. "Thank you," she said, hoping the feathered mask would help disguise her voice.

"The prince seems to be quite taken with you—his first dance of the evening and now this one."

Charlotte bowed her head.

"You seem so familiar to me. Have we met?"

Before Charlotte could think of an answer, she heard the clock begin to strike. She glanced up at the tower and saw it was indeed midnight. She had to go. "Excuse me," she mumbled and hurried off. She looked back over her shoulder and saw Gudrun following her. Panicked, she almost ran through the ballroom, weaving in and out among the dancers, not caring how rude she seemed. The clock counted down. A determined Gudrun still followed. Charlotte looked for Wilhelmina. She saw her dancing with a very pretty young woman and felt a flash of jealousy.

Down the steps she flew, to the courtyard. She stumbled and lost a shoe. It tumbled away from her. She started to chase after it, but Gudrun was close on her heels with a grim, intent look on her face. Charlotte had no time. She ran to the coach and practically leapt inside. "Hurry!" she said to the coachman. He flicked the horses with his whip and off they went. She looked out the window to see Gudrun standing there, watching. In her hands she held Charlotte's lost shoe, but then a footman came and took it from her.

It seemed to take forever until they arrived at the huntsman's cottage. Elke and Anna were waiting for her.

"Elke," she said, "we must make haste back to the manor. I have to be there before Gudrun and the others get home. I think she might have recognised me. She could be on her way home even now."

The two women helped her out of the velvet gown and back into her servant's garb. Charlotte apologized profusely for losing the shoe, but Anna assured her not to worry. She scooped up Charlotte's scattered belongings, stuffing them into the rucksack.

Elke and Charlotte ran hand in hand through the dark woods, their lanterns flickering wildly. She hurriedly emptied her rucksack so there would be no chance of Gudrun discovering it ever having been packed. To her horror she found one of the slippers. Her cold little room held so few hiding places. Fighting panic, Charlotte had still not thought of a place where she could slip it out of sight when she heard the horses and coach clattering into the courtyard. Huddled in bed, she kept her eyes closed tight when she heard her door open and felt the light of a candle on her face. Her heart pounding, she clutched the shoe to her breast while she tried to keep her breathing slow and even. Charlotte was sure it was Gudrun who stood there. It was a long while until she heard the rustling of Gudrun's taffeta skirt as she moved away.

Chapter 7

It was with some trepidation that Charlotte brought breakfast to the dining room the next morning. She was surprised that her stepmother and stepsisters were awake already and that they'd decided against breakfast in their rooms.

"How was the ball?" she asked as she placed plates of food in front of them.

"It was divine," Lisette said with a dreamy look in her eyes. "The prince danced with me. He was so handsome."

Truda pouted. "He didn't dance with me."

"He couldn't very well dance with everyone," Gudrun said. "I do think he liked Lisette though. He smiled at her at the end of their dance."

"He could have danced with me if he hadn't danced twice with that one in the rose-coloured dress and the elaborate feathered mask," Truda said.

"He probably felt sorry for her. She wasn't as pretty as Lisette."

"If she wore a mask, how can you tell?" Charlotte asked.

"A mother knows these things." Gudrun narrowed her eyes and looked at Charlotte. "And what did you do last night after we left, my dear?"

"I finished up my chores and went to bed."

"The girl in the pink gown reminded me a lot of you."

Charlotte almost dropped the milk pitcher. "Really?"

"Mama, don't be silly," Lisette and Truda both protested at once.

Gudrun ignored them. "She had your build, your hair colour. But of course, it is impossible that it was you."

"Of course."

For the rest of breakfast, Charlotte couldn't help but feel that Gudrun watched her like a hawk. Lisette and Truda seemed oblivious to the tension as they chattered on about who they'd seen and who had worn what. At long last, the three of them got up from the table. Charlotte finished her chores quickly and headed into the woods to her sanctuary. She was sure Wilhelmina would come today, and she had a lot to say to her. She couldn't believe her lover had neglected to tell her about her and Sigmund's scheme. And the most important secret of all—that she was the princess.

The church ruins were quiet. Even the animals she was caring for made no noises. She could hear only the faint sound of water. In the coolness of this green space, she could feel her nerves begin to relax. She sat on her rock and from her rucksack took out a flask of wine and an oilcloth filled with cheese and bread. The slipper, she suddenly recalled. She had meant to give it to Mina before Gudrun found it. Tomorrow, then.

Remembering the exhilaration of the ball, she was saddened that her parents weren't alive to share the experience with her. Her mother had so loved to dance, and it was at a ball very similar to this one that she had met Heinrich when she was Charlotte's age. They were married soon after. It was a story her daughter had delighted in hearing over and over. Charlotte smiled. In fact, Heinrich had been the same age as Wilhelmina—nineteen. Fate seemed to be repeating itself.

She munched on thick slices of black bread and tangy cheese. What was she going to do about Sigmund's proposal? She couldn't very well go to the palace as she was and expect the king and queen to agree to his choice of bride. The fact that she'd run away probably put an end to that arrangement anyway. And would they even have agreed to a match with a mere baron's daughter?

She turned her thoughts toward what to do about her life. She was still a baron's daughter, and Elke was right—she shouldn't be a servant in her own home. Perhaps she could appeal to the king? She could prove who she was through church records if they wouldn't take her or Elke's word. She was almost seventeen, the same age as when her mother had married. She didn't want to marry, but there weren't many options for a girl like her. She had no illusions anymore that she and Wilhelmina could live a life together, especially if Wilhelmina was a princess. Two women living as husband and wife? Could Mina become Willi permanently? It didn't seem possible. A princess could not just disappear.

"You've created quite an uproar at the castle."

Charlotte dropped her bread. "You startled me!"

Wilhelmina sat beside her on the rock and took her into her arms. "Sorry, my love." She gave her a gentle kiss. "Mmmm, you taste like sweet wine."

Charlotte held up the bottle. "It's the final batch from last year's harvest."

Wilhelmina took a long swig. "It's a lot tastier than the stuff my parents like to drink."

"What do you mean I've created an uproar at the castle?"

"Everyone's talking about the mysterious lady in pink that Prince Sigmund was so smitten with. My parents are determined to find you."

"But you introduced me to them. And Sigmund knows my name as well, and that I am your lover. We need to talk about that, by the way."

Wilhelmina stretched out on the rock and put her hands behind her head. With a grin she said, "Do you think my parents could remember the name of every woman introduced to them? And Sigmund likes to play with them, give them a hard time. He's pretending not to know your name either. It's all a game. If he appears too eager to marry you, they'll become suspicious. He's balked at it for so long."

Charlotte sighed with exasperation. "I would think they would just be glad he'd picked someone. Which brings me to another issue. Why didn't you discuss with me first the idea of marrying him?"

"I know what Sigmund told you, that he and I had plotted the whole thing. But in reality, he didn't say anything to me. I think he came up with the idea when he danced with you. Perhaps he and Josef came up with the plan?" She sat up and looked at Charlotte, her brown eyes earnest. "You have to admit it's a good plan. Then none of us would have to worry about being forced to marry someone horrible. I can see Gudrun selling you off to some doddering old fool just so she can buy her next bauble."

Charlotte shivered at the thought. "That would be just like Gudrun." She paused, then made up her mind. "Tell Sigmund I'll do it. I'll marry him."

Mina took Charlotte into her arms and kissed her neck. Charlotte shivered with delight this time. "Let him have his fun. With an entourage of footmen, he's visiting all the homes in the area, noble and peasant, and asking any unmarried females to try on your shoe. He'll marry the one it fits."

Charlotte pulled herself from Mina's grasp. "What if it fits someone else?"

"Simple. He'll ask her to produce the second shoe. Anna told me you have it."

"But—"

"Come, my love, no more talk. Let me show you how much I desire you."

Mina took her into her arms again and kissed her sensitive neck.

Charlotte felt the familiar stirrings in her loins, but this time she protested. "You've shown me many times. I want to be the one to give *you* pleasure."

Mina shook her head. "Shush, my love. I have been in torment since last night. Let me have you today. We haven't much time." She ran her hands over Charlotte's body, enjoying the swell of her breasts and hips, running her palms over the hardening nipples, tasting the sweet salt of sweat on her neck, nibbling down to her décolletage.

"Mina, oh Mina," Charlotte moaned, "but I want you—"

"And have me you shall. On the night of our weddings." She undid the ties on Charlotte's blouse and tugged on the chemise underneath. "Women wear too many clothes," she complained as she pulled the chemise up, exposing Charlotte's skin to the gentle summer breezes. She worshipped Charlotte's breasts, laving them with her tongue, teasing the nipples with her teeth.

Each time they were together, Mina became a little more bold, taking Charlotte to new heights. And each time they were together, it seemed she came to know Charlotte's body just a bit more—how she would react to each touch, tease, and lick. As if she knew exactly what each stroke did for Charlotte, and what she liked.

Charlotte moaned and squirmed under Mina's gentle ministrations, loving the tenderness, but needing and wanting more. She was no longer some naïve young girl who didn't know what she liked. She was a woman now, a woman who wanted hardness with tenderness.

Mina's hands were like fire on her skin, running over her stomach, up her inner thighs, over her hips . . . Charlotte pulled Mina's shirt from her breeches, needing to feel her skin. She ran her fingernails over the smoothness of her back. Mina shivered under her touch.

Charlotte closed her eyes and surrendered to the feelings. Letting Mina surround her, touch her anywhere and everywhere. And it did indeed feel as if Mina was everywhere all at once—her tongue and teeth on her breasts, then her inner thighs, working up to her heat. Mina's shoulders were spreading Charlotte's legs apart, her hands were clasping Charlotte's wrists, while her tongue was licking Charlotte's warm, wet centre. Her chin pushed against Charlotte, creating some of the pressure Charlotte so desperately wanted.

Charlotte struggled against Wilhelmina's hands. "Please, I need to feel you inside—" she groaned.

Mina laughed lightly and let go of Charlotte's wrists. She played with her, teasing with her fingers and tongue, occasionally thrusting her tongue just deep enough to send fiery sparks through Charlotte, making her gasp and moan.

And then Mina's fingers were fluttering inside her while her tongue worked its magic. Charlotte pushed against her, wanting more, but not knowing what. She opened her eyes and saw the blue sky. She felt the boulder hard against her back, even as she felt Mina's tongue flicking and her fingers gently thrusting. She called out Wilhelmina's name again and again as her world exploded into lights and sounds and pleasure.

All in a flurry, Truda and Lisette came into the formal dining room where Gudrun was examining the silver Charlotte had finished polishing. These last few days, Gudrun had been especially demanding. And Charlotte did not like the way her stepmother would watch her, with malice and hatred in her eyes.

"Mama! The prince is on his way here now!" Truda said.

Calmly, Gudrun began putting the silver into its velvet-lined case. "There is no need to get all aflutter. We've known that he'd be coming eventually."

"Oh Mama, it would be so wonderful if that shoe fit one of us."

"I believe it might fit you just fine," Gudrun told Lisette. She glanced from Lisette's foot to Charlotte's.

"Why not me?" Truda wailed.

"There's always that chance," Gudrun soothed. She turned to her stepdaughter, her eyes hard. "Charlotte, I want you to go into the orchard. We need apples for the streusel."

"But stepmother, the prince is trying the shoe on all women."

"Certainly not you. Why even you have said it is not possible you could have been at the ball."

"Still—"

"Go now! I don't want to see you until the prince has gone." She picked up a knife and ran her finger along its sharp edge. "Do I make myself clear?"

The look in her stepmother's eyes made Charlotte's blood run cold. And if she'd had any doubts that Gudrun knew it was Charlotte who'd been at the ball, she had none now. She hurried away as she was bid, but she did not go to the orchard as ordered. Instead, she and Elke made as if to go for the other servants' benefit, and then hid in the grand receiving room. They did not have to wait long. The heavy oak doors opened. Charlotte peeped out from her hiding place behind the heavy brocade curtains. Gudrun walked in, followed by her two daughters, Prince Sigmund, and several liveried footmen. She couldn't help but gasp when she saw Wilhelmina as Willi come in last. As Gudrun glanced about the room, Charlotte shrank back into the deep folds of brocade, hoping she wouldn't sneeze.

"You are kind to invite us into your home, Baroness," Sigmund said.

"My pleasure, Your Highness."

Charlotte peeked out again. She glimpsed Elke peeking out from behind her own curtains. The two sisters sat side by side upon the ornate couch, while their mother hovered nearby. As always in this room, Charlotte couldn't help but remember that fateful day two years ago when her father brought them home for the first time. The prince stood to one side with Willi while a footman brought over the beautiful silver shoe Charlotte had lost the night of the ball. He knelt in front of Truda. Charlotte had to stifle a laugh. The whole ritual seemed so absurd, but one glimpse of Willi and Sigmund's faces and she knew they were having a grand time with the joke.

Truda giggled and held out her oversized foot. Did Charlotte see the footman wrinkle his nose? He placed the shoe on Truda's foot.

She squealed in pain as she forced her heel down into it and then stood triumphantly. The footman shook his head.

"Truda, my dear, the shoe is much too small for you. Let Lisette try now."

Truda looked at her mother, and then with a huff, sat and pulled the shoe off. Sigmund and Willi looked at each other, grinning. Though she and Truda were about the same height, Lisette's feet were smaller than her sister's. She placed her foot in the shoe. It seemed to slide on easily. Charlotte was in shock. Gudrun had been right. With a crow of delight, Lisette stood to show that the shoe fit her almost perfectly. She lifted her skirts just enough.

"It seems a little too large," the footman said to the prince.

"Yes, the shoemaker did not do his normal perfect work this time," Lisette said. "It quite gave me blisters the night of the ball."

Frowning, the prince came over and looked at the silver slipper. Willi stepped up quickly. "You do have the second shoe?"

"Of course," Lisette said. "I just don't know where it is at this moment." She tittered and batted her eyelashes at the prince. "I didn't expect to find its match."

"You are the baron's second wife, is that correct?" Willi asked.

Gudrun nodded.

"And these are your two daughters from a previous marriage?"

She nodded again.

"I seem to recall," said Willi, "that the late baron also had a daughter from his first marriage. Is that girl here?"

"She's not at the house now, but I can assure you that she was not at the ball that night. She has not been the same since her father died. Her mind . . . Well, she prefers to behave as one of the servants." Gudrun laughed. It was a harsh sound. "She owns no clothes in which to attend such a ball."

"Still, the prince wants every girl to try on the shoe. It is too big for Lisette. Perhaps it is perfect for Charlotte?"

Gudrun narrowed her eyes. "How do you know her name?"

Willi smiled. "I know everything."

"I want this Charlotte brought to me now," Sigmund said.

Charlotte came from behind the curtain. "I am here, Prince Sigmund." She curtsied low, well aware of her drab grey dress and dishevelled hair. She could see the disbelief in the prince's eyes. At least Lisette and Truda were dressed like a baron's daughters. Charlotte sat upon the settee. The footman took the shoe from Lisette and slipped it onto Charlotte's foot. It was indeed a perfect fit.

"That proves nothing!" Gudrun said, her fury barely contained. "This girl could not have been at the ball."

"But she was," Elke said as she came out of her hiding place.

Truda let out a little shriek of fright. Gudrun took a step forward, clenching her gown furiously. It was obvious she was on the verge of losing her temper, but did not dare do so in front of the prince. Sigmund himself looked a little confused. Charlotte pulled the companion shoe out of her apron pocket.

"Would this help?"

Lisette stood. "She stole that from me!"

"All right," Willi said. "I think it's time to end the game. Prince Sigmund has known all along to whom the shoe belonged— Charlotte, daughter of the late Baron Heinrich von Hessen." She took the time to look at each woman. "We're sorry if we have offended anyone."

"But how—?"

"With the help of some friends, who gave her a beautiful pink velvet gown and the means to travel to the castle."

The prince turned to Gudrun. "I would like to point out to you, madam, that the way you have treated your own stepdaughter is deplorable. As the widow of the late baron, you are his rightful heir, but as the prince I can take the title and all the lands from you and give them to Charlotte, his natural daughter."

For a brief moment, Charlotte felt pleasure when she saw the blood drain from her stepmother's face. It would serve her right to be thrown out onto the streets, along with her horrible daughters. Then Charlotte was ashamed at her thoughts. Her beloved parents had not raised her to be mean-spirited, wishing ill upon other people even if they harboured ill will toward her. Her father, in his own way, must have loved Gudrun to marry her, and she would not take his legacy away from her.

"Please," she said, placing her hand on Sigmund's arm, "let them be. I have no wish to take away their home."

He leaned down and kissed her cheek. "That is because your new home will be with me, as my princess and then my queen."

There was a great joyousness throughout the land with the marriage of Prince Sigmund and Charlotte von Hessen. The celebration had begun weeks before the wedding and would continue for days afterward. And to show that she bore them no ill will, Charlotte had invited her stepmother and stepsisters to the wedding banquet, though they had had to scrabble for a seat at the back of the great hall with the rest of the common folk for they were not invited to sit with the royal family or the other nobility. Charlotte had looked breathtakingly lovely in her wedding gown, and radiantly happy. There was great expectation within the castle that the wedding night would produce an heir to the throne.

Charlotte came hesitantly into the candle-lit room. She had dressed with great care, wearing a diaphanous nightdress embroidered with white roses. Her golden-red tresses tumbled across her shoulders and down her back. She felt shy and very young, though she was now fully seventeen. She stopped at the foot of the canopied bed.

The sheer curtains fluttered as Wilhelmina rose from the feather pillows and took Charlotte's hands in hers. "You look more lovely tonight than I have ever seen."

Charlotte looked into Wilhelmina's eyes and saw the love reflected there. "I am beautiful for you."

Mina pulled Charlotte down onto the bed and into her arms. The smoothness of her silk night clothes felt cool against Charlotte's warm skin. They slowly undressed each other, knowing that now they were safely alone in royal bedchambers where none would dare intrude upon them.

The flickering candles gave a low, shadowy light to the room. It felt strange to Charlotte to be exposed to Mina without gentle breezes and the warming rays of the sun upon her body. But it was still nice. Better than nice, even. She sank into the big feather bed, loving how soft and plush it felt, so unlike the pine needle bed they had in her forest sanctuary.

Mina straddled Charlotte, then lowered herself carefully. Charlotte gasped out loud at the feeling of Mina lying atop her, their bare skin meeting wholly, entirely, utterly, for the first time ever. Wilhelmina was kissing her neck, running her hands over Charlotte's form. Charlotte mirrored her every move, kissing Mina's neck and letting her hands explore Mina's soft yet muscular body. As their legs entwined, each could feel the wetness of the other. Charlotte trailed her fingers across Mina's buttocks, over her hip, under her thigh, and then into the tangle of curls between her legs. It felt wondrous indeed. She sighed deeply at the touch, even as Mina sighed.

"I want you to make me yours completely, here, now, tonight," Charlotte whispered into Mina's ear, "as I will make you mine."

Mina pushed up onto her elbows so she could look into Charlotte's eyes. Her expression told Charlotte she understood. "I'm afraid it might hurt just a bit." Charlotte felt a flash of fear, then nodded. Wilhelmina moved down Charlotte's body slowly, leaving kisses like a trail of rose petals. Charlotte squirmed beneath her, breathing heavily as she arched her body toward Mina's mouth, wanting the feel of her fingers deep inside her, deeper than they'd ever been before.

Suddenly Mina stopped. Charlotte whimpered. Mina looked at her. "I don't want to hurt you," she said.

"I am yours. Now and forever. Make me thus."

Mina lowered her mouth to begin teasing Charlotte, knowing now just how Charlotte liked it—what would bring her to heights of pleasure.

Charlotte gasped as she felt the familiar pressure of one of Mina's fingers, then another. She writhed in exquisite ecstasy, crying out as Mina's fingers thrust into her. The red-hot haze of her desire made her arch and thrash about with increasing urgency. Grabbing Mina's hair to draw her ever closer, she pushed herself into Mina's mouth. She was getting closer and closer, feeling the pleasure overwhelming her and succumbing to its beautiful effects. "Please, more, now—Mina . . . I love you . . . I need you!"

Charlotte spread her legs wider to show her beloved she meant those pleas. She heard Mina groan with a feverish lust. She felt pressure inside her as she was filled with another finger, and deeper than ever before. The momentary flash of pain dissolved as waves of pleasure washed over her, sending her spiralling up into the heavens. But Mina kept on, her fingers moving in and out, her tongue taking her yet again into the throes of passion and pleasure, till she cried out . . . again . . . and again . . .

Finally, Charlotte pulled her trembling body toward the head of the bed, feebly pushing Wilhelmina away at the same time. With her body sated and her breathing returning to normal, she remembered Mina's vow. "No," she said, pushing away Mina's insistent hands, "you promised that tonight I might pleasure you."

She sat up and pushed Mina onto her back, then lay on top of her, urging Wilhelmina's legs apart so that she lay between them, much as Mina had done to her. She was nervous, not sure she knew what to do, but she started by slowly kissing and licking her way over Mina's lean, muscular frame. She smiled as Mina sighed deeply and leaned back into the pillows. She took a puckered nipple into her mouth, sucking gently at first, then harder. She moved her way slowly down Mina's body, letting her long hair sweep over Mina's skin and liking the way Mina trembled in response. She kissed and nibbled her way down, tasting and smelling the sweetness of Mina.

Charlotte moved lower still, until her shoulders pushed Mina's legs wider apart. She breathed in the scent of her, tasting a woman for the first time. Mina moaned long and deep as she guided

Charlotte's head. Charlotte licked and sucked, searching for that special spot, the one that would make Mina cry out as Charlotte had cried out. Mina's in-drawn breath made Charlotte lick more feverishly.

"Yes, Charlotte! Yes!"

Still using her tongue, Charlotte brought her fingers to Mina's wet centre. She teased and explored, then tentatively thrust two fingers inside.

"Charlotte!"

Charlotte could feel Mina's trembling increase. The muscles of her legs tightened until they were like rocks. Around Charlotte's fingers, Mina squeezed and clutched. And then Wilhelmina stiffened and let out a long, drawn-out sigh. Charlotte withdrew her fingers. She felt and tasted the gush of liquid heat. She moaned and wanted more, understanding for the first time why Mina sometimes did not want to stop tasting her either.

Now it was Wilhelmina's turn to push Charlotte gently away, as she pulled the covers over herself. She took Charlotte into her arms, letting Charlotte rest her head against her breast. Charlotte could hear the beating of Mina's heart, strong and steady. The candle nearest the bed sputtered out, leaving them in almost total darkness. The warmth of their bodies curled around them. Charlotte snuggled deeper into Wilhelmina's arms, knowing true contentment at last.

"*Ich liebe Dich*," Wilhelmina said. "Now and forever."

Charlotte looked up at her. "And I love you too."

And so it was that the good *König* Sigmund and *Königen* Charlotte, though childless, lived happily ever after, their reign a long and prosperous one. And throughout it all, the *Prinzessin* Wilhelmina and her *Prinz* Josef stayed loyally by their sides.

A Fish Out of Water

by Karin Kallmaker

"Please."

Her voice plays on my body like the tide. I rise and fall to the cadence of her words while past and present eddy in my mind, muddied by shifting sands of need and desire. She asks me if I want her. The gooseflesh along my arms says yes. The wet I can feel surging between my legs says yes. I try to say yes with the intensity of my eyes, the eagerness of my hands, the curve of my lips.

"Please say yes."

She doesn't understand that I can't give her the one thing she needs to release us both from the cage our passion has created.

I cannot say yes. Or no. I cannot speak.

Part 1

"Fly, baby, fly!" Ariel gave the cork one last shove with her thumb and whooped at the resounding pop that heralded the gush of bubbling Champagne.

"Happy New Year!" Shouts bounced off curving grotto walls that pulsated an answer in splashes of crimson and gold.

"Only thing humans know how to make that's worth stealing," Caliba enthused as she held her diamond glass under the pouring stream.

Ariel, Seventy-Seventh Daughter to Queen Vellia, drew herself up to her full height, which brought the top of her head level with Caliba's shoulder. "*Liberate*, please. Mer do not steal, you know that."

"As you wish." Caliba sipped from the glass, then sighed happily. "I've always liked the human custom of New Year's Eve. Excellent reason for a party."

A caterwaul of ill humor turned the crimson lights to burnt red.

Ariel clutched the precious Champagne bottle and turned in time to see Laveena's long sapphire-tipped nails leave four perfect scratches down the side of Zee's cheek. Blood welled in their wake.

"Oh, to the abyss with this," Ariel thought. She strolled across the room while shaking the bottle, and looked down in distaste at Laveena and Zee writhing as they fought in a tangle of legs and slapping hands. Clumps of costume and hair began to litter the floor.

Thumb over the top of the bottle, she upended the bubbling froth on both of them.

Laveena screeched with outrage. Ariel glanced worriedly at the chandelier, but Caliba appeared next to Ariel. "I'll make sure it doesn't shatter."

Zee rolled out of Laveena's reach. "I did not start that!" She angrily shook her wet clothes. Ariel was genuinely sorry that the delicate garment of rose petals was ruined, but more damage had been wrought by Laveena's nails than the Champagne.

"*You bitch!*" Laveena didn't bother to quash her mer voice. The chandelier rattled dangerously.

"My, my." Caliba examined her manicure. "You obviously missed vocabulary classes—"

Ariel quieted Caliba with a gesture. "It's New Year's Eve. No fighting. The party hasn't even really started yet."

"She stole Kareel again, took her home from a flesh party I had escorted her to!" Laveena gave Zee a poisonous look.

"Yeah," Zee snapped back. "And we had a *fabulous* time."

Laveena scrambled to her feet. "I'm going to tear your face off!"

"Quiet!" Ariel let her lights sparkle faintly. "I'll let you go party with fourth circle brats."

"Don't threaten me, Ariel." Laveena's eyes glowed orange. "I don't care whose daughter you are."

Kareel, easily setting the evening's standard for slinky, moved out of the gathered crowd. Her gown, shimmering with prized Angelfish scales, cupped her breasts and hips like a lover's greedy hands. "I've had it with you, Laveena." Her stiletto heels—a toe-pinching human affectation that suited her long legs—kissed the floor lightly as she advanced on her sometime lover. "Ariel, I know exactly whose daughter you are, and I ask you to take witness."

Ariel would for a long time regret that she didn't hide her smile. "I'm listening."

Kareel looked over the sodden Laveena, shaking her head. "We are done. Your voice has no song for me."

"You don't mean that!"

"We are done," Kareel repeated. She turned to Ariel. "I mean it this time, Ariel."

"Do you really? That's what you said last year, and the year before."

"And last century, and the one before that," Caliba chimed in.

Kareel slowly pushed her elegant bronze hair over her equally elegant bronze shoulder. "Yes. She has watched too many of those human movies. Witness it."

Laveena gasped in horror as Ariel raised her hand. "You can't do this, Ariel!"

"You're sure?" Ariel looked directly into Kareel's eyes. "Absolutely sure? I'm not going to be able to undo this one. I don't want to undo it either. This scene got boring two hundred years ago."

"Do it." Kareel closed her eyes.

Laveena leaped to intervene, but Caliba stepped in her way. It was always useful to have the tall, muscular Caliba at her back, Ariel thought. She summoned her power and cast the spell in a matter of moments. It wasn't hard for a daughter of a queen, and resolving lovers' spats was one of the few perquisites of rank a seventy-seventh daughter got to enjoy. It was a good spell, and would hold for a while. If Laveena wanted it undone she'd have to find someone stronger than Ariel. Not that there weren't plenty of mer who were stronger. The difficulty lay in getting any of them to care enough to help out the unpopular Laveena.

"This changes nothing." Laveena eyed Caliba with a near snarl. "Kareel sings for me before anyone else. Get out of my way."

"Next thing you'll be saying Kareel should be exclusive to you." Caliba shrugged. "That would be *so* human."

"Shut up, Caliba!"

Caliba struck a pose. "Kareel . . . you . . . complete me!" She spun in place, spreading her arms dramatically to appreciative laughter. "I honestly . . ." she made a loud choking noise. "I honestly . . . love you."

"I do not like that human drivel!" Laveena looked about to jump Caliba, but that would have been a mistake.

Kareel gasped and opened her eyes. "Is she speaking?"

Laveena and Caliba were continuing to trade insults. Caliba was winning. Ariel had often wished for Caliba's quick and easy wit. Ariel nodded at Kareel. "She's jabbering away."

Kareel's smile was savage. "I don't hear a thing. How wonderful. Ariel, I thank you." She bowed deeply, with her head tipped back. Ariel made sure she carefully studied the ripe pleasure of Kareel's ruby-studded breasts. To have ignored them would have been rude, especially since several times in their past she and Kareel had dallied. It hadn't been particularly well-mannered of Kareel to leave with Zee when she'd arrived with Laveena—especially to a flesh party—but Laveena had overreacted, as usual.

Laveena slipped past Caliba and seized Kareel's arm. "I know you can hear me. You *need* me! You can't walk away."

Kareel pulled her arm free, shaking her head. When Laveena made another grab, Ariel said silkily, "Do not make me do worse, Laveena. She chose and so did you."

"You had no right to do this!" Laveena's snarl was so enraged that Ariel nearly stepped backward. "Who do you think you are, working magic on me? Just wait until my aunt hears about this!"

Caliba, casually cleaning her nails with the long garnet-tipped pin that she'd slipped from her collar, said, "Yes, we know. Aunt Travesta will be here any minute to avenge you. We've heard it all before."

Laveena gave Caliba a poisonous look, but addressed Ariel, her face twisted with malice. "You have no idea what you've done, Ariel."

Ariel knew that Laveena was highly connected, but she was

hardly concerned. Laveena had managed to alienate her more powerful relatives over the last several hundred years. Travesta of the First Circle, favorite of Queen Vellia, had yet to waste her influence on such a pain-in-the-kelp niece. A daughter of the queen—even a seventy-seventh one—had precedence.

"I'm giving you a chance to change," Ariel said. "Caliba is right, you're behaving worse than a human."

"Beautiful Ariel, smart Ariel, so kind, so good, so unbelievably perfect!" Laveena added, her voice dripping with spite, "Not so perfect. Maybe I would like Kareel in my bed, but at least she's mer. You only run hot with humans!"

There was a collective gasp and Ariel fought down her rising color. "I haven't bedded above sea in decades, and you know that." She paused to laugh in her most sultry manner. "And most of those here will witness I am hardly shy at flesh parties. But since I decreed no fighting, I will forget you said that."

"I won't," Caliba muttered.

"You think you have friends? Just wait," was Laveena's parting shot. She stalked from the chamber in the direction Kareel had headed.

"She can't leave, I want a duel." Zee had not bothered to staunch the flow of blood from her cheek. "For her disgusting touch to my face and her insult to you."

"Stop," Ariel said. The party was better off without Laveena. "This is foolish."

"Are you suggesting I'm not worth it?"

Zee was too hotheaded for her own good, Ariel thought. She wished briefly for the power to fix everybody. Squabbling was boring. So far, this entire party was boring. Maybe she and Caliba could sneak off to a flesh party later. Sex would be more fun than this. It was a party night, after all, and maybe someone would have a grand entertainment to watch. "It's a holiday. No fighting tonight. I don't want to spend tomorrow explaining to some toady of my mother's why my parties turn into brawls. This matter is closed and there will be no duels. Is that understood?"

Zee finally nodded, but not until after her eyes suggested that she, too, felt Ariel had overstepped her authority. What authority, Ariel thought with a touch of bitterness. It wasn't as if a seventy-seventh daughter was truly powerful. She knew how to have a good time, and those who hunted with her had no trouble securing delicacies and entertainment. The only real power Ariel had was over whom she invited to share in the spoils of some daring and lucrative hunts. Zee wasn't willing to risk being ostracized.

Turning to Caliba, Ariel murmured, "Next year I'm revising the guest list!"

It was long after the chime of midnight when Ariel found Caliba ensconced with several hunting friends. They'd all had far too much Champagne, Ariel thought, as she woozily claimed a cushion of her own.

"She was a virgin to womantouch, I'm telling you," Morova was saying. "She sang like none I've ever had." She smiled softly. "She cries for me still."

Caliba burped. "I lost a voice this week. It's always sad."

"How?"

"Age." Caliba shrugged. "She had a sweet song, too. Her longing murmurs were constant for sixty years. A good feeding."

Primia drained her glass so sloppily most of the amber liquid ended up on her breasts. "All the ones I pick don't last. Either they don't sing for me or die of one thing or another."

"You need to stop choosing the broken ones," Caliba said with a hiccup. "You'd have more success getting song out of human men."

"I tried that." Primia's pout grew more pronounced as she dabbed at her chest. "Even Circe only gets song from every tenth one or so. And they soon forget. She keeps hoping she'll find another Ulysses."

Morova laughed. "If they still made them like Ulysses, I might try men once in a while. Oh, let me help. Can't waste Champagne."

Ariel rolled her eyes as Morova moved in on Primia, lowering her head to Primia's Champagne-drizzled breasts. Within moments, though, honesty made her admit—at least to herself—that watching Morova's agile tongue circle Primia's nipples was nearly as good as a flesh party entertainment.

"You won't catch me wasting my time with non-singers," Caliba replied.

"All of yours sing." Primia gave Caliba a resentful look. "I don't know how you get so lucky."

"She knows how to pick them," Ariel pronounced, which was a simple statement of fact. She might have added that Caliba had been given the song-sense that Primia ought to have had, but thought better of it at the last moment. "It's been too long since we've hunted."

"It's no fun." Morova lifted her mouth from the hard pucker of Primia's nipples. "Not since the edict."

"You sound as if you're not having enough fun here." Primia ran one ebony hand down Morova's bronze-tinted leg. "Has everyone been ignoring you?"

Morova parted her thighs slightly. "No, of course not." She pulled gently on the tip of Primia's delicately shaped ear. "I will likely head to a flesh party after a while. I miss hunting, that's all. Every so often a human woman can be memorable. Not as good as mer, I'm not saying that," she added hastily. "It's their songs. I'd never go above sea if it weren't for that of course."

"Songs," Caliba said with a sigh. "I could really use a few new voices."

They all sighed in unison, so deeply that their mervoices emerged. In response, the walls around them shifted from a carefree orange to a pensive blue.

A hunt, Ariel thought, would be welcome. Even more than feeling the puddles of Champagne in her blood, Ariel could hear the delicate songs of her past human lovers. They slept, and dreamed, and in their dreams remembered what the love of a mermaid had been like. Those songs were mer right for giving humans peace in

the upper seas. Everyone, including her mother the queen, was sung
for by some human woman, somewhere.

Caliba, who attracted women just by breathing, had a vast choir
singing for her. Ariel preferred her songs quiet but intense. A hunt,
she mused again, would be grand. Like Caliba, she'd lost a singer
recently. Oh, be honest with yourself, she thought crossly. You know
it's not just the song you're after.

She schooled her expression, though she thought she had always
kept her secret. Only Caliba might suspect. A night in a human
woman's arms meant far more to Ariel than just the song for the rest
of the woman's life. Laveena had been dangerously close to the truth.
Yes, it had been a long time since Ariel had indulged, but no mer had
ever come close to making her feel the way a human woman could.
Even without a real voice, or magic or the features mer considered
attractive, human women possessed something else that Ariel hungered for, something she could not quite define.

Laveena's insult had been a shot in the dark, Ariel told herself.
Nobody knew. "A hunt would be enjoyable."

"I think we've shown great restraint," Caliba said. She whispered
loudly to Ariel, "Especially you. I know how much you feed when
you go up."

Ariel felt a pang of alarm. It was as if Caliba had read her mind.
"It's the song I need." She adopted the sophisticated boredom of a
daughter of the queen. "If we could get the song some other way . . .
I suppose human women can be fun sometimes though, physically.
It's not as if they're good for anything else."

"The best ones we can't have anymore, so why even bother?"
Morova brooded into her empty glass while Primia coiled around
her. "If I'm going for song I want the women who were born for
other women. The lesbians. They sing . . . bless the kelp, do they
sing. The ones who prefer men, well, it takes three of their songs to
equal one lesbian's."

"Lesbians are off limits," Ariel said firmly. She agreed with everything Morova had said, but the queen's edict was serious. Too many

lesbians had sickened after a night with mer. If the queen discovered any of them had bedded a lesbian, the punishment could be severely unpleasant.

"Let's plan a hunt. The women at that Baptist convention last time were as plentiful as sea shells." Morova closed her eyes as Primia ran her hands across her stomach. "It's sounding very good to me."

Morova's pronounced pheromones tickled Ariel's nostrils. She avoided noticeably inhaling the scent, which was making her a little dizzy. Morova's chemistry had always been powerful but her preference for multiple partners wasn't one Ariel necessarily shared—at least not for every encounter. Morova was considered great fun at a flesh party, while Ariel herself was only sought out by those who liked intensity and privacy. A hunt, Ariel thought, was sounding better and better.

Primia stroked one of Morova's nipples. "Meantime, why don't we move on to a flesh party?"

Morova smiled. Her mervoice rippled slightly as she replied, "I'd like that tonight. Lots of different chemistries, a little of everything." She kissed Primia softly on the lips.

"Surely, you're not all calling it a night." Laveena's abrupt arrival startled Ariel. She hadn't expected Laveena to come within a league of her after the scene with Kareel and Zee. She hoped Kareel and Zee were safely away, fucking each other or someone else. Any place but here.

"I'm too tired, Laveena."

"I came to say I'm sorry, Ariel. And that I've heard the most delicious news."

Primia scooted closer to Morova. "What? Sit and tell us."

Laveena coiled up on a cushion and reached for one of the remaining sushi delicacies. It had been a fair trade, Ariel thought irrelevantly, the human secrets of sharp, fiery sake in exchange for the mer secrets of sushi. Both cultures had been well-served by that bit of détente. Mer might not need sake, but she saw no harm in wanting it now and again. Like a human woman. What *was* the harm in a little fun?

"Well," she began, "there is a party on land, and it's not yet mid-night there." Laveena licked her lips. "A room full of exactly our types. What they call Straight But Curious."

They all sat up slightly. Primia said, almost breathless, "You mean, the kind of human women who enjoy womantouch, but bond with men?"

"A group of them, all in one party. Wearing obvious indicators that say they are . . . interested. No finding out after you've got her stripped that she won't sing or that's she forbidden." Laveena shrugged. "They are also very definitely saying they're not lesbians, so if we were to *accidentally* bed one who is, well, that won't be our problem, will it?"

"Oh," Morova purred. "No problems with the edict at all!"

Ariel could not help the flush of desire that shook her. It had been a quarter-century since the edict, and Caliba was right. Hunting wasn't any fun with the queen's penalties of torture, torture and more torture in one's mind. Adding a song to her voices would be satisfying, but Ariel knew what she really wanted was to lose herself in a human woman's passion.

"Where?" Curiosity had gotten the better of her. It was too intriguing not to at least consider, though she did not want to owe Laveena anything.

"San Francisco."

"Oh," Primia moaned. "Such a beautiful city. So moist, nearly as damp as Seattle."

"I've not been to San Francisco in years," Morova added. She glanced at Primia. "We can hunt together if you like. Share our treats. Let's go."

"It's a large city," Caliba said warily. "Where?"

"This is the best part." Laveena's eyes glimmered with crimson intensity. "An entertainment establishment called The Pisces. The party is called A Fish Out of Water."

Their laughter turned the walls brilliant green.

✑

"I don't like this," Caliba muttered. "I'm cold, I'm drunk, and I don't trust Laveena."

"She's been right so far," Ariel reminded her. She looked up at the neon sign over the entrance to The Pisces. Two fish with long eyelashes and painted lips chased each other in a circle, mouths locked to the other fish's nether regions. Human women tasted different from mer, subtly so. Ariel had managed to forget that fact during the last twenty-five years, but being surrounded by human women and their pheromones was making her mouth water.

"But we've had to do nothing but hurry to get here in time. I don't like rushing anything above sea. It's not safe."

"I know," Ariel began to reply, but Laveena's return silenced her.

"We're in," Laveena announced. She pushed her way through the waiting throng. "And we have a table."

Morova said lowly, "I need new songs, Ariel. It's been a long time."

"How do we know for sure which ones are saying they're not lesbians?" Caliba hung back and Ariel felt a small pang of doubt. Caliba's instincts for trouble had saved them before. "Most of these women are really lesbians. It's unmistakable. That won't work."

Laveena beckoned to her right. "I've already started culling the selection."

A woman with long waves of black hair stepped out of the crowd. Her short black dress was tight and cut low—not as low as mer would wear on a modest day, but low for humans. Black stockings made her legs seem sinuous and long. The only splashes of color were the scarlet coating on her lips and the red rose pinned to her dress.

She didn't look at anyone but Laveena, who wrapped an arm around the woman's waist and pulled her close.

In a low tone Ariel could tell was hiding a thin layer of persuasive mervoice, Laveena said, "Why are you here?"

The woman's reply was instantaneous, though her words were slightly slurred from drink. "To meet someone like you, baby."

"What does the rose mean?"

"That I'm curious. Finding out what it's like with a woman is my New Year's Resolution. My girlfriends and I made a dare." The woman laughed. "Winner gets free drinks for a year."

Laveena brushed the back of one hand against the woman's breasts. "Well, then you'll be winning twice, won't you?"

The woman's pale grey eyes were gleaming. "Yeah, I'm not sure how I lose out. After this my boyfriend is going to have to really work."

You have no idea, Ariel thought. A little casual sex with a lesbian was what the curious woman was after. Instead she was going to have the most memorable night of her life, one she would never forget. One that would live on in the songs of her dreams. No straight human woman ever regretted a night of mertouch. Only some of the lesbians developed . . . problems.

Ariel turned her mind from that unpleasant reality. There were lesbians all around them, maddeningly ready to share a night of passion. They were all beautiful, appealing, sexual—and utterly forbidden. Their pheromones spilled into the air like blood in water, unmistakable. Ariel found it increasingly difficult to ignore the pulsing between her legs. She drew herself up proudly, not wanting Laveena to see how badly she needed more than song.

Laveena grinned at them, one hand casually caressing the woman's backside. "See? A room full."

"It's like a buffet," Primia whispered. "A fucking fabulous buffet. We could have more than one."

"I intend to gorge myself," Morova whispered.

Ariel understood Caliba's caution, but it was getting harder and harder to think. Human women needed, they moaned, they screamed, they said things no mer ever would. They even forgot who they were in the throes of their climax. Watching a human woman's face as she transformed for those few moments into a being of pure ecstasy was something Ariel could not get enough of. She didn't understand it and sometimes she envied it. The idea of losing herself to the trust of another, to feel that safe, that physically free—she had touched that space briefly with most of her singers, but she'd never even come close with mer.

She'd tried once to explain it to Caliba, but Caliba had changed the subject as if she did not want to know Ariel had those feelings. When Ariel had even hinted she might like to visit one of her singers a second time, Caliba had been obviously horrified. If your best friend couldn't understand, then who could? Ariel needed it and she made up her mind. Tonight she would have it, and add as many singers as she could. Tonight she felt like she could match Morova, woman for woman.

"I want to," Ariel told Caliba. It had been so long. "If we stick to the ones with roses, what could go wrong?"

Laveena had obviously plied the doorkeeper with a great deal of money. They were escorted to a hastily set out table half on the dance floor where they could see and be seen.

The music was painfully loud. It wasn't even music, Ariel thought. Just words and riffs cut together so sharply that it became a pounding static. She made an irritated gesture at Caliba, who strolled casually through the crowd toward the DJ's booth. Heads turned to follow the tall woman's progress and Ariel smiled. Caliba would have no regrets about the evening.

When Caliba reappeared a minute later she was grinning. "Maybe this isn't such a bad idea," she yelled over the music. "That woman was positively edible. Her chemistry was better than Champagne. Too bad she's a lesbian."

"Now, now," Ariel teased. "Behave!"

The music abruptly changed to a slower beat. The lights dimmed and dancers quickly began sultry, languid contact. Caliba had chosen well.

Primia, never shy, was the first to remove her black cloak. Ariel watched heads turn in their direction as Laveena likewise shed hers, then Morova, followed by Caliba. She went last, and they all spread their cloaks on the chairs and sat down, as on display as the dancers they watched.

Primia's gown was the most daring, and easily the most complicated. Ariel knew the spell Primia was using to keep the thin bands of orange silk over her nipples without the aid of a single strap around her shoulders or neck. In defiance of gravity, the material shimmered in place, seeming about to fall any moment. Primia always had magic to spare for such glamorous ends, and Ariel freely admitted they were very successful. Her deep brown skin was the perfect counterpoint to that brilliant hue, and being naked from the nipples up underscored the strength of Primia's shoulders, graceful neck and the regal balance of her shaved head. The gleaming orange bands swept around her long back where they loosely crossed, and then swooped to meet the rest of her dress just above the curve of Primia's supple ass. One touch from the right hand, that dress seemed to say, and Primia would be gloriously nude.

Morova had been slightly more conservative. Her body was mostly covered, though the fabric was in places as sheer as water at midnight. In deference to the incomprehensible human fetish for modesty, her nipples were obscured, and her gown opaque from hips downward. Her true glory had always been her hair, and when she went above water she wore it pulled severely to the crown of her head. Waves of thick, white hair fell from the tight knot to Morova's waist, all shimmering with a hint of aqua. And it was all natural, too. Morova didn't have to waste any energy on a glamour spell. It would be some time before she'd need mervoice to keep a woman standing very, very close. Unlike Laveena, Ariel thought, who'd needed mervoice right away to reel in a catch.

What could be seen of Laveena was surprisingly sedate, though the effect on the woman in her lap was beyond a doubt. Ariel found the black latex pants and skintight silk shirt stark and unappealing. Much like Laveena herself, Ariel thought. Laveena's real beauty had always been her eyes, but they were not in the same class with Caliba's sensuous dark blue.

She and Caliba had always hunted in matching colors and tonight was no different. Where Caliba's suit was completed with leather pants and slender mid-calf boots of sunset blue, Ariel had chosen a minuscule leather skirt and sleek sandals completely useless in the misty San Francisco night. They were not shoes made for walking. Both of them wore tight-fitting jackets buttoned under their breasts, though Caliba wore a simple matching shell under hers. Ariel wore nothing. She was hoping to be persuaded to unbutton hers, for the right, curious woman.

As usual, Caliba was drawing the most attention and the first to be asked to dance. Human women and mer alike seemed to generally prefer her sharp edges and gentle confidence. Caliba could make any woman feel gorgeous, and the art of sincere flattery came naturally to her. Human women came naturally to—and for—her, as well. A hunt for Caliba wasn't about conquest so much as generous pleasure in return for generous song.

Women were beginning to circle their table, with and without roses on their shoulders. Ariel felt a rush of something like shark blood. She craved a tasty meal tonight, and a lifetime of a human woman's remembering song. She felt Primia's intoxicating mervoice vibrating in the air as she spoke to a woman who paused to ask her to dance. They would all feed well tonight.

Laveena disappeared with the woman from the street, taking her through a door to some sort of backroom that Ariel was certain she'd see before the night was over. Bowls of supplies—not that mer needed them—were sitting on a table outside the door, and the door itself was guarded by a tall, thick-shouldered woman who looked thoroughly jaded. Even if she'd been the only woman wearing a rose, Ariel would not have considered her. There was no song left in that one.

Ariel could feel a rising pulse of mer power from the back room. Laveena was busy. She let her gaze slide over the crowd. She'd owe Laveena for this, but right now she didn't care.

That one? The woman in the scarlet dress? The straps of the dress were so thin that the rose was pinned just above her cleavage. Muscled flesh, short black hair—she had many of the qualities that often attracted Ariel. Caliba danced by with a small, dark-skinned woman who wore a clear plastic dress over skimpy pink bra and thong. Her rose was taped to the dress. The longer they danced the more responsive the woman became to Caliba's lead.

Her gaze was caught by a couple tightly entwined, hips seemingly joined. When they parted slightly Ariel could see one wore something under her form-fitting pants, and her miniskirted partner was rubbing it suggestively. Ariel swallowed hard. Human ingenuity had perhaps reached its peak with the invention of silicon. Yes, she thought, she wanted everything a human woman could offer.

A tall woman in a form-fitting white tuxedo caught her eye. Her hair was thick and black as ink, curling only slightly where it brushed her collar. Her shoulders were broad and strong, her legs powerful but agile. I'd feel small next to her, Ariel thought abruptly. She shuddered at the image of herself in the woman's arms. Her body was reacting to the woman's unique pheromones. It was wonderful chemistry. They would be very good together.

She started to get up, but then the woman turned to face her. Curse the kelp, Ariel thought. No rose. Damn. She was tempted to pursue her anyway, but with her luck she'd get caught. Being the queen's daughter wouldn't save her from punishment.

She wondered briefly what kind of lesbian would come to a party like this, to meet a straight woman who was curious. For a night of kicks? For the proverbial toaster oven accolades should the woman find she bonded better with other women? She followed the emergent lesbian culture from time to time because it was so new in human experience, and most lesbians, she had thought, avoided the curious straight woman as a danger to their emotional well-being.

What did it matter? There were plenty with roses, and she was going to feed tonight.

"Excuse me, but I have a thing for red hair and yours is simply stunning."

Ariel looked up at the woman who had stopped at the table. Green eyes sparkled with a pleasing combination of mirth and wickedness. No rose, though.

"Sorry," Ariel said. "I was hoping for one of the curious ones."

"Aren't we all? I was hoping your rose got misplaced."

"No, it didn't. I'm far beyond curious."

"I'm Mira." The woman held out her hand and Ariel politely shook it.

"Ariel."

Mira lifted an elegant eyebrow as if she didn't believe it, but only said, "A beautiful name."

"Thank you. It was my grandmother's."

"For red hair . . ." Mira touched a lock of Ariel's hair that had drifted over the back of the chair. "We're not required to pair up with only the curious ones."

"I'm on a quest," Ariel said with a flirtatious smile.

"I understand. I just want the night and no phone calls. Send her back to hubby or boyfriend or whatever. Maybe you and I could meet up another night?"

"Perhaps." Mira would have been a good time. Strong chemistry, a lot of laughing—it had a great deal of appeal—but not enough to be worth the torture. Damn the edict anyway.

"Pity," Mira answered, then she drifted into the crowd.

Ariel realized that under the music she could hear the rising of Caliba's mervoice. Had she gone to the back room already? They'd talked about taking their finds to a hotel for an extended evening. There was no sign of her, though, so maybe she'd picked someone out as an appetizer.

Morova was dancing with a caramel-skinned brunette who

moved like a cat. There were hints of mervoice from her as well. Everyone was getting ready to feed but her.

Laveena sauntered out of the back room, looking as if she'd just spent a week lounging in a warm tidal pool. A few moments later, clothing askew, the woman Laveena had taken into the back followed her out. She also looked deeply pleased.

Okay, it was time for a daughter of the queen, even a seventy-seventh one, to have something for herself, Ariel thought.

"Not yet casting a net?" Laveena leaned over to pick up her beer.

Ariel could smell the other woman's sex on Laveena's hands and her stomach lurched with excitement. Soon she would have that scent on her own hands, her face, her body. She wanted to swim. "Just about to."

"What about that one?"

Ariel followed Laveena's gesture. It was the delectable woman in the white tuxedo she'd noticed earlier. "No rose."

"Are you sure? Look—up next to her neck. On her left."

Ariel saw the rose then, nearly hidden under the woman's white collar. She felt mildly dizzy as the possibilities sank in.

Laveena's voice was as smooth as surf on a long, tropical beach. "It will be a pleasure to watch you hunt. I finished my first early just so I could watch."

Great, Ariel thought. Like I need *that* pressure. She would have to be careful Laveena didn't see that Ariel was enjoying much more than the song.

The woman in white was too appealing to ignore just because Laveena was being, well, Laveena. She was talking to a woman in hot pink and body language said it might turn serious.

Ariel crossed the dance floor, hardly aware that a path was clearing for her. The ends of her hair brushed the backs of her bare thighs and she was lost in a vision of her red hair falling over the tall woman's pale, nude body.

The woman in hot pink noticed her first and tried to turn the white-clad woman away, but Ariel neatly insinuated herself between the two. She gazed up at the tall woman, liking the intriguing eyes, green as an autumn ocean. "Care to dance?"

"Excuse me, but we were having a conversation," the woman in pink objected.

A scene would be tedious. Ariel used a hint of mervoice as she suggested, "Another will suit you much better."

The woman blinked several times and then shrugged. "You may be right." She walked away without a backward glance. Ariel watched Laveena fall into step behind the woman, with a backward leer at Ariel. Good, Ariel thought. Now she's occupied.

The green eyes warmed when Ariel looked again. "I would love to dance, if you would like."

"I would like," Ariel murmured. She let the delicious woman pull her into her arms.

They fit. That was immediately apparent. The other woman's thigh eased between Ariel's, and their dance quickly became a suggestive prelude. Ariel let her tides begin their flow. There was no reason to hold back now. Her merhair was quickly soaked.

"I'm Ariel."

"Erica," the woman replied. She tightened her hands on Ariel's waist, which only increased the pressure on Ariel's crotch. "What brought you here tonight?"

Ariel slipped her hands under the woman's tuxedo jacket. Erica's body was hot, female, and producing an increasing level of heady pheromones. "Passion," Ariel finally said.

"A very good reason." Erica stooped gracefully to bring her lips close to Ariel's ear. "I happen to be here for the same reason. And I think I've found it."

A moan of pure mervoice escaped Ariel as Erica's thigh lifted her nearly off her feet. The pressure was exquisite. "I think so, too," she managed.

They moved together for a few moments before Erica silkily asked, "Do you mind if I do the leading?"

Without a trace of humor, Ariel answered, "I prefer that." She saw Erica's eyes flood with an awareness of the power Ariel was yielding to her, and could see that Erica was deeply pleased.

Trembling, Ariel lifted her face for a kiss.

Erica studied Ariel's face. "Let's wait a minute for that."

Ariel arched an eyebrow, then heard the rising chant.

Twenty-nine, twenty-eight . . .

Amused and aroused by Erica's restraint, Ariel nipped the line of Erica's jaw with her teeth. "I can wait, but I'm not patient."

Seventeen, sixteen . . .

The sound Erica made was nearly a growl. "You want to be kissed early?"

"Early and often."

"What about made love to?"

"At least once a night." Ariel nibbled the other side of Erica's jaw. Erica thrust her thigh upward and Ariel was lifted to the tips of her toes. She made a noise of pure need that the queen's blood ought not, but she didn't care. It had been too long and she was now too close. Erica was intoxicating, wonderfully so.

"Just once a night?"

Five, four, three . . .

Ariel groaned out, "The rest of the night I like to fuck."

Erica gasped as if Ariel had struck her, and her mouth hungrily claimed Ariel's.

Happy New Year!

Erica was kissing Ariel like she meant it, like she wanted to finish Ariel right then. Erica's chemistry mingled with her own to create a heady mixture that Ariel could feel soaking into her skin, her blood. If she felt it, then Erica must as well. Her rationality slipped, and she knew she ought to worry, but it felt so good to be held by a human woman. So good to be kissed like this. The kisses were a promise they would both sing before the night was over.

Ariel rocked against Erica, ignoring the rhythm of the slow tune that humans played at midnight. Her own rhythm was rising. With a shudder she realized Erica's hand had slipped between them, and it was Erica's fingers that were rubbing against the thin fabric that covered Ariel's flowing wet. It felt so good that Ariel let herself go with the sensation. She hadn't even really used mervoice yet and they were both so hot. Their chemistry was a balance between giving and taking . . . a perfect blend. She thrust herself against Erica's fingers, thrilling as Erica put her arm firmly around her waist to hold her still and close.

With a disbelieving shock, Ariel realized she was close to peaking. Erica's chemistry blended with hers until they created something completely new to Ariel. She'd remember this night. She would sing for Erica and Erica would sing for her. It shouldn't feel so good, but it did.

"Is this what you came here for?" Erica twisted her hand and Ariel cried out as fingers sank into her swollen opening. Through a daze of heat she saw Primia's dark body pinned between two rose-pinned playmates. She cried out again.

The room spun and Ariel realized she was being carried through the door to the back. Just before she lost sight of the dance floor she saw Laveena's sharply observant eyes and her feral, pleased smile.

Erica's tuxedo gleamed softly in the dim light. The sounds of sex and fulfillment pulsated in Ariel's ears as Erica pinned her to a wall.

"This is what you came here for, isn't it?"

"Yes," Ariel breathed. "Yes." Human women could reach her this way. She could just feel her body and not worry that she shouldn't scream her needs. She could no longer smell the rose on Erica's collar and wondered, for only that brief moment, if the rose had been a lie. Erica was no stranger to women. What did it matter, Ariel asked herself. If Erica had consequences it was her own risk. The rose allowed Ariel to enjoy herself, completely.

"Yes is my favorite word," Erica said. She kissed Ariel fiercely. "Say it again."

"Yes."

"We'll make love later."

"Yes."

"We're going to fuck now." Erica unbuttoned Ariel's jacket and breathed out slowly. "Beautiful."

"Please."

"I like please nearly as much as yes," Erica whispered. She cupped Ariel's breasts and teased the hard nipples with her thumbs. "Please what?"

Daughters of the queen, Ariel thought dimly, didn't beg. Her voice sounded weak compared to the pounding of her heart. "Please fuck me."

"Spread your legs for me," Erica ordered.

"Yes," Ariel moaned. The word was becoming a prayer.

They groaned together as Erica yanked her panties to one side. Ariel felt naked and exposed in ways she never did with other mer. Erica was in her head, like she knew Ariel inside and out. It had been centuries, if ever, since a lover had held her this way.

"Yes, this is why you're here, for this." Erica sank two fingers inside Ariel, who stiffened and nearly lost her footing. Then she didn't have to worry. Erica was strong enough to hold her against the wall.

"Yes, please." Ariel felt the tingle of her mervoice. It would bring them into even closer intimacy, so she let it flare. *"Erica, love me."*

Erica's body jerked in response. "I'm going to, you're beautiful. You feel so good to me."

"Love me."

Erica lowered her mouth to Ariel's breasts, capturing her nipples with her teeth, one after the other. Ariel cried out and thrust herself down on Erica's hand.

"Bound forever by passion, sing for me."

Erica groaned. "Yes, help me, I need this as much as you do. To fuck you and have it turn out good. To fuck you and feel you come for me. *Ariel, please . . . please . . ."*

"Yes."

"Please."

Ariel lost her mervoice in the first wave of peaking. She ground her wet, swollen cunt on Erica's palm and cried out sharply, eagerly, as decades of unmet need were finally eased. She contracted hard around Erica's fingers and felt the powerful swell of her mervoice, rising in a cooing song of passionate climax. Her tide peaked with a wave of release, pouring from her filled and loved places onto Erica's powerful hands.

Erica gave a choking cry. "Yes, Ariel, yes, so good, yes."

"Bound forever by passion, Erica. Singing forever."

"Come again, I know you can, pour like that again." Erica pulled Ariel down to the mat on the floor, rolling on top of her. "Ariel, please."

Erica's mouth was devouring her breasts, sucking, biting, then claiming her tongue and lips with kisses that made Ariel tighten on the fingers still inside her body.

Erica scrabbled in a nearby basket with her free hand. "I don't want to hurt you, but I can't stop fucking you."

"You don't need that," Ariel gasped. She closed her eyes and summoned a new tide.

"Oh fuck, how do you do that? You're soaked, again . . ." Erica's hungry mouth went between Ariel's legs and Ariel reveled in the hard force of Erica's tongue on her wet flesh.

Erica was trying to tease her but her hips were moving against Ariel's shoulder. Ariel found something of her wits though Erica's tongue made it hard to want to do anything but remain exactly as she was and gush again and again.

She got Erica's pants unzipped and partially down, enough to smell what she ached to taste. Nothing compared to the silk of a human woman. Erica wanted her, was trying to open her legs for Ariel, but her knees were still trapped.

Ariel managed to get her hand between Erica's legs and thrilled at the slick waters that waited for her. She wet her fingers in the heat, then withdrew them to taste. Human women could be so sweet, so very sweet. She would have gone back for more but Erica rolled out of the reach of Ariel's hand.

"This is what we both want." Erica added another finger and Ariel cried out as she realized Erica was pushing her knuckles inside Ariel's hunger.

"*Inside me, yes.*"

Her body was quivering near another peak as Erica's tongue circled and licked her throbbing clit. She braced herself for Erica's hand. She had thought it would take all night to get to this point. How could Erica know what to do, what Ariel needed?

"*Yes! Please, Erica, sing for me!*"

"Inside you, like this." Erica groaned hard as Ariel dug her nails into Erica's bare hip, and then with a twist of her wrist, her hand was completely enveloped by Ariel's walls.

Ariel went still, her eyes tightly closed, and let her body feel the pleasure of being so tightly filled that no place inside her wasn't touched by the pressure of Erica's hand. She could let mer do this to her but it was not the same sensation of wonderful surrender. Her body, at this moment, belonged to Erica. Erica's to pleasure.

"So good," Erica was crooning. "So wet and gripping me like this. I wanted to do this to you the moment I saw you. I wanted to feel you dancing under me."

Erica gently moved her hand and Ariel let herself respond. Then it wasn't her choice anymore. Erica started to rock inside her and Ariel surged up to meet her. Soft and tender gave way to hard and primal. Time to fuck.

She rose again and again to meet Erica. Delicious Erica, so confident and able. Her tides were rising again. She told herself if she bore down any harder she'd break Erica's hand, but it felt too good.

"Let it out, baby," Erica pleaded. "Let it go again, I know you can. We both want it, let it go."

Ariel's wrenching cry was all mervoice, all her power and it enveloped both of them in a sapphire glow. "*Like this for you, all of me, have me, yours forever now, bound by passion forever . . .*"

Erica was breathing hard, her head on Ariel's thigh. Ariel felt drugged with satisfaction. She had never been so completely possessed by the power of a human woman. She closed her eyes for a moment to push away a flash of bitterness. She wanted more than one night with Erica. To share . . . more. Why was it considered sick? She would sing of Erica for the rest of her days if their one night continued this way.

She pushed away the thought of another night and focused on this one. Smiling with anticipation, Ariel thought Erica deserved a reward. She pushed the pants past Erica's knees, then scooted underneath her. She heard the wailing sounds of other lovers reaching pleasure points, even the tingle of mervoice as Morova fed.

Time to swim, Ariel thought. She pulled Erica's hips down and enveloped Erica's wet, swollen clit with her mouth.

Erica cried out, then arched her pelvis so Ariel could reach all of her. Ariel swirled her tongue in Erica's depths, drinking deeply. All that heat and wet, Ariel thought, all for me.

The taste of sex rolled over her tongue, filled her mouth. Erica moved to her haunches, lifting her dripping center out of reach of Ariel's tongue. "Want more?"

"Yes, oh yes," Ariel moaned. She arched up and found that sweet, hot flesh again. Erica's hand cupped the back of Ariel's neck, holding her where she wanted Ariel most. Ariel realized she had thirsted for years for this, for the surging wet of a lover who gave such passion so easily. Mer would never completely let go. Sex would overcome lineage and history. But Erica was nearly there.

"Don't stop," Erica groaned. She gently let go of Ariel, then fell urgently onto her hands. "Don't stop!"

Ariel had no intention of stopping, not until she felt the full power of Erica's song breaking over them both.

"*Ariel!*" It was a moment before Caliba's insistent mervoice broke into Ariel's concentration. She loved Erica's tender flesh, such heat and slickness and fire.

"*Ariel, stop!*"

Caliba was next to her now, trying to pry Ariel's hand off of Erica's rocking ass. Ariel could feel Erica tensing up as the intensity began to falter. "What is your problem, Caliba?"

"She's not wearing a rose!"

"I saw it, under her collar. Go away."

"No, there's no rose. I checked her out. We all checked her out."

Erica abruptly rolled off of Ariel, bemused and annoyed. "What's going on?"

Ariel ran her hand over Erica's jacket. "Nothing, it's just . . ." The rose was gone. "It must have fallen off. Though I can't believe you're just curious." She inclined her head for another kiss.

"I never had one on," Erica said. She scrambled to her feet, clumsily pulling up her pants. "I'm not straight." Erica sounded greatly offended at the idea.

"What do you mean you were never wearing one? I saw it. I smelled it." Ariel ran her hand over where she had seen the rose, but there weren't even pin marks. Even Ariel's highly tuned mer nostrils couldn't find the delicate scent on Erica now. Erica was steeped instead in the smell of Ariel's passion.

"You picked a lesbian, Ariel!" Caliba lowered her voice to an intense whisper. "We have to get out of here before anyone sees!"

"There was a rose!" Ariel scrambled to her feet, aware that her legs were slicked with her come. One thigh ached from the earlier strength of Erica's grip. "I saw it!"

"What does it matter?" Erica was staring at her, clearly mystified. "I only came here because I wanted there to be no question about yes. I just needed to have a good time. And we were having a really good time."

There was no way Ariel could explain. Erica was mortal, a human, bound by her own limited understanding of physics. Humans and mer had gone their separate ways a hundred millennia ago. Erica could not understand a penalty of torture for sharing chemistry with a lesbian. "You were wearing a rose," Ariel said again, barely audible over the music.

"Ariel, we have to go!" Caliba took Ariel's arm and pulled, hard.

"No, I wasn't. Let go of her!" Erica leaned menacingly toward Caliba, who responded with a glare. "I don't care who you are to her, at the moment she's with me."

Caliba turned her back on Erica. "Ariel, we must go!"

"You are with me, aren't you?" Erica was abruptly plaintive. "We were having an incredible time. I would like to leave with you, find some place more comfortable."

Ariel nearly said yes. The word trembled on her mouth. She wanted more of this woman, but everything had become so confused.

The door from the club opened and Ariel realized they were standing in a long corridor. From a few feet away a woman on her knees was watching them argue. Her standing paramour cupped the back of her head and brought the woman's mouth back to its prior business, while addressing them with a scathing, "Do you mind?"

The door remained open and Ariel's vision cleared enough to see it was Laveena letting in the light. Laveena snapped her fingers and the overhead lights came on.

Amidst exclamations of anger as women sprang apart, Laveena's voice was nevertheless plain. "Well, well, what have we here? Ariel? That one never had a rose!"

"But you pointed her out to me, remember?"

"Ariel, please. Really, you broke the edict and now you've been caught. Don't blame it on others."

Laveena smiled that evil, feral smile of hers and only then did Ariel realize what was happening. "You tricked me!"

Caliba was looking at Ariel in horror. "She's going to tell!"

Ariel swung around to Erica. "She put you up to it!" She'd been drunk on pheromones not to have sensed it before it was too late.

"I don't know what you're talking about," Erica said softly. "Can't we just go somewhere and be alone? I want to be with you. Your mouth felt wonderful. I want to touch you again. *Ariel . . .*"

"Oh no . . ." Morova had appeared, rapidly pulling on her clothes. "She's *infected*. Ariel, how could you?"

Ariel, pulsating with fear and anger, turned deliberately to Laveena. "Tell them the truth. You saw the rose too."

"Even she says she never wore a rose. After your little show tonight, you really are full of yourself, aren't you? Beautiful Ariel, she never gets caught. You might be able to block Kareel from hearing my voice, but you won't stop me from telling what I've seen!" Laveena twirled to the door and in a moment was gone.

"She did this," Ariel said desperately. "Morova, you have to believe me."

Morova slowly shook her head. "I want to, Ariel. I believe you thought you saw a rose. She says she never wore one."

Primia looked Erica up and down. "I hope she was worth it."

"I don't understand what's going on," Erica said. "I just know I want to be with you again. Can't we be together again? No one has ever been like you. I want you."

Erica was a lesbian. Erica was infected with mermadness. Ariel had infected her. *It's not fair!* She'd had no way of knowing Erica could be infected. But, a small voice reminded her, you suspected she wasn't merely curious.

Erica would not just sing of Ariel's passion, she would refuse the love of any other, eventually refuse all comfort, food . . . refuse life. For centuries the occasional human woman became fatally infected by her need for mertouch, but it had seemed pure chance and extremely rare. It was only several decades ago, with so many of human women experiencing their lesbian sexuality, that mer healers had realized the fatal infections happened only to the lesbians.

What have I done?

Caliba seized Ariel's hand and dragged her through the club, where dancers wearing fewer and fewer clothes were pairing off. Ariel saw only a barrage of bare shoulders and breasts. Roses were on the floor, petals crushed. One of them had to be the one she'd seen on Erica's jacket, but how could she ever prove it? And what did it matter? She'd infected a lesbian and Laveena knew about it. It's not fair, she thought again. The smell of roses and alcohol was both overwhelming and nauseating.

They were out on the street before Ariel pulled away from Caliba. "I have to at least tell her!"

Ariel, why are you going? I need you, need to love you . . . Ariel . . .

Erica's song was growing stronger as the hunger to hear, touch, feel more of Ariel spread in her body. It was hard to think. Erica would never stop, her last breath would be for Ariel. Some mer had become addicted to fervent, obsessive, endless power of lesbian song, and had used it to attire their egos the way a glamour spell could attire the body. Ariel could feel the thick, heady swelling of her senses as the pure longing in Erica's inner song grew. She'd understood the edict after the wave of lesbian deaths years ago. Now, finally, Ariel didn't just understand it—she felt it. Erica was already suffering.

Ariel knew she was in danger of liking Erica's pain. Her own response nauseated her.

I must find you, have you . . . don't go . . . Ariel . . . bound forever . . . stay . . . find you . . . find . . .

Caliba continued to drag Ariel down the street.

Find you, touch you . . .

"I have to go back to her!"

"You can't!" Caliba swung around to Ariel, her face contorted with misery. "I'll try to hide you, but—"

A crash overhead had them both clapping their hands to their ears. Primia and Morova, who had been following, both screamed. The sky above them opened and rain poured down so thick that the humans around them cried out and ran for cover. The street emptied within seconds, leaving the four of them to stare up into the sky.

Ariel blinked into the downpour to adjust to water vision. She heard thunder, but when her vision cleared she knew she was wrong. Not thunder, but the beat of manta rays surfing their rain to find their quarry. Ariel fought back her terror while hope died inside her.

There was no hiding from the Queen's Riders. Her mother already knew what Ariel had done.

Touch you . . . Ariel, please . . . where are you? I need you, ache for you . . .

The waterfall of rain washed over Ariel, pounding the breath from her body as the riders swept over her.

Ariel . . .

Ariel . . .

Part 2

There was no point in opening her eyes. There was no light. Even the soothing phosphorescence of the sea had been blacked out.

Ariel rolled onto her side, adding her own whimper to the echoes that dripped from the grotto walls.

No point in reaching out her hand to test if today the water she heard, gently lapping against a surface she could not see, was within reach. No point to pulling at her chains, speaking her magic or searching for a more comfortable place to rest among the gritty, fetid stones.

She could almost slip into her own mind, visit a memory or dream, a fantasy, even a nightmare, but when she paid less attention to the echoes they would become so loud she could not hear her own blood in her veins.

The only way to survive the torture was not to fight it. She let the stones hurt her skin and what was left of her muscles. Thirst tore at her throat. The chains weighed on her arms to the edge of numbness.

The perpetual darkness had even become an ally of a kind. With no light she could not tell the passage of time. She could easily persuade her mind that any moment could bring deliverance.

Sometimes she forgot why she was there. The echoes would eventually remind her she'd hurt someone. She heard someone crying for her but couldn't remember who.

When ignorance became nearly complete, the echoes gave back memory.

Erica's hand on her body, Erica's wet, hot flesh in her mouth, Erica's precise understanding of how Ariel needed to be fucked, Erica's gentleness, forcefulness, the feel of Erica's hand inside her, the wonder in Erica's voice as Ariel came for her again—it all flowed over her, every moment of it.

When those memories almost became a pleasure, the echoes took them away and she heard only the crying, pleading voice of Erica's suffering.

When she blissfully forgot why she suffered, she heard Laveena's accusing voice and her powerful aunt's accusations. There was no light for her eyes, but her mind replayed her brief trial in vivid detail, including the queen's revulsion that one of her own daughters would not only defy her edict, but actually prefer human sex to mer.

Sometimes she could convince herself it wasn't true, she didn't prefer human women. Then the echoes would parade the long line of all the women who sang for her, ending with Erica and her amazing hands. Just as those memories threatened to be pleasurable, the echoes presented visions of Erica wasting to a shell. Erica was only human, but it hurt to see her like that. Ariel didn't want to know.

She would remember ocean, sometimes, and the echoes gave her desert.

Moonlight under water at midnight—she could nearly hold the

image in her mind. Then the echoes gave her the crushing pressure of the abyss.

When her soul welcomed the abyss and tried to embrace it forever, the echoes gave her songs of her past lovers, still singing for her.

When she wanted to die, the echoes gave her reasons to live.

When she wanted to live, the echoes made sure she craved to die.

The rocks were moving. This was different, but Ariel tried not to feel anything about it. If she liked it the echoes would take the difference away. If she hated it, the echoes would give her more.

Then the floor moved like the surf, rumbling and groaning. The rocks were trembling. Ariel could hear the water swirling, but there was no light.

Something touched her feet and she screamed and tried to jump away from it, but the chains held her and then she realized . . .

Fell to her knees . . . water . . . water . . . water rushing over her feet, over her legs. She brought the salt of the sea to her face, her hair, water on her body. She was mer again. She drank from her cupped hands and felt the healing power of the sea mother inside her.

The rocks were no longer moving, but there was a terrible grinding above her. The water she knelt in receded. She crawled after it, then found herself over her head as a large wave knocked her down. She swallowed water and felt her mer lungs pull air from it. If there were no chains she could swim. Swim . . . feel the sea mother and all her children around her. She could truly be mer again.

Then she was swimming, the chains heavy but free of their moorings. She plunged downward and felt the percussion of rocks on the surface of the water, and she kept swimming down, then a boulder helped her to sink, farther, deeper, to the cold embrace of the depths.

Or at least she thought, until her eyes began to trick her, flinching from what was to her left. She closed them tightly and followed the shifting black. Black . . . then indigo behind her eyes. Indigo mutated to a color she'd forgotten the name of.

In the growing light that made her eyes hurt she saw the bubbles of her breath in the water. Only then did she know which way was up.

The chains fought her, but she swam up, toward that color. Her arms and legs screamed as she rose toward the color of something beautiful. Her wasted skin flapped in the water, slowing her down.

Up, she thought, even as her arms refused to stroke anymore. Her legs ceased their pumping and the chains began to win.

She cried out as the color faded. The echoes played their tricks, made her want the color, and now they took it away. Her destruction was complete. She would die slowly in the crushing cold of the abyss. What had she done to deserve that fate? She couldn't remember. Something bad . . . something evil. Had it been her fault? But what?

And then the sea under her changed, and she felt warmth passing under her feet. She knew that feeling, knew it from long ago, from when she had been someone else. Little Ariel had known what to do: reach down, grab hold and hang on.

Orca, brother orca, exhaled warmly again as Ariel found a barnacle she could grasp. Brother orca needed to breathe, would go up to breathe. The color, that beautiful color, was getting closer.

The sea thinned, shimmered and her eyes wanted to close from the pain of the color. Her head broke the plane of the water and she smelled fresh, salty air and saw the smile of the sky mother over her. The color . . . silver moon, silver light. Silver for freedom. Silver for insanity. She laughed into the surf and clung to brother orca, who listened to her mad story and agreed to take her toward land.

She rolled onto a beach, exhausted. The chains would not come off and she had no strength to swim farther pulled down by their weight.

She knew a day had passed because the sun rose. She had

screamed as the yellow of it stabbed into her weak eyes, but the tiny island gave no shelter. The sun set and she wept for glory of the sky mother's returned smile. Silver again.

She was still weeping when the Queen's Riders found her. They carried her into the sea again, down to the deep lands of the mer. She did not know if they returned her to her prison or to an even worse fate.

Part 3

"This is what an example looks like." Ariel shrugged as she turned back to the mirror.

Even Caliba, who loved her, could not hide her shock at Ariel's appearance. But she smiled bravely. "It will all heal."

Ariel nodded, but so far felt no real conviction. She'd soaked for hours in the bathing pool, ever since the Riders had unceremoniously dumped her in the guest chamber in her mother's hall. She still felt dirty and rough. Her flame red hair was extinguished to the shade of an ancient lobster boiled a thousand years ago. "I've had better centuries."

"I know you have, Ari. You've been through hell."

"Hell is a picnic compared to the queen's grotto." Ariel stared at her dull hair, sagging skin, even the scars criss-crossing her body from the stones she'd slept on. It *would* all heal, eventually. But she could not look at her eyes, which refused to stop watering in the low light. Not yet. She had seen the glances the guards had exchanged. She did not want to know how deeply she might have changed.

"No one will tell me anything, Caliba. What are they going to do with me? I didn't leave that place on purpose, but here I am."

"I don't think anyone knows what to do. An earthquake set you free. To put you back would defy the sea mother, maybe. They really don't know. I'm afraid the queen will think of something else."

Ariel could only nod. She was afraid of her mother's inventiveness, especially when she was in a bad mood. She let the small silence extend, still reveling in the simplicity of quiet. Finally, she asked the question she most wanted answered. "How long was I away?"

The next silence was unexpected, so she turned from her reflection to gaze directly at Caliba.

Caliba would not look at her. She was unchanged, but then Caliba had several more centuries before anything would alter in her body. She bore three more rings along the rim of her left ear—signs of increasing status—but otherwise, Caliba was as Caliba had always been.

"Fifty years?" Even to mer fifty years was a long time. "I survived long enough for it to have been enough punishment, didn't I? Forty?"

Caliba shook her head.

Ariel's voice broke. "Twenty-five? Please . . . tell me." She spun to the mirror again, surveying the damage to her body, her hands. She would heal, wouldn't she? She was a wreck, certainly, but twenty years of torture explained it. Her hands were claws.

Without meaning to she looked into her eyes.

Silver eyes, the pale color of the sky mother.

They had been deep blue, the mark of the queen's line. Their radiant color, so admired, was not a false memory left by the echoes. Now . . . she was Silver Eye, a name of respect for the old, but one of madness for the young. She had been young. Fifteen years? All her youth gone in such a short time? How could it have been only fifteen years?

She had lost the eyes of her youth forever. "Look at me," she said to Caliba's reflection.

"I can't."

"Am I so terrible?"

"One, Ariel."

"What?" Ariel momentarily went numb. "One what?"

"One year," Caliba said miserably. "The earthquake happened at midnight on the first new year since you were sent away. That's why everyone is nervous about it. It could be a sign."

Ariel lost herself in the silver of her eyes, shaking in tears, mourning her beauty. She was a shadow, a wraith, after only a year? Her life would span millennia. A year was *nothing*, and she was . . . destroyed.

"They're coming for you."

"I can't go back! I can't!" Ariel covered her ears, hearing the echoes. They'd given her freedom just to take it away. If she went back she would be utterly mad. She would rather go to the abyss where at least she knew the suffering would eventually end. Death was better. She could not go back.

The chamber door burst open and the humorless guards swept in. They dragged her sobbing to her audience with the queen, dumping her unceremoniously onto the floor.

Ariel scrambled on her hands and knees up the dais steps, and flung herself at her mother's feet. "Mercy, please, mercy. I never meant to do it, I will do anything, don't send me back, please."

Hands pulled her roughly away, but Ariel begged, with all her soul, even at the price of her soul. "I have nothing left, I can't go back, mother, please, mercy—"

"Enough." Queen Villea drew back and Ariel realized it had been a mistake to remind her that they shared blood. Even a seventy-seventh daughter had to obey a higher standard, or at least be skilled in not getting caught if she decided to break a rule.

Ariel managed to stop her flow of words, but her whimpers of fear and distress were beyond her control. The echoes washed through her mind. Show what you want, they said, and it will be taken away. She focused completely on the queen's austere expression.

A voice said coolly, "The sea mother delivered the prisoner and we risk destruction if we go against her."

Ariel found the speaker—Barwen, her eldest sister, who had centuries ago become an acolyte to the sea mother. Barwen's deep blue eyes, the shade Ariel's used to be, were filled with horror as she gazed at Ariel.

Behind Ariel another voice spoke. The hatred in it was so plain Ariel knew it was Laveena even before she turned to face her. "But her punishment is not complete."

"Look at her! She is example enough." Ariel could have cried for the strength—and the bitter truth—in Caliba's voice. Caliba had ever been better than any sister.

"Not enough! She must pay for what she did!" Laveena's eyes glowed like algae. "The lesbian will die because Ariel wanted human sex and didn't care how she got it. It's depraved!"

Ariel turned from voice to voice and the memory of her first trial washed over her. Voices twisting her in circles, accusing, never listening. The echoes gave her freedom just to take it away.

"You . . . you saw the rose, Laveena. I know you did. I never meant to hurt anyone." Ariel didn't have the anger to speak with conviction. She just said it, weak and afraid.

"She still does not recant her lie!" Laveena's powerful aunt, Travesta, was speaking now and Ariel flinched from the orange and gold show of light, all poison and pride. "She defames my niece of my clan and defies the authority of her queen. The young ones run wild, your majesty, laughing at your compassionate laws to protect the humans. She must go back as an example."

"Enough." The queen rose and her feet, which were all that Ariel dared look at, glided smoothly across the floor toward her.

"Mercy, please," Ariel whispered. "I will accept any other judgment."

"Mother, we must heed the sea mother!" Barwen was bathed in green.

"I said enough." Her mother's angry glance muted Barwen's green to a shade that Ariel thought was like a pair of eyes she had once gazed into. But whose? It was hard to remember.

"Do not beg for mercy, daughter of my blood. We do not beg. Look at me when I speak."

Ariel finally found the courage and once their gazes locked found she could not look away. A low moan escaped her as she saw the queen's lip curl in distaste.

"Silver Eye, you truly are."

"I never meant—"

The queen hissed in displeasure. "Shut up, you silly girl. If the sea mother hadn't spat you out, I would leave you in darkness forever. We share blood, but that will not save you."

Ariel knew tears were running down her face but she was powerless to stop them. "I will break."

"Yes." The queen's tone was pleased. "That is what you're supposed to do. Break and never heal. You defied my edict."

"I did not mean to. It was an accident. Truly, I never meant to hurt anyone." There had been a rose, she told herself, she knew there had been. What if she'd been mad, though, mad with lust? What if she'd only seen one because she wanted it to be there?

Travesta towered over her. "Hunting above sea to sate your sick appetites, someone was going to get hurt. But you didn't care. You weren't there for song, you were there to have your perverted sex."

Ariel shook her head. "I don't know—I was always careful."

Laveena appeared from behind her aunt. "She crawls to human women for sex. She wanted lesbian song and human flesh and thought no one would care to tell the truth about her wickedness."

Ariel saw then that Kareel stood behind Laveena. So . . . Kareel hadn't meant it after all. What had any of it been for?

Travesta silenced Laveena with a wave of her hand. "You begged for the human to touch you. You weren't there for the song." She waved a hand and the room filled with the sound of Ariel's moans: *yes* and *please*.

How did Travesta know that? Laveena hadn't been in the corridor.

Ariel found Caliba in the crowd and saw, to her heartsick horror, that Caliba was crimson with shame. "I'm sorry, Ariel. I thought if they understood how much you needed it, that you weren't sick, you just needed, and you gave as much as you took. I thought it would help."

Travesta gestured angrily. "We cannot give her mercy, my queen. Be glad you have other daughters, like Barwen, who know their duty."

Queen Villea gave Travesta a dangerous look, and Ariel hoped it meant Travesta's greed for vengeance had had the opposite effect on the queen.

Barwen spoke again, in her cool, dispassionate voice. "The sea mother *did* free her from the grotto. Her punishment might not lie below sea at all."

So much for thinking Barwen might be an ally, Ariel thought. Like everyone else, she just wanted Ariel to pay. Was it so bad, what she'd done? It had been a mistake, after all.

"If she is what Travesta claims, it would be torture to be above sea and not feed."

The queen tipped her head to one side, considering.

"It's too easy," Travesta said. "Far too easy."

"It would be novel." The queen began to smile, and Ariel felt even more afraid. "I'm tired of worrying about her fate. A seventy-seventh daughter should not be such a trouble. She needs to be an example, but I think the sea mother wants us to try another way."

Ariel felt as if she was shrinking into the floor from the heat of the queen's gaze. A seventy-seventh daughter not only didn't expect this much maternal attention, she usually tried to avoid it. All from Laveena's spite, she thought. Laveena ought to suffer for infecting the lesbian. It was Laveena's fault. The lesbian . . . then Ariel recalled the green eyes, so full of confidence and passion. Erica . . . her name had been Erica.

"It's justice that you suffer what you did, and so you shall suffer." The queen's raised hands cupped a spinning ball of fire. The room was absolutely still. Ariel knew no one would intervene now. Villea could easily make another of whatever spell she was crafting.

Ariel screamed as the ball of fire enveloped her. The queen's spell seared into her mind. She had one moment to study it, to grasp what was about to happen, then the magic unleashed and stabbed down her spine. Dignity had no point, and neither did pride. The echoes had left her nothing of either. Her body writhed across the floor.

"Suffer the lesbian's fate! You are now as infected as she is."

The collective disbelieving gasp turned the walls to umber.

"But that is a death sentence!" Barwen actually sounded as if she cared.

The queen raised an imperious hand. "I am not done."

The fire around her was fading. As the pain left her, Ariel felt something else. Longing. Needing . . . needing a touch, the nearness of someone. Not anyone, but Erica. It was a different kind of fire, licking over her skin and then into it, sinking into her muscles, her blood. Desire began to pump steadily through her heart and into her mind. *Erica.* She needed Erica. She hurt without Erica.

"Because the sea mother sent you back, it is remotely possible she wants you saved for reasons of her own crafting. I will not risk her displeasure. I have also given you the cure. If you can resist the infection's call until the end of this new year, the cure will work on you, and you will be free. If you peak in any way or cause another to . . . you will die, just as the lesbian shall."

"Still too easy." Travesta was displeased. "She can isolate herself for a year and be cured."

Queen Villea gave Travesta a look that would have had anyone else on their knees. "Do not suggest that I don't know how to design torture."

Travesta paled. "I did not mean that, your majesty."

There was a tense silence. Ariel wished her mother would decide to practice torture games on Travesta. Travesta and Laveena, anybody but her.

Finally, the queen turned back to Ariel, but her words were for Travesta. "She will go to the lesbian. She really has no choice, poor thing." In spite of her words, her mother's smile was edged with cruelty. "But there is one more thing."

Ariel let out a low moan. Her body was searing with need for the lesbian's touch.

"Your song was used to lure the lesbian, to beg for her, used like the Sirens, luring an innocent to her death. If you sing or speak, use words in any way, you will lose the cure. You will not sing for her, or for anyone. You must hold your tongue—in both ways!"

There was mild, appreciative laughter at the queen's cleverness.

Ariel's entire body seared with arousal and fire. Erica, she needed Erica, now. She wanted to speak, at least to moan.

The queen cupped Ariel's chin in hand and gazed one last time into Ariel's eyes. "One sound, Silver Eye, one noise, one word, and you will lose the cure. You understand, don't you?"

Ariel nearly said Yes. She nodded instead.

The queen's grin was triumphant. "I see that you do."

Ariel trembled with wanting to moan. She needed Erica's chemistry, her breath, her tears. *Was this what Erica felt?*

"Yes." The queen seemed to read Ariel's mind. "This is how she feels, which is why we cannot let stupid girls like you infect those born to love women. I think that not only do you seek the sick pleasures of human sex, you like to feed on the lesbian's pain. And that cannot be allowed."

A protest died on Ariel's lips before she spoke. She hadn't liked Erica's pain. She'd hardly thought about it.

The queen's voice rose, addressing the gathering. "In those distant times when we chose to separate ourselves from the petty land-breathing barbarians, we made a choice. We took our knowledge and sank our island and found splendor in the depths. They still scratch on the surface of their world. Humans are self-destructive and limited, and we will not go their way. But because of the genetic bond that once existed between us, we hold back our power and leave them in peace. I am queen because I silenced the Sirens, ended their petty games with pitiful sailors. I will sacrifice one of my daughters to remind all of us what happens when we mingle too closely in human fate."

Ariel shook briefly with a fit of rage. None of this was fair. She hadn't meant for any of this to happen.

Her mother rose and gestured at Laveena. "Any last words for the one who injured you?"

Ariel wanted to back away as Laveena towered over her. "You were beautiful and charming, but no longer. Good Ariel, so sweet and pure—no more." Laveena knelt so her words would whisper into Ariel's ear. Ariel cringed at the force of Laveena's pheromones enveloping her. "You may have your uses when you return, though."

Trembling, Ariel could only stare. Her body burned with desire for Erica, and Laveena's chemistry was making it even worse. Maybe she deserved to be punished, but did she deserve this? To want to debase herself to someone who wanted her destroyed? To beg for what would surely break her in ways the echoes could have never reached? The effort it took not to arch herself up for Laveena's taking brought tears to her eyes.

Queen Villea said, "I do not think you will last a week without feeding on her human lusts. You will lose the cure, and we will not see you again. You want human life, so you shall be one and die in the shortness of their days. But I tire of this. I will swim now." The queen pointedly took Travesta's hand and left without another glance for anyone.

The room began to empty, mer of all clans making sure to stare as they passed Ariel, though none spoke. Ariel knelt, shaking, with tears standing on her cheeks. Barwen turned her back. Barwen—and all of her sisters—had all had their times above sea, but none of them, their rigid spines seems to say, had ever done anything perverted. Their crimes were now Ariel's, and Ariel would pay for them all.

Laveena paused at a distance. "How does it feel, Ariel? What? Catfish got your tongue?" Caliba growled, but Laveena only laughed. "Still the trained shark? If you're her friend tell her the only way out. Persuade her to do the smart thing. I might respect her if she took it."

Laveena swept out of the chamber, Kareel on her arm. Ariel looked enquiringly at Caliba.

Caliba had tears in her eyes. "You'd never think of it, you're too innocent. Laveena I'll bet thought of it right away. What does it say about me that I know what she was getting at?"

Thoroughly confused, Ariel spread her hands.

"You can't bed her if she's dead. She dies, the temptation dies."

Ariel gaped, shocked to her core at the idea. She was being punished for carelessly infecting a human, but it was acceptable to murder her instead?

Caliba was shaking her head vehemently. "Of course you won't—it's just the kind of warped thinking Laveena specializes in."

Another wave of craving Erica's touch swept over Ariel, and she forgot Laveena even existed. *Erica, I need you.*

Fire seemed to lick at Ariel's nipples, as intense as the nip of Erica's teeth had been.

Caliba was the only one who did not leave her. Even Primia and Morova had scurried out. Of all those who had ever hunted with Ariel, enjoyed the pleasures and parties, only Caliba stood by her.

"Stay," Caliba urged her. "One year, here, and you'll be well. I'll take care of you. Take care of it. We'll get through it together, the way we have through everything."

Ariel wanted to believe that she could stay, but her body's burning fire was like nothing she had ever felt before. It was difficult to think of anything else. Caliba could not possibly understand. Being close at least she would know where Erica was. She had to be close to Erica now. Her arms ached to hold Erica, even though what was left of her rational mind told her it was just a physical drive. She knew nothing about Erica's life, her dreams. What if they burned for and yet hated each other at the same time?

No, she thought. *I may be thinking with my heart, but that night with Erica was like no other.* She trembled at the memory. At least they could hold each other and breathe in their chemistry. Whatever she shared with Erica it could never be as sick as Laveena's suggestions.

But are you strong enough, the echoes seemed to whisper, strong enough to hold her and not have her? Be held and not sing? Maybe Laveena is right. The only way you can live is if she dies. She's dying anyway, isn't she?

Never, Ariel thought. I never meant to hurt her and I won't do worse. I will suffer through this rather than turn into Laveena!

Her mother had done well, Ariel thought bitterly. She was given freedom and a prison in one step. No matter how she tried, Ariel would never be capable of that kind of subtlety.

"Stay here and in a year you will be free." Caliba touched her arm.

Ariel jerked away as if she'd been stung. She shook her head violently.

Caliba drew back. "Stay . . ."

Ariel closed her eyes, shaking her head. Caliba tried once again to take her in her arms, but Ariel pushed her away.

"Go then. I will be here when you get back. Everything can be the way it was."

Ariel would have laughed at Caliba's naïveté, but even laughter had been taken away. Nothing would ever be the same. How could Caliba not know that? Even if Ariel survived, she was changed.

Finally, her eyes trying to say good-bye, Ariel turned to the door. She took nothing with her but the too-big finery Caliba had lent her.

The last Ariel saw of the lands of the mer was the Grand Pool, access to all other places. She sank into its depths, took in oxygen through her merlungs, and wearily began to swim. She did not have to seek resonance of the sky mother or sense the movement of the tides to find her way.

Her body knew where Erica was.

☙

Ariel slipped out of the surf and rested on the rocky beach. Every league of the ocean's crossing, and every step she took now, brought her closer to Erica. Soon she would be with Erica, breathe in her chemicals, her essence. Touch her, hold her tightly. The fires would subside when they touched. It would be easier to think then.

She had thought salmon stupid for destroying themselves to return to a place they had long forgotten. They swam upstream on pure instinct, unthinking, blindly following a physical drive.

She was now one of them, Ariel thought. Instinct was all she seemed to have.

She walked the tidewater, wading until the stony beach gave way to sand and the sand finally to a narrow bridge leading to an empty country road. At the top of the headlands she looked back at the rolling sea. The pang in her heart felt like a goodbye. She didn't know if she would go back, and if she did whether she'd be welcome in the places she'd called home for centuries. She felt a longing for it but it was nothing, *nothing* compared to the burning craving in her body for Erica.

She walked for hours, following the winding lane. One lone car passed her, but it did not stop. Her feet knew the way to a place she'd never been before. The foggy, dank day showed no passage of time until it began to fade. She walked and felt Erica slowly grow closer.

She had no idea what she would do when she found Erica, how she would live. All she knew was that she had to be close to her. Maybe then she would be able to think.

She stopped several times at puddles of rain water, slaking her thirst and cooling her face. Her body felt as if she was on fire, and nothing would ease it but Erica's presence. Her reflection in the mirrored water showed her hair hanging in clumps of knots. Her skin was sallow and sagged like the most ancient acolyte's. What would Erica think of her? Inside she could hear the increasing volume of Erica's suffering, hungering to find Ariel, to find peace from the longing. But could a broken mermaid—who had no explanations to offer or passion to give—meet any of Erica's needs?

Erica sang for a beautiful woman, one she could make love to, one who would sing back. What could Erica see in her but a lined face, rough hands and ruined skin? Erica would look into her eyes and see the madness. Ariel burned with needs of her own. Erica could hardly want to . . . touch her. Might be compelled to touch her, but wouldn't . . . want to.

She held back a moan as she realized that Erica could regard her with the same horror and helpless desire that she herself had felt that morning looking at Laveena. Hating and wanting in the same breath. It was one thing to be bedded for passion without love, but quite another to be taken in desperation laced with disgust.

What was she thinking? They were not going to bed. No making love, no fucking, none of whatever anyone wanted to call it. It would be better if Erica did indeed hate her and wouldn't touch her, then the year would pass and she would be cured. That Erica would eventually die wasn't something Ariel could change.

Part of her wanted to linger forever in one of the ponds. Water was mildly soothing. But whenever she stopped moving she could only hear the echoes playing their tricks, as if she was yet in the grotto. She no sooner believed water would ease her when all the physical ache of being constantly, deeply aroused would wash over her skin. The weariness of walking made the ponds call out with promises of peace.

Her nipples were sore from standing erect. A slick of arousal seeped through her pants, and she could feel a rash starting where her wet thighs rubbed. She was an animal in heat, she thought. Crawling after her fix, wanting to get fucked and not caring how as long as the itching inside went away. Who could possibly want that? Only another animal.

Erica wouldn't want her. Erica was not an animal. But that's good, a small, quiet voice said. If Erica doesn't want you, you'll get the cure. Then she heard the vicious echo of Laveena's spite: if she does want you, then kill her and you'll still get the cure.

I will not do that, Ariel thought. *I would rather succumb to this burning desire, use mervoice to have her, give up the cure, give up my life rather than become anything like that evil, twisted bottom feeder.*

Her blood pounded in her veins, swelling her tender flesh and flushing her skin.

I am lost in this fire, with no hope of its easing. I can no longer hear any dream song except hers, which twines with such hunger and despair that I don't want to listen. It begins to match my own song, as if we sing different parts of the same tune. The song will not end and no amount of singing or listening will stop it. My prison is hers is mine.

Darkness came swiftly and with it a deepening of the chill. The country road had not yet led to civilization, though she could feel its pulse over the next set of wind-brushed hills. Her feet turned away, still seeking Erica in the rolling coastal landscape.

She had selected the left-hand route at a fork in the road several miles back. The increasing dark was not a problem—mer vision had its uses, even out of water. She was still startled, however, when her path rounded a curve and was completely blocked by a wide golden gate. It was obviously electronically locked and secure, though still decorative. The narrow bars were wide enough to peer through, but only a cat could have slipped past. She could see no house or lodgings beyond the curving drive, but Erica was there, somewhere.

The drive was gravel, but marked by clumps of weeds. What she could see of the gardens was unexpectedly wild. Bushes looked as if they had once been clipped and manicured, but more recently left to grow freely.

There was no sign or street number, just a telephone box she presumed would announce her presence to the occupants of whatever remote manor lay out of sight. She could not speak so that was useless to her. She could probably entice the gates to open, but humans and mer alike did not care for unwanted guests. Perhaps that was not a bad idea, she thought. If she could get arrested, she would be prevented by force from being with Erica.

There might be a time when she was desperate enough to try that, but she had to at least see Erica first. She had to know if it was possible to touch and not fall into bed.

She didn't know what to do about the locked gate. She waited for an hour for a car to come or go, any sign of life to offer her a legal way to get inside.

Ruefully, with what was left of her humor, she acknowledged that Ariel, Seventy-Seventh Daughter to Queen Vellia, was not equipped for this situation.

The cold worsened and fog settled around her, quieting even the sound of wind moving the branches overhead. She felt the cold, too, which surprised her. Mer swam with icebergs and relished it. It had to be the infection, the unending desire, and her ordeal in the grotto. She had been drained, and felt so empty except for the ache.

Erica was close and she could feel it. To walk away, even for the night, would take more strength than she had.

She was as imprisoned as she had been in the grotto, only this time the echoes were the song of her longing matching the song she could feel inside from Erica.

I need you, Ariel, want to be with you. To feel your touch again, to drown in your voice.

Ariel could not help but respond with her own deep wishes. *I'm here, Erica. Look for me and you will find me.*

The scuff of a shoe on the drive brought her to her feet. There was a figure in the darkness, wrapped in black.

Her body knew it was Erica.

She sprang to the gate, unable to keep herself from thrusting her hands through it. So close . . . so close. To touch . . . so close.

Out of the dark, Erica said calmly, "Go away."

Ariel wanted to call out, to beg. She did not care one whit that mer weren't supposed to beg. She would beg, if only she could use words. She stretched her arms as far as they would go, reaching. She couldn't bear being so close and not touching. How could Erica just stand there?

"I don't want you here. I don't know what you did to me, but I will have no more of it."

Ariel turned her hands palms up and slowly slid to her knees, a supplicant, pleading. Erica's words were firm and she meant what she said, Ariel could tell. But her face was in shadows, and Ariel still heard the inner turmoil and longing that was at odds with her order for Ariel to go away.

"I'm sick to death of you. Of thinking about you, wondering where you went, how you could leave me like this, addicted to you. So go."

If only she had words, Ariel could explain, could at least answer the questions. She fought down a tearful moan. *Open the gate and take me in your arms. We will both feel better for it. We have to, because feeling the way we do now is unbearable.*

Erica took a step closer. Ariel could almost make out the strong line of her nose and jaw. "Don't you have anything to say for yourself?"

Ariel shook her head violently no.

"Why are you here? Why can't you just leave me be? I was better this last little while. Getting over it finally." Erica's voice thinned with unshed tears. "You have no idea. No mercy, do you? Leave! Or I'll call the cops."

Ariel slumped back on her haunches, and held the bars of the gate in her hands. Every moment she could see Erica and not actually touch her seemed to double the agony. Her brain felt as if it was boiling.

Another scuff of shoe on the cement made her look up. Erica had moved closer, and her face was now visible in the dim light.

Ariel held in her gasp, but just barely. Erica's face was etched with pain, the hair at her temples stark white. But it was her eyes that shocked Ariel most. The sharp, tantalizing green was gone. Silver for age, silver for madness, Ariel thought, now she has my eyes and I have hers. My recklessness or Laveena's spite, what does it matter?

I should go, leave her. Let her at least believe she can overcome this. But Ariel could not make herself go.

"Why won't you leave?" Erica took another step. "Why does it hurt so much to remember you? Why does it hurt to look at you?"

Ariel could only shake her head.

"Answer me!" Erica came two steps closer, her heartbreak transmuting to anger.

Answers wouldn't comfort Erica for long. Ariel rested her forehead on the cold bars. How had she thought Erica would happily accept Ariel into her life, into her arms—and take no for an answer? She couldn't think. Her mind overflowed with images of Erica's hands on her body. Her mouth watered at the memory of Erica's wet cunt in her mouth.

The queen had said the whole point was for Ariel to break. Something was breaking. She was just a salmon. Maybe if she threw herself hard at the very thing that would destroy her she would find a way to go on, to save herself.

She rose slowly and opened her court jacket. She let it fall to the ground around her feet. She grasped the hem of the shirt and pulled it roughly over her head.

"Oh please . . . please don't." There were tears in Erica's eyes to match the choking sound in her voice. "You really don't have any mercy, do you? What do you want from me?"

The cold bit into Ariel's already chilled body. She kicked off the shoes and winced at the cold pavement. She heard Erica whimper as she unbelted the too long trousers, and another whimper as she pushed them down her hips.

She stood naked, offering only one thing as she pressed her body to the frigid bars. She extended her hands as far beyond the bars as she could reach, fighting the shivers that were making her knees threaten to buckle.

"No, no," Erica was repeated, "please no. Don't do this, please . . . I can't. I can't."

Ariel tried to say with her eyes, her offered body, her pleading hands, that she needed Erica to touch her. Touch was the only comfort they could have.

"Go away!" Erica knocked Ariel's hands down as she lunged at the gate. Ariel braced herself for Erica's strike.

Erica cried out when her fingertips touched Ariel's face. Ariel felt a wave of faintness at the effort it cost her not to scream.

Not pain . . . ecstasy.

Erica's hands cupped her face and then Erica was kissing her hungrily through the bars, her mouth nearly savage. Ariel filled her hands with Erica's hair, holding back the moans building in her throat. Her mervoice wanted to sing, but Ariel held that in as well. She touched Erica's cheeks, her neck, her shoulders. After the torture, any pleasure was welcome. After the day of infection, touching Erica was clearly the only thing that would help.

She felt Erica's hands on her breasts, fondling them where they pressed between the bars. Her pelvis arched and she longed for Erica to have her again. All her thoughts circled in a whirlpool of need until the only focus was her desire for Erica. She could not even remember what it had been like to have control over her body.

Erica's hands left the exploration of her breasts, her ribs, her hips, and in the minute it took to open the gate all the pain returned. Erica caught her hands and pulled Ariel into a full embrace, and the ecstasy came back, heady, driving, inescapable. Then Erica pushed her away.

"Get dressed."

Numbly, Ariel obeyed. Erica wasn't saying she had to go. She would do anything to stay. She dressed quickly, then looked hopefully at Erica, her heart pounding.

Erica's eyes were burning with a mixture of lust and despair. Ariel could read it easily because her own gaze matched it. Finally, Erica said, "Follow me."

"Are you hungry?"

Erica's question brought Ariel back from her intense study of Erica's home. The driveway ended at a very large house. All the windows were dark except one. A single, wan light burned over the wide double doors.

When Ariel didn't answer, Erica looked over her shoulder. For a moment Ariel could only think of that night, and Erica's face framed by the collar of her white tuxedo. The rose had been there, she knew it had been. The light flashed on the white at Erica's temples and the silver of her eyes. What did it matter, Ariel thought. Erica was infected and dying, and now she was as well.

"You haven't said a word." Erica studied her in the light over the entry. "You said plenty that night."

Ariel nodded. She remembered everything they had sung between them.

"Can you talk?"

Without thinking, Ariel truthfully nodded yes.

"You can, but you won't?"

Ariel realized then that lying would have been easier. There was so much she wanted to tell Erica, so much truth, it just hadn't occurred to her she might need to be ready to lie. It was too late to change her story, so she simply nodded.

Erica's eyes flared with sudden anger. Her nostrils flared slightly while her lip flared with contempt. "So you're somebody else's toy now, is that it? Then why are you here?"

Ariel shook her head, trying to say with her eyes that she wasn't playing a game. Perhaps doubt showed in her eyes, because she abruptly remembered the way Laveena had made her feel, like a puppet to be enjoyed.

Erica turned away, and her question did not seem directed at Ariel. "Why do I want you?"

The sound of the door swinging open echoed through the seemingly empty house. The foyer was barren of all furniture, the walls devoid of everything except the outlines of paintings no longer there. From somewhere in the dark came the solitary drip of water.

Ariel felt washed over with the memory of the grotto. If she stepped over this threshold it would be another prison, one her body would not let her leave no matter how the ground shook.

Erica turned to look at her and their silver gazes locked.

Was it pity that she felt? Or was she as weak as the queen had said, unable to resist? Weak for staying, or weak for going? Was she really thinking that she was here for Erica's sake? She should be honest with herself. Nothing she had done had ever been for Erica's sake.

Erica lowered her gaze and turned away. "Go then."

Ariel stepped inside and let the future claim her.

She drank the offered water thirstily and ate the cheese and crackers, though both tasted like sawdust. At least Erica had turned on more lights. It was the kitchen faucet she had heard dripping, but now it had stopped.

The house was quite large, and quite empty. That much was obvious. The table where they ate was so far the only place to sit that she had seen.

"Ariel."

She looked up at Erica.

"Why are you here? Drop the silent act. Whoever she is, if she treats you this way she doesn't deserve your slavery."

Ariel gave Erica a puzzled frown.

"I'm talking about this." Erica leaned across the distance that separated them and yanked up the hem of Ariel's shirt. "You didn't have these that night. Anyone who beats you like this, who cuts you—how can you stay? How can you go on playing her game?"

She shook her head, though she knew there was no way to make Erica understand any of it. Was she the queen's toy—yes, maybe so. But it was no game, it was her life.

It wasn't Erica's life, though. Erica was already doomed. At least one of them would live. You should have gone, she told herself. *You should have left. You can't save her. You can only make her hurt more.*

She opened her mouth to speak, then closed it again, shaking her head. Even if she had words she wasn't sure Erica could understand.

Erica's hand was still on her ribs, hot and shaking slightly. The fingers tightened and Ariel swallowed hard. Then Erica was pulling Ariel over to her lap, and Ariel felt drunk on the pleasure of it weaving with the memory of Erica's strength that night, the way Erica had carried her into the back, and held her against the wall.

Erica kissed her hungrily as she pushed the shirt up to expose Ariel's breasts. "I can talk for both of us, baby. I know you feel this."

Ariel nodded. It was hard to hear over the pounding of her heart.

"Do you remember my favorite word?"

Again, Ariel nodded.

"I need it. I won't have you without it."

She wanted to moan, deeply from her chest, when Erica's fingertips lightly circled her nipples, then tweaked gently. Her pelvis arched.

"I know you want this. I want it, bad. I can't get you out of my head and my entire life is gone. I know somehow it'll all be right if I can have you. Just say it, and we can go to bed."

Ariel wanted to push Erica's hands away. Wanted to push them down. Wanted to pull Erica's shirt off and feel their breasts shocking alive against each other. No sound, no climax, but everything else they could have. But did everything else matter without peaking, without their mutual song?

She didn't know how long she writhed on Erica's lap. She was soaked and aching to feel Erica's hands between her legs. Erica had buried her face in Ariel's neck, breathing hard and fast. Their chemistry had merged and was stripping away all of Ariel's resistance.

Ariel had thought nothing could match the echoes for torture, but being so close to Erica and yet not singing with her was worse. She had not thought she would survive another year in the grotto and yet an hour of Erica's chemistry was unraveling every intention. If Erica stroked her, she would use her voice. Give up her life for the pleasure of Erica's touch.

"Dear heaven, what are you?" Erica surged to her feet, tumbling Ariel to the floor. For a moment, Ariel thought Erica would kick her, but instead Erica twirled toward the door. "After what you've done to me, is one word too much to give?"

Erica did not ask her to leave. Maybe she didn't have the strength. Maybe she thought Ariel would break down. If she'd had any pride left, Ariel might have thought that pride was what kept her silent and out of Erica's bed. But she had no pride. It was fear of losing the cure that had her huddling in blankets on the chilled floor of the bedroom next to Erica's. She chose the wall closest to Erica's bed and slept little, hearing the song of Erica's dreams churning with the anguish of wanting Ariel.

At night there was Erica's song, during the day Erica's anger at Ariel's silence. She'd left pens and pads of paper for Ariel's use, and been livid when Ariel had pointedly sat on her hands. How could Erica possibly understand the subtlety of Queen Vellia's mind? No words . . . writing would not have escaped her intent.

Ariel's attempts to ease Erica's anger in other ways all failed. Erica didn't want to eat, to dance, to play. She didn't want company, not Ariel's company. Sometimes she would stay in her room all day. Then she would quit the house from dawn to dusk, prowling the grounds and the overgrown garden, always returning in a mood more foul than the one she had left in.

Deeply lonely, Ariel found herself sleeping at odd hours or sitting miserably in the garden. She would suddenly realize it had gone dark while she was maundering. One day Erica stormed past her, dropping a blanket on her lap. Only then did Ariel realize it was bitterly cold. For a long while, it was the only contact she and Erica had, and Ariel slept with the blanket every night after that. The steady pulse of her need was the only way she marked time.

She had never been truly alone. Even the echoes had been a kind of company. It was a novel experience to be studiously ignored. It hurt to feel Erica's desire, to hear her ever-continuing song, and not give way. It hurt . . . but she breathed in enough of Erica's chemistry to get through the day without weeping. Well, most days.

On a bleak, gray day that was nearly spring but felt still caught in winter, Ariel was walking the estate's perimeter fence when she made a most marvelous discovery. The walk had become a familiar one, and the gentle motion had slowly restored some of her health. She was never too far from Erica that the pain ruined the pleasure of the walk.

At the midpoint she realized she had been so depressed that morning she hadn't eaten and her body was refusing to go on much further. She cut across the middle of the small wood, thick with eucalyptus and oak, to return to the house. To her surprise, she found herself on the edge of a good-sized pond.

It was not a portal to any other waters, but there were fish. Ariel put her hands into the water and they crowded around her fingers, the little voices simple to hear. Her face ached as she smiled for the first time in weeks, but the joy quickly faded to concern. The poor things were all unhappy. The pond was choked with weeds and silt. The koi, in particular, were about to give up.

Well, ignoring Ariel was one thing, but helpless little fish! Ariel stomped her foot indignantly and marched the rest of the way to the house. She fumbled her way through several storage areas, mostly empty, and found a discarded shovel and a rake. Tools and some magic would save the fish and at least provide her with a distraction.

She was a long way from the house and she could feel that Erica was not immediately near. She stripped off her clothes and waded into the frigid water. The rake was nearly useless, she soon discovered, quickly clogging with the heavy bracken and silt. With a sigh of something that could have almost been pleasure, she submerged and blinked her eyes to adjust to water vision. Mud made it hard to see, but her hands could find weed root. They were easy to pull out of the soft bottom soil.

She worked until she was dizzy with hunger and fatigue. She waded out of the thoroughly stirred up pond and summoned the drying spell, then stepped into her clothes. In the watery afternoon light she saw that she had only cleared a quarter of the worst weeds. She left the tools and wearily walked back to the house.

The knob of the large patio door was still in her hand from closing it behind her when she heard Erica's angry voice.

"Where have you been?"

Ariel stared at her with surprise. Erica hadn't missed her in days, maybe weeks. She was about to shrug apologetically when she remembered the poor neglected koi. She tossed her head with all the regal dignity of a daughter of the queen's blood and walked pointedly toward the kitchen.

"If you leave here I won't look for you." Erica followed Ariel to the kitchen. "I spent a fortune the first time. I won't do it again."

Bring me some shells and I'll repay you, Ariel thought. When she had the cure maybe she would do just that. Obviously, Erica had once had money, but those days were past. She was about to turn back to Erica, and try to indicate in some way that she was sorry, when Erica grabbed her by the arm and spun her around.

"Stay or go, but tell me why."

The rush of pleasure from the touch of Erica's hand was so intense that Ariel couldn't focus on what Erica was saying. Her body tingled and she saw sparkles behind her eyes.

Erica shook her, hard. "Why are you doing this? Why did you show up here? You're like some drug. I'm losing my mind!"

Ariel could only nod frantically. She understood how Erica felt. She was wet again, just from Erica's touch.

"What does that mean, Ariel?" Erica pressed her against the counter. "Where's the yes I know you are dying to give me? Look at you, it's all over you."

Erica's hands cupped her breasts and Ariel arched into her. It was shockingly good.

"I should have never touched you. Not that night, not now. You want me."

Erica pulled the shirt up, baring Ariel's breasts. Her fingers traced the lines of scars that crisscrossed Ariel's torso. "These are healing," she said softly. "You don't eat enough."

Neither do you, Ariel wanted to say.

"Ariel," Erica whispered. "I want to hold you, sleep with you, it's not just fucking."

Ariel closed her eyes. Humans tended to equate sex with love—it was a counter to their guilt fetish. Erica was not in love with her.

She shuddered when Erica's fingers abruptly closed on her nipples and tugged sharply.

"Ariel, please. Why can't we have a normal life? Why can't you just say yes and we can move on?"

She wanted to laugh at Erica's foolish simplicity, but then Erica didn't know she was dying, and had no idea she held a mermaid in her arms. The irony wasn't fair to Erica. None of this was fair to Erica. The queen said humans were not their playthings, but what was this game of the queen's but toying with Erica all the more?

You can't fix it, Ariel told herself. You can't change this, you can't make anything better. The only thing you have control of is the cure.

"I want this, too." Erica's hands went around Ariel's waist and then she lifted Ariel onto the counter. "I've never been with anyone who made me feel the way you did. Like I knew all your secrets and passwords. Like I was some god reading your mind."

She nudged Ariel's legs apart, and it was all Ariel could do to keep from grinding her pelvis against Erica's stomach. The ache that never went away grew so intense that her eyes wanted to roll back in her head.

Erica grasped both of Ariel's wrists in one hand and pressed them into the cabinet above Ariel's head. She held Ariel firmly and gazed into her eyes.

"Say yes, Ariel."

Ariel's entire body shook as Erica trailed one finger slowly down her breast, then circled her nipple several times. Then she was firmly pulling on the puckered flesh, toying with the nerves that seemed to explode inside Ariel's brain.

"Say yes."

Yes was her prayer, Ariel remembered. She wanted to give herself to it, swim in it and drown. Her tides were surging. Her hips rocked to the edge of the counter and she felt that hard pressure of Erica's body there, pushing back against her own.

She was close. She clamped her lips together, though she didn't remember why it was necessary. She tried to move away, but her body screamed for her to stay.

"Say yes, and we'll make love at least once tonight, the way you said you liked to."

Ariel's breath was catching in her throat. She wanted so badly to moan.

"You want to come, don't you?"

Ariel convulsed at the suggestion, nearly pulling her wrists out of Erica's grasp. She wanted to give herself but all the reasons she should not were so confusing now.

"Just say yes, and we'll fuck for weeks. I'll lose myself in your body."

Why was yes wrong? Why was she not supposed to be with Erica? Who . . . who was she that she couldn't say yes?

She hung suspended in that moment of not knowing who she was, utterly lost in her desire. She had always wanted this. It had seemed an ideal she would never reach. She lived inside the moment, and wanted the ecstasy, the screaming, the surge of her pouring wet.

The moment seemed perfect, so why did she hurt? Why was her soul edged in sorrow and guilt?

Say yes, Ariel, yes, I need you . . .

Erica . . . Erica was touching her, wanting to take her, love her. But it wasn't real. It was a sickness. Ariel was a disease to Erica.

The moment of perfect desire was sand under the surf, washing away to nothing. Erica did not want her and without any chance for pure, clean song between them, Ariel could not remember why she had wanted to feel this way.

Erica let go of her wrists and staggered back. Only then did Ariel realize she was shaking her head no.

"Why?" Erica was as pale as the moon's light, but her eyes were hot with anger. "You want it, I want it. You're a walking fucking temptation, and I want to tear your clothes off every time I see you. Why won't you say yes?"

Ariel pulled her shirt down and buried her face in her hands. She wanted to scream, wanted to sob, but she held it all inside, caught in a whirlpool of silent grief. It was a long time before she realized Erica had left the room.

Days, then weeks, even months passed, and Erica pointedly would not stay in the same room with Ariel. If their paths crossed she quickly adjusted and it wasn't long before Ariel instinctively went the opposite direction, too. It hurt to be near Erica, hurt to be away, hurt to breathe. Hurt to move, hurt to think . . . she hurt. In her bones, in her muscles, in her heart, she hurt.

The only time she didn't hurt was when she was working in the pond. She dug out weeds until her hands ached. Communing with the little creatures was simple and undemanding. She wasn't alone, and that was what mattered.

During her exploration of the far end of the pond from where she began, she discovered a leaf-clogged pump. She knew nothing of how such things worked, but she cleaned everything she could reach. A search revealed the controls concealed inside what appeared to be a solid rock. To her delight, the pump gurgled into action. Moments later, a small, musical waterfall cascaded down what she had thought was merely decorative rock.

Within a few days the water had cleared to the point of being able to watch the gleaming fish dart back and forth. She visited the pond every day, hunkering down with at least her hand below the surface. Some days she stripped and waded. It wasn't deep enough to swim, but she could float and twist. It became her small slice of something like home.

The days were growing longer, and most afternoons the fog lifted, allowing for warming sunshine. The nights remained black with the frustrated song she shared with Erica. Ariel didn't know how to break Erica's anger. She wasn't even sure she deserved to try. What had she brought Erica except pain? What could she ever offer Erica besides unwelcome news and, eventually, an eternal good-bye?

On a bright afternoon with the waterfall tinkling in a light breeze, the overhead sun lanced into the pool and the surface shimmered with a light Ariel recognized. She had not thought this pond, far from the sea and so darkened with mud, could ever be healthy enough to act as a window. She let the surface still, then leaned slowly over it, her mouth near enough to kiss the surface. She breathed out, slowly, and below her an image spread.

She saw swimming colors and a barrage of faces—Caliba, who was never far from her thoughts, and some of her sisters. They all shimmered with gaiety and light, no worries, no cares. The breeze made the images waver for a moment, then the spell broke completely.

After that, she was at the pond every day from the moment the sun came into position until it faded. The glimpses of home were brief, but she felt, finally, she could bear this year. If Erica was too far away, Ariel ached to know where she was. If she was too close, Ariel burned to be touched. But this middle range they had found left Ariel with some control, while memories of home helped warm the cold inside her. Only at night, in closer quarters, did the physical longing surge up, leaving Ariel's thighs perpetually wet.

≪≫

Ariel thought it must be nearing summer, because sunflowers broke ground in the garden, and reached for the light. They reminded her of anemones, so brilliant and pleasing. She caressed their silky petals as she wandered her way to the pond. The day was warm. Yes, it must be summer, she thought.

When the sun moved over the pond, the visions from home were spangled with light and laughter. Ariel longed to touch or hear, to at least laugh. She watched hungrily until the spell broke, wondering if anyone there ever remembered her. More than a little depressed, Ariel slipped out of the baggy sweat clothes Erica had lent her, and slipped into the water.

She floated on her back, listening to the faint clicks and whistles of the fish happily searching the pond for bits of food. The sun was warm on her breasts and face. Smiling to herself in an unusual flash of innocent pleasure, she turned several slow somersaults in the water. Easy and graceful, she let her hands touch the bottom while her feet waved happily above the surface in the sun.

A concussion hit the water and Ariel flipped skyward in surprise. When her eyes flicked back to air vision she saw Erica standing next to the pond, a rock in one hand.

"What are you doing?"

Ariel just stared. What the kelp did it look like she was doing?

"You were under forever."

With a silent sigh, Ariel swam toward her clothes. She frowned, annoyed. With Erica here she couldn't use a drying spell. She'd be wet all the way back to the house.

"Is this where you've been hiding?"

Ariel shrugged.

Erica knelt by the water's edge. "I thought the fish would all have died by now. The pump broke and I didn't have the money to fix it. Smartest thing I ever did with my inheritance was pay cash for this place, but . . ." She stared down into the water. "The fish are beautiful. Thank you."

The compliment was welcome, and Ariel wished there could be

more. But the infection they both suffered was the only reason Erica wanted to be close. Ariel wanted to go home, go back to hunting with her friends and enjoying the life of the first circle. She only hung on Erica's every word because of the infection too. It had nothing to do with the gentleness in Erica's voice, or the way, sometimes in an unguarded moment, Erica looked at her with something more than hunger.

Ariel climbed out some distance from where Erica was kneeling, but realized that she would have to walk past Erica, naked, to get to her clothes.

"They are beautiful, like you."

Ariel flushed, but only nodded. She gathered her things and hurried toward the house, not stopping to put anything on. Erica was too close and Ariel could feel her pulse starting to throb. Control was easier if she didn't fully inhale Erica's chemistry.

Erica was following her and Ariel ran, her hair streaming water down the backs of her calves. She couldn't be naked with Erica.

"Ariel, please wait. I won't touch you."

Erica's plea was so earnest that Ariel had to stop, even though it wasn't Erica's control she was worried about.

Erica stood a scant foot from her. "I can't take this. I can't even look at those fish and not think about your skin. Everything I see is you."

Please, Ariel wanted to whisper. Then she asked herself, "Please what?"

"I've waited, waited for something to happen. Waited for you to say yes. You want to, I can feel it. God knows I want you. I will *never* forget that way you responded to me. No woman has ever been that way for me, and I don't know how you did it. You made me feel like you were saying yes to *me*, not the rich hot butch who knew how to fuck. Your yes was real. Real."

Ariel nodded. She had wanted Erica as much as Erica had wanted her.

"I want you, not just in bed. Not just coming on my hands

though . . . God, Ariel, I want that too. But that night you smiled at me, and spoke so softly. Even though the sex got hard, we weren't hard."

Ariel closed her eyes. She knew what Erica meant.

"Ariel . . . even if we don't . . . I feel good when I hold you. I feel better."

Ariel opened her eyes and realized that Erica had gotten even thinner. She seemed all eyes and sinew. What was Erica asking for? Comfort?

Trembling, Ariel told herself that comfort was something she could give. They both wanted more, but comfort wouldn't lose Ariel the cure. And it might ease Erica's time. Until that moment Ariel had not seen past the moment when the cure was unleashed in her body. She supposed she had thought she'd go home. And leave Erica to do what? She would stay, Ariel decided, stay with Erica, until it was over.

She slowly lifted one hand and brushed her fingertips the length of Erica's jaw.

Erica sighed, and gently pulled Ariel into her arms. "I just need to hold you."

Ecstatic fire seemed to lick over Ariel's body. The feel of Erica against her, holding her, was so welcome and so needed.

"It's okay, Ariel. I'm not asking for yes right now. Just this."

Ariel ached to say yes. She told herself that the moment she was cured she would say yes. She would stay with Erica until Erica's ending. Was that pity? Compassion? Erica's pain was real, and Ariel had been the unwitting cause. Trembling with the effort to be gentle, she kissed Erica softly on the lips.

They stood like that, in the dappled sunlight, for some time. Ariel knew the tears on her cheeks weren't just her own.

"Thank you," Erica finally murmured. "I don't understand, but I feel better."

They walked toward the house in silence. In the kitchen, Ariel paused to pull on the clothes, then filled the tea kettle.

"So, you do some sort of water acrobatics?"

She nodded and smiled. It was somewhat close to the truth, close enough that her eyes sparkled.

"I thought you were drowning. I can't swim. I was too busy with horses when I was growing up."

Ariel looked a question and Erica seemed to make up her mind. "Bring your tea into my room."

Ariel had only glimpsed the inside of Erica's large bedroom. There was a sparse seating area with a settee and a low table crowded with books and papers. A massive desk with cubbyholes and a computer dominated another corner of the room. The bed, its four thick posts devoid of curtains or tapestries, was also massive, but it was a perfect compliment to large picture windows facing the woods. In the distance there was either fog or sea, she couldn't tell which.

She tore her gaze from the bed, too easily picturing herself spread out on it, and Erica's naked body on top of hers.

Erica set several albums down on the cluttered table, and Ariel joined her on the settee. "This is Algonquin, isn't she a beauty?"

Ariel studied the photograph of a very young Erica. She was dwarfed by the large chestnut, but her face beamed with confidence. Ariel outlined the splash of white on the horse's head and nodded. A beautiful creature, but not as lovely as the shining child that stood next to her.

They turned the pages and Erica let the stories pour out of her. "Dressage isn't so hard, it just takes a good horse and patience. I loved going to competitions, and I had so many friends. I met an English princess and an Egyptian sheik, and it all seemed so charmed."

The light outside faded as Erica showed Ariel her life. She'd been everywhere in the world, and her voice was mixed with fond memory and an edge of unhealed grief.

"I think I would be in a different place if Daddy hadn't died when he did. Mom sent me back to boarding school after the funeral and I guess I thought nothing would change. Then she got remarried, and that asshole . . . Dad's money was in trust from his great-grandfather. When he died the trust moved on to my brother. He was supposed to provide for mom and me, but he didn't like her new husband. Don't blame him. The jerk spent mom's money like it was water. But when my brother found out I was gay, that was enough excuse to cut me off too. So he kept it all."

Erica's voice was laden with annoyance, but not true anger. "I was fine, because I hadn't wasted the education I got, and I went into international consulting and kept up my riding and my girlfriends . . . and life was good. I had an inheritance from Dad and I bought this house because I'd never lose it. No matter what, I'd have it."

She shut the last album abruptly. "And I've kept it." Her eyes were shadowed, and the tender smiles were gone. "You can't take away a person's primary residence, no matter how much it costs."

Ariel didn't understand what Erica meant, but she could hear that there was an untold story. She gently touched the back of Erica's hand.

"What?" Erica look at her in the low light for a long moment, then shook away Ariel's touch. "I did think you were real, Ariel. That you wanted *me*, not Erica, horse goddess and heiress. But I don't know what you really wanted."

Maybe there was too much truth in her eyes, Ariel thought, as Erica suddenly snapped, "A good fuck, wasn't it? That's all you were after. I was just a stud."

Ariel wanted to retort that Erica had been looking for the same thing. She tried to say it with her eyes. *You were just there for pussy, for someone to coo Yes and Please in your ear.*

"Don't give me that look, like I'm to blame. Okay, fine, sure, I wanted to fuck somebody. And I fucked you, you sure liked it enough. I'd have called you again. I'd have wanted to see if we could keep on feeling that good together. We were too easy and too fabulous together for a one-night stand. But that's all I would have been to you, huh? A fuck, and good-bye? So don't give me that look."

Ariel turned her face away. Suddenly the proposition that mer deserved human song in exchange for allowing them the surface of the seas didn't seem so persuasive. Don't feel for them, don't pity, don't love, the queen cautioned. Just use their bodies and leave them singing for you, as if bodies and souls and hearts were not connected.

"Doesn't anything get through to you? Don't you feel me?"

Ariel nodded, and turned to face Erica again. She cupped Erica's face, trying to say that maybe she didn't understand everything, but she was still sorry.

Erica pushed her roughly back onto the settee. "I don't need your tender pity. That isn't what I want from you."

Erica yanked down Ariel's pants, her voice choked with bitterness. "I had a life before you. I had dreams that weren't hell. All I wanted that night was to remember how good it was to hear yes. To be wanted. You wanted me."

Ariel frantically nodded yes. Sea mother help me, Ariel thought, I can't say no. She's the one with all the self-control. Weak human? Erica was stronger than Ariel was. Erica tossed Ariel's pants on the floor and Ariel spread her legs. She was all yes.

Erica leaned over her, pinning Ariel's shoulders to the cushions. The crotch of her pants ground into Ariel's exposed flesh, setting off explosive shocks on Ariel's skin.

Erica gazed down at her, watching Ariel respond to the pressure of her hips. "Just say yes, Ariel. I have to have yes. Say yes and I will fuck you for days." *I want to fill you completely, touch every good place until you scream from pleasure. Please, Ariel . . .*

Ariel wrapped her legs around Erica's hips. It felt so good. She was very close and thought hysterically that she no longer cared about the cure. She opened her mouth to give Erica what she asked for.

But even as the word formed on her tongue, Erica was letting her go. "Why do I want you? Your yes was nothing but a lie."

Ariel sat up slowly, her head swimming, and realizing how close she had been to losing it all.

"I'm sorry, Ariel, I shouldn't have touched you like that. Please . . . please go."

Ariel picked up her pants, aware that the smell of her arousal was plain in the air. The only reason Ariel would make it to the cure was because Erica was strong. Ariel would live and Erica would die.

She slept against the wall nearest Erica's bed, dreaming of her hair strewn over Erica's long, lean body. They danced and writhed together in every imaginable, twisting position. They sang freely of their passion, planned more nights of pleasure and days of laughter. Ariel turned mountains of shells into a waterfall of golden coins and Erica galloped along the beach where Ariel communed with the sea. Then a cloud passed over the ocean, and the ground trembled. Erica's strength was gone and Ariel's song of love turned to a siren's lament.

Their routine altered after that. Their daylight contact was fleeting. Erica stayed in her room, even when summer heat stifled the air. But at night she would wander the house and find Ariel, and hold out her hand. Ariel went with her and they would move together across Erica's bed, never touching where they ached most to be touched. Their legs would tangle, their pelvises rock, and the kisses—needy, bruising, dueling kisses—seemed to last for hours. Erica would finally push Ariel away and fall into restless sleep. Ariel would doze lightly, waiting for the least sign that Erica wanted to hold or be held again. It was a long way from comfort, but she could think of nothing else that would make either of them feel better.

She begs me to say yes. Any other lover would have just taken me by now. My eyes say what my mouth won't. I'm not sure I care about the cure. The days are so long when she won't let me near. And these nights are a torture beyond the grotto. Every inch of my skin is aware that she is within my grasp. My every thought tells me to touch, to take. I am supposed to break, but I already feel so broken I do not remember what being whole felt like. Always the thought torments me that I will find wholeness, but only in her arms.

Wind blew red and gold leaves from the trees, and their soft fall against the glass reminded Ariel of the whisper of surf on sand. It was a chilly fall night, but the bed was hot from the hours of Erica making love to her until both of them could hardly breathe. She pushed Ariel's hands away when Ariel tried to touch her back.

"I only want one thing from you, Ariel. Say yes."

Ariel could easily see Erica's silver eyes in the dark. She lifted her hand again, only to have Erica press it back to the mattress. Ariel found herself struggling, then she pushed Erica hard and tried to feel her breast through the T-shirt Erica rarely removed. Erica slapped her hand away and then Erica was on top of her, her anger right at the surface.

Ariel arched her back with a noiseless moan that shook through her whole body. Erica's hand was stroking her swollen, aching flesh, playing in the folds and slick, endless wet, just as she had that night.

"This is what you want, isn't it? I ought to just give it to you! You like it rough? I can do that."

Ariel braced herself, holding back her whimper.

I want to fuck you to pieces. I want you Ariel. You're everywhere, everything. Tell me what you want. Erica's song was edged with desperate violence, and Ariel felt a brush of fear. Ariel knew she flirted with losing the cure, and flirted with Erica's losing control. If Erica snapped and did fuck Ariel, would it mean losing the cure was Erica's fault? Is nothing ever your fault, she asked herself. Would it be just another unfairness, if Erica doesn't stop this time?

Erica rolled off of her, her breath coming in ragged sobs. "I scared you, I'm sorry."

Ariel crawled across the bed to hold Erica, not understanding anything except that it hurt parts of her that had never been touched before to see Erica cry so helplessly.

Erica shook her off after a few minutes. "Don't touch me right now. I might not stop next time. I don't care if that's how you want it. I won't do that again."

Ariel cupped Erica's face and turned her so they were looking into each other's eyes. She shook her head, raised her eyebrows, tried to say she didn't understand, but she wanted to.

"My life is running down a drain. I can feel it. The night I met you was the last time I felt alive."

Ariel rearranged herself and pulled Erica's head into her lap. Her fingers played lightly over the white temples.

Erica sighed deeply. "When you have nothing but money and everyone thinks you live like some prince, nobody expects you to be good at anything but partying. So that was my goal in life. To be a good party. I liked women and I liked sex, and so along the way I decided to be a good fuck."

Ariel nodded with a tender look she hoped said she understood. What other goal in her long life had she ever had except to be fun?

Erica didn't seem to notice. "This girl I picked up in New York was wild and I'd been to a few clubs and seen the serious players do their thing. Maybe she thought I was a serious player. Maybe . . . I don't know. There were things I wouldn't do. She begged, and begged, and one night finally started a fight. I don't mean yelling. I mean with her fingernails. I didn't want to hurt her. But that's what she wanted."

Ariel knew the sound of a bitter ending. Erica's voice was laden with it.

"I got angry when she clawed me again and I just lost it. She kept screaming she wanted it and so I fucked her, mad and half-drunk and holding her down. I swear, I swear to you I thought that was what she wanted. I didn't know different until the letter arrived from this lawyer she'd hired. Maybe it was all meant to be a scam. But she had a doctor's statement saying she'd been sexually abused, and they had a sample of my blood. The scratches from her nails, she'd clawed my hand and some got smeared on her . . . somewhere down there. And I'd go to jail unless I paid. And then I'd pay anyway."

Ariel knew about ironic fate. She knew all about it. And she understood now more than ever how words sometimes lacked all clarity.

"I should have just left. Somehow it got out even though she was the one doing the hitting. I know I shouldn't have fucked her because I was angry. Even if that was what she wanted, wanted me to lose control. I'd always asked her before we did anything rough. That night—I just don't know. Maybe she thought she'd hold me up for money. Maybe she tried to say no and I didn't hear her. I play it back in my head, Ariel. I hear the echoes of her crying and moaning, and it's like torture."

Ariel closed her eyes. A single mistake, a lapse in better judgment. It was all too familiar. What if, that night, she had realized that even with a rose, Erica had to be a lesbian? She ought to have seen it, and avoided her. She ought to have worried regardless of roses and games about inadvertently infecting any human woman. It wasn't blameless to be ignorant that she was a lesbian—dying was dying and dead was dead. How often had she joked with her hunting friends about their above-sea lovers being *only* humans?

"She got her money. My lawyers said the evidence was good, and we paid. That was the last of my inheritance money and everything I'd saved working. I had to sell my horses, Ariel, all of them. I didn't care about the paintings and the Chinese rugs and the cars and the shit like that. But I lost my horses."

Erica rolled off of Ariel's lap and buried her face in the mattress. "And then after I thought she was out of my life, and I'd settled my last few investments and decided to live quietly, I went out on New Year's Eve. I thought I'd find someone willing and sweet, who would say yes, and we'd have a really good time. I needed a clear, honest yes. Everything was going to get better."

Ariel stroked Erica's back and felt the tight, knotted muscles through the shirt. She circled them lightly, hoping to ease Erica's discomfort. She knew the rest of the story.

"Then I met you. I thought we were great together. It was just getting good. We . . . fit. We clicked. I felt whole again, when I was inside you. Something was right about the way we moved together. And then you ran away."

She rolled out from under Ariel's hands. "Why? Why did you leave me? Why can't I stop thinking about you? I spent what money I made working on detectives. Then I just couldn't work anymore, I couldn't focus on anything but you. I would try to follow conversations and get lost. The money ran out and I lived on selling the remaining paintings, one by one. Where did you go? Why are you here? I feel cursed, Ariel. Like if I let myself want something it's always taken away."

Erica's suffering was so much like Ariel's in the grotto that tears spilled down Ariel's cheeks. Erica touched them, and put her wet fingers to her lips, tasting Ariel's salt.

"Tears for me? I don't want them, Ariel. I would like to stop feeling like I'm the primary amusement of some twisted, lesser god."

Ariel swallowed hard and wanted to answer, wanted somehow to comfort Erica's confusion. For a moment Erica looked as if she could read Ariel's regret, but then she turned her face away. "I want to sleep. Could you—go in the other room tonight?"

Ariel left in silence, but she heard Erica's tears, streaming in the dark toward a bleak sunrise. *Ariel, Ariel . . . why . . .*

The seasons turned again, and Ariel noticed that Erica's shoulders had become like razors. Her powerful legs had lost all their tone and even if she'd had the chance, Ariel wasn't sure Erica could have stayed on a moving horse. She hardly ate now. She grew more tired, and sometimes asked Ariel to nap with her during the day, to spoon and hold her. "It hurts but it doesn't. I feel better with you here."

Ariel understood that only too well. It might have been comforting, even, if she hadn't also heard the truth in Erica's song. *I need her near me, I don't know why. I hate this feeling, and I dread every new day. Ariel, I want you, say yes for me . . .*

Winter sunlight was infrequent, and her glimpses of home grew rare. Caliba was always at a party or a gathering. Ariel thought she saw signs that she had caught the queen's eye. Her clan would be happy. The glimpses left her feeling sad and empty. Didn't anyone miss her? Had they only liked Ariel because of what Ariel provided in the way of fun?

Ariel's daily walk to the pond and a nightly ritual of a long hot bath were her only comforts outside of Erica's arms. A dash of bath salts she had found in the bathroom cupboard, and carefully eked out, made it something like the bathing pools of home. She missed home, missed the ease of that life, all the things that made being mer so fortunate. And yet as she pictured that life she could pick out no particular day that was better than another. She could recall only moments of passion, and nearly all of those had been bedding human women. Had she ever really belonged in that easy life? It felt all wrong now, and she wasn't sure she could go back and not feel the ill-fit of that life against her skin.

She submerged herself in the water, breathing easily. It felt good to use her mer lungs. She opened her eyes to watch the shimmer of the water's surface, so beguiling. From her earliest breath she had asked to find out what was on the other side of that shimmer. When she got out of the tub she'd dry herself and join Erica in bed. Erica said she liked Ariel's hot, soft body at her back. She said it made the winter go away.

The light changed and she realized that Erica had come into the bathroom. She'd never done that before. Ariel hastily lifted her head out of the water, breathing hard, as if she'd had to hold her breath. She wasn't prepared for Erica's hands cupping her face, pulling her further up for a desperate, wet kiss.

"I can't do this, Ariel. Please say yes, please."

There were two days left of the year. She would say yes in two days, yes to anything Erica wanted. She tried to say that with her mouth, her eager tongue, but how could Erica understand?

Erica was lifting her out of the water, pulling Ariel's warm, wet body into a full embrace. Two more days, Ariel told herself, even as she arched against Erica with her body's perpetual yes. Two more days.

"I can't," Erica repeated, over and over. "I won't."

Ariel put her arms around Erica's shoulders as she kissed her throat. Erica usually pulled back by now, but she sighed instead and cupped the back of Ariel's head, guiding her down to the breasts that had hardened under the now wet T-shirt.

Her heart hammering with desire, Ariel bit the prominent nipples and reveled in Erica's moan.

Then Erica was pushing her away, getting to her feet. "We're going out. You like to play games, so that's what we'll do. God knows I should have done this when you showed up. How could I have put up with this for nearly a year? It's like time has no meaning when I'm with you." She indicated a bundle of clothes on the counter. "Those are for you. Relics of a past."

Ariel took the proffered clothes, and just didn't know what to think. Erica rarely left the house, and when she did it was on foot. Groceries were delivered and no other tradespeople had ever called. She hadn't thought a human could live so disconnected from her world.

"I don't have my millions any longer, but there's enough for a night on the town. Get dressed."

Ariel waited for Erica to leave before she explored the clothes. The very short black skirt was made of leather, as short as the one she had worn that night. The blouse was sheer. The hose were held up by a garter belt that was the only undergarment. The shoes were a mere strap of leather over stilettos so high she was on tiptoe.

Below sea she'd wear less and think nothing of it. She'd accept compliments and roving touches without a blush. What she displayed she liked to have noticed and appreciated. But above sea, it was different. This outfit made her feel powerless. Did Erica want her hurt? Not that she blamed Erica for being angry and bitter. She thought that Erica had begun to suspect that she was sick.

And how about you, Ariel, she thought. Her cheeks were hollow, her skin a sickly pale shade, like a flower grown without enough light. Her hair had never recovered from the grotto and if she looked close, she could see flecks of white at her temples. She was sick, too, and could feel something she never had before: the breath of mortality. It frightened her. She should live another thousand years. Even if she did, she would feel every year's passing from now on.

She made her way to the foyer, her heart pounding with uncertainty. Erica looked her up and down without smiling, but offered a calf-length black overcoat to shelter her from the night air. It matched the one Erica wore. All Ariel could see of Erica was her long legs encased in soft leather trousers.

A cab was waiting. They drove down the wandering country lane, then turned away from the sea, crossing the last set of hills into the glowing lights of human civilization. In a few minutes they emerged from a tunnel and the dazzling panorama of San Francisco sparkled on the other side of the straits. Ariel had hunted more than once under the graceful bridge they traveled over, but she'd never experienced it this way. She would have liked to look more openly at the night lights, but Erica's dark mood was frightening her.

They stopped at a club not unlike The Pisces, but the crowd outside wasn't the effervescent party gathering from that fateful New Year's. Brooding silence was broken only by the pulse of low-toned music. Women in leather walked in varying shows of power, muscles flexing in gloved hands or heavy boots mastering the pavement.

"If you can't say yes to me, maybe you can to one of them. Somebody has control of you and maybe someone here can break it. It's been nearly a year, Ariel. We're strangers and yet we're not. I don't know why you won't talk to me, why you won't let us have what we both want." Erica laughed, and it reminded Ariel of the queen's cruel smile. "There are women here who won't care that you don't talk."

Ariel was shaking as she got out of the cab. She had often fantasized about a night like this, about giving herself completely in a way other mer seemed not to understand. But reality was different from fantasy. She had always loved sex with human women but now she was scared. She didn't understand what Erica hoped to have happen.

Was Ariel supposed to beg for it to stop or to begin? Would a yes torn out of her in pain truly satisfy Erica?

Erica wouldn't look at Ariel as they crossed the sidewalk to the club door. Inside, her coat was taken away and Erica roughly ushered her deeper into the club. The music was painfully loud. Ariel just kept looking into Erica's face. What did Erica want her to do? Erica didn't know Ariel's life was at stake. But you knew, she reminded herself, you knew when you met Erica that her life could be at risk. You didn't care. Why should Erica care about your life?

How much was she going to have to pay tonight for the suffering Erica had endured? Would it make any difference at all? I'll do it, she thought desperately. I'd do anything if I thought it would help her. But this place is a mistake.

The first woman Erica let get close to them never looked at Ariel's face. Her long red hair was lightly touched and approved. She was just flesh and wet, an object. Fantasies had held moments like these, and it had seemed what she wanted. What could she do? Without mervoice she couldn't manipulate any of them, either. She had no weapons here. She realized, then, she was as close to being human as she had ever been.

It was terrifying.

Erica was nodding and they were getting up, looking at Ariel expectantly. Ariel began to shake her head, then pull back, but Erica was stronger. With Erica's body straining against hers Ariel flashed back to the club, to that night. She wanted Erica, not a stranger.

Their struggling hiked up her skirt and Ariel felt another pair of hands on her, grasping her hips. She was flipped around and the woman taking them to the back stared down into Ariel's exposed crotch.

"She's hot for it, isn't she? There's really only one way to get a firecat like this under control."

The open-handed slap across her face caught Ariel by surprise. She fell to her knees, stunned. Her fear catalyzed to anger and she let her magic surge. She would use her mervoice if she had to. She'd rather die with Erica than let anyone abuse her. She hadn't said yes to this but she was sure as kelp going to make it understood that she was saying no.

In that moment, Ariel realized she did have some control over what happened to her. She had choices she had ignored. Nothing in her life was decreed. She would not be made even more of a victim.

She began to rise, but Erica stood protectively over her, shouting in the other woman's face, "I told you not to hurt her! That wasn't the deal."

"You told me she liked it hard and you wanted to hear her scream, asshole. Don't waste my time because you can't stomach the scene."

Erica lowered her hands and Ariel saw a tremor run over her body. "You're right, this was a mistake." She held a hand down to Ariel, who scrambled to her feet.

"Don't ever bring your fucking face back in here, got it?"

Erica nodded tightly and Ariel moved in a daze toward the exit. She shivered even after the coat was around her shoulders, and the condition only worsened when they were outside. They walked toward a busy thoroughfare where Erica successfully waved down a cab.

The silence between them wasn't so much angry as it was bleak. Erica stared out the window. Ariel tried to distract herself with the lights of the city, then the graceful arc of the Golden Gate Bridge. Yes, she thought, she'd swum under it, had looked up at the pleasure craft and ferries, heard the laughter, and she'd wanted to join that world.

She could not be less than she was. Yet it had never crossed her mind that she could be more than she had been. She was mer, but was that all?

"Did you want to look at the bridge for a bit?"

Erica had noticed Ariel's craning for a better view. Ariel wasn't sure if Erica really meant the offer, but after a moment she nodded. She wanted to see it with Erica and wasn't sure there'd be another chance.

Erica paid the driver to wait and they walked slowly along the brightly lit span. The wind was biting but the view in all directions was breathtaking. Ariel could feel the sea moving hundreds of feet below her. The sea sang to the bridge, the bridge to the wind. It was deeply comforting. She lifted her face to the brief hint of mist.

Erica touched her face gently and Ariel felt a surprising wave of peace. The tenderness in Erica's touch was equally unexpected, and she turned to look at Erica, her eyes shimmering with unshed tears.

Erica tried to smile, leaned to kiss her, then burst into wracking sobs.

Ariel had thought human women only lost their essence during the height of sex, but Erica fell to her knees, surrendering to her grief. Arms wrapped around her stomach, she rocked as she cried. Ariel knelt on the ground in front of her and offered her shoulder, but she wasn't sure that Erica knew it was her.

All my fault, Ariel thought. I set the tidal wave in motion, though it was never my intent.

"I thought I was crazy. I hated you." Erica wiped her face with her hands while her shoulders continued to shake. "I thought we wanted the same thing, that magic yes. All I had to do was figure out how to get you to say it for me again. And everything would be fixed."

Ariel nodded. Yes, they both wanted to lose themselves again, get lost together. Humans made such noise about love, but it seemed to matter nothing without trust. Maybe they were both infected with each other, but Ariel no longer believed that was why she trusted Erica. It had grown over nights in Erica's arms, of living with Erica's honesty. Even when Ariel gave all the wrong signals, Erica had kept to what she felt was right: Ariel's yes.

"Who is she? What did she do to you? Why are you still her prisoner after a year of being away from her? I've waited . . . and waited . . . and hoped. And teased you until I thought my body would explode. *I don't understand!*"

Tears trickled down Ariel's cheeks. This day was nearly done, and tomorrow night, seconds after midnight, she could explain it all. But

Erica seemed to need answers now and Ariel had no way to give them.

Erica cupped Ariel's face, her hands hot with tears. "I saw your face in the club, Ariel. You're not into that scene, so I don't understand why you won't talk. Why you won't say yes and let me help you!"

Ariel felt a pang of confusion, a feeling that something wasn't as she expected. What had she brought Erica besides pain and suffering?

"I know you hurt, Ariel. I know how much. I just want to make it better for you. You don't have to love me back. But at least let me love you. Just say yes."

Silver on silver, their gazes locked and Ariel felt herself falling into Erica's depths. Little humans, scratching the surface of the world, puny voices and souls, they have nothing to offer mer. Ariel had always thought those were lies. She didn't think humans were little, and she proved it by desiring and admiring their sex.

Until that moment, looking into the shining reality of Erica's inner self, Ariel realized she had never seen Erica for all that she was. She had thought Erica incapable of anything useful but sex.

"Ariel, please, let me help."

Ariel staggered to her feet. She understood none of this, she thought hysterically. How could Erica feel that way? If Erica knew she was dying and Ariel had been the one to infect her, Erica would never want her, never want to help her.

Ariel didn't deserve that kind of commitment. She was a vapid, empty party girl, with no direction in her long life, no more than any of her kind. They had been born with gifts and guarded them jealously. Humans didn't deserve the benefits of mer? Maybe it was the other way around. Maybe mer didn't deserve what humans could give so freely.

Ariel backed away, shaking her head. She couldn't watch Erica die. Neither could she take any more from Erica than she had. Erica didn't need Ariel. That Ariel needed Erica was the reason Ariel had come to her. It had always been about what Ariel wanted. Never about Erica.

She could leave, she realized abruptly. She really could. She didn't want to hurt Erica anymore, and so found the will to go. After nearly a year, what she wanted no longer mattered. She could try to do the right thing, finally, and leave Erica in peace.

She walked away, not toward the cab, but toward the city. Erica did not deserve to be burdened.

"Ariel, please. Don't go."

She looked back. Erica had risen and was clutching the bridge railing, seemingly dizzy. Ariel wanted to say she was sorry, but was actually glad she could not. It was utterly inadequate.

"I can't . . . I can't lose you again."

With every step Ariel ached more, but she made herself walk on. Weak fool, she cursed herself. *She lived without you for a year, and you lasted hardly a day before you crawled to her. Let the queen send me back to the grotto, I'll laugh all the way there.*

She only turned back because she heard a shout of alarm.

Before she could also cry out, Erica flung herself from the top of the railing, and her body plummeted toward the black onyx of the ocean's surface.

Ariel ran to the place where Erica had let go, shoving aside the onlookers who had tried to grab Erica back to safety.

She didn't stop at the railing. She called her magic and flew over the barrier, spreading her body on the wind.

Part 4

She fell, it seemed, for hours, surrounded by wind, mist, and dark broken only by the glitter of stars. Magic spread her thinly over the vapor, and she experienced briefly what it meant to be a bird.

The sea rushed toward her as the desperate magic dissolved, and she knew then what it was to be a stone. The shocking cold of the water claimed her with a violent, numbing blow. For moments she could not breathe, could not tell up from sideways in the black.

But she could hear Erica's song, ululating through the water like the lament of whales. Erica was alive, but the song was fading.

Ariel swam toward the song. She thought it was down. Every joint in her body felt wrenched, but she pressed on, deeper, where it was cold and the current was merciless.

Ariel ... Ariel ...

When she saw a flash of silver she knew she had found Erica.

Erica's eyes were open but vacant. She didn't struggle as they sank into the close, chilled depths.

Ariel breathed in the sea and exhaled into Erica's mouth, sharing air and life. She stripped them of useless shoes and the heavy coats, shared air again, and then used Erica's trousers to tie Erica to her.

They belonged nowhere, not together, not apart. She could not let Erica die this way.

Why save her, the old echoes argued. She is going to die anyway. She's close—she jumped because she can feel it. You know she's dying. This might be best. Another day and you will be cured. Let her go. This is quick, nearly painless, she's nearly gone as it is. If she dies then you will certainly have the cure. You could go home. You should have killed her when you arrived, and been sure of it. She is *just* a human, after all.

Shut up, Ariel wanted to scream. For a moment the current was so strong and the cold so intense that the insidious voice tempted her. She could just let go. There was no one to know. Erica *had* jumped, and maybe it was better this way. She could go home, back to her old life.

Ariel began to swim, her strokes desperate against the fierce current. Erica was going to die anyway, and Ariel could not fix that. But she could save Erica now, and in a day at least answer Erica's questions. She owed Erica answers. It was only fair, only right. She didn't want Erica to die.

She made little headway against the constrained sea that poured through the narrow straits separating bay and ocean. Erica was a dead weight and sharing air left Ariel dizzy. She swam, holding Erica against her, in black waters, alone and cold. There was no brother orca this time, no little fish or sky mother to guide her.

She is human, and worthy of life, worthy of my protection. Any emotion becomes a bond, something new. And with that I can change. I can be what I wasn't, all from caring for her, for wanting to be with her. I gave her suffering and she gave me back love. She does not deserve to die.

Ariel's hands and feet were numb before she realized that swimming had grown easier. The tide had changed. It was as if the sea mother took pity, though why was beyond Ariel's reckoning. She did not deserve such mercy, but Erica did. A current bolstered her weary strokes, and when she had to rest, to breathe for both of them, Ariel felt held up by calm waters.

The beach was sharp with small rocks, and even though she was unconscious, Erica moaned as Ariel dragged her over the stones and out of the water. She had reached the same small cove where she had come ashore in her search for Erica. Ariel fought back a moan of despair. They were hours from help. Erica was blue with cold and could not walk. Ariel hardly noticed that her confusion and worry about Erica's safety was louder in her blood than the infection.

Think, Ariel. You are not a salmon, think!

She used some of her strength on a drying spell and immediately felt better. She looked at Erica's inert body, and wondered why it wouldn't work for her as well. Ariel had never heard of mer ever using anything but protective magic against a human, but she now heartily believed that she knew far less about humans than she had ever suspected. She pulled Erica against her and invoked the spell again, giving it more power. To her delight—and relief—it worked. Erica was dry. Another spell for warmth and Erica's skin began to lose its blue cast. Perhaps, Ariel mused, that was why Erica had survived the fall. Some of Ariel's magic had caught her as well, easing the impact with the water.

She needed to get Erica home, fill her stomach with something hot. She seemed so fragile now. Where once Ariel had felt small next to Erica, now she felt, if not larger, certainly stronger. Moving on land was not easy, however, and the prospect of carrying Erica anywhere was daunting.

She had magic she could have used all along, she reminded herself, but she'd been selfish and helpless, thinking only of the next minute, the next hour. She had not lost her magic, she scolded herself, but she'd obviously lost every ounce of sense.

There was no help to be had above sea, and she could not carry Erica. Leaving Erica for a moment, Ariel waded into the water. The tide eddied around her calves as she thought only of Erica's limp form and how desperately she did not want Erica to die.

When a small mouth nudged her foot she nearly yelped in surprise, but she recognized the touch and had to smile. Unlikely help, but the offer was kind.

The tiny turtle slowly poked its head above water. It could have been cousin to any of those in the pond. Ariel touched the spotted shell, then carefully lifted the creature until her silver eyes could look directly into the turtle's black ones. *Thank you, but I fear land is as unkind to you as me.*

Moonlight broke through the thin clouds as the turtle continued its calm regard. For a moment, her vision dazzled, Ariel thought she saw something quite different on her palm. She would never have thought of something so audacious, but if the turtle was willing to try, perhaps the sea mother would pity them all.

She smoothed one damp finger along the fragile green throat and sought wisdom in the old eyes. Was that a wink? Perhaps. We'll try, Ariel thought. I'm the queen's blood, after all, sick though I may be.

She thought of everything she had ever learned, or ever seen done. Her mother could do this, and she was certain Barwen could as well. They'd say it was simple illusion. The turtle was still a turtle. All that mattered was what Ariel and Erica believed.

She set the little creature safely in the sand at her feet, squeezed her eyes shut and invoked the only spell she thought might work. Then—like a foolish youngling—she was afraid to open her eyes to see what had happened.

There was soft noise, a whicker of hello. Ariel's eyes flew open and she looked in amazement at the mare with wise black eyes that stood gazing at her. More mist than substance, the mare tossed her light green mane, as beautiful as any creature in Erica's photo albums.

Erica stirred, then rolled to her side, coughing. "Where are we?"

Kelp if I know, Ariel wanted to say. The mare whickered again and Erica abruptly glanced up.

"How did . . ." Erica staggered to her feet. "Where did she come from?"

The mare nudged Erica's head, then licked her hair. With a helpless laugh, Erica put her arms around the horse's neck.

Ariel felt washed over with an emotion she could not name. She had seen Erica passionate, angry, bitter, hurt, devastated, but this was completely new. Erica was happy, radiantly so. Whatever she had made Erica feel, Ariel knew it had had nothing of this kind of simple joy in it.

Was this regret she felt? Pity? What could this feeling be that it hurt so to know she had never made Erica laugh? Sex was one kind of pleasure, but—a concept so foreign that Ariel thought for a moment the world was revolving backward—sex was not the only pleasure that nourished. Erica was glowing and Ariel wished she was the reason. But it wasn't her. It was the horse's breath and tickling nose. An animal could make Erica happier than Ariel ever would.

"How did we get here? I don't remember. There was that club, but we left."

Ariel took a deep breath. How could she pantomime anything that would make sense? Erica, however, didn't seem to expect an answer.

"Oh, Ariel, look at her." Erica ran her hands over the horse's neck. "She's beautiful, isn't she? Eerie color in the moonlight, but she's a lot like Sea Foam, one of my favorites. Is she going to take us home?"

Ariel nodded. Erica's face was alight with joy as she led the mare to a rock. Scrambling up, she looked as if all her worries and pain were a thing of the past.

She extended a hand down to Ariel, then lifted her lightly to perch in front of her. "I think we'll have to call her Sea Foam, don't you?"

Ariel nodded, then clutched Erica tightly as the mare ambled toward the road.

Hooves sounded incredibly loud in the night. In a matter of minutes Ariel felt as if she'd been thoroughly jolted in every possible direction. Erica murmured something and her hips moved against Ariel's ass in a way that was almost sexual. Sea Foam tossed her head and broke into a happy canter. Erica laughed into the night and the happiness of her inner song washed over Ariel like a healing wave.

They flowed toward home as if they rode a landward tide. Erica was holding her tight and Ariel felt that indefinable feeling again, rich and magical, but not any kind of magic she'd ever experienced before. She had never suspected that a human woman could be so strong, so deep, so resilient. Just because their lives were short did not make them weak, did it?

Had she dwelled her entire life in pretty, sparkling shallows? Only now, after a year of living in Erica's sphere was Ariel aware that this silent, painful life was still better than her life before, better because Erica was near.

Erica's strength had shown her that there could be light in spite of dark, laughter because of tears, even love where there had only been obsession. Erica had only despaired because of Ariel. Ariel would change a thousand turtles into horses if that would ease Erica's pain.

Their journey seemed edged in magic, though Ariel had never felt more human. What seemed hours later Erica opened the gates, and Sea Foam trotted up the drive to the house.

Ariel slid to the ground, holding back a moan of discomfort. Her back and thighs screamed with red hot cramps. She had barely enough time to steady herself when Erica tumbled after her.

"God, I hurt," Erica whispered hoarsely. "It has been so long since I've had that much fun, but I'm going to feel this for days."

Ariel tugged Erica's arm, wanting her in the house where it was warm and there was something to eat.

"We have to rub down the horse," Erica murmured.

Sea Foam pranced away a few steps, then lowered her head to

nudge Erica's face. She likewise nuzzled at Ariel, fixing her with a long, solemn gaze.

Ariel nodded. A debt was owed, and she would repay it someday if she could.

Sea Foam lifted her head to the stars as she turned to gallop toward the gate.

"Where is she going?" Erica tried to stumble after the departing horse, but Ariel held her back. In the distance there was a whinny of glee, then the sound of hooves faded into the night. Ariel realized that the horizon was glimmering with the coming dawn.

They walked back to the house in the rising light and Ariel realized that this was her last day of silence. Tonight she would get the cure, and she would tell Erica everything, every bitter and hard truth. I'll stay, she thought. *Not because she needs me or because it's the right thing to do, but because I feel more and am better when she is near.*

She was vaguely aware of the hot shower and warm sheets. Erica was kissing her lovingly, softly, and spreading lotion on her raw thighs and pelvis. The sensation of Erica's slick fingers brought a cascade of shivers that began at the top of Ariel's head. She felt so much, and it was so confusing. Ariel wanted to weep, but not from pain. Erica had to be exhausted, but she was making the effort to be gentle and thorough in the care of Ariel's hurts.

I haven't earned this, Ariel thought. I don't understand.

It felt so good that she realized with a shock she was close to a very different kind of peaking than she had ever experienced before. Words wanted to spill out of her mouth. She wasn't sure she had the strength to stop them any longer. It felt so right, so easy, so safe. She wanted to moan as she closed her eyes with a deep, silent sigh. Never once had it crossed her mind she could make Erica's life better in any way except sex. Likewise she had never considered that Erica had more than sex to offer her.

Safe, warm, loved . . . Oblivion swept over her with the soothing peace of a tropical sea.

◈

She woke with a start, and Erica's arms were instantly around her. "It's okay, I'm here. I've just been watching you sleep."

The dream slipped away from recalling and Ariel sighed into Erica's arms. Watery sunlight of late afternoon spilled through Erica's windows. She stared drowsily up at Erica, who looked as if she'd been up for some time. But the light also revealed deep hollows under Erica's eyes, and a yellowish cast to her skin. She had probably not eaten, Ariel worried, and the traumas of last night had taken a heavy toll.

"For a long time I haven't wanted to be alive the way I did when I woke up this morning. I have been bitter about everything I lost, but this morning I wanted to move on, finally. Then I saw myself in the mirror." Erica swallowed hard. "I'm dying, aren't I?"

Stunned, Ariel stared into Erica's eyes until she couldn't hold her gaze any longer. It was a minute before she remembered to breathe.

"You're like . . ." Erica put her hand on Ariel's heart. "You're like an angel come to watch over me."

Ariel shook her head violently. She was no angel, all the kelp knew that.

"You must be, Ariel. I dreamed about you day and night for a year, and just when I thought I would go mad, you came to me. Though I don't understand so much, you still have comforted me. And last night—I remember now what I did last night. And somehow you saved me in my darkest moment."

Ariel was still shaking her head. She wasn't so sure if saving Erica had been her intent. Being with Erica to wherever that fateful jump would lead them—that had been all she had been thinking of.

"What are you, Ariel? What's going to become of us?"

What purpose had secrecy served her? She had spent the entire year waiting for it to be over, wallowing in self-pity and wanting what she could not have. She had wasted a year of Erica's life, quite possibly the last year, when she could have made a real difference. Bring her seashells by the truckload and Ariel could turn them into gold. There could be a dozen Sea Foams in Erica's life, giving her more real joy than Ariel ever would. The infection was a sickness of soul, of spirit, as well as body. If she had worked to keep Erica's spirit healthy, then the body could follow. But she'd been too caught in her own pain to care about Erica's.

She drew Erica out of the bed, pausing only briefly to wrap herself in one of Erica's long, warm robes. She led Erica by the hand out to the patio and through the still weed-choked garden. Some minutes later they neared the pond.

"How is this an answer?" Erica seemed too weak to resist. "I need to lie down all of a sudden."

The sun was on the pond, but would not be for long. Ariel drew Erica to the edge and they knelt side by side. Ariel gave Erica a meaningful look, then bent to blow softly on the surface.

"What's supposed to happen?" Erica sounded tired and puzzled.

Ariel gazed hopefully at the surface of the pond. Maybe the light wasn't strong enough or the magic wouldn't work with a human witness. Either way, the surface remained dark.

"I feel strange, Ariel. I don't know what it is." Erica touched the surface of the water for a moment. "Like I'm going to float away, and the only reason I don't is you."

Forgetting the water, Ariel looked at Erica in alarm. She was pale and drawn now, and seemed as mistlike as the mare of last night. When Ariel touched Erica's knee she was almost surprised to find it solid.

Erica lifted her hand, coiling it in her own. "Your touch is the only thing I can feel anymore." She brought Ariel's hand to her breast. "I don't care about yes. I think there's no more time to worry about that. Please, Ariel . . . we never did make love and I would like to. Before . . . it's all over."

It wasn't just the day that was ending. Erica's breathing was increasingly shallow. Her eyes seemed almost feverish. But her hands were direct and still strong on Ariel's body.

"I think it's the only thing that could save me. Please Ariel . . ." *Say yes, Ariel, please, love me, for always.*

All the frustrated desire of the past year welled up inside Ariel's body, so intense she wanted to cry out. But where she had begun this year feeling only the empty ache of lust, the desire she felt now was mingled with something that touched other parts of her soul. Her heart was pounding with a confusion of fear and excitement. What was happening? Why did her hand in Erica's fill her with warmth and tenderness? How could that driving ache for Erica's sexual touch seem pale next to these completely foreign feelings?

"Ariel . . . Grant my wish." Erica's eyes glittered with tears. "I need to be with you one last time. I love you." *I love you, Ariel, please.*

Ariel's heart was beating so fast and high in her throat she could not breathe. How could Erica love her? Human love . . . no mer would ever want it, but that could only be because they did not understand it. Ariel felt as if she was growing, but on the inside, deepening in ways she did not begin to comprehend. Someday she might understand it all, but only if she had Erica's love to help her.

Her life hung in the balance. If she spoke now, and said the one word she longed to give Erica, her days would be numbered incomprehensibly short. She would eventually wash away in the tide, drifting and lost, a stranger to her home. If her yes eased Erica's sickness, Erica would still die, like all mortals. So what would her sacrifice have been for?

For love, she thought. It would have been for love.

Erica's sigh was faint, and Ariel realized her eyes had taken on a glassy cast. "I think I'm going, Ariel. I feel so odd. Make love with me, before it's too late."

The year was nearly done, but Erica might not see it. The cure seemed pointless now. Ariel did not want to be cured. She wanted Erica in her blood, in her heart, buried deep and inexorably into her soul.

She stared at the glittering surface of the pond, reaching her decision. The sun now sparkled on its surface and there were images to see, faces she knew gathered in yet another celebration. She saw Caliba, a diamond glass raised in salute, chanting something. Ariel had once longed to be able to hear, but it didn't matter anymore. Erica mattered. Erica was everything in ways the infection had never caused.

Erica drew Ariel close and gazed steadily into her eyes. "I don't need your words, my love. I can see it in your eyes and I trust your eyes. I wish I had learned that sooner."

She pulled Ariel on top of her, twining her hands in Ariel's long hair. "You don't have to make a sound, Ariel. Our bodies know what to do."

Erica's hands faltered while opening Ariel's robe, but Ariel helped, unknotting the tie and pushing the heavy cloth off her shoulders. *So beautiful, Ariel. We made something that night, and I have loved you ever since. Please . . . say yes.*

The glow in Erica's eyes was wonderfully intoxicating, more than Champagne, more than any voice could be. She cupped Ariel's breasts with tender intensity. Her gaze seemed to see inside Ariel's mind, inside her body.

Ariel's mouth dropped open as Erica's fingertips found her nipples and tugged gently. Erica knew . . . somehow she knew. Weak, turning to mist, Erica still knew what made Ariel feel good. Ariel felt as moldable as wet sand in Erica's hands. Erica increased the pull on Ariel's nipples until Ariel bent forward, and their mouths met to the sound of Erica's deep moan.

The kisses were urgent, and Ariel's head was spinning. She had not ever wanted Erica more than she did at that moment, her heart brimming with emotion and her mind swirling with the realization that love was more intimate than sex.

Erica gently massaged Ariel's thighs. Her tide was rising and Ariel realized it would take only a few strokes inside her to reach her peak. Every nerve in her body, singing with love, burning with lust, wanted this moment. All of her was screaming yes. She swallowed reflexively. It had been so long since she'd made any sound at all, and now she wondered if she could.

She turned her head to focus on the stroke of Erica's fingers and saw Caliba, still chanting. She could almost make out the words.

She wanted to say yes. But if she waited until midnight, Erica might not be conscious enough to hear it. She loved Erica, as much as her unpracticed heart could feel. She needed to find the words, and now. Erica was slipping away, and more time with Erica was worth any price.

What was Caliba saying? So familiar . . . Erica's fingers slipped inside Ariel, and Ariel shivered so hard she could not breathe. So familiar.

Erica's soft moan brought a flash of clarity to Ariel's seething mind. She did not need to hear Caliba to know what she was saying.

Thirty-five, thirty-four . . .

Mer time . . . It was nearly midnight at home. The queen would have set the cure to midnight for mer. No other time mattered. In spite of the winter sun overhead, midnight was *now*.

Erica was inside her, fingers finding the places inside Ariel that gushed with wet. It felt so good and Erica knew exactly what to do. Ariel wanted to lose herself in the moment. The sun was out, but it was midnight. She tried to focus, but Erica's touch was driving away all her rationality.

Twenty-three, twenty-two . . .

"Please, Ariel. Let it go. Come for me this last time. I don't have long, and I have only this to give me strength. There is nothing without you. Please."

Ariel could hear the countdown in her head. Already she fancied that a tingling had begun in her brain, the early signs of the queen's latent spell. She had only to last less than a minute and she would give Erica her yes.

Erica's hand faltered. "The light's going . . ."

Ariel could feel the sunlight on her back. Erica's eyes were closing. No, Ariel, thought, it could not be so close. Erica had to survive. She caught Erica's falling hand and brought it to her face. So wet, so close . . . Erica had only ever asked for one thing.

Eleven, ten . . .

She was desperate enough to try anything. If she was wrong then she lost even a chance of helping Erica, and at the moment, her entire being was devoted only to that. Erica could not die. If she did, Ariel could not think of any reason to live. The queen's spell was alive now, waiting for the moment to come, radiating heat throughout Ariel's shoulders and back. She patted Erica's face frantically, searching for some sign of consciousness. Had she waited too long? Was Erica already gone beyond recalling?

Two, one . . . Happy New Year!

The queen's spell burst into flames inside Ariel's mind, and it grew in strength as it played out the elements of the cure. Ariel could feel the growing ball of fire and desperately, with all her concentration, she sculpted part of the spell to envelop Erica as well. She risked losing it completely, of never being healed, but any kind of future with Erica was better than none at all.

She cleared her unused throat. Through the fire that was enveloping them both she managed the only word that mattered. "Yes!"

She convulsed when the fire exploded in her nerves and she did not let go when Erica stiffened in agony, pounding her fists into Ariel's sides and back. Erica was trying to escape the burning, but Ariel knew the only way out of the fire was through it. She held on, not knowing she had the strength. Phoenix or ashes, the difference no longer mattered to Ariel.

Together was the only place they belonged.

"Erica, wake up, look at me," Ariel said hoarsely. "*Yes.* Yes, for you."

Erica gasped with pain, and her eyes opened wide with shock. Ariel reached for her mervoice and let its full power swell between them. "*For you, for us. My yes is forever yours.*"

Erica cried out again, her eyes rolling back in her head.

Ariel's mervoice rose to her own cathartic scream. There was no reason to hold back her agony. Birds winged into the air as she let go of the torture, let go of her soul, and sang for the joy of that single moment. Steeped in pain, only one thing mattered—they were together.

She sang of all her years, of who she had been, and what she had become by knowing love. She sang for Erica every story, every secret, every thought, yielding not just her past but her inner being. She felt, for a moment, like the angel Erica believed her to be, answering all of Erica's questions.

Their essence spilled between them, blending, pooling. Ariel had to give up everything. Less than everything would leave them both with nothing.

"Yes, Erica."

Erica shivered violently, then her body surged under Ariel's. They teetered on the edge of the pond. Ariel had only a moment to realize that she would have to let go of Erica to keep them from falling in. She would not let go. The spell wasn't done. She clutched Erica to her and they toppled into the cold waters.

Erica panicked. She tried to escape Ariel's grasp, but Ariel clung. It was Erica's life she was protecting. She breathed in water and shared air with Erica. Her mervoice rippled through the chill. *"Whatever comes, Erica, we will be together. My yes is true."*

They struggled against each other for a few more seconds, then the flames around their bodies winked out. Erica blinked, seemingly conscious. Ariel leaned forward to share air again, but Erica turned her head.

Ariel pushed off from the pond's bottom, taking Erica with her toward the surface. Erica pulled back and Ariel paused, her hair drifting between them.

"Ariel."

"What's wrong, Erica?" Ariel pushed her hair out of the way so she could study Erica's face.

Then she realized she was looking at Erica, who did not know how to swim, drifting comfortably under the surface of the water. Her green eyes followed Ariel's every move. Ariel swam closer, her heart pounding in her ears. Green eyes . . . Erica's eyes were no longer the silver of madness.

A wild hope surged inside Ariel. Some of the cure had worked for

Erica. Something had helped. That was all that mattered. Erica would live. Ariel stared in amazement at how calm Erica was, breathing naturally, with no sign of her earlier panic. Breathing, Ariel thought . . . she's *breathing*.

As coolly and competently as any mermaid, Erica turned a somersault in the water.

"*I think I'm having a very good dream,*" Erica pronounced.

Ariel shivered as the delight of Erica's mervoice wrapped around her. Mervoice—Erica should not have mervoice. She had given Erica more than a cure, it seemed.

Rising to the surface, Erica beckoned to Ariel. They clambered onto the soft ground next to the water. Without thinking Ariel cast a drying spell for herself.

Erica immediately did the same, grinning. "I understand everything now. I don't really believe what just happened, but I felt as if I was touching death, and now . . . that's all gone. Because you sang for me, Ariel." Erica settled on the bank near the water and pulled Ariel onto her lap. "You sang for me with an angel's voice."

"I'm no angel. Just a mermaid, and maybe not even that, anymore."

Erica gasped. "I wasn't wrong—you did speak, didn't you?"
Ariel nodded. "Yes."

Erica cupped her face. "Your eyes tell the truth, don't they?"
"Yes."

I love her yes, and I will never get enough of it. Ariel, I want you and love you. "You know that's my favorite word?"

Ariel's lips curved. "Yes." Erica's song was still vibrant in Ariel's mind. The infection was cured, and Erica had no reason to sing now, but she did. For love, Ariel thought. She sings for love and so . . . and so do I.

Eagerly pulling Ariel's mouth to hers, Erica laughed for joy. Ariel felt the wonder of being something that gave Erica happiness, not pain. The feeling was better than anything she had ever felt, and it was addictive. She wanted to feel it again. "Yes, Erica, love. Yes. Always yes."

They stretched out on the soft ground, tangling in Ariel's hair, mouths bruising in the haste to kiss and enjoy another wonder, and another.

Erica's teeth grazed Ariel's jaw as their breath mingled. "Time . . . time to enjoy this."

"We have all the time in the world." Ariel arched up to meet Erica's playful, wet kiss. Her tides were rising unsummoned, uncompelled. Her body ached for Erica, and it felt wonderful to want and know that want would be fulfilled. "Please."

Whatever they had become, they still had this, Ariel thought. Erica's hands knew how to touch her and this time there would be no stopping Ariel from learning every crevice of Erica's body with her mouth and fingers. They would not have just one night, but all the nights that counted.

All the pasts had led to this present and only this present could give them a shared future.

With a laugh, Ariel rolled on top of Erica. Her gaze was distracted by shimmers on the surface of the water. It was already the new year in the land of her past. Bright with color and motion, the scene had once been all Ariel had thought beautiful and necessary. Now she wanted much more, and with Erica she had found the missing pieces of her soul.

She saw Caliba standing abruptly still, seemingly staring into Ariel's eyes. Then Caliba smiled sadly, waved a hand, and the images misted over, as if they would only be dreams for Ariel now.

"Look at me, Ariel," Erica said in a low voice. "*Look at me.*"

The green of the autumn sea merged with the blue of midnight. "I love you, Erica. I had no idea what that meant, but you taught me."

"We will go on learning." Erica kissed her softly. "But right now I want you to sing for me, Ariel."

Ariel closed her eyes and let the pleasure of Erica's touch sweep over her. With it was the knowledge that the only reason Erica ached to touch her was love. Their happiness was a choice.

Ariel's voice soared for Erica, with all her passion, and when Erica's voice joined hers it was a song no mer nor human had ever heard before.

"Please."

Her voice plays on my body like the tide. I rise and fall to the cadence of her words while past and present eddy in my mind, muddied by shifting sands of need and desire. She asks me if I want her. The gooseflesh along my arms says yes. The wet I can feel surging between my legs says yes. I try to say yes with the intensity of my eyes, the eagerness of my hands, the curve of my lips.

With all my heart, with the soul that loving her has grown in me, I give her the only word that has ever mattered: Yes.

Eternally yes.

Contributor Bios

Barbara Johnson has always been a lover of fairy tales, and being the femme that she is, always wanted to be the princess. Alas, she never lived in a castle although she's visited several, and is more like Brier Rose than Princess Aurora. With her partner of 30 years, Barbara, like Brier Rose, lives in a house near the woods, where she is surrounded by a menagerie of animals, both wild and tame. Naiad Press published her four novels, *Stonehurst*, *The Beach Affair*, *Bad Moon Rising*, and *Strangers in the Night*. Her short stories have appeared in numerous anthologies, including Bella Books' *Back to Basics: A Butch/Femme Erotic Anthology*. "Charlotte of Hessen" marks her long-awaited return to publishing.

Though she hadn't realized she wanted to grow up to be a lesbian, **Karin Kallmaker** fell in love with her best friend at the age of 16, and still shares her life with that same woman, and their two children, more than a quarter century later. The author of more than a dozen romances and a half-dozen fantasy-science fiction novels (including three Lambda Literary Award Finalists), she recently began expanding her repertoire to include explicit erotica. As Karin says, "Nice Girls Do."

Therese Szymanski hails from the Motor City and now lives in the Nation's Capital. An award-winning playwright, she believes in erotic freedom and maximizing the erotic content of life. Best known for her Brett Higgins Mysteries / Motor City Thrillers, including *When Evil Changes Face* (a 2000 Lambda Literary Award Finalist) and *When Good Girls Go Bad*, she is also the author of numerous erotic, horror and romance short stories in a variety of anthologies, including several for gay men which came about as a dare. She also edited Bella Books' first anthology, *Back to Basics: A Butch/Femme Anthology*.

As a four-year-old, **Julia Watts** forced her poor mother to read her "Beauty and the Beast" every night for a solid year. "La Belle Rose" is no doubt the perverse result of this childhood obsession. In addition to being a fairy tale fan, Julia is the author of six novels, the most recent of which,

Finding H.F., won the 2002 Lambda Literary Award for young adult fiction.

Publications from
BELLA BOOKS, INC.
The best in contemporary lesbian fiction

P.O. Box 10543, Tallahassee, FL 32302
Phone: 800-729-4992
www.bellabooks.com

ONCE UPON A DYKE: NEW EXPLOITS OF FAIRY-TALE LESBIANS by Karin Kallmaker, Julia Watts, Barbara Johnson & Therese Szymanski. 320 pp. You've never read fairy tales like these before! From Bella After Dark. ISBN 1-931513-71-6 $14.95

FINEST KIND OF LOVE by Diana Tremain Braund. 224 pp. Can Molly and Carolyn stop clashing long enough to see beyond their differences? ISBN 1-931513-68-6 $12.95

DREAM LOVER by Lyn Denison. 188 pp. A soft, sensuous, romantic fantasy.
ISBN 1-931513-96-1 $12.95

NEVER SAY NEVER by Linda Hill. 224 pp. A classic love story... where rules aren't the only things broken. ISBN 1-931513-67-8 $12.95

PAINTED MOON by Karin Kallmaker. 214 pp. A snowbound weekend in a cabin brings Jackie and Leah together... or does it tear them apart? ISBN 1-931513-53-8 $12.95

WIZARD OF ISIS by Jean Stewart. 240 pp. Fifth in the exciting Isis series.
ISBN 1-931513-71-4 $12.95

WOMAN IN THE MIRROR by Jackie Calhoun. 216 pp. Josey learns to love again, while her niece is learning to love women for the first time. ISBN 1-931513-78-3 $12.95

SUBSTITUTE FOR LOVE by Karin Kallmaker. 200 pp. One look and a deep kiss... Holly is hopelessly in lust. Can there be anything more? ISBN 1-931513-62-7 $12.95

GULF BREEZE by Gerri Hill. 288 pp. Could Carly really be the woman Pat has always been searching for? ISBN 1-931513-97-X $12.95

THE TOMSTOWN INCIDENT by Penny Hayes. 184 pp. Caught between two worlds, Eloise must make a decision that will change her life forever. ISBN 1-931513-56-2 $12.95

MAKING UP FOR LOST TIME by Karin Kallmaker. 240 pp. When three love-starved lesbians decide to make up for lost time, the recipe is romance. ISBN 1-931513-61-9 $12.95

THE WAY LIFE SHOULD BE by Diana Tremain Braund. 173 pp. With which woman will Jennifer find the true meaning of love? ISBN 1-931513-66-X $12.95

BACK TO BASICS: A BUTCH/FEMME ANTHOLOGY edited by Therese Szymanski—from Bella After Dark. 324 pp. ISBN 1-931513-35-X $14.95

SURVIVAL OF LOVE by Frankie J. Jones. 236 pp. What will Jody do when she falls in love with her best friend's daughter? ISBN 1-931513-55-4 $12.95

LESSONS IN MURDER by Claire McNab. 184 pp. 1st Detective Inspector Carol Ashton Mystery ISBN 1-931513-65-1 $12.95

DEATH BY DEATH by Claire McNab. 167 pp. 5th Denise Cleever Thriller.
ISBN 1-931513-34-1 $12.95

CAUGHT IN THE NET by Jessica Thomas. 188 pp. A wickedly observant story of mystery, danger, and love in Provincetown. ISBN 1-931513-54-6 $12.95

DREAMS FOUND by Lyn Denison. Australian Riley embarks on a journey to meet her birth mother . . . and gains not just a family, but the love of her life. ISBN 1-931513-58-9 $12.95

A MOMENT'S INDISCRETION by Peggy J. Herring. 154 pp. Jackie is torn between her better judgment and the overwhelming attraction she feels for Valerie.
ISBN 1-931513-59-7 $12.95

IN EVERY PORT by Karin Kallmaker. 224 pp. Jessica's sexy, adventuresome travels.
ISBN 1-931513-36-8 $12.95

TOUCHWOOD by Karin Kallmaker. 240 pp. Loving May/December romance.
ISBN 1-931513-37-6 $12.95

WATERMARK by Karin Kallmaker. 248 pp. One burning question . . . how to lead her back to love? ISBN 1-931513-38-4 $12.95

EMBRACE IN MOTION by Karin Kallmaker. 240 pp. A whirlwind love affair.
ISBN 1-931513-39-2 $12.95

ONE DEGREE OF SEPARATION by Karin Kallmaker. 232 pp. Can an Iowa City librarian find love and passion when a California girl surfs into the close-knit dyke capital of the Midwest? ISBN 1-931513-30-9 $12.95

CRY HAVOC A Detective Franco Mystery by Baxter Clare. 240 pp. A dead hustler with a headless rooster in his lap sends Lt. L.A. Franco headfirst against Mother Love.
ISBN 1-931513931-7 $12.95

DISTANT THUNDER by Peggy J. Herring. 294 pp. Bankrobbing drifter Cordy awakens strange new feelings in Leo in this romantic tale set in the Old West.
ISBN 1-931513-28-7 $12.95

COP OUT by Claire McNab. 216 pp. 4th Detective Inspector Carol Ashton Mystery.
ISBN 1-931513-29-5 $12.95

BLOOD LINK by Claire McNab. 159 pp. 15th Detective Inspector Carol Ashton Mystery. Is Carol unwittingly playing into a deadly plan? ISBN 1-931513-27-9 $12.95

TALK OF THE TOWN by Saxon Bennett. 239 pp. With enough beer, barbecue and B.S., anything is possible! ISBN 1-931513-18-X $12.95

MAYBE NEXT TIME by Karin Kallmaker. 256 pp. Sabrina Starling has it all: fame, money, women—and pain. Nothing hurts like the one that got away. ISBN 1-931513-26-0 $12.95

WHEN GOOD GIRLS GO BAD: A Motor City Thriller by Therese Szymanski. 230 pp. Brett, Randi, and Allie join forces to stop a serial killer. ISBN 1-931513-11-2 $12.95

A DAY TOO LONG: A Helen Black Mystery by Pat Welch. 328 pp. This time Helen's fate is in her own hands.   ISBN 1-931513-22-8 $12.95

THE RED LINE OF YARMALD by Diana Rivers. 256 pp. The Hadra's only hope lies in a magical red line . . . climactic sequel to *Clouds of War*.   ISBN 1-931513-23-6 $12.95

OUTSIDE THE FLOCK by Jackie Calhoun. 224 pp. Jo embraces her new love and life.
                                                             ISBN 1-931513-13-9 $12.95

LEGACY OF LOVE by Marianne K. Martin. 224 pp. Read the whole Sage Bristo story.
                                                             ISBN 1-931513-15-5 $12.95

STREET RULES: A Detective Franco Mystery by Baxter Clare. 304 pp. Gritty, fast-paced mystery with compelling Detective L.A. Franco   ISBN 1-931513-14-7 $12.95

RECOGNITION FACTOR: 4th Denise Cleever Thriller by Claire McNab. 176 pp. Denise Cleever tracks a notorious terrorist to America.   ISBN 1-931513-24-4 $12.95

NORA AND LIZ by Nancy Garden. 296 pp. Lesbian romance by the author of *Annie on My Mind*.   ISBN 1931513-20-1 $12.95

MIDAS TOUCH by Frankie J. Jones. 208 pp. Sandra had everything but love.
                                                             ISBN 1-931513-21-X $12.95

BEYOND ALL REASON by Peggy J. Herring. 240 pp. A romance hotter than Texas.
                                                             ISBN 1-9513-25-2 $12.95

ACCIDENTAL MURDER: 14th Detective Inspector Carol Ashton Mystery by Claire McNab. 208 pp. Carol Ashton tracks an elusive killer.   ISBN 1-931513-16-3 $12.95

SEEDS OF FIRE: Tunnel of Light Trilogy, Book 2 by Karin Kallmaker writing as Laura Adams. 274 pp. Intriguing sequel to *Sleight of Hand*.   ISBN 1-931513-19-8 $12.95

DRIFTING AT THE BOTTOM OF THE WORLD by Auden Bailey. 288 pp. Beautifully written first novel set in Antarctica.   ISBN 1-931513-17-1 $12.95

CLOUDS OF WAR by Diana Rivers. 288 pp. Women unite to defend Zelindar!
                                                             ISBN 1-931513-12-0 $12.95

DEATHS OF JOCASTA: 2nd Micky Knight Mystery by J.M. Redmann. 408 pp. Sexy and intriguing Lambda Literary Award-nominated mystery.   ISBN 1-931513-10-4 $12.95

LOVE IN THE BALANCE by Marianne K. Martin. 256 pp. The classic lesbian love story, back in print!   ISBN 1-931513-08-2 $12.95

THE COMFORT OF STRANGERS by Peggy J. Herring. 272 pp. Lela's work was her passion . . . until now.   ISBN 1-931513-09-0 $12.95

CHICKEN by Paula Martinac. 208 pp. Lynn finds that the only thing harder than being in a lesbian relationship is ending one.   ISBN 1-931513-07-4 $11.95

TAMARACK CREEK by Jackie Calhoun. 208 pp. An intriguing story of love and danger.
                                                             ISBN 1-931513-06-6 $11.95

And watch out for further New Exploits coming in 2005 from Barbara Johnson, Karin Kallmaker, Therese Szymanski and Julia Watts!